NIGHT

SCHOOL

C.J. DAUGHERTY

Katherine Tegen Books is an imprint of HarperCollins Publishers.

Night School
Copyright © 2012 by C. J. Daugherty
www.epicreads.com

Library of Congress Cataloging-in-Publication Data
Daugherty, Christi.
Night School / C. J. Daugherty. — 1st U.S. ed.
    p.   cm.
Summary: After her third arrest in one year, sixteen-year-old Allie's
parents send her to Cimmeria Academy, a boarding school, where she finds
herself exposing the dark secrets of the school and her classmates.
ISBN 978-0-06-219385-8 (hardcover bdg.)
[1. Boarding schools—Fiction. 2. Schools—Fiction. 3. Interpersonal
relations—Fiction. 4. Conduct of life—Fiction. 5. Supernatural—Fiction.]
I. Title.
PZ7.D26213Nig   2013   2012022151
[Fic]—dc23   CIP
                                                                     AC

Typography by Erin Fitzsimmons
13 14 15 16 17 LP/RRDH 10 9 8 7 6 5 4 3 2 1
❖
First U.S. edition, 2013

First published in the UK by Atom, an imprint of Little, Brown Book Group.

To Jack
Who always believed

ONE

"Hurry up!"

"Will you chill out? I'm almost finished." Her jaw set, Allie crouched in the dark, painting the last *k* as Mark knelt beside her holding a flashlight. Their voices echoed in the empty corridor. The light beam illuminating her work quivered when he laughed.

A sudden snapping sound made them both jump.

Fluorescent lights flickered and buzzed above them, then flooded the school hallway.

Two uniforms stood by the door.

Allie dropped the can of paint slowly without taking her finger off the trigger, causing the last letter to stretch freakishly down the door of the headmaster's office to the dirty linoleum floor.

"Run." As the word left her lips, she was already flying down the wide corridor, the rubber soles of her sneakers squeaking hollowly in the emptiness of Brixton Hill School. She didn't look back to see if Mark was behind her.

She didn't know where the others were, but if Harry got caught again, his dad would kill him. Rounding the corner at speed, she turned onto a dark stretch of corridor. At the end of it she saw the red glow of a fire exit sign.

A thrill of power rushed through her as she ran toward freedom. She was going to make it out. She was going to get away with it.

Crashing into the double doors, she shoved hard against the bar that should have freed her.

It didn't budge.

Unbelieving, she shoved again, but the door was locked.

Bloody hell. If I hadn't just been vandalizing the place, she thought, *I'd alert the local paper.*

Feverishly, she scanned the wide corridor. The police were between her and the main entrance. The only exit at this end was locked.

There had to be another way out.

She held her breath to listen. Voices and footsteps were heading her way.

Resting her hands on her knees, she let her head drop low between her shoulders. It could *not* go down this way. Her parents would destroy her. A third arrest in a year? It was bad enough when they made her go to *this* godforsaken school. Where would they send her now?

She ran to a nearby door.

One, two, three steps.

She tried the handle.

Locked.

Across the hall to another.

One, two, three, four steps.

Locked.

She was now running toward the police. This was crazy.

To her relief, though, she pulled the third door open easily. A supply closet.

They left the supply closet unlocked but locked empty classrooms? This school is run by idiots.

Slipping in gingerly among shelves of paper, mop buckets, and electrical equipment she couldn't identify in the gloom, she steadied her breathing. Behind her, the door swung shut, latching with a solid click that sounded deafening to Allie.

Her breath caught. It was darker than she'd expected. She held her hand up in front of her face—right in front of her face—and she couldn't see it. She knew it was there; she could feel its existence. But not being able to see it was instantly disorienting. Reaching out to steady herself, she gasped as a top-heavy pile of papers begin to slip. She struggled to rebalance it without being able to see it.

Outside the door she could hear faint voices; they sounded far away. She just had to wait a few more minutes and they'd be gone. Just a few more minutes.

It was hot, airless.

Stay calm.

She counted her heavy breaths . . . *twelve, thirteen, fourteen . . .*

But it was happening. That feeling of being encased in concrete, unable to breathe. Her heart pounding, rising panic burned in her throat.

Please calm down, Allie, she begged herself. *Just five minutes and you'll be safe. The guys'll never tell.*

But it wasn't working. She felt dizzy, suffocated.

She had to get out.

As sweat streamed down her face and the floor seemed to swing beneath her, she reached for the door handle.

No no no . . . it can't be.

The inside of the door was completely smooth.

Frantic, she felt the entirety of the impassive door, then the wall around it. Nothing. There was no way to open it from the inside.

She shoved the door, scratched at its edges with her nails, but it would not give. Her breath came harder now.

It was so dark.

Curling her hands into fists, she pounded on the smooth, unyielding door.

"Help! I can't breathe. Open the door!"

There was no response.

"Help me! Please?"

She hated the pleading tone in her own voice. Sobbing now, she put her cheek against the door and gasped for air as she slapped the wood with her hands.

"Please."

When the door opened, it did it so suddenly that she fell forward helplessly, straight into the arms of a police officer.

He held her at arm's length, shining a flashlight into her eyes, taking in the wild hair and tear-streaked cheeks.

He grinned over her head at the other cop. That was when Allie saw Mark, his head down and his cap missing. His arm was firmly in the grip of another officer, who grinned back.

Against the constant rumble of a police station on a summer Friday night, Allie heard her father's voice as clearly as if he were standing in front of her. She stopped twirling her hair and looked anxiously at the door.

"I can't tell you how much I appreciate this. I'm very sorry for the bother," she heard. The tone in his voice was one she knew quite well: humiliated. By her. She heard another male voice she couldn't quite make out and then her dad again: "Yes, we're taking steps, and I appreciate your advice. We'll discuss this and make a decision tomorrow."

Decision? What kind of decision?

Then the door opened, and her gray eyes met his tired blue ones. She felt her heart twist in her chest just a little. Unshaven and rumpled, he looked older. And very tired.

He handed a few papers to the female officer, who barely glanced at them before adding them to her stack of paperwork. She reached into a drawer and pulled out an envelope containing Allie's things, which she shoved across the desk to Allie's father. Without looking at either of them, she said robotically, "You've been released into your father's care. You're free to go."

Allie rose stiffly and followed her dad down narrow, brightly lit corridors to the front door.

When they were outside in the cool summer air, she breathed deeply. Relief at being out of the police station mingled with anxiety about the expression on her father's face. They walked toward the car in silence.

From across the street her father unlocked the door of the black Ford, and it beeped its incongruously chirpy welcome. When he started the engine, she turned to him earnestly, her eyes filled with explanations.

"Dad . . ."

He looked straight ahead, his jaw tense. "Alyson. Don't."

"Don't what?"

"Don't talk. Just . . . sit there."

After that, their journey was silent. And at their house, he got out of the car without a word. Allie scrambled after him, the worried feeling in the pit of her stomach growing.

He didn't seem angry. He seemed . . . empty.

Allie walked up the stairs and down the hallway, past her brother's empty room—these days she could pass it without looking in. Or wondering.

In the safety of her own bedroom, she studied herself in the mirror. Her hair was tangled, black paint was smeared on her temple, and mascara was smudged under her gray eyes. She smelled of stale sweat and fear.

"Well," she told her reflection, "maybe it could have been worse."

The next morning, her parents called her into the living room. Early.

Still half asleep, Allie sat in the soft burgundy armchair; her expression already resentful.

Her parents sat side by side on the sofa across from her—like a prim firing squad.

"Alyson . . . ," her father began, then faltered.

Putting her hand on his knee, her mother took over. "We've been talking about what we can do to help you."

Uh-oh.

6

"Obviously you've not been happy at your current school." She was speaking very precisely and slowly. Allie's eyes darted from one parent to the other. "Now that you've broken into the school, set fire to your records, and spray-painted 'Ross is a dick' on Headmaster Ross's door, it's rather obvious that they're not very happy with you, either."

Allie fought the urge to giggle nervously. Giggling now really wouldn't help.

"This will be the second school to ask us, very politely, to send you somewhere else to study."

Allie was stunned. "They kicked me out?"

"Not yet." Ice fairly dripped from her mother's voice. "But they will."

Her father leaned forward and looked Allie in the eye for the first time since he'd picked her up at the police station.

"We understand that you're dealing with everything that's happened, Alyson," he said. "But graffiti, truancy, vandalism . . . enough, okay? You've made your point. We get it."

Allie opened her mouth to defend herself, but her mother shot her a warning look, so she closed it again.

Now it was her mother's turn again. "Last night, the very helpful police liaison officer suggested we send you to a different school. Out of London. Away from your *friends*."

She said the last word with bitter contempt.

"We made a few calls this morning, and we've"—her mother paused, glancing across at her father almost uncertainly before continuing—"we've found a place that specializes in teenagers like you."

Allie flinched.

"We've spoken to the headmistress, and she's agreed to accept you. Starting now."

"Now . . . what?" Allie's voice rose in disbelief. "Like *today*? But the summer holiday just started!"

"The school is called Cimmeria Academy," her father said as if she hadn't spoken. "It's a boarding school."

Boarding school?

The words reverberated in Allie's head.

They have got to be joking, she thought, but she knew they weren't.

"It will be difficult for us to afford, but we think we must at least try and stop you from throwing your whole life away. You're a juvenile now in the eyes of the law, but you won't be for long." Without warning he slapped his hand hard on the arm of the cream-colored sofa. Allie jumped. "Come on, Alyson! Wake up. You're sixteen years old. This has to stop."

Allie listened to her heart pound.

Thirteen beats. Fourteen, fifteen . . .

She couldn't believe how bad this was. It was unbelievably bad. Record-setting levels of badness were happening right now in this room.

"Look, I know I messed up. I feel really, really bad about it." She turned to her father, imploring. "But don't you think you're overreacting? Dad, this is crazy!"

He shook his head sadly.

"It's too late," he said. "The decision has been made. We leave this afternoon. Until then no computer, no phone, no iPod. And no leaving this house."

When her parents stood up, it felt like the judge was leaving the courtroom. In the emptiness they left behind, Allie exhaled shakily.

After she'd packed her things (her iPod, phone, and computer having been gathered by her parents and carried away first), Allie stared at her open closet for long minutes trying to decide what to wear.

What do you wear when you don't know where you're going?

She finally opted for skinny jeans and a long black camisole with the word *Trouble* scrawled across it in sparkly silver. She brushed her dyed red hair and left it loose.

Studying herself in the mirror, she thought she looked pale. Scared.

I can do better than this.

Grabbing her liquid eyeliner, she applied a thick black swoosh to her eyelids, then coated her lashes in mascara. Next she dived under the bed and pulled out a pair of dark red, knee-high Doc Martens, lacing them up over her jeans. The boots were well-worn and scuffed.

When she walked downstairs a few minutes later, her expression was mutinous.

Looking at her outfit, her mother sighed dramatically but said nothing. She just picked up her purse and headed for the door.

Outside, the sun shone brightly. It was a hot afternoon, and kids pedaled by on their bikes, shouting at each other happily. On a normal day, Allie would have been heading to the park to hang out with Mark and Harry and talk about last night's exploits.

Instead, she stopped and looked back at their ordinary London row house, trying to memorize it. It wasn't much, but it had always been home, with all of the emotional beauty that word implied.

Now it just looked like every other house on the street.

TWO

As London's crowded streets gave way to rolling green fields dotted with white sheep dozing in the warmth, Allie felt a wave of loneliness. The mood in the car didn't help. Her parents barely acknowledged her presence.

She had no idea where the school was, and the town names whizzing by didn't help much (*Guildford, Camberley, Farnham . . . whoever heard of them?*). Then they left the motorway and began to wind their way up and down hills on tiny country lanes surrounded by high hedges that blocked any view, through minuscule villages (*Well, Dippenhall, Frensham . . .*).

Finally, after more than two hours, they turned down a narrow dirt track. Her father slowed the car to a crawl as the road passed into thick forest where the day was cooler and quieter. After a few minutes of jostling and bumping as her father swerved to avoid deep holes in the road, they arrived at a tall iron gate.

Then they stopped. The rumble of the car engine was the only sound.

Nothing happened for a long minute.

"Do you need to beep the horn or push a buzzer or something?" Allie whispered, taking in the forbidding black fence, which extended into the trees as far as she could see.

Before her father could reply, the gates shivered and then, with a clanging metallic sound, swung slowly inward. Inside, the forest continued, and the sun barely filtered through the thick branches.

Allie stared into the shadows ahead.

Welcome to your new school, Allie. Welcome to your new life.

The gates locked into place with a shudder.

Feeling her throat closing, Allie focused on breathing. She really didn't want to have another panic attack right now. But she couldn't shake an overwhelming sense of dread.

Her father pulled the car forward onto a smooth gravel drive that rolled through thick trees. After the rutted dirt road outside the gates, the drive was so smooth that the car seemed to float.

After a few minutes the drive emerged from the trees. Blinking in the bright sunlight, she saw an enormous Gothic edifice of dark red bricks. The three-story structure looked as if it had been ripped from another time. Its jagged roof jutted sharply in peaks and turrets, topped with what looked like daggers of wrought iron stabbing the sky.

Holy crap.

"It is an impressive building," her father said.

Her mother snorted. "Impressively ghastly."

Terrifying. The word they are looking for is terrifying.

The second the car stopped moving, the front door of the school swung open and a slim, smiling woman slipped out and ran lightly down the stairs. Her thick, dark blond hair was held back loosely with a clip, and it curled up at the ends as if it were happy to be there. Allie was relieved to see how normal she looked: her glasses were pushed up on top of her head, and she wore a creamy cotton cardigan atop her pale blue dress.

Allie's parents climbed out and walked over to meet her. Lagging behind, Allie reluctantly opened her door and left the backseat of the Ford. She didn't close the door.

"Mr. and Mrs. Sheridan, it's so nice to meet you in person." The woman's voice was warm and lilting; she smiled easily. "I hope the drive wasn't too tedious for you. The traffic can be awful between here and London. But at least the weather is lovely today, isn't it?"

She had oddly beautiful golden brown eyes, and Allie noticed a faint accent, but she couldn't identify it. Was it Scottish? It added delicacy and complexity to her words, as if they were filigreed.

After more pleasantries were exchanged, the three turned toward Allie. Her parents' smiles disappeared, replaced with the cultivated blankness with which she'd grown uncomfortably familiar. But the headmistress smiled at her warmly.

"And you must be Allie. Welcome. I'm Isabelle le Fanult, the headmistress at Cimmeria Academy. You can call me Isabelle."

Allie was a bit surprised to hear her nickname, rather than "Alyson." To be told to call a headmistress by her first name seemed weird, too.

But quite cool.

Isabelle turned her smile back to Allie's parents. "I'm afraid it is our policy that parents bid farewell to their children here," she said. "When the students cross the threshold, they start their new lives as Cimmeria students, and we like them to do that independently."

Allie's father lifted her two small bags from the trunk and set them down on the gravel.

Picking up the larger bag, Isabelle stepped away tactfully.

Allie's father turned to her. "Work hard and drop us a line now and then." He looked sad as he gave her a quick hug.

Her mother smoothed a strand of hair out of Allie's face and whispered, "Please give this place a chance." For just a second she hugged Allie tightly, and then she let go and walked to the car without looking back.

The whole time Allie stood stiffly, her hands clenched at her sides.

When the car disappeared into the shadows of the forest, she took a gasping gulp of air. Only then did she realize she hadn't been breathing.

When Allie turned to the headmistress, she found her watching her soberly.

"It's always difficult the first time." Isabelle's voice was gentle. "It gets easier."

Allie didn't want anybody's sympathy right now. And she didn't know who this woman was. With a curt nod to show that she was perfectly fine, she picked up the second bag and turned to face the enormous Gothic school building.

Isabelle headed briskly toward the steps, saying over her shoulder, "Just follow me. I'm afraid we have a little distance to go."

Her voice faded as she walked inside. After a moment's

hesitation, Allie walked after her.

"You'll find this building is simply endless . . . ," Isabelle was saying, but Allie hardly heard as she gaped at the vast entrance hall.

Inside, it was dim and cool, the bright sunlight filtered into colorful shade by a stained-glass window far above her head. The ceilings were at least twenty feet high, held aloft by thick stone arches. The stone floor had been polished smooth by thousands of feet over hundreds of years. Candleholders five feet tall stood like sentinels in each corner. Some walls were covered with old tapestries, though Allie didn't get a good look at them as she hurried after the headmistress.

From the entrance hall they moved on into a wide hallway with dark wooden floors, then up a grand staircase with a heavy mahogany banister, polished to a high sheen. Isabelle's espadrilles made a soft shushing sound as she skipped upward, all the while reeling off facts and figures about the building. Allie was a bit dazed by it all—the staircase was Edwardian, or had she said Victorian? The dining room was Reformation . . . or was it Tudor? Classrooms were in the east wing, but what did she say was in the west?

At the landing, Isabelle turned left and walked down a wide corridor, then climbed a narrower flight of stairs that led to a long, dim hallway lined with wooden doors painted white.

"This is the girls' dormitory. Let's see, we've put you in three twenty-nine. . . ." She hurried down the hall until the appropriate number appeared, and swung the door open.

The room was very dark and small with a single, bare bed, a wooden dresser and desk, and a freestanding armoire. All except the desk were painted the same clean shade of white. Isabelle flipped a latch Allie couldn't see, swinging open a wooden shutter covering an arched window. Instantly the room glowed with golden afternoon light. She pushed the window open and a breeze flowed in.

"All it needs is a little fresh air," she said cheerfully. "Your uniforms are in the wardrobe. Your parents gave us your sizes, but let us know if anything doesn't fit. You should have everything you need."

She paused as if expecting a response, but unable to think of anything to say, Allie stared around her, speechless.

"Shall I leave you to get settled, then?" Isabelle headed toward the door. "Dinner is at seven. Mealtimes are strict—please be on time. Oh, by the way . . ."

She turned back. "I noticed you've been having trouble in English lately, so I've added you to my own class. It's a special seminar with a smaller class; I hope you'll find it interesting."

Overwhelmed with information, Allie nodded silently; then, realizing that words were required, she said haltingly, "I . . . I'll be fine."

"There's endless information about the school and your classes in the envelope on the desk. I'll send a prefect around to introduce herself and answer any questions you might have." Isabelle tilted her head to one side, studying her. "I'm very sorry about what happened with your brother, Allie. And I do hope you'll be happy here. I think this is the right place for you."

Without waiting for a response, she left. The door closed behind her with a quiet click.

Allie exhaled. For a long minute she stood still in the silence of the small, bare room as her mind whirled with questions.

What am I doing here? And, while we're at it, where is here, anyway? She looked at the door as if she could see the headmistress through it. *Why would they tell her about Christopher? That's none of her business.*

Shutting off the noisy thoughts that were beginning to cause her brain to pound, she lifted a bag up onto the bed and busied herself with unpacking. When she opened the dresser drawers, she found most were already full of T-shirts, shorts, and sweaters, all in white or midnight blue, with the Cimmeria crest above the heart.

Curious, she opened the armoire to find neatly pressed dark blue skirts, white shirts, and blue jackets. As she rummaged through the back of the wardrobe, though, her fingers came across something much too light and filmy to be a uniform.

Pushing the hangers back so she could see, she found three delicate ball gowns hanging gracefully among all the workaday clothes.

What are these doing here?

Running her fingers wonderingly across the silky fabric of a white gown, she tried to imagine herself wearing it, nibbling canapés and making small talk.

Her own bitter laugh surprised her.

Not my world.

She shoved the dresses back into the armoire roughly and turned to the desk.

The envelope Isabelle had left her was thick. Inside was a

map of the building, a class schedule, and a slim, black folder on
which was written:

Inside sheet after sheet had been written out by hand in a
similar dramatic, curling script.

What the hell . . . ?

Holding the papers in her hand, Allie lowered herself slowly
to the chair. She'd read no farther than the first line when someone tapped lightly on her door.

Before she could say a word, the door swung open and a
pretty girl in a Cimmeria uniform walked in. Her straight, white
blond hair brushed the tops of her shoulders, and she wore pink
Birkenstock sandals.

Noticing that her pedicure matched her shoes perfectly, Allie
felt awkward and tomboyish.

When was the last time I painted my nails?

She got the feeling the girl was trying not to stare.

"Allie?" She had a husky voice that didn't seem to match her
appearance. "I'm Jules, the prefect for your class. Isabelle asked
me to meet with you."

"Um, thanks."

There was a pause. Jules raised one perfect eyebrow inquiringly and tried again. "She thought you might have questions
that I could help you with?"

Allie struggled to think of interesting questions. And failed.
"So," she said after an uncomfortable pause, "are we supposed to
wear a uniform every day? All the time?"

Jules nodded. "Whenever we're anywhere on the grounds, we wear the uniform. There's a whole section on it in the papers Isabelle left for you."

"I was just sort of reading them." Allie wished she didn't sound like such an idiot. "But there's a lot to read."

"It's a lot to take in on your first day," Jules conceded. "I think my first day would have been awful, but my brother was here already, so he helped. Lots of kids have relatives who went here—do you?"

Shaking her head, Allie said, "I'd never heard of the place until . . . like, now."

Something flashed in Jules's eyes that Allie couldn't read, but she said only, "Well then, I better show you around."

Allie took a step toward the door but Jules glanced at her outfit meaningfully.

"Why don't you change first?" Flushing, Allie crossed her arms across her chest as Jules added, "I'll wait outside."

As soon as the door closed behind her, Allie yanked open the wardrobe door and pulled out a white shirt and neat blue skirt like the ones Jules wore and threw the outfit on the bed.

Had Jules been making fun of her clothes? She couldn't be certain, but she was so . . . perfect.

Of course she was making fun of me, Allie thought bitterly. *That's what girls like her do.*

Girls with perfect pedicures . . . She unlaced her boots violently and kicked them under the bed.

Girls with perfect hair . . .

She launched herself at the wardrobe to find acceptable shoes but unearthed only practical rubber-soled black oxfords and prim, schoolgirl white socks. She made a face as she pulled them on.

Stupid perfect girls.

Checking herself in the mirror on the back of the door, she felt self-conscious about her heavy makeup—it looked odd juxtaposed with her uniform. Jules wore only lip gloss.

But there was nothing to be done right now.

Smoothing her tangled hair with her hands, she walked out.

Jules was leaning against the wall. "Now you look like one of us," she said approvingly as they walked down the narrow hall.

Allie didn't know what to think about that.

"This area used to be the servants' quarters," Jules explained, oblivious to Allie's simmering resentment. They turned back toward the stairs. The building felt busier now, with uniformed students talking and laughing everywhere.

"Did Isabelle take you to the common room?"

Allie shook her head.

"What was she thinking? It's the most important room in the school." Jules spoke with such a flat cadence that Allie wasn't sure whether or not she was joking, so she smiled cautiously as they walked down the stairs.

"Most of us are in the common room after class, whenever we're not doing our prep," Jules explained.

"Prep?"

This time she had no problem reading Jules's face. It was as if Allie'd asked her to define "air."

"Homework." She opened a door at the foot of the stairs, and they stepped into a comfortable room with leather sofas, Oriental rugs scattered on the floor, a piano in one corner, and floor-to-ceiling bookshelves stacked with books and games. The room was empty save for one deep chair, where a boy sat watching them over the top of an ancient-looking book. He had straight black hair, a firm mouth, and huge dark eyes surrounded by thick lashes; his feet were propped casually on a tabletop painted like a chessboard. He studied her with a mixture of insolence and open curiosity that she found unnerving. She tried to keep her expression blank, but his lips curved up into a knowing smile. She could feel herself blush, and she wrenched her gaze away and looked back at Jules, who was watching her expectantly.

Say something.

"There's, uh . . . no television? Or . . ." She thought she heard a stifled chuckle from across the room, but she refused to look at him again.

Again she saw bafflement on Jules's face.

"No, definitely not." Jules' voice was stern. "No TV, no iPod, no laptops, no cell phones . . . No twenty-first century, really. Surely your parents mentioned this to you?"

As she listed off the things the students couldn't have, Allie's heart sank with each word. In answer to Jules's question, she shook her head mutely.

Of course not, Allie thought. *Because my parents knew if they'd told me that, they'd never get me in the car.*

Clearly astonished, Jules gathered herself enough to explain. "How odd that nobody told you. It's one of Cimmeria's big selling points. We're expected to learn how to amuse ourselves in more traditional ways. Like conversation and reading. Trust me, they'll keep you so busy with prep, you won't have time for TV anyway." Jules turned to walk out of the room. "It's all in the packet. . . ."

That stupid packet. It will take me all bloody night to read it and learn more about how rubbish this place is.

Without looking back at the boy in the chair, she followed the prefect out of the room.

"So, you've got a little while until dinner, and I'd suggest you read through the packet," Jules said. "That stuff is really important."

Allie stopped herself from screaming in frustration.

Back in her room, she flipped through the stack of papers on the desk and tried to focus on class guides ("Students must be in their seats before the instructor begins each class . . ."), but her thoughts returned to the boy in the leather chair. The way he'd looked at her had been so . . . disconcerting. Like he was trying to get a reaction out of her. She twirled her pencil between her fingers, remembering the way his dark eyes had studied her.

Turning over another page, she glanced down at her watch.

Balls.

It was one minute until seven o'clock. Where had the time gone? Dinner was starting.

Dashing out the door at top speed, she barely avoided colliding with a girl with short blond hair who hurtled past her.

"Watch it!" the girl yelled without breaking her stride. Allie stepped in right behind her.

"Sorry! I didn't see you."

The girl didn't look back, and they both ran downstairs and skidded to a stop at the dining room entrance. Without exchanging a word, they walked into the room with the same air of contrived insouciance—as if they'd been chatting casually on the way down. The blond girl glanced at her and winked before sitting at what appeared to be her regular table, judging by the way everybody there greeted her.

Only then did Allie really look around her. The room was enormous and elegant. At one end a gigantic fireplace, so big she could have stood up in it without bumping her head, was unlit. Candles sparkled on round tables swathed in white tablecloths. Plates in the school colors and crystal glasses glittered in front of each seat.

The air smelled of something delicious, but being alone in a room filled with strangers made Allie's stomach tighten into a tiny knot. Spotting an empty chair nearby, she slid into it as if it had *refuge* painted on the back.

Conversation at the table died instantly. Seven pairs of eyes turned toward her.

"Is it okay if I, uh . . . sit here?"

Before anyone could answer, the door to the kitchen opened and waitstaff appeared, dressed in black and carrying platters of food. Somebody placed a clear glass jug of water at Allie's elbow. Until that moment she hadn't realized how thirsty she was, and she longed to fill her glass but waited to see what everybody else was doing. Nobody moved.

"Please do."

She followed the voice, with its French accent, to her left side, where a boy with tawny skin, thick dark hair, and exquisite blue eyes was watching her.

"Excuse me?"

"You asked if you could sit here," he said. "Please do."

She smiled at him gratefully. "Thank you."

He smiled back, and she thought she might actually melt into a puddle on the floor. He was gorgeous.

"You're welcome. Would you be so kind as to pass the water to me?"

She handed him the pitcher and, to her relief, he filled her glass before his own. She drank half of the glass very quickly, and then served herself from the platter of beef and potatoes he passed to her. Silence fell again.

One of us should talk, she thought, glancing at him from underneath her eyelashes. *He's probably waiting for me to say something.*

"Allie," she blurted out before she could stop herself. Then, inwardly cursing, she added, "I mean—that's my name. I'm Allie. And . . . I'm . . . new. . . ."

Her inane words trailed off mercifully as she contemplated kicking herself to death as soon as dinner finished.

But his smile was understanding.

"I'm Sylvain." In his musical accent it sounded like he'd said "Sil-VAN." She committed it to memory. "Welcome to Cimmeria."

"Thanks," she said, relaxing a little.

The food was delicious. She hadn't had anything to eat since an awful, stilted breakfast in London, and now she ate ravenously. As she speared the last piece of potato into her mouth, though, she glanced up to find everyone watching her—her throat tightened, and she chewed with difficulty, then reached for her glass of water, which she noticed too late was again empty.

Sylvain picked up the glass and filled it for her. His eyes glittered in the candlelight like blue fire.

"You're from London." The abrupt voice came from a red-haired girl across the table, and Allie looked up in surprise.

"Yes. How did you . . . ?"

"They told us a new student was coming. You're Allie Sheridan." The redhead stated this matter-of-factly, as if she were reporting the day's news.

Allie's reply was guarded. "So they tell me. Who are you?"

"Katie." None of the others volunteered their names.

Uncomfortable under their combined gaze, Allie longed to fill the awkward gap in the conversation. But small talk had never been her strong suit.

"This school is . . . huge," she fumbled after a long silence. "The building is kind of scary."

"Is it?" Katie sounded taken aback. "I think it's beautiful. Everyone in my family went to school here. Didn't your parents go here?"

When Allie shook her head, Katie arched one perfect eyebrow as the girls on either side of her murmured to each other.

"How strange."

Allie felt her hackles rise.

"Why is that so strange?" she asked, in a tone Mark or Harry would have recognized as dangerous.

Katie tilted her head to one side. "Most of the kids here are legacy—I am, Sylvain is, and Jo is, too."

Allie looked at her blankly. "Who's Jo?"

Katie seemed bemused. "The girl you came in with."

"Miss Sheridan." The booming voice came from behind her seat, and Allie turned sideways to see its owner, a balding man who looked to be her father's age. He was very tall—well over six feet—and although he wore a tired-looking suit, he stood with almost military carriage. Allie sat up straighter.

The room fell silent.

"Has anyone explained to you the rules on meals at Cimmeria?" The look he gave her felt like contempt.

"Yes." Her voice quivered slightly, and she hated that.

"All students must be in this room before the start of every meal. You cut it a little too close today. As did you, Miss Arringford." He spun on his heel and pointed at Jo, who regarded him fearlessly. Turning back at Allie, he said, "Don't let it happen again. New or not, the next time you're late, you'll face detention."

He strode away, his heels making a clicking sound in the hushed room.

Allie stared at her empty plate, feeling the room's eyes on her. Her cheeks flushed with anger. She had been *two seconds late*. He had no right to humiliate her in front of the entire school for that.

I can't believe it. I just got here and I'm already in trouble.

Looking over at the nearby table, she saw Jo watching her. When their eyes met, Jo gave her a cheeky smile and another wink before returning to talking and laughing with her friends as if nothing serious had happened. As Allie watched, a boy rubbed Jo's arm and she rested her head on his shoulder for a moment, smiling at something he'd said.

Allie felt both better and worse.

The others at her table were talking to one another now, pointedly ignoring her. All except Sylvain, who looked concerned.

"Who was that?" she asked, folding and unfolding her linen napkin, pretending that what had happened wasn't that important.

"Mr. Zelazny," he said. "History teacher. A bit officious, as you can tell. He sees himself as the school's enforcer. I'd like to say that you shouldn't worry, but in reality you don't want to get on

26

his bad side. He can make your life . . . unhappy. If I were you, I'd be early for meals for the next few days. He will be watching you."

"Great." She sighed.

All around them students began rising from their tables and walking out. Allie saw that they left their plates and glasses on the table.

"Don't we help clear the tables?" she asked, surprised.

The girls next to Katie giggled.

"Of course not," Katie said. "The staff do that."

Allie turned back to Sylvain, but his seat was empty. He was gone. She could hear more giggling and whispering around the table, and she'd had just about enough of that today, so without another word she joined those walking to the door.

Her shoulders sagged under the weight of the day. What she wouldn't give to go back to her room and listen to her iPod while texting Mark and Harry about the weird people she'd met today. But that world seemed very far away from Cimmeria's stuffy, antiquated universe where technology didn't exist and people were too pampered to pick up their own plates and carry them to the kitchen.

In the hallway students were streaming outside into the fading daylight; others headed to the common room. They all seemed to be traveling in cheerful groups, talking and laughing.

Alone, she climbed the stairs toward the girls' rooms. Her feet felt so heavy, she might as well have been climbing Everest.

Twenty-four steps to the second floor, twenty more to the third, then seventeen steps down the hall to her room.

Once inside, Allie saw that somebody had been in while she was at dinner. The window was closed, although the shutter was still open. The bed was now covered in crisp white sheets and a fluffy white duvet; a dark blue blanket was folded neatly across the footboard. The clothes she'd thrown on the floor had disappeared, replaced by a pair of soft, white slippers. Two white towels were folded up on the chair with a bar of soap on top. The papers on the desk had been straightened into a neat pile.

Somebody around here's a clean freak.

Kicking off her shoes, she picked up the packet of papers she'd tried to read earlier and threw herself onto the bed. She'd only made it through half of it, though, when her eyelids drooped. For a second, she let her head rest on her course schedule.

She woke with a start—as her head jerked up, a page stuck comically to her cheek. Pulling the paper off, she glanced at the old-fashioned analog alarm clock on her desk. It was just ten. She couldn't believe it was so early—she was exhausted.

Grabbing her toothbrush, she headed down the hall to the bathroom. As she stood at a row of white sinks, brushing her teeth, she studied herself in the mirror. Did she look older now than she had a week ago?

She felt older.

Back in her room she closed the shutter over the window and climbed into bed. But when she switched off the desk lamp, the room was plunged into total darkness. It was *way* too dark. In a slight panic, she groped for the lamp, knocking over her alarm clock, which fell to the floor with a musical thud.

Jumping out of bed, she stubbed her toe hard against the chair and hopped on one foot, cursing, before reaching out to open the shutter. The early moonlight bathed the room with a soft glow.

That was better.

She lay in bed watching the stars appear in the sky. She'd counted one hundred forty-seven breaths when she fell asleep.

"Allie, run!"

The scream came from ahead of her in the darkness. Allie didn't know why anyone felt it necessary to say that anyway—she was already running, and running as fast as she could. Her hair flew behind her, and although she couldn't really see the trees clearly—she could just make out their shapes—she could feel the branches grabbing at her clothes, the twigs tearing her flesh. The forest floor was uneven, and she knew that eventually she would lose her footing. You can't run blindly in the dark through the woods. It's impossible.

Suddenly, just behind her, she heard footsteps and felt the air move as if someone were right . . .

Hard fingers cut into the skin on her left shoulder and she cried out, swatting whoever it was with her hands, beating them away from her.

Then she heard a contemptuous laugh right behind her and, screaming, she was pulled off her feet by hands she couldn't see. Allie sat bolt upright. Disoriented, she scrambled into the far corner of the bed, her back to the wall and her arms wrapped around her knees protectively. Her heart pounded.

Then she remembered.

Cimmeria. School.

That dream again. She'd been having it for weeks. Each time she woke up sweating.

The room was still dark—the clock showed that it was just after 12:30. She felt wide-awake and anxious, and yet somehow still groggy, as if nothing were real.

Untangling herself from the sheets, she climbed out of bed

and leaned across the desk to look outside. The moon gave the world an unearthly blue glow. She clambered up onto the desktop and opened the window, closing her eyes as the cool breeze flowed over her. Resting her chin on her arms, she gazed out into the night. She breathed the fresh air in deeply. The smell was unusual to her—pine needles and loamy soil rather than the exhaust and concrete of the city she was used to—but she found it comforting.

Suddenly she heard footsteps . . . above her? Was that possible?

Straining to see above her window, she could have sworn she saw a shadow moving on the roof.

She sat still for a moment, listening, and thought she could hear, very faintly, a susurration of voices above her.

Goose bumps crawled up Allie's arms, and her breath came in short gasps. She fought to calm down.

You're just imagining it, Allie. It's nothing. The wind.

Staying as still as she could, she listened, her head against the window frame, her hand on the latch, ready to slam it shut if needed.

But this time she heard nothing. Even the wind had quieted.

She sat like that for half an hour, until her head nodded against her chest. Then she closed the window, latching it tightly.

When she'd climbed back into bed, she lay awake for a long time, watching shadows cast by trees in the moonlight dance on the ceiling.

THREE

Allie opened her eyes to find the room flooded with daylight. In the hazy space between sleep and wakefulness she thought that, with its pure white walls and pristine white duvet, it looked like heaven.

It was only six thirty, but she could hear voices in the hallway as she stretched and yawned. The room was cool with the fresh morning air.

She sat up straight and stared at the wide-open window.

Hadn't she closed it last night?

I'm sure I did. Pulling the covers up to her chin, she replayed her actions from the night before in her mind. They just didn't jibe with what she was seeing in front of her.

The more she thought about it, though, the more she began to doubt her own memory.

I was so tired. Maybe I just dreamed that I closed it. Maybe it was all a dream.

But it had seemed so real.

When she climbed out of bed, she kept her eyes on the window, as if it might suddenly do something unexpected. But it never moved as she pulled on her robe and slid her feet into her slippers, and in the end, she wrapped her shampoo and toothbrush in a towel and hurried down the hall, readjusting her anxieties to direct them to the shared bathroom scenario ahead.

In contrast to its echoing emptiness last night, the room was now steamy and busy, but there was one free shower. Relieved it wasn't one of those everybody-naked-in-a-brutal-concrete-cube shared showers, Allie pulled the curtain closed behind her and stepped in to find a private changing area in front of a spacious white shower cubicle. Both were spotless.

This wasn't so bad, actually. In the hot spray she felt better almost immediately. Later, with her wet hair wrapped in a towel, she found a free sink to brush her teeth and didn't really mind how busy it was. Swathed in a thick white robe like everybody else, she was less conspicuous as the new girl.

Back in her room she combed her damp hair and reached for her makeup bag. Pulling out her eyeliner, she prepared to add her customary swoosh, but something stayed her hand. Should she? Nobody here wore much makeup. Somehow it felt odd applying her London cosmetic shield in the sunny countryside. She hadn't worn much makeup until last year. Until everything fell apart. In the mirror her eyes clouded. Shaking her head to clear the dark thoughts, she applied a quick line of black above her top lashes and a layer of mascara for good measure.

But nothing more.

She stuffed her papers and pens into a dark blue tote bag she'd found in the wardrobe and, swinging it over her shoulder, headed downstairs at seven o'clock on the dot, well ahead of the seven thirty breakfast deadline.

In the doorway of the dining room door she paused in surprise—it had been transformed. Huge windows along one wall
let in sunlight, diffused through white blinds. Gone were the
twinkling candles and sparkling glasses. Most of the tables were
empty and topped only with plain white tablecloths. Food was
piled on buffet tables: ten kinds of cereal, a steaming cauldron
of porridge, and stacks of bread ready for toasting. Heated silver
serving platters held eggs, bacon, and sausages.

As soon as she smelled the food, she was starving again. She
piled her plate with toast, cheese, and scrambled eggs, then
poured herself a glass of apple juice before claiming a seat at an
empty table. She didn't recognize anybody in the room, which
was, in its own way, nice. Smearing butter and black currant jam
on her toast, she took a huge bite.

"Is this seat taken?"

Trying not to chew with her mouth open, Allie turned to see
Sylvain standing beside her. She shook her head and struggled
to swallow gracefully but failed, wincing as the food went down.
For the first time she thought his smile reached his extraordinary
eyes.

"No . . . I mean . . . Yes. You can sit here. Please."

Ignoring her awkwardness as if he hadn't noticed, he sat down
next to her. His plate was piled with eggs and bacon, and he'd
balanced a cup of coffee on top of it all, which he now carefully
dislodged.

"How did you find your first night?" he asked, glancing up
from his rearranging. "I looked for you in the common room but
couldn't find you."

Her heart jumped and she looked determinedly at her cheese so that he wouldn't see how pleased she was that he'd looked for her.

"I had a lot to read last night. I thought I'd better learn as much as I could before today to, you know, get ready. Big day and all that."

He nodded and bit into his bacon. "I remember that from my first day. They seem to want you to learn everything about Cimmeria all at once. I think the information they give you is more than"—adorably, he seemed to struggle to think of the English words he was looking for—"the school in size, if that makes sense?"

Charmed, she couldn't help but smile. "I know exactly what you mean. It's disproportionate."

"Yes. Disproportionate." He smiled back at her and Allie's heart jumped again.

Stop that, she told herself firmly. *He's just being polite.*

Silence fell and she hurried to fill it.

"So," she said, "does everybody hang out in the common room a lot? It looks okay."

Great small talk, Allie. Really smooth.

He didn't seem to notice her inanity as he sipped his milky coffee. "The common room and the library are where people are most nights. In the summer on warm nights many of us choose to be outside, though. I was outside last night, playing night cro-quet. That is why I was looking for you. I thought you might want to join us."

Allie's fork stopped halfway to her mouth.

"You were playing croquet at night? In the dark?"

"It's more fun that way. You know, I've found that many games are more exotic if played at night." His eyes held hers for just a second too long.

Warmth rose in her cheeks and she tore her eyes away from his. Her gaze skittered around the room.

Chair, table, girl-with-ponytail, window, chair again . . .

When she glanced back at him, a slight smile played at the edge of his lips as he watched her face.

He's flirting with me. Definitely.

"Football without lights, for example," he continued thoughtfully, "although that can be a bit . . . rough."

He balanced a piece of toast on his fingertips while he considered the possibilities. "And tennis with fluorescent rackets on a moonless night is incredible. I think you'd love it. I promise to find you the next time we play—wherever you are."

She watched as if hypnotized while he took a bite.

"Allie. How nice to see you again."

Katie's sarcastic words pulled Allie out of her reverie as the girl and a group of her friends sat down at their table. Allie recognized some of them from the night before.

"And Sylvain. What a surprise."

Katie's long, curly red hair contrasted brilliantly with her milky, translucent skin. In the soft light, she seemed illuminated. Her group of perfectly styled friends watched Allie with amusement.

"I was just leaving, actually." Sylvain's voice was icy.

But when he turned back to Allie, his gaze warmed. "We have English together, I believe. It's Robert Browning this week, in case you want to read before class. See you then."

He walked away before she could ask him how he knew what

classes she was taking, but when he reached the doorway, he turned back for just a second. When their eyes met, Allie felt as if somebody had draped a warm blanket across her shoulders.

After he was gone, she smiled at her apple juice.

"Sylvain's lovely, isn't he?" Katie's crisp west London accent cut into her reverie. Allie looked up to find she was watching her knowingly. "Those dreamy eyes and that melty accent. His girlfriend's lovely, too, isn't she?" She turned to the brunette beside her, who nodded and giggled.

"She's staying in France this summer." Katie delicately consumed a segment of grapefruit as Allie felt her emotional balloon burst. "But she'll be back next term."

Ah. Girlfriend. Right. So much for that, then.

She was not surprised to find the inevitable crushing blow of early romantic disappointment following hard on the heels of hope. Frankly, that was how things usually went for her. When she'd first met Mark, there'd been something there. For two weeks it had been obvious to everybody that they'd get together. Until one night he'd shown up with a perky, diminutive blonde named Charlotte who had a penchant for miniskirts and hot pink nail polish.

After that he was just Allie's friend.

"How nice for him," she said resignedly. "Well . . . I have to go, too."

She stood up and walked away quickly, stopping herself at the last minute from looking for a place to take her plate and glass. Hearing giggles behind her, she straightened her spine and did not look back.

Outside the dining hall Allie joined other students

walking down the wide hallway with oak wainscoting toward the classrooms in the east wing. The walls were lined with oil paintings—most were huge portraits of nineteenth-century men and women in formal attire staring down at her haughtily. A few portrayed Cimmeria from different perspectives, most from the hill outside with thick forest in the foreground.

Her first class was biology; climbing the staircase to the second floor, she found the room near the top of the stairs.

The handful of students who'd arrived early were sitting in pairs at tables arranged in long rows as a tall, distracted-looking man with wire-framed glasses and unruly brown hair flipped through papers at the front of the room.

"Hi," Allie said to get his attention. "I'm Alyson Sheridan. I'm new."

He peered at her over the top of his glasses and shuffled his papers again at length, finally emerging with one, which he waved triumphantly.

"Of course you are. A transfer student, how lovely. But I have you down as 'Allie.' Which do you prefer?"

"Allie," she said, surprised. School records always had her down as Alyson.

"Then Allie it is." He was shuffling papers again distractedly. "I'm Jeremiah Cole. The students usually call me Jerry. Please take the second seat on the right there, next to Jo."

She glanced in the direction he pointed to see the blond girl from dinner last night waving vigorously.

"I'm so glad it's you. I do hope you're good at biology," she said as soon as Allie walked up. "I think all the sciences are diabolical— dead baby animals and parasites—what are they trying to tell us?

37

Crikey, we got into trouble last night, didn't we? Does that always happen to you?"

She had a contagious smile—white, even teeth, deep endearing dimples, and little crinkles around her tiny nose—and an incredibly posh accent. Allie smiled back at her before her brain realized she wanted to do it.

"It does always happen to me. If you hang around with me, it will definitely happen again," she said.

"Brilliant!" Jo beamed at her. "This is going to be *amazing*."

As Allie pulled out her notebook, Jo whispered, "Isn't Jerry *adorable* for an old guy? I had a crush on him my whole first year here."

Allie studied the teacher. He looked like somebody's dad. A nice dad. But a dad nonetheless.

"I like that you can call teachers by their first names here," she said noncommittally. "My last school was so strict we practically had to call them 'Officer.'"

Laughing, Jo looked like she wasn't sure whether or not to believe her. "You're going to have to tell me more about your life," she said. "It sounds much better than mine."

Don't count on it, Allie thought. But she just smiled.

Jo showed her where the class had reached in the book. "It's disgusting," she said cheerfully. "Today I think we're dissecting."

As if on cue, Jerry called for quiet.

"This morning we'll be looking at the general internal construction of amphibians, thanks to the sacrifice of this little fellow."

Reaching under his desk, he pulled out a dissection tray containing a dead frog, spread-eagled and pinioned, its pale belly curving at them vulnerably.

"Oh, bollocks." Jo grimaced.

"Who can tell me why we're dissecting a frog rather than some other poor creature?" Jerry asked, looking at the class over the top of his glasses. "Why do we torment these innocent pond dwellers? How about you, Allie? Has everybody met Allie, by the way?" He pointed at her and everybody turned to look. "Is this something you studied at your school in London?"

In the glare of attention, Allie felt the color drain from her cheeks.

"I . . . I guess . . ."

"Because a frog's anatomy is so much like man's." The voice, deep and pleasing, came from behind her.

"Mr. West," Jerry said, glancing without warmth toward the speaker, "is correct as usual, although he could wait his turn. The anatomy of the frog is somewhat similar to human anatomy. . . ."

Allie turned around in her seat to see who had saved her, and instantly recognized the boy from the common room yesterday. He was staring at her with those big dark eyes. But before she could thank him, he turned away. Flushing, she turned back to the front.

Science was not her best subject, and so she tried not to think about "Mr. West" again, and focused instead on Jerry's lesson about frogs.

She didn't look back again.

"You took loads of notes," Jo said as they were walking out. "I'm so psyched that you're really into science. I need a friend who's a science geek."

"I'm not that into it," Allie admitted. "I just think I'm going to have to work to catch up. This class is way ahead of my last school."

"This *is* a really hard school," Jo said. "But it's fun, too. Although it does have too many freaky rules."

Thinking about the ban on computers and phones, Allie nodded. "Totally."

Pretending to straighten her bag strap, she asked casually, "Hey, who was that guy who saved me from the frog question? Jerry called him 'Mr. West.'"

With a knowing look, Jo lowered her voice confidentially. "Carter West," she whispered. "He is totally hot. But he's a mess. So you probably shouldn't."

Allie was so intrigued she didn't bother to deny interest. "How is a he a mess?"

"He thinks he knows everything and that everybody else is shallow. He's infuriating. Constantly in detention. Half the teachers hate him, and the others treat him like, I don't know, he's their kid or something. And he's a notorious womanizer. He gets what he wants and then he's not interested anymore. You'd be better off working that Sylvain thing you've got going."

Allie blushed. "I don't have anything going with Sylvain."

"Well, I think he's got something going with you." Jo elbowed her.

"Actually, I heard he has a girlfriend in Paris."

"First I've heard of it." Jo seemed genuinely surprised. "Who told you that?"

"The redheaded girl. What's her name . . . Katie?"

"Oh, Katie Gilmore." Jo's voice dripped with contempt. "She's such a liar. Don't listen to a word she says. She's always had a thing for Sylvain and he's never been interested in her at all. She must really hate the way he's just fallen for you."

Allie kept her expression blank, but inside she was churning.

So Katie wants to mess with my head, does she? Fine then.

Game on.

The day was a brain burner of new classes, new teachers, and new classmates, and of finding out the truth about just how much schoolwork she needed to do. She had Mr. Zelazny for history, which seemed like a nightmare, but to her relief, aside from a brief hard stare when she first walked into his classroom, he treated her like everybody else.

Her next class was Isabelle's English seminar, and as she walked in, the first person she saw was Sylvain, leaning back in a desk, his long legs stretched out gracefully. He was talking to the boy beside him, but she noticed that he was watching her as she walked up to Isabelle.

"Hi, Allie." The headmistress smiled. "How has your first day been so far?"

"So far so good," Allie said, only lying a little.

She handed Allie a syllabus. "We're reading Robert Browning today. Are you at all familiar with his work?"

In between classes, Allie had read the Browning in her textbook. "I've read 'Life in a Love,'" she said.

"What do you think of it?"

Allie fidgeted. "It was all right."

Isabelle tilted her head to one side, looking unimpressed. "Is that your full review?"

Allie hated poetry, but now seemed like a bad time to mention it. She leaned on the edge of a desk as she fumbled for the right words. "To be honest . . . it seemed a bit . . . you know, stalky."

For a second the headmistress looked as if she was going to argue, but then she stopped herself and handed Allie the class syllabus. "Fair enough. Sit anywhere you like."

The desks were arranged in a circle, which somehow made choosing one more difficult. After a moment's hesitation, Allie chose a seat at random. When she sat down, she saw that Sylvain was still watching her. She raised her hand hesitantly, and he smiled at her before turning back to the boy beside him.

Isabelle stepped into the circle and leaned against an empty desk.

"I hope everybody read some Browning last night. I'm curious to hear what you all thought. He had a unique style that rebelled against many of the accepted rules of poetry of the time, so I thought some of you might relate to his approach. I presume you've all had a chance to meet our new student, Allie. Allie, I don't want to embarrass you, but would you please read the first few lines?"

Oh God.

Standing uncomfortably, she held her book close to her face and cleared her throat.

> *Escape me?*
> *Never—*
> *Beloved!*
> *While I am I, and you are you,*
> *So long as the world contains us both,*
> *Me the loving and you the loth*
> *While the one eludes, must the other pursue.*

At Isabelle's nod, Allie slipped gratefully back into her desk.

"So, what is Browning saying here?" The class regarded the headmistress in silence. Allie was fairly confident that she knew, but no way was she going to say anything right now.

"It's about obsession."

Somehow Allie hadn't seen Carter West come in, but he was sitting just a few desks away from her.

Isabelle nodded. "Care to elaborate?"

"As long as they both exist on the same planet, he has to be with her," Carter said. "He's in love with her, but it's more than love. It's everything. He thinks they were meant to be together, but she doesn't. So his life is spent trying to convince her."

"Interesting theory." Isabelle glanced at Allie. "Anyone else?"

Allie slid down in her seat.

"Ismay," the headmistress said, turning to a familiar-looking brunette. "Can you read the next few lines?"

Allie chanced a sideways glance in Carter's direction and then looked away sharply. He was looking right at her.

"What is it with the boys in this school?"

Allie and Jo were walking to the library. Classes had ended for the day, and Jo had intercepted her on the way back to her room and suggested they study together.

"What do you mean?" Jo asked.

"They stare," Allie said. "A lot."

Jo smiled. "You're pretty. And new. Boys stare at pretty new girls."

"I'm not *that* pretty. Boys didn't stare at me like that in London."

"I think you're pretty," Jo said. "Maybe they just"—she

shrugged—"want you to notice them."

They both giggled. Allie pretended to sag under the weight of her book bag. "I can't believe how much prep I need to do."

Jo nodded. "They really bury us in the summer, because if you're here for the summer term, it's because you've got, like, promise."

"Promise?" Allie raised her eyebrows.

"You know, potential. Whatever. There's loads more students here in the autumn and winter terms, but summer break is for extra studying, mostly for advanced students—the brainiacs. Everybody else gets the summer off. That's why I don't mind being here in July." Jo pushed open the library door and lowered her voice to a whisper. "We have the place to ourselves, and the people who are here at this time of year are the coolest."

I'm not here because I'm smart, Allie thought with a frown.

As they walked into the library's hush, she breathed in the rich mix of leather, old books, and lemony wood polish. The room stretched farther than she could see through a forest of dark wooden bookshelves that reached to the ceiling fifteen feet above their heads. Each row had its own rolling ladder giving access to the highest shelves. The floor was covered with thick Oriental rugs that captured the sound of their footsteps. Ancient, wrought-iron light fixtures that surely must have once held candles hung several feet below the ceiling on thick chains, so that the books on the top shelves were lost in the shadows. Heavy wooden tables topped with green-shaded lamps were surrounded by leather chairs; many were already occupied by students, dwarfed by the stacks of books piled around them.

Intimidated by the display of studiousness and its

accoutrements, Allie tried to push back a wave of insecurity. She was already so far behind: How would she ever catch up? For the first time in a long time she cared about failing.

She followed as Jo wound her way to a table neatly placed to provide a good view of the main study area while managing to be slightly out of the sight line of the librarian's desk. They stacked their books onto the table and settled into the big leather chairs. They were immersed in history when two leanly muscled arms wrapped around Jo from behind, pinning her to her seat. She gasped and then giggled as a handsome blond boy appeared near her shoulder, kissing her neck lightly.

"Gabe, stop it! You haven't met Allie yet. And you need to, because Allie is a goddess." Jo's face glowed, and Allie felt a twinge of envy chased by a brief surge of guilt for having felt it.

Gabe gave her a welcoming smile, his hazel eyes glittering in the lamplight. Reaching around Jo, he held out a strong hand with square, neat fingernails. "Hello, Allie. I've never met a goddess before."

"There's a first time for everything," she said, trying to look goddesslike as she shook his hand.

Brushing a kiss on the top of Jo's head, he sat down across the table from her and pulled her notebook closer so he could see it. "What are you two working on? Ah, history. Good to see you studying so diligently."

Jo rolled her eyes at Allie. "Gabe's a year ahead of us. Sometimes it makes him pompous."

He laughed and swished the end of a pen lightly up her arm. "Not pompous. Just experienced."

Jo giggled again as Gabe turned to Allie. "So you're the famous

Allie Sheridan everybody's talking about."

Allie was startled. "Everyone's talking about me? Why would they talk about me?"

"Relax." He smiled. "It's just because you're new. Fresh meat. Those of us who are here year-round can start to feel a bit cut off from the rest of the world. So a new student in the summer is about as exciting as it gets. Plus there's the whole Sylvain thing. . . ."

His voice was ripe with suggestion as it trailed off, and he and Jo both smiled at her as if she'd done something wonderful.

"Oh, for God's sake." Allie had heard enough of "the whole Sylvain thing." "I'm sorry to disappoint you, but there isn't a Sylvain thing."

Jo leaned toward Gabe. "Allie's in denial. I think they're meant to be together."

Allie bristled. "I'm not in denial."

"Either way," Gabe said smoothly, "everybody's noticed that he's interested in you. And we're all intrigued."

"Why is it so intriguing?"

Jo leaned toward Allie, her eyes sparkling in the lamplight. "Sylvain is kind of . . . special. His parents are very . . . Let's just say they're important people. And just . . . look at him, you know? He's got those muscles and those cheekbones. . . ."

Rolling his eyes, Gabe flipped pages in her notebook.

"Lots of girls over the years have tried to get his attention, but nobody's ever really succeeded," Jo continued. "Not properly, anyway. But then you came along and suddenly it's like he has this huge crush."

All this talk about Sylvain made Allie feel pressured, and she always hated that feeling. She leaned back in her chair and crossed her legs.

"Well, I'm sorry to disappoint everyone, but I'm not sure I'm interested."

Clearly surprised by this response, Gabe looked up from Jo's notebook.

Answering his unasked question, Jo said, "I think she's into somebody else."

"Oh, really? Who?" Gabe said, and she gave him a significant look.

"Carter." She wrinkled her nose when she said it.

"Oh no." Gabe leaned toward Allie intently. "Seriously. You can't. Not West. He's the single worst guy you could go for here."

"Thanks, Gabe. I never knew you cared."

Recognizing the rich deep voice instantly, Allie froze in her seat, trying to figure out how to dissolve into the leather and never be seen again.

But Gabe was undaunted. "Oh, get over it, West. You know it's the truth. You haven't exactly made a name for yourself around here as a reliable, trustworthy boyfriend."

Giving Allie an apologetic look, Jo stacked up her books briskly. Color was high in her cheeks. "I was just about to dash to the common room for a break before dinner. Should we all go?"

She and Gabe both stood up, but Allie was immobilized with embarrassment, pinned to her seat like that frog on the dissection tray.

Besides, she told herself, *leaving now would look cowardly. And I'm not a coward.*

She raised her chin to meet Jo's eyes. "No thanks. I'm going to

47

get through a bit more before I take a break."

Over Carter's shoulder Jo mouthed, "I'm sorry," at her before walking toward the door with Gabe.

Without waiting for an invitation, Carter sat down in the seat Jo had just left. Allie pretended to write a note to herself in her history notebook. But her mind was spinning.

So he now thinks I've got this major crush on him. So what? Let him think it.

She counted two breaths in and out.

"Hey," he said.

Looking up from her notebook, she saw that he was leaning forward. His face was close—his dark eyes looking right into hers. She thought, inanely, that his lashes were really long, and his eyebrows straight and fine.

Somehow she kept her face expressionless, but her burning cheeks surely betrayed her.

"I don't think we've been properly introduced," he said. "I'm Carter West."

"I know," she said. "I'm Allie Sheridan." She willed her voice to be steady and unembarrassed, and for a change it cooperated. She held his gaze fearlessly. Or at least she hoped it came across as fearless.

"I know." His smile seemed mocking as he settled comfortably in the chair. "We should talk."

"Should we?" she said coolly. "What about?"

"You."

"Terrific," Allie said. "Well, my favorite color is blue and I love puppies. Your turn."

"Very funny," he said, looking like it wasn't very funny.

"Oh yes," she said. "And I'm very funny. Sorry, I forgot to mention it earlier."

He was beginning to look exasperated. "That's really useful, thanks. But what I was wondering is, what are you doing at Cimmeria? New students never join in the middle of summer term. So you must be somebody."

Put off by his investigative tone, Allie leaned away from him and crossed her arms. Her embarrassment was beginning to fade—replaced by irritation and suspicion.

She twirled her pen between her fingers. "I won a contest?"

"Funny," he said, although his face said it wasn't. "Seriously. Never be afraid to be honest. What brought you here really?"

So he wasn't going to let go. Fine then.

She raised her chin and met his eyes directly. "I got arrested."

He shrugged. "So?"

"Three times."

"Oh."

"In one year."

He gave a low whistle. "Right. You've been busy. But getting arrested doesn't get you into Cimmeria. This isn't a reform school. Why are you here?"

Stung, Allie could feel her temper rising, but she fought it back. "To be honest, I have no idea. My parents told me that I was coming here, and then here I was. They said it specializes in kids like me. Whatever that means."

"Interesting." He studied her curiously, as if she were a puzzling display in a museum cabinet.

She shot him a sharp look. "What's so interesting about it?"

"Some troubled kids do come here, but not in the summer

term. All the summer term students are high academic achievers—advanced students."

A flash of resentment shot through her, and she glared at him.

Do I have "too stupid to be here" tattooed on my forehead?

She stacked her books in angry piles.

"I guess it's impossible to consider the idea that I might be troubled *and* smart." She spat the last word out. "Well then, I better get on with studying, right? I'll have to really work hard to keep up with all you geniuses."

"Hey." He looked startled. "Don't be so sensitive. I'm just trying to figure you out."

And that was all it took. After Katie and Jules and Zelazny, her parents and the police, she'd had it. She shoved the books into her bag and spun around to face him.

"Well, don't. Okay? Don't try to figure me out. Don't try to analyze me. And, while you're at it, quit insulting me. You see me in class and overhear a conversation and think you know me. But believe me, you know *nothing* about me."

She stormed out of the library and ran up the stairs, her muscles straining at the speed with which she took them.

. . . fifty-two, fifty-three, fifty-four steps . . .

She just made it to her room before the tears came. The bag dropped from her nerveless fingers, and leaning back against the door, she slid down to the floor with her face buried in her hands and sobbed quietly. Why was she here? Everybody treated her like the village idiot who'd slipped in when the guard's back was turned. She could feel her breath growing shallow, and she fought back against an oncoming panic attack. But the edges of her vision started to go black.

She counted her breaths, the boards on the wooden floor, the books on the shelves, and the panes of glass in the window until she felt herself regain control, and her sight began to return to normal.

When she felt better, she climbed to her feet. Opening the door, she checked to see if the hall was empty before hurrying down to the bathroom to splash cold water on her face. As she smoothed her hair back, the door opened and Jules walked in. Her eyes took in Allie's tear-stained cheeks and a worried look flashed across her face.

"Hey, Allie. How are you settling in?"

Allie didn't feel like faking it. And she didn't feel like talking about it. She just wanted to be someplace else.

"Everything's great, Jules." Her words dripped sarcasm but she couldn't help it. "Everybody's being so nice. It's all just . . . great."

Before Jules could react, she opened the door and ran down the hall.

She'd never felt more lonely in her life.

Allie awoke with a start and sat up in the wooden chair. Her back ached. Outside the pool of light cast by the desk lamp, the room was dark.

What time is it?

Her brain foggy, she turned the alarm clock to face her. Two o'clock in the morning.

Must have fallen asleep at my desk.

She was sitting in front of the open window, a stack of papers spread out in front of her. After her meltdown she hadn't been hungry, so she'd skipped dinner and stayed in her room to catch up on her reading.

The last thing she could remember was reading The Rules.

After finishing her homework, it had occurred to her that she'd never really read them, and she'd pulled them out of the desk drawer. They were so strange and proscriptive that at first she couldn't believe what she was reading.

Welcome, Allie.

Cimmeria Academy is a unique place in which to learn, and we are very glad to have you here among us. The school has, for many years, operated according to rules set out long ago by its founders.

All new students are given a handbook when they first arrive to teach them the rules that must now guide them. This is your personal handbook. Please keep it safe, and use wisely the information it gives you. There is much to learn, but perhaps it's best to start with the most important rules first.

1. The day begins at 7 a.m. and ends no later than 11 p.m. Outside of those hours you must be in your dormitory. If you are outside of your dormitory wing during those hours without permission, you will be punished.

2. No one may leave the school grounds without permission from staff and parents. Any student who does so will be punished severely and could be expelled.

3. The woods around the school are home to wildlife, and so they can be dangerous; please do not enter them after dark or alone. This is for your own safety.

4. Classrooms are open to you only during scheduled class times. Unless you have special permission, you must

not enter the classroom wings outside of these hours.

5. *Only teachers are allowed in the teachers' wing. If you need to speak with a member of staff after hours, please let your prefect know.*

6. *You may write to your parents and friends as often as you like, but phone calls are for emergencies only. Speak to the headmistress if you believe an emergency exists.*

7. *Students in certain advanced areas of study take part in Night School to prepare them for life after Cimmeria, so you will sometimes hear them working late in the evening. Only very few select students are offered this opportunity; if you are not among them, you must not attempt to interfere with or observe Night School, and the fourth floor of the classroom wing is off-limits.*

Suddenly she heard again the noise that must have awakened her. It was a kind of scrabbling on the roof. Moving fast, she switched off the lamp. Then she held her breath. And listened.

A scratching sound above her head. Then a skittering noise as something small was dislodged and rattled its way down to the ground.

Allie covered her mouth with her hand. *What the hell is going on?* Shoving papers aside as quietly as possible, she scrambled up on top of the desk and slid across to peer outside. Resting her arms on the cool wood of the windowsill, she leaned forward. There was no moon tonight, and clouds obscured the stars. She could see nothing but darkness.

She closed her eyes and concentrated on listening. At first she heard nothing, and then in the distance a shout. A few seconds later, a faint scream.

Her eyes opened and she strained to see the grounds below.

Suddenly, much too close, a noise—a creaking sound, like footsteps on old wood. Right above her head.

Allie ducked and jerked her head back inside.

Whatever that was, it was on the roof.

She thought she saw something dart across the grass into the woods down below. She held her breath to listen. Was that . . . laughter?

Her ears hurt from trying to hear. She closed her eyes again to focus. As she did, she heard a voice whisper so faintly she wasn't sure she hadn't imagined it: *"It's okay, Allie. Go to sleep."*

Jumping off the desk, she spun around, her arms raised defensively, to take in the whole bedroom. It was dark, but there was enough ambient light for her to see that she was completely alone.

Again she heard a very faint noise that sounded almost like a boy chuckling.

Her breath came in short, frightened gasps. None of this made any sense. It felt unreal, and she shook her head fiercely as if trying to wake herself up.

But I am awake. And I am alone in this room.

She stared at the open window as if it were the thing behind all of this. Then she slammed it shut and latched it firmly. Once it was tightly closed, she propped a stack of books in front of it and set the desk lamp on top of that.

If it opens again tonight, I'll know it wasn't me.

Climbing back into bed, she pulled the comforter up around her like a shield and watched the darkness with wide-open eyes.

FOUR

The alarm's jarring ring woke Allie from a deep sleep the next morning at seven. Groggy, she swatted it several times before finding the off switch.

Still in bed, she stretched languorously, then sat up sharply as last night's events came flooding back.

Another weird night. A dream that wasn't a dream. What was with that voice? It had seemed so real.

Now the books and lamp were still propped against the closed window where she'd put them last night. At the front of the stack was the cover of her handbook—*The Rules*.

Could reading that have freaked me out so much that I started hearing things? She shivered. *Maybe this school is driving me crazy.*

"He just gives me the weirdest looks all the time," Allie said. "He's always staring at me. And he seemed so arrogant in the library. Like he was so cool and I was . . . nobody."

She and Jo were in the dining room as the lunch crowd waned, twirling salad leaves around their plates and talking about

Carter. Jo had insisted Allie tell her everything that happened after she and Gabe left the library. Allie was giving her an edited version of events.

With a guilty flush she remembered Carter's maxim: "Never be afraid to be honest."

But then, Carter is a dick.

"He probably just wants you to crush on him." Jo wrinkled her pert nose. "He wants everyone to crush on him."

"Have you ever crushed on him?" Allie asked.

Jo wrinkled her perfect nose. "God, what a wretched thought! Besides, I've got Gabe."

"True." Allie was relieved to have a chance to change the subject. "Tell me about him. How long have you two been together?"

Jo brightened. "Let's see. We've been together more than a year now. When I first came here, I went out with this guy Lucas, but then I met Gabe and it was just . . . like, forget it. He's the coolest guy I've ever known. The funniest. The sexiest. The . . . everything." She laughed at her own giddiness.

"I can't believe you've been going out a whole year," Allie said. "I don't know anybody who's been together that long."

"It's my longest relationship. Maybe because we're both here so much of the time." She toyed with her food. "I mean, some kids here, like, never go home. They're just always here. Like this is their home. And we're their family."

"Who does that?" Allie asked curiously.

"Lots of people. Carter. And Gabe. And, well . . . me, I guess."

Allie couldn't hide her surprise. "You never go home?"

"Long story." Jo's clear blue eyes clouded, and Allie got the feeling this wasn't the time to pry.

Suddenly Jo looked around the room, which was nearly empty. "Oh, crap. What time is it?"

They reached for their bags and ran out the door, down the hallway, and up the stairs. As they neared the second floor landing, they were both giggling hysterically.

"Late again!" Allie said as they careened down the corridor and divided to go to their separate classes.

"We are so busted." Jo giggled breathlessly.

Allie stopped at the closed door to her history class to catch her breath, then opened it quietly. In the awful sudden stillness, the students all turned to look at her.

"Miss Sheridan." Mr. Zelazny insisted on keeping an old-fashioned chalkboard in his room, and he was standing in front of it now, glaring at her. "Class started two minutes ago. I know you're new, but I presume you know our rules on tardiness."

Allie nodded mutely.

"Yes? Good. Well then, see me after class."

Allie trudged to her seat, her eyes downcast.

I can't do anything right.

No matter how hard she tried to change her life, it didn't work. Trouble was her default setting.

At the end of class she waited for the others to leave, pretending to organize her books until the room was mostly empty. Then she walked up to Mr. Zelazny's desk. He was writing and did not immediately look up. She cleared her throat timidly. After a moment, he raised his head and fixed her with an icy glare.

"I'm very sorry to have to speak to you a second time about tardiness in your first week. It is a very bad sign for your future at

Cimmeria Academy. I know the other teachers say you have great promise, but I must say I haven't seen any sign of it."

An angry flush rose to Allie's cheeks, but she bit her lip and said nothing. He handed her a handwritten piece of paper.

"This is your detention notice. Tomorrow morning at six thirty, meet the group outside the chapel and hand the teacher this."

Allie couldn't believe it.

"Six-thirty in the *morning*? But tomorrow's Saturday!"

His expression of cool disinterest did not change. "I've only given you one day's detention, Miss Sheridan. If it happens again, I will make it a week."

"Zelazny is such a bastard!" Jo was furious. "You were only, like, two minutes late. I don't know how he could do that to you when you're still in your first week."

It turned out that Jo's French teacher hadn't even noticed she was late as he'd been discussing an impending trip to Paris and hadn't realized that class should have begun. Jo had few comforting words for her.

"I've done detention so many times I've lost count. It's totally common here because the rules are so strict. If you veer even a step outside them . . ." She made a pistol out of her fingers and fired them into the air. "There are always at least ten students in it. But it's bloody hard work, so brace yourself."

Allie was puzzled. "Isn't it just reading or studying?"

"Oh no. Not at Cimmeria." Jo's tone was wry. "Here it's hard labor. You'll either be painting something or weeding, planting, clearing . . . God knows. It's always something that makes you sweat. It only lasts a couple of hours, but it can be horribly dull if they give you something awful. But you know, at least you'll get to meet the other troublemakers."

Allie rolled her eyes. "Oh, great. Lucky me. Like I don't know enough troublemakers already."

As they talked outside the dining room, the students streamed in for dinner. Allie watched the laughing groups passing her with a touch of envy. They all seemed so at ease—they already knew all the rules and how everything worked here. They probably never got detention. Or if they did, they didn't mind.

Zelazny probably thinks they're all awesome.

With a smile, Jo reached for her hand and pulled her into the dining room.

"Right. I've had enough of you being the new girl, all suffery and miserable. Come with me—you need to meet everyone. You're about to make a whole bunch of new friends."

Leading Allie to her usual table, Jo made her sit next to her. And amid the raucous rumble of pre-dinner conversation, she raised her voice enough to be heard.

"Everybody, this is Allie. Allie, this is everybody."

"Come on, Jo, you could be more specific." The heckler was about Gabe's age and sat across the table from Allie. His glossy light brown hair was just long enough to fall over his right eye. "I'm not everybody. I'm Lucas."

The others hooted derisively, but his smile was friendly and contagious, and she couldn't help but smile back.

One by one the others at the table laughingly gave their names. Rachel was sitting next to Lucas. She had almond-shaped eyes and glossy dark curls, her skin was tawny, and she had a nice smile. There was a slim girl named Lisa, with long, straight fair hair and a hesitant smile. Ruth was athletic and unsmiling with messy shoulder-length, dark blond hair. She sat next to Phil, who was cool looking with very short dark hair and trendy glasses. Allie got the feeling they liked each other.

There was an early excited buzz of conversation ("We've been hearing all about you. . . ." "What do you think of Cimmeria?" "Isn't Zelazny a . . ." "Shhh! Careful, he's right over there. . . ." "Do you like it here?"), before everybody moved on to other subjects. But by the time the meal was over, she was being treated as if she'd always been at Cimmeria—as if they'd known her all their lives. They seemed to actually like her, and to her surprise, Allie liked them, too. Maybe she had little in common with them—they were all so rich and groomed, how could any of them understand the kinds of things she'd been through? But there was something charming about them. They were so relaxed together. As Jo had said, they were almost like a family. And Allie felt as if she were tantalizingly close to being part of that.

She hadn't really felt like she'd had a family in a while.

After dinner, Jo took her to one side.

"Want to do something?"

"Sure." Allie shrugged. "Like what?"

"Have you explored the grounds yet? Or have you just been imprisoned inside with dusty books and me?" Jo asked. Allie's smile seemed enough of an answer for her.

Hooking her arm through Allie's, she directed her through the flow of students to the tributary heading to the door.

They wandered out across the drive, which in the evening

light had lost the ivory luster that Allie remembered from two days ago. Now it just looked like an ordinary gray gravel path. The smooth green school lawns stretched out in all directions, and the long shadows of the trees reached out for them as Jo led the way onto the grass.

"Where's Gabe tonight?" Allie asked.

"He's working on some special project, I think it's going to keep him busy until curfew." Jo smiled indulgently. "Okay, FYI? See that path through the trees there?" She pointed at a row of pine trees across the lawn of the east wing. Allie could just make out a path going into the woods. "That leads to the chapel. That's where you need to go tomorrow."

Then she pointed in the opposite direction at a pathway that wandered from the west wing of the school building down to the tree line.

"Over there," she said, "there's a summerhouse just beyond the edge of the woods. You can't really see it from here. Sometimes we have picnics there."

"So what's farther out in the woods?"

Jo's grin was quizzical. "Trees?"

Allie laughed. "No, I mean, are there more buildings? Or things to do . . . ?"

"I think there are a few houses far in the woods where staff or teachers live, but I don't know for sure. We don't actually do much in the woods, and they kind of discourage it because of, I dunno, health and safety or something. You'll like the chapel, though. It's really old."

They walked around the west side of the building and then behind it, where stone steps led up through a series of terraced lawns edged with colorful flowers. Beyond the last stretch of grass, the ground rose steeply up a lightly forested hill.

"There's an old tower at the top of the hill." Jo pointed and Allie could faintly make out a stone structure. "It looks like there used to be a castle or something there, but it's just ruins now. The tower's kind of cool. You can climb to the top and see everything. Some people say they can see all the way to London, but all I see are trees and fields. It's supposed to be haunted, but that's all bollocks."

They skirted the foot of the hill until they reached a long stone wall.

"What's this?" Allie asked.

"You'll see."

After a few minutes they came to an ancient wooden door sealed with an incongruously modern combination lock. With the speed that comes of practice, Jo spun the three numbered wheels, and the lock clicked open.

She opened the door and walked through, ducking to avoid the low doorframe. Allie followed, and Jo carefully closed the door behind them, pocketing the lock.

"Oh, wow." Allie breathed, taking in the huge, cultivated, walled garden. The air had a cool scent of damp, loamy soil. Vegetables stood in rows of military precision, straight as rifle barrels. Fruit trees crowded at the back, their branches heavy with apples tumbling over the wall against the evening sun. Around the edges fragrant flowers spilled over in vivid pinks and whites and purples.

A stone path ran around the edge of the garden, and Jo struck off down it. "Welcome to my favorite place at Cimmeria."

"It's amazing! Are we allowed to be here? How do you know the combination?"

"It's just this random thing," Jo said. "I had to work here on detention my first year. At first I really hated it—getting up at six every day—but by the end of the week I realized I was going to miss it. I don't know why. I'm really good at the whole gardening thing, and this place is . . . I don't know. Peaceful, I guess."

Allie wondered what she'd done to earn a week of detention, but since Jo didn't volunteer it, she decided not to ask. Besides, it seemed pretty easy to get detention around here.

Turning left onto a path that cut across the middle of the gardens, Jo led her past a classic fountain where a pretty young girl in flowing gowns with a slightly damaged nose tipped a pitcher of water eternally onto rocks, around a blueberry thicket, and then onto the granite path on the other side.

"Now I volunteer here after class and on weekends. I come here sometimes when I want privacy."

A wooden bench was tucked away amid the lush purple wisteria enrobing the walls, and Jo perched on it, gesturing for Allie to do the same. Allie pulled her feet up onto the seat and wrapped her arms around her knees, breathing in the cool scent of the flowers.

"We can talk here," Jo said. "In fact, this might be the only place in Cimmeria where nobody is going to overhear us. As you've noticed, this is a really nosy school. How are you doing, anyway? It must be totally weird for you to be here. I remember my first few days— this place completely freaked me out."

"It's going to sound crazy," Allie said, "but I hate it here. And I kind of love it, too."

Jo gave her an easy smile. "I actually completely understand. But go on."

"It's so different from any school I've ever been to, you know? And it's a lot of work. But it's . . ." Allie thought for a minute. "It's not my life. And that's what I like about it. It's not my life the way it's been for the last two years, and anything's better than that."

Jo considered her for a moment, and when she spoke again Allie could hear the hesitance in her voice. "When I came here, I'd flunked out of my last school. And that was *after* they caught me and my ex-boyfriend passed out on the roof. We'd drunk an entire bottle of vodka, and we broke into the school and . . . well. Anyway, my parents were unbelievably pissed off. But the thing is, it was supposed to be this great school, but it was just . . . stupid. The classes were too easy, there was nothing to do, and it was full of other rich kids like me biding their time until university—which will, of course, be Oxford or Cambridge."

She dropped one leg and swung her foot back and forth.

"My parents sent me here next. I think they thought I'd hate it, but after I got used to how weird it is, I was totally into it. I love how hard the classes are, how bizarre some of the teachers are, and how weird it all is. It's just kind of perfect. Since then, I've been okay. Great, actually. It's like I'm in the place I need to be."

Something about the way Jo confided in her touched Allie's heart. And her story was clearly something she didn't share very often. She got the feeling Jo was trying to get her to open up to her. But Allie hadn't opened up to anybody in such a long time, it seemed impossible.

Resting her chin on her knees, she thought about what to say.

"I guess what I'm saying is . . ." Jo touched her arm, and Allie raised her eyes to meet her gaze. "I can tell something bad happened to you. If you ever want to talk about it, you really can tell me. I won't tell anybody else."

I can't talk about it, Allie thought.

A long pause followed, and she knew Jo was waiting for her to say something.

"I don't really know . . . how to talk about this stuff. . . ." Allie squirmed on the bench, staring out over the garden, where the flower heads waved in a light breeze. She'd never talked about what had happened with Christopher. It was just too hard. Nobody would get it.

Yet part of her wondered if she'd feel better if she did. And there was something about Jo that made her want to confide in her. She seemed like somebody who might understand.

"You don't have to say anything," Jo said. "We can talk about other things."

"No." Allie was surprised by her own vehemence. "It's okay. Maybe it would be good for me to tell somebody this stuff."

As she tried to shape her thoughts into words, Jo waited quietly.

"My life has been . . . kind of crazy lately." Allie paused, and then decided to go ahead. "I had, I think, the perfect life until a year and a half ago. I was the perfect daughter, got perfect grades, my parents loved me. Then one day . . . it all ended."

She stopped and looked up at Jo. "You know, I haven't told this story to anyone. Ever."

Saying nothing, Jo nodded and waited.

Allie took a deep breath; her next words came out in a rush. "So I came home from school one day and the police were there.

My mum was crying, my dad was shouting at the cops although I could tell he wanted to cry, too. It was chaos.

"My brother was missing. And they never found him."

Jo reached for her arm. "Allie, Jesus! That's horrible. What happened? Did he . . ."

"Die?" Allie finished her thought. "Who knows? We've never heard from him again."

"I don't understand. What happened?"

Allie thought for a second.

"See, Christopher and I, we were super close. He was like my best friend my whole life." Her voice was calmer now and steady. "Other kids fought, but we never did. We hung out together all the time. He's two years older than me, but he was always completely patient with me. He just didn't get tired of me the way some older brothers get tired of their little sisters. When I was little, he used to meet me after school every day and walk me home. He'd help me with my homework, watch TV with me. My parents work a lot, but I never minded because Christopher was always there. And even when I was older, he'd check up on me. Just sort of show up after school, like it was a coincidence or something. And he'd do his homework at the same time I was doing mine, so if I got stuck on a question he could help.

"About six months before he disappeared, though, he started acting funny. He stayed out really late, got into trouble with Mum and Dad. He was never around, and he didn't have much to say when he was there. I felt like I was kind of losing him. When I tried to talk to him about how he was, and was everything okay, he would walk away. Like he would literally get up and walk out of the house and not come back for hours. His grades went from

66

great to terrible. My parents were completely freaked out, but they couldn't do anything to help. He wouldn't let them."

She stopped, remembering endless arguments and slamming doors. A night bird sang an elaborate melody.

When she spoke again, her tone was emotionless. "Anyway. He left a note. My parents wouldn't tell me what it said, but I overheard Mum on the phone one day talking to someone about it. She had it memorized. It was the meanest thing I've ever heard. It said, 'I'm leaving. I'm not hurt; I'm not on drugs. I just don't want to be a part of this family anymore. I don't love you. Any of you. Don't follow me. Don't try to find me. I don't need your help. You will never see me again.'"

"Oh my God," Jo whispered. When Allie looked up, she saw that her eyes were filled with tears, which she dashed away with the back of her hand. "Oh, Allie."

Allie focused on staying distant from the story she was telling, pretending, as she sometimes did, that it had all happened to somebody else. "So then it all fell apart. I guess I had a nervous breakdown. I couldn't, like, talk. I sat in Christopher's room for days on end. I didn't go to school for months. They sent me to a counselor, who I hated. My mum and dad argued with each other all the time, and I was just this . . . nuisance they had to deal with."

She glanced up at Jo with pain in her clear, gray eyes. "It was like when he left, he pulled the stopper from our lives and drained everything good out. They didn't love me anymore. And I felt nothing at all." She gave a shaky sigh. "Feeling something became really important to me. So I started drinking, but that's kind of the opposite of feeling anything, you know?"

Jo nodded, and Allie could see in her eyes that she did understand. So she kept going.

"I hung out with people who hurt each other. I got into a lot of trouble. Getting arrested was really scary, so I did that a few times. I . . ." She held out her left arm, exposing three neat, thin white scars between her wrist and the inside of her elbow. "I cut myself for a while. And that hurt, which was good. But it was also totally stupid. And it felt fake. Like, if you do it to yourself like that, it's not real. It's cheating. So I don't do that anymore."

She rushed through the end of her story as if she couldn't wait to be done with it. "Anyway, the last time I got arrested, my parents had pretty much had enough of me. So here I am. They've got an empty house now." Her voice was hollow. "And I don't even have that."

Spontaneously, Jo threw her arms around her and hugged her fiercely. Then she leaned back and held her shoulders, locking her gaze onto Allie's. "Okay. That's bloody awful. But you're here now. And you're alive. I just met you, Allie, but I can already tell you're awesome. And you might have a horrible family, but your life from now on is up to you." The fervor in her expression took Allie by surprise, but it also touched her heart. "I want you to promise me that you'll give this place a chance. Cimmeria straightened me out. It's my home now, and these people are my family. It can be the same for you."

Something seemed to break inside Allie. Something that had been strung tight in her chest for so long. She hugged Jo and fought back tears. "Okay." she whispered, her voice quivering. "I promise."

Jo pulled Allie against her so that her head rested on Jo's

shoulder, and they sat quietly on the bench for a moment, each lost in thought. Allie felt awkward. Hungover. Tired.

"It's funny, this place," she mumbled. "Time seems sort of compressed here. I can't believe I've only been here two days. This will be my third night, but I feel like I've been here for weeks."

Jo seemed to understand just what she meant. "It's like life concentrated. More happens here in a week then happens outside in a month." Her lips quirked up. "I like that."

Curled up on the bench, they talked idly as the daylight ebbed away and shadows filled the garden.

"I can see why you like this garden." Allie stretched her arms above her head, running her fingers through the smooth leaves and waxy flowers of the jasmine behind her. "It's kind of magical. Like that book you read when you're little—*The Secret Garden*. Did you read that?"

Clearly pleased that Allie had made the connection, Jo grinned. "I've always—"

Her words were interrupted by the sound of something crashing loudly at the far end of the garden. They both jumped.

"What the hell was that?" Allie asked, staring into the gloom, noticing for the first time how dark it had become.

"I don't know." Jo said. She peered at her watch, holding it closer to her eyes to see its hands. "Oh, bugger! It's nearly curfew. We have to get back."

She was standing up, reaching out to Allie, when they heard the sound again. Then footsteps.

"What the . . ." Clearly puzzled, Jo shouted, "Who's there?"

The footsteps stopped.

They stood frozen, listening. "Jo," Allie whispered. Her heart was pounding, but she didn't know why. When had it gotten so dark? "Couldn't it just be a gardener or . . ."

They both heard the growling sound at the same moment.

Jo grabbed Allie's arm.

"Jo, seriously. What the hell is that?" Allie whispered.

"I don't know," Jo hissed. She was leaning forward, looking in the direction of the sound.

"Should we . . ." Allie took a step away from the noise.

"Run?" Jo said.

"Yeah."

"On three. One. Two . . ."

The quiet was shattered by a crash that seemed to come from the shadows inches away from them.

With a startled scream, they hurtled down the footpath. Jo held Allie's hand tightly.

"Stick with me," she said breathlessly, and raced off the path into the orchard. In the darkness they zigzagged between the trees, and Allie could feel dropped fruit squelching sickeningly under her shoes. She tried to distinguish whether she could hear footsteps aside from their own, but they were going too fast—it was impossible to tell.

Then something touched her head and she screamed, batting at the air around her. Jo dragged her to the left, around the tangle of blueberry bushes and into a rose garden. Thorns tore at their hands and clothes. Twigs snapped under their feet.

Something grabbed Jo and lifted her off her feet, dragging her inside a room built into the wall. She opened her mouth to scream but a hand covered it, muffling her.

Allie reached for her, panic sending adrenalin in a rush to her heart.

"Shhh." Gabe held one finger to his lips and looked into Jo's eyes. She threw her arms around him and buried her face in his neck.

Gabe reached out for Allie, but now somebody was holding her arms, too. She looked up wildly to see Sylvain's blue eyes watching her steadily in the darkness as he pulled her into the dark room.

He mouthed one word: "Quiet."

FIVE

Gabe encircled Jo in his arms protectively as Sylvain pulled Allie behind him. She watched as the boys stared through the open door, their eyes alert.

Something crashed through the garden, and Allie jumped at the sound, but it sounded farther away than before.

Then a guttural sound she couldn't identify. A man's voice?

And after a few seconds . . . silence.

When a few uneventful moments had passed, Gabe and Sylvain exchanged a look, and then, as if they'd been given a signal, they began walking quickly into the garden. Gabe scanned the area around them, then looked back and nodded. Sylvain reached for Allie's hand, and they all ran silently out into the garden, down the path to the gate, and out onto the lawn. Wordlessly Jo handed Gabe the lock, and he secured the garden door behind them.

For the first time Allie became conscious of the fact that Sylvain still held her hand; her face was near his shoulder. He had a distinctive scent, like sandalwood and spice, and she inhaled deeply. His grip tightened, and she looked away quickly.

Faint streaks of light still glimmered in the sky as they walked through a back door that took them directly into the central hallway. In the light, Allie saw that a trickle of blood ran down Jo's pale cheek. Gabe frowned with concern.

"You're hurt," he said. "We should take you to the nurse."

"It's not that bad . . . ," Jo said, but when he insisted, she didn't resist.

As the two walked away, Allie felt again the curious ache of envy. As if he'd sensed it, Sylvain stepped toward her, his eyes searching her face.

"Are you wounded at all?" Her heart fluttered and she hoped he wouldn't notice.

Until that moment she hadn't paid any attention to herself, and now she glanced at her hands but could find no wounds.

"I'm fine." She looked up at him. "Sylvain, what was out there?"

"I don't know," he said. But his eyes dodged her direct gaze.

Something about his tone didn't ring true. She could sense that he was holding something back—something important.

"I think we should tell Isabelle," she announced. "She should know there was some sort of . . . I don't know. Break-in, I guess?"

He looked doubtful. "That might not be such a good idea." His voice was calm and reasonable. "She's probably asleep. And I don't think it's as serious as a break-in. Everyone is fine now, and you do not want to appear to overreact, no?" He had, Allie thought, a rather lovely smile. "Maybe first thing in the morning would be better."

Even though she wanted to disagree, Allie could see the logic— they had, after all, seen nothing. But after the excitement in the garden and the rush of the rescue, she wanted to do something. To go back outside and look for whatever that was. Or at least to sit and talk about what had happened. There was no way she could sleep.

"Maybe we should go check on Jo?" she suggested hopefully.

"She's okay—Gabe's with her." Sylvain paused and then continued with some reluctance, as if he knew what her response would be. "Listen, it is past curfew. You should go to bed and we will deal with all of this tomorrow."

Allie couldn't believe what she was hearing. "What, seriously? No, Sylvain! I want to talk about what happened. Be completely honest: What did you see out there?"

Sylvain's reply was carefully framed.

"I am afraid I saw nothing. Perhaps it was some sort of animal. Maybe you disturbed a fox or a badger." As she opened her mouth to protest, he held up his hand to stop her. "You're tired, Allie. And I'm tired, too. And I don't want to get detention."

She wasn't tired. Not at all. But arguing about whether or not she was tired wasn't really any fun.

"Fine then." Her tone was brusque.

As she turned to go, he caught her wrist and held it gently.

"What? No good-night kiss?" he said, smiling teasingly. "No 'you're my hero, Sylvain'? Not even a 'thank you for rescuing me, Sylvain'? You should never go to bed angry, *ma belle* Allie."

She yanked her wrist free of his grasp.

"Whatever," she said, stalking away.

"Sweet dreams," he called after her with a light laugh.

She ran up the stairs without looking back.

The next morning Allie was up at six and feeling oddly energetic, as if the adrenalin from last night still rushed through her veins. Standing in front of her wardrobe, she wondered what to wear for hard labor, finally deciding on a pair of exercise pants, tennis shoes, and a white T-shirt with the school's insignia on the breast. She clipped her hair back and, grabbing the detention notice, headed downstairs at a trot.

Her stomach grumbled, but it was too early for breakfast. Taking a chance, she peeked into the dining room and found it empty save for one table, which held bacon sandwiches on a warming platter alongside a silver ice bucket filled with water bottles. She tiptoed into the room with some hesitation.

They must be for us. . . .

Picking up a sandwich and a bottle, she looked around the empty space.

"Thank you," she whispered, holding the bottle of water aloft in salute.

Munching on the sandwich, she made her way through the quiet entrance hall and down the front steps. The morning air was cool and the sky overcast. Leaves of grass dropped chilly dew on her ankles.

In a weird way, it was actually quite nice being out on the grounds alone.

In her head, she went over the experiences of the night before and practiced describing it all to Isabelle while not sounding crazy. It wasn't easy.

As she walked past the tree line and into the shadows, she shivered—it was colder out of the sun. The path was arrow straight, shooting under pines and bypassing thorny brambles.

Feathery wings of ferns brushed delicately against her calves, but she barely noticed as she continued her mental vivisection of the evening before.

After about ten minutes the path arrived at a low stone wall, which it followed for about fifty feet to a gate opening into a shady churchyard, where aged gravestones leaned higgledy-piggledy under leafy trees amid deep, soft grass. An old garden bench rotted slowly against the wall in a pool of sunshine, and she could hear a stream nearby.

An ancient stone chapel stood in the middle, and a small group of students clustered near the door looking bored. Allie breathed a quiet sigh of relief when she saw that they were all dressed much like her. Seeing nobody she recognized, she kept to the fringes of the gathering, leaning against the elaborately gnarled trunk of a yew tree.

She'd barely got comfortable when the door of the chapel opened and a woman appeared in the doorway. Casually dressed in dark linen trousers and a white button-down shirt, she'd knotted her long dark hair loosely on her head. She held a clipboard in one hand.

"Can I have all notices, please?"

As the students walked up, she took their sheets without comment. Allie handed her the notice Zelazny had issued, and the woman stopped and smiled.

"You must be Allie." She sounded as pleased as if they'd met in the dining room over a cup of tea. "I've heard a lot about you from Isabelle. I'm Eloise Derleth, the librarian. You must stop in and say hello. Isabelle left some books for you at my desk."

With that she stepped away briskly, raising her voice to call out to the entire group. "I know you're all eager to find out what today's work will be. So I won't keep you waiting. Please follow me."

The students rolled their eyes and giggled as they trooped along behind her. Allie hung back, making up the last of the rebellious party.

Eloise led them around the side of the chapel to a shed at the back of the churchyard, where a man in the black work outfit worn by the staff at the school waited.

"Today you're going to be clearing the churchyard," Eloise explained. "Mr. Ellison will give you the tools you need and assign you tasks for the morning. Good luck!"

With a cheerful smile, she walked briskly down the path and out the gate. Allie headed over to join the group lining up in front of Mr. Ellison.

"I'm dividing you up into teams." His voice was a rich, resonant baritone, and as he handed out tools, Allie marveled at the sheer size of him. He must have been six and a half feet tall; his arms were thick and strong, probably from working outside all his life. His skin was the color of espresso, and he had a calming manner.

"These are my weed trimmers here." He gestured at a group of boys he'd already armed with noisy devices. "They'll trim around the graves, while this group here"—he pointed at two boys and a girl pushing lawn mowers in various directions—"do the main clearing."

Allie was the last in the queue. As she walked up, Mr. Ellison gave her a friendly smile.

"And you two will be my rakers."

Two?

Spinning around, she found Carter standing behind her, gazing innocently at the gardener as he handed over their rakes. Too surprised to move, she stared, astonished. Carter thanked him politely, then turned on his heel and strode off, carrying both rakes in one hand.

She hurried after him, hopping gingerly past the graves and stumbling on the uneven ground as the angry mosquito buzz of grass cutters filled the air.

"What are you doing here? And where are you going?" she asked sharply. And when he ignored her: "Hey! Are you listening to me?"

Carter didn't seem at all concerned. "I'm here because I have detention," he said calmly. "Why are *you* here? And can you please just chill? We need to wait a few minutes for the mowers to work. They'll give us something to rake. Right now I'm getting out of their way. You should do the same."

Furious as she was at his patronizing tone, she nonetheless saw that he had a point. And she followed him as he walked across the graveyard. He didn't stop until he got to the yew tree near the front of the church. Then, leaning the rakes against the trunk, he stepped up on a bulging tree root and climbed onto a low branch, where he sat comfortably with his legs hanging down. Holding out his hand to her, he raised his eyebrow questioningly.

Muttering under her breath, Allie ignored his hand and pulled herself up. She slid out along the thick, gnarled branch away from him, then sat with one leg dangling and the other propped on the branch.

Spinning a twig between two fingers, he studied her with

open curiosity; she pretended he wasn't there at all and watched the lawn mowers make grass disappear in uneven rows.

"Look," Carter said, distracting her from her reverie, "I've been wanting to get you alone so that I could apologize."

She glanced at him suspiciously, but he didn't seem to be making fun of her. In fact, he looked uncharacteristically uncomfortable.

"I gave you the wrong idea the other day in the library," he said. "I know you thought I was saying something I wasn't. I think you have as much a right as anybody else does to be here. Okay? Please believe that."

Although she nodded, her expression must still have betrayed her doubt, because he sighed with frustration.

"I feel terrible about this. You must think I'm a complete dick."

She nodded again, this time with an ironic half smile, and he laughed. His laugh was contagious, and despite a nagging voice in her head that said he was still probably making fun of her, she found herself smiling back at him. "I knew it," he said. "And I don't blame you. I just hope you believe me. I didn't mean what you thought I did. Not at all. I hate the snobs at this school. I won't be one of them. Can we start over? Pretend this is the first time we've talked?"

The voice in her head told her not to trust him. But then, the voice in her head didn't trust anyone.

"Sure," she said finally.

"Good." He seemed genuinely relieved. "Now we're at the beginning again." Looking out over the garden he said, "Right. Well, that break was short and sweet. Looks like Mr. Ellison is waving us over. We'd better get started."

He jumped down from the tree, landing smoothly, and turned to help her down. Rolling her eyes, she ignored his outstretched hand and lowered herself to the ground.

There was something cynical and self-deprecating about his smile when she glanced up at him as she dusted off her hands.

"Something tells me that life with you around is going to be interesting, Allie Sheridan," he said. Before she could respond, he turned to pick up the rakes and headed off toward the other students. "Off to work we go."

Watching his loping stride, she followed him into the graveyard.

As she walked, she read the names engraved around her. The gravestones gave little away (EMMA LITTLEJOHN, BELOVED WIFE OF FREDERICK LITTLEJOHN AND MOTHER OF FRANCES LITTLEJOHN 1803–1849 GOD GRANT YE REST), but she found herself unable to pass without reading and thinking about the occupants, wondering if they'd had happy lives and what brought them to this place.

Forty-six. Not really that old, she thought. Her own mother was probably at least that old.

Handing Allie a rake, Carter began combing the grass and leaves expertly into large piles. As she worked alongside him, Allie whispered an apology to each grave.

Sorry to disturb you, Mrs. Coxon (1784–1827). I'll just be a moment.

But her pile was a mess and she lost half of the grass on the way to the stack.

"You're really great at this," Carter said.

"Shut up!" She laughed. "Give me a break. I've never done this before."

"Never done what? Raked?" He seemed genuinely surprised.

"Yeah, I've never raked." She shrugged.

"How have you never raked? Don't your parents make you do anything?" His tone was disapproving.

"I live in London, Carter. We don't have a yard. We've got, like, a patio with pots of flowers around the edge. I've swept it plenty of times, but I've never raked."

He worked in silence for a few minutes, then, without looking up, said, "London must be full of kids who've never done anything like this. That is so weird to me. I can't imagine not working outside, getting my hands dirty."

Leaning against her rake, she marveled at how efficiently he worked.

"Where are you from?" she asked.

He made a sweeping gesture at the land around them. "You're looking at it."

"What, you live around here?"

"I live here. Here is home."

Puzzled, she raked for a few minutes, then stopped again, brushing a stray strand of hair out of her eyes.

"But where did you live before here?"

He stopped, too. "Nowhere. This is where I grew up. My parents worked here as part of the staff. I'm here on scholarship. I've never lived anywhere else."

"Your parents are teachers?"

Still working, he answered her without looking up. "No. My parents were part of the staff." He emphasized *were* and *staff*.

"So"—still puzzled, Allie worried the grass with her rake—"they don't work here anymore?"

"No." His voice was cold. "They don't let you work here after you're dead."

Allie froze. He worked furiously; she could see the muscles move under his shirt.

Here lie Mr. and Mrs. West. . . .

"Oh God, Carter. I'm sorry. I didn't know."

He kept raking. "Of course you didn't. How could you? Don't worry about it."

Dropping her rake, she walked over and touched his arm.

"I'm really sorry."

Jerking his arm away as if her touch scalded, he glared at her. "Don't be. And seriously? I don't want to be here all day, so would you help?"

Stung, she picked up her rake and walked a few graves away. For the next hour they worked in silence. Allie's back and arms ached, but she'd made several impressive piles of leaves and grass. She looked over at Carter several times, but he never met her gaze.

Gradually, the awful buzzing of the garden equipment declined, and after another ten minutes or so it stopped altogether as the last grass trimmer was turned off and returned to Mr. Ellison, who was carefully organizing the returned supplies.

"I think we're done here."

Allie was so lost in her work that Carter's words startled her and she dropped her rake into the pile of grass. As she picked it up, the strand of hair escaped again, and she brushed it back absently. His eyes followed her hand.

"Here," he said, "turn around."

She looked at him doubtfully but after a moment's hesitation did as he asked. Standing behind her, he smoothed the errant lock, gently winding it into her clip. She stood very still. His light touch on the nape of her neck gave her goose bumps. After a few seconds the touch stopped, but he said nothing.

When she turned around, he was walking to the chapel carrying both rakes. She hurried after him, tripping over a tuft of grass.

"Here you go, Bob," Carter said, handing the rakes to Mr. Ellison.

"Thanks. You in trouble again, Carter?"

"Always."

Mr. Ellison had a deep chuckle that Allie liked instantly. She smiled up at him and stuck her hands into her pockets.

"I hope we did an okay job, Mr. Ellison."

He smiled at her kindly. "It looks great, Miss Sheridan. Thanks for your help."

As they walked down the path, he called after them, "Don't let Carter get you into any more trouble."

Without waiting for her, Carter strode across the churchyard ahead of her and then out the gate.

Briefly Allie wondered whether she should try and catch up with him, but she decided against it. Instead she walked at a leisurely pace, hoping he'd get far ahead of her.

A few minutes later, though, as she rounded a bend, he was standing on the path, kicking a stone into the trees. Avoiding his eyes, she walked past him without a word.

"Allie, wait!" She could hear him running after her, but she didn't look at him until he caught up and began walking alongside her, backward.

"Here's the thing," he said, walking as easily as if he were facing the right direction. "I seem to have behaved like a dick again."

"No worries," she said coolly. "At least you're consistent."

She was surprised when he laughed.

"Okay, I deserve that. I'm sorry I snapped at you. I'm just really sensitive about . . . some things." His eyes darkened and he kicked a rock off the path.

Thinking about Christopher and how sensitive she'd been about his disappearance, Allie thawed a little.

"It's cool," she said. "I'm over it."

"You sure?" His eyes searched hers hopefully.

"Totally."

Satisfied, he turned until he was facing forward again and walked beside her.

"Have you recovered from last night, then?" he asked.

A frown creased her forehead. "How do you know about last night?"

"Nobody has any secrets at Cimmeria," he said. "I heard Jo got hurt running in the dark."

Allie wondered how honest she should be. She wanted to talk about it with somebody, but she was afraid Carter would make fun of her.

"It was scary," she admitted.

"What exactly did you see?"

"Nothing," she said. "I mean, it was too dark. We just heard . . ."

She didn't know how to explain it.

"What did you hear?" His dark eyes were hard to read.

"I heard something growl," she admitted, "like a dog. But I heard footsteps, too. The human kind."

When he didn't respond, she slowed her pace.

"What do you think it could have been?" she asked. "I mean, do people have dogs here? Like teachers or . . . staff?"

"No dogs," he said shortly.

"Well, somebody has a dog," she muttered. "Or somebody growls."

He stopped so suddenly she nearly ran into him.

"Honestly?" he said. "I think it was some of the guys teasing you. Trying to scare you."

For some reason she hadn't expected that, and she felt embarrassment warm her cheeks.

"Why?" she asked. "That's stupid."

"Because they're childish," he said. "And bored. And you're new. They did it for fun."

The idea that a gang of boys would make fun of her did seem plausible. And it hurt, though she tried not to show it. As they walked down the path, she stared at her feet, swallowing hard. But something about his explanation didn't ring true. Because what about Jo? She'd been there, too.

As she thought it through, she decided there were only two possibilities. Either the incident had been an elaborate hoax, in which Gabe and Sylvain had both participated. Or Carter was lying to her.

She glanced up at him from under her eyelashes—he was staring straight ahead.

"You know, Gabe and Sylvain rescued us," she said casually. "Were they in on it?"

Carter's mood darkened. "Oh, they rescued you, huh? How heroic." He turned to look at her. "What's going on between you and Sylvain, anyway? You've only been here a few days, but I hear he's already staking a claim."

She couldn't resist rising to the bait.

"That's ridiculous," she said a bit snappishly. "Nobody's claiming anybody. Sylvain's just been nice to me. He seems like a nice guy."

"Sylvain? Nice?" Carter scoffed. "I doubt that very seriously."

She glared at him. "You know what? Sylvain has been nothing but nice to me since I got here. Unlike just about everybody else."

Grabbing her arm, he turned her to face him. "Just . . . be careful, Allie. You haven't been here long enough to know how things are here. You can't trust everyone—"

"Let go!" She yanked her arm loose angrily. But before she could reply, she heard Sylvain's distinctive voice.

"Allie. There you are. I was just coming to find you." He appeared out of the shadows, walking down the path from the school. His eyes narrowed when he saw who Allie was with. "Carter. Of course. I should have known you'd have detention today. You always do."

His tone was light, but there was something more serious underlying his words.

"And somehow you never do." Carter's voice was laced with contempt as he shoved past Sylvain and stalked away toward the school.

When he was gone, Sylvain turned to Allie, who stood watching them both with a puzzled frown. "Did something happen? You look upset."

"It was nothing," Allie said as Carter disappeared around a bend. "He's just a bit of a jerk, isn't he?"

"I think that describes him perfectly," he said. "So how was detention? Awful?"

"It wasn't too bad. Just one blister." She held up her right hand, where a white bump had formed on her palm at the base of her ring finger.

"Tragic." He lifted her hand up to his lips and lightly kissed it. Allie shivered.

"I have decided you should never do manual labor," he said. "It's not your style. You should have servants feeding you, while you wear silk. . . ."

The absurdity of the idea made her laugh. "Yeah, they could peel my grapes while I count my diamonds. . . ."

"You joke." He smiled. "But it could happen."

She was hyperconscious of the fact that he still held her hand as they began walking down the path. "*I'm afraid* this is not a social call. Isabelle would like to see you."

Worry tightened Allie's stomach muscles. She wasn't really surprised that the headmistress would want to see her, given that she'd been given detention her first week at Cimmeria. But she was so hoping not to be in serious trouble for a change.

Sighing, she decided to change the subject. "About last night . . ."

"Ah yes," he said. "The brutal attack in the garden."

His tone was teasing, but Allie was serious. "Who was that? I heard footsteps, and some kind of dog."

"I think the footsteps you heard were probably Gabe and me," Sylvain said. "And what you thought was a dog was probably a fox."

"A fox that growls?" Allie asked dubiously.

"It could have been trapped in one of the sheds and distressed." Sylvain shrugged. "It is not unusual."

Allie studied his face closely. "Carter said he thought it was some boys making fun of me."

"That is ridiculous." Sylvain frowned. "I would know if that happened."

His response was spontaneous, and Allie was surprised to feel a rush of relief that it hadn't been a big gang harassing her. But relief was followed by a flare of anger for Carter.

"Yeah," she said coolly. "That's what I figured."

As the path reached the school's grassy lawn, though, something occurred to her.

"Why did Isabelle send you to get me rather than one of the junior students?" she asked.

"Oh, I was at a prefect meeting and we were chatting," he said. "It's not unusual. She knows we are . . . friends."

Even as she clocked the way he hesitated ever so slightly over the word "friends" (*Does he think we're something more?*), she kept her expression blank. "I didn't know you were a prefect."

"Didn't you?" he said teasingly. "Well, now that you know, you must do everything I say. Because I am the boss."

Laughing, she pulled free of him. "Oh, is that how it works? Well, we'll have to see about that."

Without warning she darted across the lawn. She heard Sylvain laugh and then the soft thud of his footsteps in the grass as he tried to catch her. They reached the front door at almost exactly the same time.

"I was first," Sylvain said, and something about his

competitive expression made Allie laugh.

"You were second." She tried to keep a straight face, but when he opened his mouth to argue, she burst out laughing again.

"What's so funny?" he asked. But she saw that he was trying not to laugh, too.

At that moment the door swung open and Zelazny stepped out. Allie's giggles evaporated.

"Miss Sheridan." It might be Saturday but the history teacher still wore a suit and tie, and his voice oozed disapproval. "I'm gratified to see that you are taking your morning of detention so seriously."

I've been arrested by less grumpy men, Allie thought.

But before she could speak, Sylvain stepped forward.

"It is entirely my fault, August. I have been trying to cheer Allie up because she was so sad when I found her on the path after her difficult morning of detention. Please do not judge her for my actions."

Looking somewhat mollified, Zelazny marched past them. "Glad to hear it, Sylvain. Keep up the good work."

"Of course," Sylvain said, steering Allie through the entry hall as she struggled not to laugh out loud.

When they were in the hallway, Allie sputtered with laughter, but Sylvain shushed her. "Not here," he whispered. "His hearing is exceptional."

But somehow even that seemed hilarious, and she covered her mouth with her hands to stifle her own giggles.

"I don't want to see you trapped in detention for an entire week," Sylvain said, but his eyes sparked with amusement.

They walked past the common room, stopping under the

main staircase. She was about to ask him what they were doing there when he tapped once on the carved oak paneling and, from somewhere, she heard Isabelle's muffled voice invite them in. But only when Sylvain reached for the handle did Allie see the door, neatly hidden in the woodwork. Inside, Isabelle sat at a large desk, surrounded by stacks of papers.

"Good luck," Sylvain whispered in her ear as he turned to walk away. The warmth in his expression was almost palpable, and Allie's heart beat faster.

"Come in, Allie," Isabelle called.

After a moment's hesitation, she stepped into the room. It was a spacious, windowless room with a fireplace, its carved mantelpiece topped with unlighted candles. One wall was entirely covered in a tapestry—a knight with a sword and a damsel by a white horse. Two leather chairs faced Isabelle's desk, and she gestured at one of them.

"Please," she said, "sit down."

Amid the papers on her desk was a laptop, and she snapped it shut as Allie perched on the edge of the soft chair.

Allie looked at the device longingly.

Modern life still exists.

Pulling off her glasses, Isabelle rubbed the bridge of her nose before leaning back in her chair. "How was detention this morning?"

"Fine, I guess." Allie shrugged. "I mean, it was hard work but it was fine."

She waited for the lecture to begin.

Isabelle smiled at her kindly.

"Allie, you mustn't feel singled out. Mr. Zelazny is, as you probably know by now, famed at Cimmeria for his strictness. He sees to it that a week never goes by without at least a few students working in the gardens or organizing the old storerooms. But I've asked him to give you more time to adjust before he includes you in his punishment rota again. I think it's a little early to expect you to do everything according to The Rules."

Her words stunned Allie to speechlessness. Sympathy was the last thing she'd expected.

If Isabelle was surprised by the lack of a response, she didn't show it. Instead, she studied Allie curiously. "And the incident last night—we should talk about that. Sylvain said some sort of wild animal frightened you in the garden?"

A flicker of irritation stung Allie. Why hadn't Sylvain included her in that conversation?

"Well, we don't know what it was," Allie said. "It crashed through the garden and . . . chased us, I guess. We thought we heard it growling or something." Her own words sounded silly to her. "What do you think it could have been?"

"Sylvain suggested it could be foxes. We do have rather a lot of them around," Isabelle said.

Frowning, Allie tilted her head to one side. "There are lots of foxes in London, but I've never heard one of them growl or seen it chase people."

"Well, this is the country." Isabelle shrugged. "Foxes are wilder here—the urban foxes in London are practically tame. A vixen can be very protective of her cubs. Still, I've asked the grounds staff to look out for any other sort of animal, but I just can't think of what else it could have been. I'm very glad you are both okay."

She sounded sincere, and Allie was gratified that she hadn't made her feel like an idiot.

Isabelle was moving on to other issues now, though.

"How are you doing, really? Are you making friends? Sylvain tells me you're doing well, and that you and he are getting along famously, and I'm glad to hear that. He is one of our best students."

Allie blushed. It was weird to think that Sylvain, who flirted with her constantly, discussed her with the headmistress.

"I'm okay," she said, sliding back in her chair and toying with the hem of her T-shirt. "I'm friends with Sylvain and Jo, and I've met a few other people. Everybody's been sort of nice, except . . ." She bit her lip.

Isabelle looked at her encouragingly. "Except?"

"Oh, you know." Allie crossed and uncrossed her ankles. "Katie Gilmore? She's a bit bitchy."

Isabelle sighed. "I know Katie can be . . . difficult. She is studying at a university level now—her math abilities are stellar. That's why she's here. But because of her childhood, she has a hard time interacting with students who are not as privileged as she is—she's been too sheltered by her family's wealth." Isabelle polished her glasses with a clean cloth. "I hope you two find a way to get along." She put her glasses down and leaned forward, her expression serious. "But we do not tolerate bullying of any sort, so if she goes too far, I want you to feel you can come talk to me or to Jules."

Katie was clever? Allie couldn't believe it. She just seemed like another spoiled little rich girl. Somehow knowing she had hidden depths made things worse. It was harder to hate her if she couldn't fit her into an easy box.

"Anything else aside from that?" Isabelle asked. "Your

coursework is looking fine so far. You're certainly doing very well in my class. Any problems academically?"

Allie shook her head. It was true the work was hard, but it was more interesting than the work at her last two schools and she found that, actually, she enjoyed it.

"Any homesickness?" Isabelle asked. "I've noticed that you haven't asked to phone your parents since you arrived. Would you like to phone them? I know it says emergencies only in The Rules, but I'm happy for you to talk to them, since you're new."

Again Allie shook her head—more vigorously this time. "I don't want to talk to them right now," she said. "I want some time without them."

Isabelle's expression was hard to read, but something told Allie she understood.

"Of course," she said, adding, "but if you ever change your mind, come to me."

The conversation had now skated onto thin ice for Allie, who fidgeted in her seat, hoping she'd soon be released.

Nothing escaped the headmistress's attention, and she stood up with a weary stretch.

"Well, I suppose I should free you to have lunch and enjoy the rest of your weekend."

Needing no more invitation, Allie leaped to her feet and headed for the door, but Isabelle's voice stopped her just as she was about to open it.

"Please, Allie," she said, "don't hesitate to come to me with any problem, however small or large. I am here to help you. I am absolutely not here to get you in trouble. You are safe with me."

Her words seemed heartfelt and Allie smiled shyly. "I will."

"Oh God. Please make the torture end." Jo fell facedown onto her biology book.

Sitting across from her at the table in the library, Allie threw a pen at her.

"Yep," Gabe said, closing his book, "we need a break. I've still got a bit more to do, but nobody's saying I can't do it later. It's Saturday afternoon, it's a beautiful day—who wants to go outside?"

Without raising her head from her book, Jo stuck her arm straight up in the air. "Me," she said, her voice muffled by biology.

"Allie?" he asked, stacking his books.

She shook her head. "I've had enough of the great outdoors today, thanks. I think I'll explore the building."

Jo's head popped up; her blond hair stood on end. "The building's cool. Ask Eloise to show you the study chambers. They're wicked."

She seemed largely recovered from the night before; the cut on her cheek was closed with two flesh-colored butterfly bandages, and there were no other visible wounds. Allie hadn't yet had a chance to talk with her about what had happened—she was dying for a few minutes alone, but Gabe had scarcely left Jo's side all day. Now he stacked her books with his as the two stood up to leave.

"See you at dinner, if not before?" Allie asked hopefully.

"Defo," Jo said, smiling.

When they were gone, Allie stretched and looked around. The room was mostly deserted.

Eloise sat at an old-fashioned raised librarian's desk, lined with cubbyholes, slim vertical shelves, and narrow drawers with brass handles. Perched on a high stool amid a world of paper and polished wood, she was busy flipping through a library card file and didn't see Allie walk up.

"Uh . . . hi?" Allie's voice was hesitant.

"Oh, hello again," Eloise said, straightening.

The librarian's dark hair was pulled back in a loose style from which tendrils escaped; purple-framed glasses perched at the end of her slender nose.

"Are you here for those books I told you about? I've set them aside for you."

Reaching under the desk, she pulled out a stack of books tied together with twine. A card on top read "For Allie."

"I believe it's some extra reading for your English class."

Allie had already forgotten about the books the librarian had mentioned that morning, and frankly, she thought she had enough to read already.

But still . . .

"Thank you," she said politely, putting the books in her bag. "Actually, I was just going to explore the building and Jo said there were some cool study rooms or something in here?"

Eloise looked blank for a minute, then brightened. "You must mean the carrels in the back. They're quite something. Let me get the keys."

She removed a crowded key ring from a hook behind the front counter. Allie followed her along what seemed like hundreds of years' worth of Oriental rugs and past endless rows of shelves.

"This place is huge," she said, looking up to the ceiling.

"Just be glad you don't have to dust it," the librarian replied chirpily. "Mind you, if you get detention again, you might get that chance."

Her joke surprised a laugh out of Allie.

"Please, no," she said glancing at the rows of towering bookcases.

"Don't worry." Eloise smiled. "If you behave yourself, it'll never happen."

They turned a corner and the room opened out into a space with fewer bookshelves and more tables surrounded by deep leather chairs.

"This area is reserved for advanced students," Eloise explained, choosing a key from the ring in her hand. "Here we go." The walls were paneled with elaborately carved dark wood. Eloise inserted the key into a lock so skillfully hidden in the woodwork that Allie couldn't see it at all. A door that until then had been virtually invisible opened silently.

Isabelle flipped a light switch and stepped back. Allie walked into an illuminated room about eight feet wide by six feet long with a low ceiling. Inside the windowless space was a desk with a lamp, a leather chair, and a small bookcase. Dominating it all was an elaborate mural.

"Wow!" Allie's breath came out in a gasp.

"Wow indeed." Eloise looked at her over the tops of her glasses. "These study rooms are part of the oldest part of the building. We're not at all certain what their original purpose was, or why somebody . . . Well, take a look."

Stepping into the center of the room, Allie turned a slow circle to take it all in. The painting seemed to tell a story: men and women armed to the teeth and fighting in a field, overlooked by enraged cherubs under a stormy sky.

The scene was chilling.

"How does anybody study in here?" she whispered, finding it impossible to speak out loud. "I'd spend the whole time ducking for cover."

"It doesn't seem to bother anyone else." Eloise looked at the swinging swords. "But I can't say I disagree with you."

She stepped out of the room. After a last glance around, Allie followed, and Eloise locked the door behind them.

"Are they all like this?"

The librarian nodded. "They're very similar. The paintings in each room tell a different part of the same story. This is the main battle painting. It seems to be the last in the series."

She walked down to the end of the paneled wall and unlocked another hidden door. Turning on the light, she gestured for Allie to follow, and they stepped into the small study room. This room's paintings showed the same people, the men in hats and formal attire, then women in elaborate long dresses. They appeared to be talking in a circle, in front of what looked like a smaller version of the building she was in now.

"We think this is the first in the series," Eloise said.

"Is that Cimmeria?" Allie asked.

"Before the expansion," Eloise said. "The painting is of that time—early eighteenth century."

"What's it all about?" Allie asked. "Some kind of war?"

Eloise was studying one of the faces. "Nobody really knows anymore. The school lore is that the building was originally built by a single family. Some kind of disagreement divided them, and they essentially went to war with one another—the winning side kept the estate. But none of that is recorded in the school records, and let me tell you, if it was I would know; I'm also the school historian."

As they walked out of the room, Allie was lost in thought.

"Weird," she said. "I mean, how could something so important just get lost?"

"Things do," Eloise said. "Especially if nobody wants to remember it."

"I really do not want to study in those rooms," Allie said firmly.

"Luckily, you've got another year before you're advanced enough to sit back here." Eloise gave her a bright smile. "So you're safe for now."

SIX

As Allie walked out of the library and down the hall to the class-room wing, she was still thinking about the strange paintings. As it was a Saturday, the rooms were empty and silent, and she idly climbed the staircase past the familiar lower rooms and up to the fourth floor. Only advanced classes were held up here, and she'd hoped the floor would have some air of mystery, but she was disappointed to find that it looked exactly like the lower levels—a wide hallway with a polished wood floor. With the lights off, it was lit entirely by daylight filtering through classroom windows.

Her rubber-soled shoes rendered her footsteps nearly silent as she peeked through open doors at desks waiting in patient, ghostly rows.

She wasn't sure when she first heard the voices—just murmurs—perhaps midway down the hall. She stopped walking.

Someone shouted and there was a crashing sound, followed by a concerned wave of voices that seemed to be trying to calm things.

Allie was poised to turn back when a door at the end of the hall opened and a figure stepped out of the shadows.

Instinctively she ducked into the nearest doorway and hid in the shadows behind the door, listening. At first she could hear nothing but the sound of her own breathing; then, after a moment, she could hear the faint sound of footsteps heading her way. She counted her breaths.

. . . ten, eleven, twelve . . .

The footsteps paused.

She stopped breathing.

"Allie?" Carter whispered, his voice harsh. "What the hell?"

He reached in and grabbed her arm, pulling her roughly toward the stairwell. She was too surprised to protest and stumbled alongside him. He hustled her down the stairs to the third-floor landing, where he turned her to face him.

"What were you doing up on the fourth floor?" His fingers dug into her upper arm.

"Exploring," she said, struggling to free herself from his grip. She tried to appear calm, but she knew she sounded defensive.

"Exploring what? The classrooms?"

Feigning nonchalance, she shrugged. "Yeah. Sort of. It's not off-limits or anything, is it?"

He stared at her in disbelief.

"Allie, did you ever actually read the information you were given when you started here? Or do you think rules are just optional for you?"

Sarcasm dripped from his voice, and now Allie could feel anger growing in the pit of her stomach.

What is wrong with everybody at this stupid school?

"I read enough to know it was boring," she snapped. "Now will you quit being a psycho and let me go?"

She forced her arm free from his grip. "Bloody hell," she said, rubbing her shoulder.

"The fourth floor is for advanced students and Night School only," Carter said, as if he were talking to a child. "You could get into serious trouble if they catch you there. You must *never* go up there."

She shot him a glare. "Overreact much? Jesus. You'd think I killed someone."

His expression did not change. "Seriously, Sheridan. I'm starting to think you like getting in trouble."

Turning on her heel, she stomped down the stairs, firing over her shoulder, "Well, from what I hear about you, West, you'd know all about that."

He didn't reply.

At dinner that night, Allie was still distracted by her fight with Carter. His words stung, in part because they rang true. Why hadn't she paid attention to all the rules? For the first time it occurred to her that she actually wanted this school to work out. She was tired of starting over.

It got harder each time.

Lost in thought, she played uninterestedly with her food as Jo and the others talked with their usual animation. She could just make out the sound of rain against the windowpanes. It had been gray all afternoon, and now it was pouring down. She was so deeply entangled in a complex net of her own thoughts that bits of the conversation floated by her like flotsam.

"Twenty pages by Tuesday!"

"Most amazing smile . . ."

"What is this meat, anyway?"

"Mystery meat."

Laughter.

"I heard a teacher say it's supposed to rain for the next three days."

A chorus of groans.

Allie glanced up, puzzled.

"It's so boring here when it rains," Jo explained. "The common room will be packed. We should get there early if we want a seat."

As soon as they'd finished, they hurried out and down the hall. Jo claimed a sofa in the middle of the room, kicking off her shoes and tucking her feet underneath her. Allie sank into a deep leather chair across from her. They were just settling down when Gabe walked up.

He, like Allie, had seemed distracted. "I can't stay," he said apologetically. "It's this stupid project."

Kissing Jo, he whispered something in her ear that made her smile, then hurried out.

Finally, for the first time since the previous night, Allie and Jo were alone. At last, Allie would have a chance to talk with her in private.

"What should we do now?" Jo asked. "Do you want to play Trivial Pursuit?"

"Not right now." Scooting forward in her chair, Allie leaned toward Jo and lowered her voice to a whisper. "Jo, what *was* that last night? What does Gabe think?"

Jo seemed puzzled. "Well, there was some sort of crazy fox or something . . . I don't know. It all happened so fast."

Disappointed, Allie leaned away from her. "That's what Sylvain said. But, come on, Jo, that didn't sound like a fox."

"What do you think it sounded like?" Jo asked.

Allie shook her head. "I don't know. Something with big teeth."

"A bear?" Jo suggested impishly. "A dragon? A *wookie*?"

"Jo, seriously!" Allie's frustration was reflected in her tone. "What happened last night was real. Gabe and Sylvain took it seriously. They didn't seem to think we were being silly. They were . . . well, not scared, but like, into it. Now I feel like everyone's trying to make us think we were hysterical. Or like it was some big joke. But I think there was something out there."

Jo made a soothing gesture with her hands.

"Look, Allie, something definitely happened, but it was dark, and I don't think anybody knows whether or not it was really dangerous. We could have just scared ourselves. Gabe says some people went out last night looking for whatever it was, but they didn't find anything." She smiled. "Don't get too freaked out."

Even though she was unconvinced, Allie didn't want to appear obsessed, so she nodded reluctantly.

"So. Back to what to do tonight," Jo said. "If not Trivial Pursuit . . . Backgammon? Something else? Checkers? Tic-tac-toe?" Then she cocked her head. "Have you ever played chess?"

Allie's expression must have given her away, because Jo's face took on a determined focus.

"Seriously? That's outrageous. Well, I'm about take care of that right now."

Jumping off the sofa, she knelt beside the table in front of them and pulled a shoebox-size wooden box from underneath it. From it she began to pull out glossy pieces. Setting the black pieces on her side, she handed Allie a white knight.

Allie held it up and made a neighing sound. Jo gave her a withering look.

"Pony," Allie said weakly.

"Get serious, Allie," Jo said. "This isn't a game. Not really. Because chess is really war."

When Allie made a face, Jo pointed at the piece she still held. "That is not a pony. That is a knight that kills." Pointing at a square on the board, she said, "Put it there."

Trying to look serious, Allie placed the knight where she was told, but shooting Jo a rebellious glance, she murmured "Good horsie" under her breath.

Jo ignored her and picked up a pawn.

"These are your foot soldiers. They have the least freedom and the least power, but because they're willing to sacrifice themselves for their betters, you can't win without them."

Setting it down, she picked up two more pieces. In her right hand she held a piece shaped vaguely like a minaret. "The bishop. Slick and dangerous, he has huge power. I think of him as the queen's dirty boyfriend." As Allie laughed she waved the tall, regal piece in her left hand. "The king. Almost always weaker than you'd think—all the pieces protect him, but he almost never helps anyone else, because if he does he could die."

Allie cupped her chin in her hand. "This is like Shakespeare, only . . . lamer."

Now Jo picked up a slender, crowned white piece and handed it to her. "The queen. She's a complete bitch. But if you want to win, you have got to work with her."

"Great," Allie said. "What happens next? And at what point do I begin kicking your ass?"

Jo handed her the white pieces. "If you practice and work hard? Maybe by your twenty-seventh birthday. I've been playing chess since I was five. Set yours out the way I've done mine, then I'll beat you for the first time."

Allie arranged her pieces as a mirror image of Jo's.

"So tell me a more about your friends," she said, picking up the queen. "Lisa and Lucas seem nice, but Ruth and Phil I couldn't really tell . . ."

Jo nodded. "I think you'll really like Lisa—she was my first friend at Cimmeria. Ruth's cool but she's kind of, I don't know, intense, I guess. Phil's okay—he tells terrible jokes when he loosens up. But he's kind of shy around new people."

"And who was the other girl . . . ? I've forgotten her name. She didn't sit with us last night."

For a second Jo looked blank, then she brightened.

"Oh. Rachel. She's a friend of Lucas's really. She doesn't usually hang out with us. She's a total brainiac."

At that moment, Ruth ran into the room, breathless, her clothes soaked and her wet hair dropping beads of water.

"Jo."

She stood in front of them, panting, her hands clutching her sides as if she'd run very fast. Water puddled on the floor at her feet.

The queen still in her hand, Allie froze. Jo seemed speechless, but Ruth didn't wait to be asked.

"It's Gabe."

SEVEN

Jo jumped to her feet, sending chess pieces scattering across the floor.

"What . . . ?" She looked confused. Fearful.

"He's hurt. Phil too. It went wrong."

Jo seemed to be stunned to immobility. Whatever had happened, Allie knew it couldn't be good. Concerned, she moved to Jo's side.

"What happened?" she asked Ruth. "What went wrong? Where are they?"

Ruth gave her an appraising look; out of the corner of her eye, Allie thought she saw Jo nod almost imperceptibly.

"The summerhouse," Ruth said finally. "I'm going to get Zelazny and the others to help."

When Jo still didn't react, Allie decided to take charge.

"Come on." Taking Jo by the hand, Allie pulled her toward the door as Ruth ran down the hall in the opposite direction.

Allie and Jo dashed through the grand entry hall, where they skidded to a stop on the stone floor and shoved the heavy wooden door open. Outside the rain pelted down.

Allie turned to Jo. "Which way?" She shouted to be heard above the noise of the storm as thunder rumbled above them.

Jo pointed past the west wing. They hurtled down the drive, then onto the wet grass and out toward the woods. Allie could hear her own ragged breathing ringing in her ears, the sound of rain . . . and nothing else.

A few minutes later she saw an elaborate Victorian gazebo through the trees. It was empty. They ran up the stairs and looked around, panting. Allie bent over with her hands on her knees, trying to catch her breath.

Jo pointed into the woods. "There."

Allie peered into the rainy gloom but could see nobody.

Then she heard a shout that seemed to come from deep in the forest.

Allie looked at Jo to see if she'd heard. She was staring off into the trees, her lips parted.

"Did you hear that, too?" Allie whispered.

Her eyes still fixed on the forest, Jo nodded.

"It's Gabe."

More shouts, but still they could see nothing. Then, after a few minutes, shadowy figures came into focus, walking out of the woods. Allie could make out Carter and Gabe. They seemed to be holding somebody up between them. She couldn't see who it was.

"Oh my God." Jo was still whispering. They stood up.

As the boys walked up the stairs to the summerhouse, Allie

could see that they were wounded. A cut on Carter's forehead bled freely. Gabe had blood on his hands and shirt. He looked angrily at Allie.

"What the hell are you doing here?"

Before she could reply, Carter interceded. "Not right now, man. We've got enough problems."

Gently, they laid down the person they carried.

Jo gasped. "Phil. Oh no!"

"You're going to be okay," Gabe said to Phil. "Can you hear me? Sylvain's gone for help."

Jo tugged at his arm, turning it over to reveal a jagged cut on his wrist.

"Gabe," she breathed, color disappearing from her face.

What the hell is happening? Allie thought, looking at the disaster scene in front of her. *And why isn't anybody else asking that question?*

On his knees beside Phil, Carter tore a strip from the end of his shirt and tied it tightly around the unconscious boy's leg. Then he tore another one and held it up to Jo. "Tie this around Gabe's wrist."

But Jo seemed unable to move. She held the white fabric as if she didn't quite know what it was.

Allie stepped over. "I'll do it."

As she reached for the fabric, Jo let it fall from her hand.

The makeshift bandage fluttering, Allie turned to Gabe. "Hold out your hand."

Still scowling at her, Gabe lifted his arm and Allie wrapped the strip expertly around his wrist and hand, weaving it into a tight bandage, then tucking the end in so the fit was snug.

"Hold your hand above your heart until the bleeding stops," she intoned automatically.

Turning back toward Phil, she saw that Carter was watching her.

"You're bleeding, too," she said.

"I'm okay."

"I can see that," she said with gentle sarcasm. "But someone should look at that cut."

Hearing footsteps running across the grass, Allie looked up to see a group of people heading their way. As they neared, she saw Sylvain was in the lead, Zelazny and Jerry right behind him. Zelazny glanced at Allie with irritation.

"What is she doing here?" His tone was accusing.

Sylvain's eyes met Allie's for a second, then he returned his focus to Zelazny. His voice was soothing. "We'll find out later—first we must deal with this."

"How bad is it?" Jerry said, checking the tourniquet.

Carter looked worried. "Not too bad, but he needs a doctor. He's bleeding a lot."

"What about you?" Jerry asked.

Blood dripped down Carter's face and onto his soaked white shirt, but he didn't look up. "I'll be fine. I need a couple of stitches."

"Okay, you and Gabe get to the nurse. Sylvain, help me with Phil. Everybody else, get back inside." Jerry glared at Allie. "Now."

His tone left no room for argument, and on his last word they all moved at once. He and Sylvain carried Phil by draping his arms across their shoulders, and Zelazny hurried ahead of them.

As if she'd been shaken awake, Jo turned to Gabe and hugged him.

Allie and Carter followed them out of the gazebo and back toward the school.

"What the hell was that all about, Carter?" she asked, hoping they were out of earshot of the others. "Why was everybody all ninja all of a sudden? What the hell is going on?"

"It was nothing," he said. "An accident. It happens."

"It *happens*?" she asked, disbelieving. "An accident in the woods in the pouring rain in which half the student population ends up bleeding to death . . . happens?"

The dark look he shot her was made even more murderous by the blood streaming down his face.

"Has anybody ever mentioned you've got an exaggeration problem?" he said.

"No," Allie replied without hesitation. "Anybody ever mention you've got a dickhead problem?"

After that, they didn't speak.

As the rain pounded down on them, she cast a sideways glance at him from underneath lashes so covered in raindrops, it was like looking through a waterfall. He was staring ahead, his jaw set.

When they reached the school steps, Isabelle stood at the top in a long white raincoat. The rain made a dull plastic sound as it pounded against the hood.

"Carter. Allie. Are you okay? Carter, you look horrible."

"I'm fine," Carter insisted. "I just need a couple of stitches."

Isabelle scrutinized him, then turned to Allie. "And you? Are you hurt?"

When Allie shook her head, water poured onto her nose.

"Good. Carter, get to the nursing station. Allie, would you come with me, please?"

Without waiting for a reply, she walked back inside briskly.

As Allie turned to follow her, Carter grabbed her elbow. She thought he looked like a victim in a horror film.

"Come find me before curfew," he said in a low voice. "I'll be in the great hall." Then he sloshed into the school, leaving a trail of water in his wake.

Frowning, Allie let her eyes follow him down the hall.

"As if," she muttered before hurrying after Isabelle.

In her office, Isabelle handed her a soft white towel, and Allie rubbed the water roughly out of her hair and then wrapped it around her shoulders, shivering. Now that she was inside, she felt cold.

"Please sit down." Isabelle perched on the edge of the desk, watching her. Allie was conscious of the low timbre of classical music playing from hidden speakers.

"You're sure you're okay?" Isabelle asked. When Allie nodded, she continued. "Good. I just want to talk to you for a minute, and then I'm going to send you off to get some dry clothes. You're not in any trouble, but I just need to know what happened tonight."

Allie looked at her, puzzled. "I don't . . . ?"

"I mean, what were you and Jo doing out at the summerhouse? Tell me what happened from the beginning."

Wrapping the towel more tightly around her shoulders, Allie thought quickly. Was someone in trouble?

Am I in trouble?

"We were just . . . looking for Gabe," she said carefully. "Jo wanted to surprise him by sneaking up on him, but we couldn't find him. We went to the summerhouse to get out of the rain, and then we saw the boys coming out of the woods. . . ."

She felt uncomfortable lying to Isabelle, but the whole thing felt wrong. When Ruth had come to get them, she'd looked frightened. She'd been white as a sheet. *Ruth wasn't supposed to tell us anything.* Allie's instincts told her to cover for her, even though she didn't know why.

Isabelle watched her closely. "Then what happened?"

"We knew right away that something was wrong, but nobody would tell us what happened." The last bit sounded self-pitying, but really why was everybody being so secretive?

"Is that everything?" The headmistress gave no indication at all that she didn't believe her, so Allie decided it was time to ask some questions of her own.

"Do you know what happened?" she asked. "Carter refuses to tell me, and everybody else acts like I've done something really wrong."

Isabelle leaned back in her chair. "I'm sorry about that, Allie. They shouldn't behave like that. You're new, and there's no way for you to know. I'm not quite clear yet as to what happened or how Carter and Phil got hurt, but I intend to find out."

"It's just," Allie said, "it looked really bad."

Isabelle stood up. "I think it looked worse than it was. I'm told nobody was seriously injured, and sometimes games just get a little too rough. It's nothing for you to worry about. I will speak with those involved."

Isabelle dropped her hand to Allie's shoulder and squeezed it lightly as she walked by her to the door, which she held open for her.

Every instinct in Allie's body told her Isabelle was lying.

"Thank you, Allie. I'm glad you're okay. You don't need to worry about Phil—he's already being seen by medical staff. And it is clear to me that Carter's wound is superficial."

Allie didn't see the point in asking more questions. Something had obviously gone horribly wrong. But Isabelle wasn't going to tell her anything.

What could have happened to them all out in the woods? And why won't anyone tell me?

Back in her room she changed into a dry skirt and sweater, dumping her wet clothes on the floor. She wanted to get back downstairs before curfew and find out how everyone was doing.

As she dabbed on pale pink lip gloss in front of the mirror, though, her hand stopped. *Should I go meet Carter?*

It wasn't that she really wanted to meet him. She was just curious. Why did he want to meet her alone? And why in the great hall? She'd never even been in there.

She checked the clock. It was only ten. There was still plenty of time until curfew. If she hurried, she could go to the great hall and see what Carter wanted and still have time to talk with Jo.

As she dashed down the stairs a few minutes later, she passed no one. Even the ground floor hallway was eerily empty.

Where is everyone?

"Allie." Sylvain's silky French accent caressed her name, and she spun around to find him right behind her. "I was hoping to run into you. I was concerned—are you okay?"

He'd changed into dry clothes, and as he pulled her into a warm hug, she breathed in his clean scent.

As he released her, his fingers delicately traced a line down her back to her waist.

Goose bumps.

"I'm fine."

She tried to think of an excuse for what she was up to. Something told her he wouldn't be happy to know she was on her way to meet Carter.

"I was just looking for Jo . . . ," she said.

"I believe she is with Gabe."

He stood so close to her, she could feel his breath on her cheek—faintly redolent of coffee.

"What were you and Jo doing in the summerhouse anyway?" His tone was casual, but something about his manner sent off warning signals. "Zelazny was very cross to see you there."

Is he investigating me?

"It was before curfew," Allie argued. "I don't see why everybody cares that we were outside. We just wanted to go outside. So we did."

"In the pouring rain."

Allie was tired of being questioned. "We thought it would be fun," she said shortly. "And you know what? I could ask you the same question. What were *you* doing outside in the pouring rain?"

He studied her curiously, as if he saw something new in her he hadn't noticed before.

"Fair enough, *ma belle*." For the first time she heard cool distance in his voice.

She'd touched a nerve.

"How's Phil?" she asked, trying to move to safer ground.

"He is fine—but he lost some blood. It was a bad fall."

As she opened her mouth to ask what had happened out there, he spoke again.

"You should have something warm to drink," he said. "Come with me. There's hot chocolate and coffee in the kitchen."

"No." Allie's response was more panicked than the situation called for, and Sylvain raised one eyebrow in surprise as she fumbled for a reason. "I . . . There's something I need to do. Let's talk tomorrow? I have to run. . . ."

Her explanations fading, she dashed past him to the library. It was deserted—even the librarian's desk was empty. Running across the soft rugs down to the stacks, Allie disappeared into the shadows between two tall bookcases.

This is so stupid. Why am I hiding from Sylvain? He won't follow me anyway. Why would . . .

The library door opened and closed again. She held her breath. After a moment she heard Sylvain call her name twice, softly. Then a long pause. Then the door opened and closed again.

To be safe, Allie stayed where she was a few minutes longer. When she'd heard nothing after counting slowly to two hundred, she stepped out of the stacks, opening the library door to peek out into the hall. It was empty.

She sighed with relief. Wondering even as she did it why she was relieved.

Tiptoeing down the hallway, she hesitated in front of the grand carved great hall door, then pushed it tentatively. It swung open without a sound.

Inside, the lights were off but she could see a faint glow at the far end of the vast ballroom. She could just make out a few tables and chairs scattered around, but otherwise the cavernous space was empty.

"Carter?" she whispered.

A voice made a ghostly *woooo* sound that echoed around her.

She rolled her eyes. "Cut it out, West."

His chuckle echoed around her.

As she neared the light, she saw that he was sprawled in a chair with his foot propped up on a table between two lighted candles. His forehead was neatly bandaged and he was wearing clean, dry clothes. He was holding a book, which he now dropped lightly on the floor.

There was another chair next to him, and he gestured at it.

"Sit."

"Don't tell me what to do," she muttered as she sat.

He smiled darkly. "Sorry, I thought I was being polite."

"How's your head?" she said, changing the subject.

He waved the question away impatiently. "I'm fine."

There was a moment of silence.

"So, what's up?" Allie asked to break the stillness. "Why did you want to meet me here? In case you're hoping, I don't dance."

"I like it here." He shrugged. "I'm always here. They never check it; I don't know why."

Lifting his foot from the table, he turned to face her. "I just want to know how you and Blondie ended up in the summerhouse tonight right when everything went down. Gabe said he left you both safely in the common room on the verge of a girly conversation about . . . I don't know . . . shoes or lipstick or whatever girls talk about. Fifteen minutes later, you're at the summerhouse in the pouring rain tying bandages. How did that happen, Allie?"

She dodged his eyes, angry to be asked this question yet again. "Bloody hell! Why is everybody so obsessed with this? For the thousandth time, Jo just wanted to look for—"

"Oh, give it a rest, Allie," he said shortly. "I'm not Isabelle."

Surprised by his vehemence, she fumbled for something to say.

"I . . . uh . . . well—"

"The truth would be good," he said, interrupting her stuttering. She thought about his words from the library: *Never be afraid to be honest. . . .* The same instinctive worry that stopped her from telling Isabelle told her not to tell Carter, either. But she had to find out what was going on around here, and if anybody would know, he would.

"Ruth," she said at last. "She came and got us."

In the candlelight, his eyes were fathomless. She stared into them for a long, silent moment looking for a reaction but saw nothing.

When he spoke, though, his voice was cold.

"What did she say?"

Allie crossed her arms across her torso, visualizing Ruth standing in front of her, water streaming from her hair and dripping onto the floor. Fear on her face.

"She said Phil and Gabe were hurt. And something weird. I think she said, 'It went wrong.'"

Another long silence. "Have you told this to anyone else?" His voice was tight.

"No," Allie said. "Not yet. . . ."

Carter came out of his chair so fast that later she couldn't remember seeing him do it. He grabbed her by her shoulders.

With his lips a few inches away from hers, he spoke in a harsh whisper. "You must never tell anybody else what Ruth did. Swear it."

Allie stared up at him, and her lips moved for a second before any sound came out.

"Yeah, sure. Okay, I won't tell anyone." She shoved him away. "Get off me, Carter."

As if he'd just realized what he was doing, he let her go.

"You're freaking me out." Allie rubbed her shoulder. "What is your malfunction?"

Trying to look casual, he leaned against a pillar.

"Sorry. But Ruth shouldn't have done that, and people might be . . . She might get in trouble. I don't want her to get in trouble, so you really can't say anything."

"Hey," she said icily. "That's not a problem. And while we're all about honesty, maybe you could tell me what tonight's performance was about? How did you all end up cut to pieces in the middle of the forest?"

Crossing his arms, he looked at her coldly. A long silence fell.

"Okay then." She stood up. "Thanks for the inquisition and the threats and everything. It's been really awesome. But I should probably be going."

Carter stared at her as if there was something else he wanted to say. In fact, she could almost pinpoint the moment when he decided not to say it.

"You make a good bandage," he said instead. "Where'd you learn to do that?"

She wanted to walk out in disgust. But she stayed. She wasn't sure why. Maybe just curiosity.

"South London," she said. "First-aid class. Girl Guides."

He raised one sardonic eyebrow. "You were in the Girl Guides? No way."

She couldn't figure out why they were having this jovial conversation after he'd just gone all creepy on her, but she decided to go along with it.

"Yes way. I was a kid then, but that stuff stays with you. Bandage tying. Butterfly catching. Jam making. I can do it all."

He barked a short laugh, but Allie didn't smile. "What's really going on around here, Carter? Did you guys get in a fight? It looked really bad."

His eyes went blank again. If he'd closed a door in her face it couldn't have been more clear.

"Just let it go." he snapped. "And don't ask anybody else either. Nobody will tell you a thing and people will get angry. I'm serious about that, Allie." He looked at his watch. "It's nearly eleven. We have to go."

Without warning, he blew out the candles and the room plunged into darkness.

Blinded by the sudden blackout, Allie turned toward where she thought the door might be and promptly tripped over something in the darkness. Carter caught her. For just a second they stood face-to-face. Though he was wreathed in shadows, Allie thought he looked almost sorry.

But I'm probably wrong about that.

"This way." He led her by the hand through the dark room with the confidence of somebody who'd done it many times. His fingers felt warm and strong against hers, and something in her responded to his touch. But some other part of her really didn't want him touching her right now. Conflicted by everything that had happened, she moved stiffly beside him, her hand loose in his.

When they emerged blinking into the lights of the hall, she pulled her hand free of his in a deliberate motion.

"It's eleven, Sheridan," he said roughly. "You should hurry. You don't want detention again."

"Yeah, sure," she said sarcastically. "Blood and gore we can have. But Allie out after curfew? That would be a disaster."

"Good night, Sheridan," he said, firmly.

She turned for the stairs. "Whatever, West."

"You have to trust me, Allie."

Carter's eyes looked into hers intently but she resisted.

"Why would I trust you?" she asked. "You don't trust me."

They were standing in the great hall. It was filled with lighted candles—they glittered on windowsills, tabletops, and in hugely tall candelabra. The heat they gave off was intense.

Carter's eyes glittered in the light. "But I can help you. . . ."

Someone banged on the door loudly. Threateningly. Allie felt her heart pound.

"They're here," he said.

The banging came again, more insistent this time. The noise was almost deafening, and Allie covered her ears.

"Who is it? Who's here, Carter?"

His voice was urgent. "You have to trust me. Do you trust me?"

Over his shoulder she could see the door was cracking under the strain of the pounding.

"Yes!" Allie cried, reaching out for him. "Yes! I trust you."

Gasping, Allie sat up in bed clutching the duvet in tight fists.

A loud bang made her jump, but it was only the wooden shutter thrown against the wall by a stiff breeze coming through the open window.

Climbing up on top of the desk to look out the window, she saw the storm had worsened during the night—the trees swayed, and leaves, freed from their branches, rode the wind high above her.

The air smelled fresh as she latched the window tightly into place and climbed back into bed.

Pulling the covers up she muttered aloud, "Get out of my *head*, Carter West."

EIGHT

When classes resumed on Monday, Allie had the disconcerting sense that none of the weekend's events had actually occurred. Everyone took their normal seats in class at the normal time. And Jerry and Zelazny treated her exactly as if they'd never seen her wrap a bandage in the pouring rain.

Sylvain wasn't in English class, but Carter arrived late as usual and just smirked when Isabelle gave him an exasperated look. If he hadn't still been wearing a bandage on his forehead, Allie might have thought she had imagined the entire thing.

But over the next few days, rumors were rife about what had occurred down in the woods that night. Everybody knew that people had been hurt, but there was widespread confusion over just what had taken place. When word came that students were now forbidden to go out onto the grounds, it only made the gossip worse. Nobody seemed to know that Allie and Jo had been there, though, and the most common rumor was that the boys had run afoul of the same fox Jo and Allie had encountered, although everybody was openly skeptical of that story.

Phil didn't return to class that week, but Ruth, who seemed to warm to Allie after that night, said he was recovering and would be back soon.

Given the fact that they were all, as Allie saw it, under house arrest, at least the weather was terrible. Throughout the week the rain was unrelenting. It was not as heavy as it had been on Saturday, but it was steady and the days were gray.

At the same time, the teachers seemed to be amped up on educational adrenaline, and Allie spent every available minute studying to try and keep up with her assigned work.

Stumbling out of the library late Thursday night, she was so dazed, it took her a moment to realize Sylvain was walking beside her. When she finally looked up and saw him, he laughed at the startled look on her face.

"Hello, lovely Allie. Where have you been? I haven't seen you since the weekend."

Suddenly wide-awake, Allie felt her heart beat faster, but she tried to act like seeing him was no big deal. She hoped he wouldn't ask where she'd disappeared to when she ran away from him the other night. That would be difficult to explain.

"I've been here." She gestured at the library door behind them. "Just trying to keep from being so buried in homework that I'm never seen again."

He nodded. "I know. The teachers are suddenly very busy making work for us."

"Yeah. What's up with that? Are they always this evil?"

When he smiled, his blue eyes sparkled like the sea in the sun.

"No, this is unusual even for Cimmeria. I think it's possible they are keeping everybody too busy to try to sneak outside."

Allie tried to hide her surprise at his honesty.

"Because of the other night?" she asked.

"Perhaps." He shrugged, but his eyes told her she was right.

She looked longingly toward the front door. "I'd love to go outside. . . ."

"Are you bored?" Taking her hand, he pulled her closer to him. "I could read your palm. Perhaps that would amuse you. And then I would see into your soul."

"You can read palms?" Her voice was doubtful, but she liked the feeling of her hand in his.

"Of course." He smiled. "Can't you? It's easy."

He had long, slim fingers; his skin was smooth and warm. Turning her hand over, he ran his fingertip down the shallow lines of her palm with a touch as light as a cat's whisker.

As they stood close together studying her hand, their heads nearly touched. The air between them felt warm.

"You have a very long life line," he murmured, tracing a line from her wrist to the middle of her palm. "And your heart line is strong. See this line here?" He ran his fingertips along a line that ended between her thumb and index finger. She shivered at the delicacy of his touch. "Do you know what that means?"

Mute, Allie shook her head.

"It tells me you are in love with someone. Or maybe that you will be soon."

Her body tingling from his touch, Allie tried to think of a witty reply, but before she could speak the library door swung open.

Jo said, "Hey, Allie, don't forget the . . ." When she saw Sylvain, her voice trailed off. "Oops, oh dear, I think I forgot my . . ."

Improvising badly, she ducked back inside. A moment later the door opened again and a group of students walked out chatting. Allie could hear Jo whispering at them "No, wait a second. . . ."

Sylvain dropped Allie's hand with a regretful smile. "I should like to explore that topic further with you sometime," he said.

"Yes," she said, flustered by his attention. "Let's . . . that would be . . . fun. . . ."

"Perhaps we could meet after dinner on Saturday?" he said. "If you are free?"

"Sure," she said, trying not to sound as breathless as she felt.

He smiled. "Good. I'll find you in the dining hall. See you then."

"See you then," she parroted back.

The pace of schoolwork never let up, even on Friday, when all the students were given research papers to complete over the weekend. When assignment slips were handed out in history class, Mr. Zelazny's neat handwriting glared at Allie from the page:

3,000 words on the socioeconomic impact of the English Civil War on the agrarian society of the day

Due Monday. No exceptions. No excuses. The library was so crowded on Friday afternoon that, once every seat was taken, students spilled out into the hallway, where they sat on the floor in small clusters, their books and papers spread around them.

"We look like refugees," Jo muttered as she and Allie carried armloads of books out to a free spot near the school's front door.

"It's mad. How long can they keep this up?" As she spoke, Allie was balancing a china cup of tea on a century-old history book and lowering herself to the floor.

"Good question," Jo said, snatching the cup from its precarious perch before it could crash to the stone floor.

"Thanks." Allie settled down with her back against the wall.

Jo took a sip of Allie's tea. "I should have gotten one of those. Now I'll just end up drinking yours."

"And we definitely should have gotten cookies," Allie said.

"We're idiots."

Allie shuffled her books, a frown of concentration creasing her forehead. "Where's Gabe today? I've hardly seen him or Sylvain all week."

Jo was choosing a notebook. "Dunno. He said he had something to do and would do his paper later."

"Weird," Allie said. "The teachers are being so tough, but Sylvain and Gabe don't seem to mind."

Jo shrugged. "Nobody's telling me much about what's going on. Gabe and I had a fight about it, and we never fight."

"Boys suck," Allie said, opening her book.

Having finally found the right notebook, Jo was now focused on finding something it contained, and she rustled through its pages as she spoke absently. "All I know is the Night School kids are out every single night, and I'm sure it has something to do with what happened the other night. But it's top secret."

Allie stopped and stared at her, a brittle, yellowing book page still gripped between her fingers.

"Wait. You know who's in Night School?"

Jo froze, guilt spreading across her expression. "No. Not

really. I mean, I kind of . . . guessed. Anyway, a few are pretty obvious about it."

"Like who?"

"I don't know, really," Jo said carefully. "I mean, just guessing, it could be Sylvain, and Phil, maybe Lucas, and possibly Gabe and Carter, I mean, but who knows?"

She was lying so badly Allie would have laughed if she hadn't been so surprised.

"You mean you think your own boyfriend is in it, but you're not sure?" she said.

Jo looked around to make sure nobody was paying attention to them, then leaned toward Allie and lowered her voice to a whisper. "Look, it's really supersecret, you know? You get in a lot of trouble if anybody finds out you've said anything about it. I mean, a *lot* of trouble."

"So we really shouldn't be talking about it now?" Allie whispered.

"No," Jo hissed.

Allie returned to her book, turning one slow page after another, but her mind was still whirling around what Jo had told her.

She leaned forward again. "No girls?"

Jo gave her a significant look.

"Loads," she said.

"Who?" Allie wasn't going to let this go.

"Maybe Jules," Jo whispered so quietly she could hardly hear. "And Ruth."

For half an hour after that they worked in silence, save for the sound of notes being scribbled and pages turned. Then, without warning, Allie's head popped up.

"That explains the way Carter reacted last Saturday," she said, as if their conversation had never paused.

Jo looked intrigued. "Why? What? And . . . when?"

Allie explained about Carter chasing her away from the fourth floor.

"Interesting," Jo said when she finished. "During the day? That's kind of weird."

Allie twirled her pen again, getting ink on the side of her hand. She rubbed at it futilely. "What exactly is it that they do, anyway?"

Jo didn't look up from her book. "No idea."

Allie was still rubbing her hand. "I've always had the feeling that Carter knew what was really going on. So this would explain why."

Jo gave her a look.

"What?" Allie asked, cocking her head.

"Nothing."

Allie picked up her pen, but Jo was still looking at her.

"*What?*" Allie said again, giving her a light shove. They both giggled.

"Well, it's just . . . you know. You and Carter."

Allie quit laughing. "What about me and Carter?"

"I don't know. He just sort of always picks on you."

"Yeah, I've noticed," Allie said dryly. "That would be because he's a psycho."

"No. I mean . . . I don't know. Something about how he picks on you interests me."

Allie frowned. "Jo, what the hell are you talking about?"

"Oh, it's nothing. It's just that I thought for a little while there he liked you, and I know you liked him, and now it's like you two hate each other."

"It happens." Realizing she'd inadvertently used Carter's words from the other night, Allie winced.

"Hmm . . ." Jo's voice was doubtful.

"There's no 'hmm' about it," Allie said. "All he does is order me around and tell me what to do and not do. Yeah, he's good-looking and everything, but I don't like him."

Jo drew a squiggly line on her notepad and then drew over it again until it was bold. She gave it a forked tongue.

"You know all that stuff Gabe and I said about Carter?"

Allie nodded.

"Well, it was true. But he's been different since you came here. I haven't seen him with any girl since then."

Allie smiled broadly. "What? In two whole weeks? I mean, seriously. What restraint! He must be totally in love with me."

They dissolved into a fit of giggles.

"Anyway, in more sane news, Sylvain asked me to meet him tomorrow night after dinner," Allie said. "I think it's kind of a date."

"Ooh, a real date." Jo's grin was impish. "Seriously, forget everything I said about Carter. I'm just being silly. I'm so excited that you're the one who's going to get Sylvain. All the girls will be terribly jealous of you."

"I'm sure that will make them all be very nice to me." Allie's tone was sarcastic, but Jo arched an eyebrow knowingly.

"If Sylvain's your boyfriend, they won't dare be anything but nice."

Before Allie could ask what she meant, Jo said in her firmest voice, "Right, enough frolicking. We need fifteen hundred words before dinner, which is in"—she checked the delicate gold watch on her wrist—"just over three hours."

"Fascist," Allie said.

But she was already writing.

At dinner that night all discussion centered on rumors that the school grounds were now opened to students "within reason." The problem was nobody knew what that meant.

"Does it mean we can go outside again without dying?" Lisa asked, flipping her long hair over one shoulder.

"Nobody died, Lisa."

Allie thought Gabe's tone was unnecessarily sharp.

Lisa just shrugged and nibbled her salad.

"I'll bet it's perfectly safe," Phil said, his voice deliberately measured, "but I was just thinking of going to the common room."

"Same here," Gabe said quickly.

"Not me. I'm going out. I've had just about enough of inside," said Jo, her voice emphatic, but her eyes not meeting Gabe's. He was staring at her intently, but she looked around the table pretending not to notice.

"Jo . . ." His tone was ominous, but she just shot him a warning look.

"What?"

Throwing his napkin down, Gabe shoved his chair back and stood up, muttering, "I'm not hungry anymore."

He stormed out without looking back.

There was a brief awkward silence while everybody pretended not to notice what had happened right in front of them. Allie saw Phil and Lucas exchange a look.

Ruth tried to distract everyone by launching into a story about a science experiment, but her voice gradually trailed off.

"Right, well, I'm pretty much done. Jo?" Allie said loyally.

Jo gave her a grateful smile and followed her out. Allie waited until they were far enough away from the table to be certain they wouldn't be overheard.

"What was that about?"

Jo was hurrying down the hall, and for a second she didn't answer. When she did, her tone was bitter. "Well, obviously Gabe doesn't want me to go outside because it's not safe. And obviously Gabe wants to act like I'm a child and he's the parent and can tell me what to do. Which I *hate*. I've already got two useless parents, thanks. I don't need another."

She moved through the ornate entrance hall so quickly that Allie was nearly running to keep up by the time they reached the front door. Jo shoved it open impatiently and they both stopped, side by side at the top of the stairs.

"Well," Allie said, looking up at the innocent blue evening sky, "it looks perfectly safe to me."

"I hope it isn't," Jo said. "Last one to die loses."

Laughter softened the impact of her words as she dashed down the stairs. After hesitating for a split second, Allie followed, and they hurtled onto the empty grass. For a few minutes they danced on the lawn, twirling circles in the freedom of the fresh air.

"Wait," Allie said breathlessly, reaching for Jo's arm. "Where are we going?"

They slowed to a more leisurely pace.

"Good question. Someplace where Gabe won't find me and drag me back inside like a caveman." She thought for a moment. "Have you ever been in the chapel?"

Allie made a face. "No, but I've raked its grass."

"Oh yeah. I forgot that detention thing. It's actually pretty cool. There's some old poetry on the walls in, like, a million languages. It's super old."

The chapel was out in the woods, where the guys had been hurt. Allie glanced in that direction uncertainly—Jo's manic behavior was starting to worry her.

"Is it safe to go right now?" she asked. "I mean, with all that's been happening?"

"Probably not." Jo's smile was wicked. "Are you coming or what?"

Without looking back, she headed off across the grass toward the trees.

NINE

The evening sun glinted off Jo's bright blond hair as she sped across the lawn. Allie was right on her heels. Although she was still worried about what could be out there, as her feet carried her swiftly across the smooth lawn, she felt a rush of exhilaration so powerful that she laughed out loud. She loved jogging but, with so much going on, she hadn't been out for a run in ages.

Maybe tomorrow . . .

When she caught up with Jo a few seconds later, she tapped her on the shoulder. "Hurry up!" she shouted, passing her.

Once they were in the forest, though, the blue sky disappeared, and with it the light. In the shadows cast by the tree canopy above them, they slowed to a walk, and some of Allie's courage left her.

"It's so dark in here," she said.

Jo didn't seem concerned. "Forests are like that. You city girls just don't understand the countryside. There's only one thing to do in spooky forests." She gave Allie a light, joking shove. "Run."

As they ran down the well-trodden path, the wild ferns lining it on either side brushed softly against their ankles. Their laughter echoed hollowly off the trees. But Allie was still jumpy. The sounds of the forest—wind blowing branches, a birdcall, a twig snapping underfoot—all made her nerves twitch.

Now that she thought about it, this didn't seem like such a great idea. Something didn't feel right.

Why am I so worried?

But even as she debated whether or not to say something, Jo called over her shoulder. "See? We're here already."

The chapel wall was just ahead, and in the churchyard—fewer trees and more light. As soon as she walked into that glow Allie felt better, but Jo was already at the door, putting both hands inside the iron ring to lift the latch, and then leaning back and pulling on the ancient door with all her weight. It opened with a groan. Inside, the fading sunlight was fractured by yellow and red stained-glass windows into shards of colored light, and despite the natural chill from the stone floor and walls, the room seemed warm.

Standing just inside the door, Allie couldn't believe what she was seeing.

"Holy crap," she whispered.

Jo watched her with a knowing look. "Good, no?"

Tiptoeing into the middle of the room, Allie turned in a slow circle. The walls were covered in paintings. Some were words—most of them obviously poems—others were images. The paint was faded to rusty red, ivory yellow, and graying black, but it was clear, and it was easy to imagine how bright it must once have been.

"This one freaks me out." Jo walked over to the back of the chapel, where a painting of simple figures showed a devil with a pitchfork prodding naked suffering souls into a variety of horrible fates with the help of gleeful troglodyte-like demons.

Allie wrinkled her nose. "Eeeuw."

"Exactly. This is nicer." Jo pointed at nearby painting of a gnarled yew tree rich with fruit and birds. The roots twisted into the words *Tree of Life*.

All around the painted images were words in ancient languages. Allie studied the Cyrillic letters of one.

"Do you understand any of it?" she asked Jo.

"A little. Some is Greek." Jo gestured to symbols painted on a rood screen, then turned to a wall beside it. "And that's some form of Gaelic. Most of it's Latin, though."

On the wall above the door a phrase was painted in elegant red letters. The color was bright enough that Allie wondered if it had been recently restored. She stepped back to see it clearly.

"*Exitus acta probat?*" She sounded the words out and then looked at Jo quizzically. "Do you know what that means?"

"'The result justifies the deed,'" Jo replied without hesitating.

Allie looked back at the words.

"What's that about?" she mused. "It seems kind of strange as a 'Hey, welcome to church!' quote."

"Damned if I know." Jo was spinning down the aisle in a dizzying dance.

Frowning slightly, Allie turned her attention to an elaborate painting of a dragon, whose tail twirled down nearly to the floor as a dove flew just out of reach of its claws.

"This is incredible," she breathed.

"And now that you've seen it, can we go?" Carter leaned against the doorframe—his arms crossed loosely, his eyes watchful.

Allie jumped. "Carter! You scared me."

But while she didn't show it, she felt relieved to see him. Jo was weirding her out, and now they could walk back together. Safety in numbers.

"You shouldn't sneak up on people," she said tartly.

"I didn't sneak." His tone was cool. "I walked. Isn't that how you got here?" When he turned to Jo, his voice warmed. "How's it going, Jo?"

She was at the opposite end of the chapel, pretending to study a painting.

"We're fine here, thanks, Carter. You can tell Gabe I don't need his help." Her voice was steady, but she didn't meet his eyes and her jaw had a stubborn set.

"Hey, I'm not Gabe's minion." His hands made a placating gesture. "It's about to get dark out there, and I just thought I might offer you ladies an escort. Why? Is Gabe looking for you?"

The look she gave him was withering. "Give it up, Carter. I know he sent you. He always sends somebody to follow me around."

"Honestly, Jo, Gabe doesn't know I'm here," he said. "Have you two had a fight or something?"

Carter's face was so earnest that Allie was inclined to believe him, but Jo moved to the altar, as far away from him as possible.

"Something," she said coolly.

Pretending she was studying the wall paintings, Allie made her way over to Carter, who still stood by the door.

Staring intently at a delicate painting of a white rose, she whispered, "How did you find us?"

Just as quietly he replied, "I followed you."

Their eyes met and glanced away. Allie's skin tingled.

"What's up?" His lips barely moved when he spoke, but his head inclined toward Jo.

"I don't know," she replied. "It's like she's not . . . her."

"Whisper whisper whisper!" Jo's angry voice cut through their conversation, and they turned to see her standing at the altar, palms flat on the pulpit, glaring at them. "Why don't you two just kiss and get it over with?"

Allie stared at Jo with her mouth open. She felt like she'd been punched.

What the hell is wrong with her?

But she tried to keep the wounded tone out of her voice. "Hey, that is so not cool, Jo. Look, it really is getting dark and I'd like to get back. Come with me?"

She held out her hand. Jo studied her for a moment and then walked across the nave to her.

"Fine. Whatever. Let's go." Her tone was reasonable, and as she took Allie's hand, she gave it a squeeze. But Allie had the uneasy sense that something still wasn't quite right. When they got outside, the light was fading, and the woods looked darker and more ominous than before.

Jo balanced on her toes on the front step.

"Hey, Allie, remember what I said about the only way to go through the scary woods?"

Allie gave her a puzzled look. "What? Run?"

At that, Jo took off down the path at surprising speed as Carter and Allie stood in front of the church staring after her.

"What the hell?" Carter looked up at the sky like he hoped it held some sort of answer.

"I have no idea what is going on," Allie said. "I think she fought with Gabe and now she's just, like, lost it. Big-time."

"Oh, great." He sighed. "I thought she was done with this stuff."

Allie shot him a puzzled look. "What? She's done this before?"

"She used to do her crazy act whenever anything went wrong, but she hasn't done it in a while." He seemed exasperated. "Now I've got to go make sure she gets back to the school or Gabe'll kill me—will you be okay? I'll come back for you if you want."

"You don't have to come back," she said. "I can keep up with you."

They took off through the gate, and at first she matched him step for step. But as they ran through the first stretch of darkened woods, something occurred to her.

"We left the door open," she said, slowing to a jog.

"What? At the church?" Carter stopped running. At first he looked doubtful, but then he slapped himself on the forehead. "Damn. You're right. We should go back and close it."

But he didn't move. He looked in the direction Jo had run, then back at the church as if he couldn't decide which problem was more important.

Seeing his indecision, Allie knew what she had to do.

"I'll go back," she said. "I'll close it up. You catch up with Jo."

"Are you sure?" he asked doubtfully. "It's getting dark and it's nearly curfew."

But Jo was not being rational and she was out there in the dark on her own. And while Allie wasn't thrilled about being in the woods by herself, she knew it was the right thing.

"We'll get in trouble if it's left open," she reasoned. "And I really don't think it would be great for Jo to be quizzed by Zelazny right now. Besides, what if a fox gets in and eats Jesus?"

He burst out laughing, and for a second all the stress left his face.

"Okay," he said. "But I'll double back for you as soon as she's inside."

"Don't worry about me—I'm not afraid of the dark," she lied. "It's all good."

"Thanks, Sheridan." She could hear the relief in his voice. He took off for the school, his final words floating back on the breeze. "I'll come back."

"Don't!" she shouted after him. He gave no indication that he'd heard.

The moment he was out of sight, though, her bravery abandoned her. *I could just leave it open,* she thought looking down the empty path. *Maybe nobody would know it was us.*

Then she thought about how awful it would be if anything happened to that amazing chapel—what if it rained all night and the Tree of Life was ruined and it was all her fault.

She turned around and headed back through the gloaming to the chapel.

The pool of golden light that had illuminated the churchyard earlier was gone now. Allie walked toward the old chapel door, looming open like a leering maw.

Taking a deep breath, she pushed her weight against it. It didn't move at all. After a moment she realized it was held open by a black metal hook that fixed it in place. Even after she'd freed it from its hobble, though, the door was incredibly heavy. She gave it a good shove, and it was closing with a reluctant creak when, just for a split second, she saw something move between the shadows inside.

Allie froze, staring into the darkness. Then, as the door continued to close, she sprang into action, grabbing it and digging in her heels to try and hold it open. But the old door had a mind of its own now, and nothing she did would stop it. It latched shut with a resounding clang that seemed to echo through the trees.

Allie's heart pounded and she stared at the closed door.

Holy crap, what was that?

A sudden flutter of wings above her head made her jump, but it was only birds flying up into the darkening sky from a nearby tree.

With her hand on the heavy iron ring that served as a door handle, Allie considered her options. Someone was definitely inside—she'd seen them.

Unless it was a trick of the dark.

I should go. Get back to the school, she thought. *I'm just spooked.*

Then she imagined what Carter would have done if he were here. He would have opened that door without hesitating and demanded to know who was in there.

"But he's a moron," she muttered unconvincingly. It didn't really matter, of course. She already knew what she was going to do.

She turned the ring.

Yanking the door open with effort, she leaned inside without actually stepping through the door.

"Hello?" she called. The room was so dark now that she could barely make out the drawings on the wall. "Is anybody there?"

The only sound she heard was her own voice echoing back at her. But the silence that followed had a weight to it as silences always do in ancient buildings, and she felt goose bumps rise on her shoulders. She was just about to step inside when she heard quick footsteps cross the churchyard behind her.

Spinning around, Allie crouched down as if to avoid a blow . . . there was nobody there.

There was no sound but the wind in the trees.

Squinting, she peered into the thicket around the church. Every sound made her jump.

You know what? Screw this.

With all her strength, she shoved the door to. As the latch was still clanging shut, she ran to the churchyard gate, slamming it behind her with a careless bang. Looking neither right nor left, she ran down the path, speeding up as her muscles loosened until she was hurtling through the woods. But as she sped around a curve in the dark, she skidded on a stone and went sprawling, hitting the ground with such force that the breath was knocked out of her and she gasped for air, clutching her sides.

She took a second to try and calm down. As her breathing steadied, she picked gravel out of a scrape on the palm of her hand while building up the courage to look at her knee. Blood oozed from a shallow wound and ran down her leg. She hoped it looked worse than it was.

Air hissing through her teeth, she pulled herself to her feet and experimented to see if her leg could hold her weight. It hurt, but it worked, and she limped down the path, cursing under her breath.

The path seemed endless now. After what felt like hours, she stopped to rest her leg. It hadn't taken nearly this long to get to the chapel, had it? Had she taken a wrong turn?

A rustle in the trees stopped her fretful thoughts. She held her breath and listened.

"Carter?" she asked tentatively.

The noise stopped.

A moment later she heard it again, only now it seemed to be on the other side of the path. Allie spun around to face it, squinting as she tried to see through the trees.

"Hello?" Her voice shook; she tried to steady it. "Who's there?"

Silence.

"If this is some sort of a joke, it's not funny," she shouted into the dark, but now she hurried down the path, limping as quickly as she could.

. . . twenty-five steps, twenty-six, twenty-seven . . .

The sharp crack of a breaking twig behind her made her jump. She froze in her tracks. *That rustling sound again. But closer. Much closer.*

Now, ignoring the pain, she ran down the path, jumping over roots, feeling rocks skitter under her feet but keeping her balance. Her fists pumped the air beside her.

After a minute she turned to look over her shoulder—the path was empty. But when she turned back to the front, someone was standing right in front of her.

She screamed and skidded, but Sylvain's hands caught her and pulled her close.

"Hey . . . hey!" He looked at her with concern. "Are you okay? You're bleeding. What happened?"

Her words came out in broken phrases as she panted. "There was . . . somebody . . . the chapel . . . in woods." Her voice was breathless and frightened.

His hands tightened on her arms. "Did they hurt you?"

They?

Allie shook her head, trying to catch her breath. "No . . . fell. But . . . could . . . hear someone . . . nearby. I think . . . he was watching me. I heard him breathing."

"You're shaking." Sylvain pulled her into a hug. "Come on, let's get out of here." With his arm supporting her, she hobbled toward the school.

They both heard the footsteps at the same time.

"Do you hear that?" Allie whispered.

Sylvain nodded and looked in the direction of the sound, pushing Allie behind him. She peered over his shoulder as Carter stepped out of the woods. His face darkened when he saw Sylvain.

"Sylvain, I didn't know you were here." Carter's voice was cold, and he looked at Allie. "What's wrong? Are you okay?"

Stepping out from behind Sylvain, she nodded, feeling like an idiot. "I fell. And I could hear something moving in the woods."

"Must have been me. I took a shortcut." Turning to Sylvain, he said, "We should get her back. Do you want me to take her?"

Sylvain shook his head. "No, it's fine. I'll take her. You have work to do. Make sure there's nothing out there."

Allie could sense Carter's reluctance, but then Sylvain pulled on her arm and she walked with him.

Her leg was getting stiff and the pain worse; walking was increasingly difficult. She said nothing, but she was limping much more and Sylvain noticed.

"Is it your leg?" he asked, brushing the hair out of her face.

"I'm sorry," she said. "I'm being a baby. It doesn't hurt that much." But her lie was clearly not convincing.

"Don't be ridiculous," he said, and without another word he scooped her up off her feet and carried her down the path.

Allie couldn't believe it.

"Put me down, Sylvain," she protested. "I can walk."

She wriggled in his arms, but he only held her more tightly.

He really is quite strong, she thought.

"It's easier if you don't fight me," he said, a smile curving his lips up softly. "Come on, Allie. You can hardly walk. We need to get back. Just put your arms around my neck."

Reluctantly, she did as he said. Now that she was off her leg, the pain had lessened. Against her will, she found she enjoyed the oddly weightless sensation of being carried for the first time since she was a child. She wanted to rest her head on his shoulder and just give in to it. But she held herself stiffly in his arms.

They had been closer to the building than she knew, so it was only a few minutes before he was climbing the stairs. Someone opened the door for them, and she turned her head to see Zelazny standing in the lighted entry hall.

"What happened?" he barked.

Allie opened her mouth but Sylvain answered for her.

"She fell in the dark."

"Of course it's dark. It's nighttime." Zelazny did not sound sympathetic, and Allie hoped she hadn't broken another of his stupid precious rules. But he just gestured down the hallway. "Take her to the nurse. Somebody else fell earlier—she's in the dining hall with them now. Get in line."

As he walked off, she could hear him mutter, "Falling down. It's just clumsiness if you ask me. . . ."

"I don't need a nurse," Allie protested, but Sylvain ignored her, carrying her straight to the dining hall.

The nurse, who wore white scrubs with the Cimmeria logo, was wrapping the sprained wrist of a girl Allie didn't recognize as Sylvain set Allie down in a chair. ("Night tennis gone wrong," the girl said, sighing, when she left.)

Tutting at Allie's knee, the nurse cleaned the wound with an antiseptic liquid that stung so much Allie tried to get up and leave (Sylvain wouldn't let her), and then applied an ointment and bandages so gently she barely felt them at all.

The whole time, Sylvain stood beside her, one hand resting on her shoulder.

"Don't run any marathons in the next few days, love," the nurse chirped as Allie and Sylvain walked out the door, "and you'll be right as rain."

Allie thought it must be after curfew by now—the halls were quiet as Sylvain helped her up the stairs to the girls' dorm.

"Do you want me to walk you to your door?" he asked when they reached the top. His smile was somehow both innocent and sexy at the same time, and Allie had to laugh.

"I think I can make it from here," she said dryly. "But thanks for rescuing me. Again. This is getting to be a thing with us. Let me rescue you next time. For variety."

Keeping her weight on her good leg, she turned to go, but he grabbed her hand and pulled her back. Before she had time to react, he leaned down and kissed her. It was a long, deep kiss. "You're welcome," he whispered as he let her go.

Surprised, Allie stepped backward too fast, stumbling over her own feet and colliding with the wall behind her. Color flooded her cheeks as she righted herself.

"I . . . so . . . .thanks . . . Well, good night."

As she turned to limp down the hallway, she saw Sylvain try not to smile.

TEN

"So . . . what happened last night?"

It was Saturday morning. Allie sat in the quiet common room on the opposite end of a deep leather sofa from Jo. Each wore the same dark blue knee-length skirts and white, short-sleeved shirts, and each held a white mug of tea in her right hand.

They'd headed here together just after breakfast, where Gabe had not joined them.

Jo's clear blue eyes evaded capture, flitting around the room anxiously before finally coming to rest on Allie. "Gabe can be a bit . . . controlling." On the last word her voice was so low, Allie leaned in to hear it. After a pause, Jo's left hand waved the thought away. "And I hate that. Sometimes."

She paused and Allie waited.

"So." Jo sighed. "Yesterday he was just acting a bit too much like my dad. Do this, don't do that. Don't question me. And if he thinks he can get away with that, he's wrong. And . . . well, now we're not speaking. He was in the common room when Carter and I came in—"

She interrupted herself, shooting Allie a worried look. "By the way, Carter went back and got you, right?"

Allie nodded. "That's a story, too, but let's talk about this first."

Jo sipped her tea. "Gabe was there, and he was just so up himself. It was all the 'I told you not to go out. . . . You should've listened' bollocks that makes me just . . ." She balled up her right fist and shook it. "So I told him what he could do with his advice and went to bed. Haven't seen him since. I hope you weren't too freaked out last night. I really didn't think Carter would leave you alone. That must have been a bit scary—you've never been out there at night alone."

"It was fine. We were worried about you. I . . . wanted him to go."

Jo set her cup down on the table and drew her legs up, wrapping her arms around her knees. "So what happened after I took off? Were you okay? Carter was totally worried about you and really cross with me for making him leave you alone."

"Was he?" Allie was surprised to hear it—he'd seemed so irritated when he'd come back for her. "He did come back. But by then I'd run into Sylvain on the path. And the weirdest thing happened, Jo."

Lowering her voice to a near whisper, Allie said, "Sylvain kind of ordered Carter away. He was like, 'Go get back to work.' What's that about? I could tell Carter didn't want to do it, but he did it anyway."

Jo rolled her eyes. "It's just some Night School crap—Sylvain outranks him, I guess."

Allie slid down the sofa so that her head rested on the back of it and her legs stretched out toward the table, revealing the clean, white bandage. Jo clocked it instantly.

"Oh, babe, what happened to your knee?"

"I fell down on the path last night. Like a total klutz." Allie held up her left hand to show the scrape on the palm. "Scarred for life."

Jo groaned. "Oh, God, it's all my fault. I'm so sorry I had a complete flake-out, Allie. Now Gabe's pissed off and you're wounded. I'm such a mess."

Her contrition seemed genuine, and Allie felt an instant need to make her feel better about things.

"Don't be silly," she said. "It's nothing. It barely hurts." Then she gasped and buried her face in her hands. "Oh, God. I can't believe I haven't told you yet. Sylvain kissed me."

"He did?" Jo sat up straighter. "When? And wherewhyhow?"

With her face still covered, Allie's voice was muffled. "And he carried me down the path when my leg hurt."

"Oh my God—he so fancies you." Jo sighed. "That's the most heroic thing ever. Tell me about the kissing."

Peeking over her fingertips, Allie told her what happened.

"And it wasn't one of those friendly-on-the-cheek things, either," she concluded. "It was a proper kiss. With tongues."

Jo gave her a joking shove. "So? Was it good?"

"Yeah, I suppose." Allie sank down farther into the cushions, her cheeks bright red. "Okay. Yes. It was definitely very good."

"And don't you have some sort of date thing tonight?" Jo nudged her again. "Come to my room after and tell me *everything*."

Then she sat up straighter. "Hey, that reminds me, the Summer Ball is in three weeks. Sylvain will probably ask you to go with him tonight! What will you wear? Tell me now."

She was so irrepressible, Allie had to laugh at her. "God, you're like a child. I don't know anything about this ball thing. What are you going to wear?"

"I bought the dress on my last trip to London." Brightening visibly, Jo described the silver sequined minidress and matching sandals she'd found in a boutique on London's posh Bond Street.

She gave Allie an appraising look. "Have you got a dress?"

Thinking about the dresses in her armoire, Allie nodded hesitantly. "Well . . . kind of. There are a couple of options, and one vintage dress that I love. But I don't know what I'll do for shoe—"

"You'll come to my room!" Jo interrupted her. "I have—God, I don't know—a million pairs of shoes. Problem solved." She grabbed Allie's hand. "We can do the whole girls-getting-ready-together thing. We'll do each other's hair and makeup. We'll be gorgeous."

Allie hesitated, then confessed, "Look, I've never been to a dance before. Not a real one. I mean, my schools just kind of didn't do that sort of thing."

Jo waved her worries away. "You'll love it. It's old-fashioned, but not . . . you know, stuffy. Everybody looks beautiful. Even the teachers. You wouldn't believe how some of them scrub up. It's really cool. When Sylvain asks, you have to say yes."

"But what will I do if he doesn't ask?"

They both sat in silence for a moment, pondering the true horror of potential datelessness.

"I could always go with Zelazny," Allie said finally. "He seems nice."

They both dissolved into laughter.

That night as supper ended, she sat in the dining room with Ruth, Lisa, and Lucas. Jo had left with Gabe earlier, and they'd all exchanged knowing glances as the two walked away. ("Massive make-up make-out session ahead," Lisa predicted.)

"I think we should go outside," Ruth said. "It's hot in here and it's such a warm night. We'll stay close to the building. We could just sit on the grass and talk."

Lucas looked doubtful. He opened his mouth, but the voice from behind Allie came first.

"I agree. It's a good night for croquet, don't you think?" Allie turned around to see Sylvain standing behind her.

After pausing for just a second, Lucas shrugged. "Okay then. Let's go."

As soon as Allie stood up, Sylvain reached for her hand. They walked out side by side. He leaned toward her. "I think you'll like it. Croquet seems boring during the day, but at night it's much better."

His breath tickled her ear and she gave a delicious shiver.

She smiled up at him, then raced forward, pulling his hand. "Come on then. Don't dilly-dally."

Outside, the others were pulling supplies out of a small storage room near the front door. They all helped to put the wicket hoops in the turf. "We need a sixth," Lucas pointed out.

"I'll go get Phil," Ruth said, hurrying back inside.

Allie saw that Lisa was blushing—she was clearly pleased to be Lucas's partner, but he hadn't noticed yet.

Then Sylvain interrupted her reverie.

"While we are waiting for Phil, there is something I need to do." His tone was businesslike, and Lucas only shrugged.

Sylvain turned to Allie. "Would you come help me?"

Frowning slightly at this turn of events, she shrugged.

"Sure."

Taking her by the hand, he pulled her around the side of the building so quickly she had to run to keep up. When they rounded the corner, he stopped.

She looked around, puzzled. "Where are we go—"

Without warning, he pushed her up against the stone wall and kissed her hard. In an instant, surprise turned to desire and she wrapped her arms tightly around his neck, kissing him back. He was, she thought, very good at this—she had never kissed anybody like this in her life, and she didn't want it to end.

When he stopped, they were both panting.

"I'm sorry. I couldn't wait one more minute," he said, his blue eyes holding hers.

"Do it again." Allie said, pulling on his shoulders.

He smiled. "If you insist."

The second kiss was longer, and if possible, more passionate as his lips traveled down her neck and his hands tightened on her hips.

"We should go join the others," he whispered regretfully after a few minutes, his breath warm against her throat. He brushed her swollen lips lightly with his thumb. "They'll be wondering where we are."

"Stupid them," Allie whispered.

He smiled and stepped back from her, although he still held

her hand. "Now we shall enjoy the croquet."

"Yay," she replied weakly. "Croquet."

As they walked back around the corner, she could see that everyone had been waiting for them, including Carter. His eyes told her that he knew exactly what they'd been doing.

"Allie! Sylvain." His tone was mocking. "This is great. What have you been up to?"

Surprised by his aggression, Allie flushed with anger. She thought they'd had a moment out in the woods when they understood each other and maybe could be friends.

But now he seemed worse than ever.

Sylvain pulled her closer. "Unfortunately, Carter, our teams are set already. We do not need another player."

"I didn't come to *play*." Carter put the emphasis on the last word. "I came to see how Allie was doing after her fall last night."

He turned from Sylvain to her.

Allie felt as if a cool breeze had chilled her skin. "I . . . I'm fine, Carter. Thanks."

She faltered under his gaze, which seemed to challenge her. As if she'd done something bad, disappointed him in some way.

"That's great. You do seem *much* recovered." His words dripped sarcasm. "Did you hurt your lips, too? Or is that from something else?"

Allie's hand flew up to cover her mouth as Sylvain took several steps forward.

"Why are you still here, Carter?" he asked icily.

Carter stared at him, unflinching. "I just wanted to see if what I suspected was true."

"Seen all you need to see?" Sylvain's voice was low and menacing.

"Hey, everybody," Ruth stepped between them. "Come on. Stay calm. Let's not get into something here."

Carter ignored her. "Oh, I've seen enough, Sylvain."

With a sigh, Ruth stepped out of the way. They were now standing no more than a foot apart, glaring at each other. Allie wrapped her arms around herself.

They stood glaring for another moment until Carter turned to Allie. His eyes were dark and intense.

"Don't believe anything he tells you. He's a liar."

Allie heard gasps and a murmur of disapproval. Although she was thoroughly confused, she raised her chin defiantly.

"I don't need advice from you, Carter. I make my own decisions."

Anger flared in his eyes, but without another word, he stormed off into the woods.

Looking down, Allie saw that her hands were shaking.

What is wrong with him?

"Well, that was unpleasant." Sylvain swung a mallet with casual brutality; Allie could see the anger in the set of his mouth, but his voice was light. "Let's get on with the game. Allie, shall we be blue?"

Her head still ringing with Carter's warning, she nodded mutely.

When everybody was setting up, she whispered in his ear, "What was Carter talking about?"

He brushed her hair back from her forehead with gentle fingers. "I think he fancies you, *ma jolie*. Perhaps he is jealous."

That didn't seem likely, though, and as he walked off to take his shot, she frowned with thought. Why did Carter hate Sylvain so much?

She couldn't imagine the evening being anything other than miserable now, but to her surprise, it was kind of fun. The hoops were treated with light-absorbing paint, which meant that the darker it became, the more they glowed. The mallets had LED lights activated by clicking a button on the handle. The balls glowed whatever color they were painted. This made the lawn gradually more colorful as darkness fell. In the end, they could hardly see one another, but they could follow each other's movements through the lighted mallets and rolling colored balls.

Ruth was very good and showed Allie techniques to keep the ball moving in a straight line. When Allie managed to knock one of Phil's balls off the playing area, he groaned in mock agony.

"I've taught you too well!" Ruth laughed.

By the time the game was over and they began putting the equipment away, Allie found that she was joking with Ruth and leaning comfortably against Sylvain, who had draped an arm casually across her shoulders. But as the conversation waned, he caught her eye and she felt a tingling sensation of anticipation.

"You have the most beautiful eyes," he whispered. "They are translucent, like your soul." After saying a quick good-bye to the others, he turned back to her. "Walk with me?"

Her throat tightening, she gave an eager nod.

They walked through the dusk to the far side of the school building. When they were alone, he stopped and pulled her into his arms.

He whispered into her ear, "I've had a lovely evening, Allie.

I'm glad Carter didn't upset you too much."

She smiled at him. "I had a good time, too."

And she had, despite everything.

Then he pulled her close and nuzzled her neck before lifting his mouth to hers, and Allie felt all her concerns melt away. He could do the most amazing things with his lips. Her heart pounded and her breath came in short gasps as he kissed her ears, licking her earlobes delicately. Reaching her arms up, she twisted her wrists behind his head.

When Zelazny shouted, "Curfew!" from the back door a few minutes later, Sylvain sighed against her neck.

Allie wasn't ready for him to stop. "Do it again," she insisted.

He smiled, his hands still warm on her waist. "It's curfew. We have to get inside."

"One more time?"

Tantalizingly he leaned toward her. Lifting her face, she parted her lips in anticipation, but he just pecked her quickly on the cheek.

"Inside, young lady, before you get detention."

"Curfew!" Zelazny shouted again. "Last call!"

With Sylvain's arm draped possessively across her shoulders, they walked to the door. As they joined the crowd streaming in, they passed Katie and Jules. When Allie saw the venom in Katie's expression, she smiled at her beatifically.

Allie: one; Katie: nothing.

ELEVEN

When Allie went down to breakfast the next morning, Jo was waiting impatiently outside the dining hall.

"How was it?" she asked without preamble, following Allie in. "Tell me everything."

As she piled scrambled eggs and toast on her plate, Allie laughed at her. "You're so nosy."

"He kissed you again, didn't he?" Jo said. When Allie nodded, she squealed. "He so fancies the pants off of you. Did he ask you to the ball?"

"Nope," Allie said. "So maybe he just likes kissing me."

"He *will* ask you," Jo said confidently as they walked to their usual table.

"Carter was totally weird last night, though." Allie told her what had happened, and Jo frowned.

"That's not like him," Jo said. "Do you think he's jealous?"

"No way." Allie was firm. "He hates me. The way he acted last night . . . it was like I repulsed him. And I don't know what was going on between the two of them, but it was seriously intense. I thought for a second they'd get into a fight."

"Carter wouldn't dare," Jo said. "He'd be in unbelievable amounts of trouble if he did. Anyway, who cares? Sylvain is so into you! And he's so going to ask you to the dance."

Throughout the week the ball was the only subject of conversation—who was going with whom, what they would wear, how everyone was allowed champagne and there was no curfew at all.

Sylvain was involved in a major project, so she rarely saw him. But the way he looked at her each time they saw each other made it clear that Saturday night was not an aberration. He couldn't keep his hands off her. When they passed in the hallway, he would pull her into a hug or run his fingers down her arm. Every time the encounter left her slightly breathless, and hungry for more.

But he still hadn't asked her to the dance.

At the same time, Carter completely ignored her. Whenever she saw him, he looked over her head. In class, their eyes never met. He treated her like she didn't exist.

After the last class on Friday afternoon, Allie headed straight to the library in hopes of finding an obscure book of poetry for Isabelle's English assignment.

When she pushed the door open, it slammed into someone on the other side.

"Sorry," she said automatically, then stopped. Carter glowered at her in the doorway.

When he started to walk by her without saying another word, she'd had enough.

"Hey!" she whispered, grabbing his arm. "What's wrong with you?"

With clear reluctance he stopped. "Nothing."

"Oh, really?" she said. "Then why are you so broken?" Shoving her way past him, she stormed into the library. She heard the door close behind her but didn't look back.

Then, grabbing her arm, he turned her to face him.

"You do not get to call me broken," he hissed in a stage whisper.

She could see how angry he was, but she couldn't have cared less. "I can call you whatever I want, Carter," she whispered, shaking his hand off. "And the way you've been acting lately is not normal. It's totally lame."

"Define normal for me, Allie," he whispered angrily. "Is Sylvain normal, for example?"

A chill ran down her spine. "What kind of question is that? What's he got to do with the way you treat me?"

"Nothing." But his eyes said different. His dark brows were lowered, and she could sense the tension coiled within him before he spoke again. "*Everything*. How can you be so stupid? I thought you were clever, but you're just another stupid girl. You don't know the first thing about him, or about this school, and yet you'll make a public spectacle of yourself with him."

Her eyes widened. "I'm not—"

"Not what?" he interrupted her. "Not falling for Sylvain's well-practiced lines? Really? Because to me it looks like you're falling for it."

He was so angry, she felt panic rise as she tried to reason with him.

"Carter, I don't understand—so I'm seeing Sylvain now. So what? Why do you care? You hate me anyway."

He stood so close to her that she could feel his breath on her cheek. He smelled of sandalwood and cinnamon. "You think I hate you?" Those deep, dark eyes held hers. "I don't. I just thought you were different."

When she opened her mouth to argue, he put his finger lightly over her lips. Her eyes stared into his for a long second. She could taste the salt of his skin on her tongue.

Then he swore under his breath and walked away.

"The question of the day, Allie, is should you wear your hair up or down?" Holding a wide-tooth comb, Jo studied Allie's head intently. It was Saturday morning and they were in Jo's room. Allie sat in front of a mirror. They were surrounded by the gowns from Allie's wardrobe and shoes from Jo's limitless supply. Jo had insisted that they needed to "practice."

Allie twisted a strand of hair around her finger and then released it. "Does it matter? The dance is in two weeks and Sylvain still hasn't asked me to go with him. I might as well dye my hair green and shave it into a mohawk."

Jo held one pair of shoes up to a dress, considered it, and then tried another pair. "Sylvain is going to ask you to go with him," she said. "I have it on the best authority."

Allie looked at her hopefully. "Really?"

"Really." Jo pointed a kitten heel at her accusingly. "So get serious. Hair up or down?"

"Um . . . I don't know." She picked up a brush and ran it through her hair. "So . . . who's Lucas going with?"

"Lisa, of course." Jo's voice was muffled as she pulled out another pair of delicate shoes.

"And Carter?"

"I hear he's asked Clare." Jo set down the shoes. "I think up would be best."

"Who's Clare?"

"Small, blond, pretty. In our biology class. Third row over. He hooked up with her last year, then kind of dumped her. Everyone was furious with him because she's so sweet. Seems like they're getting back together."

Allie studied herself in the mirror. *Why should I care who Carter goes with?*

She pulled her hair up with her hands. "What a complete bastard. Yes, I think you're right. Up could work."

Jo smiled. "Excellent. Once we choose a dress, I'll know what to do with it." She spread the three dresses out on the bed and studied them.

"These are fabulous! Where'd you get them?"

"They just appeared in my armoire." Allie shrugged. "I don't know where they came from. But I didn't have one of my own, so . . ."

"Isabelle, I'd imagine." Picking up a black gown, Jo checked the label. "Vintage. Nice. I wonder how she knew you didn't have one."

"No idea."

"She knows everything. She's like God." Jo held the dress out to Allie. "Right. Strip and try this on. Today we decide what you'll wear to the ball, Cinderella."

The black dress was long and fitted. It brushed Allie's ankles, had a high neck in the front, and was backless. It was incredibly sophisticated.

"Lovely," Jo said, studying the line of the dress. "Bit too old for you."

"Totally. I look, like, thirty." Allie pulled it over her head, dumping it back on the bed. The next dress was white, with a long straight skirt and spaghetti straps.

"Gorgeous!" Jo pronounced. "Summery. Virginal."

Allie wrinkled her nose, then twirled in front of Jo's mirror. "It's a bit clingy," she said doubtfully. The dress hugged every curve, leaving little to the imagination.

"But you pull it off," Jo said. "It looks amazing with your coloring, and I have the perfect shoes for it."

The last dress was Allie's favorite. Dark blue silk and knee-length, it had a full skirt with a built-in organza petticoat. Its low, beaded V-neck plunged just far enough in the front, and the back was high. The sleeves were tight and ended just below her elbow. It fit like a glove.

When Allie pulled up the side zipper and turned around, Jo gasped dramatically, her hand to her heart. "You look *amazing*. That is a dress you should wear every single day of your life. Except at the Summer Ball."

Allie gawped at her. "Why not?"

Jo was "It's a winter dress. Everybody else will be in light summer frocks and you'll be sweating in heavy silk. Save it for the Winter Ball. It's much more important than the Summer Ball anyway. Hide this dress away until then, though."

Jo seemed so certain, Allie couldn't see the point in arguing with her. She knew little enough about clothes, having always been a blue-jeans-and-boots kind of girl. On the rare occasions when she'd dressed up for weddings, her mother had chosen her outfits. But she had to admit the white dress suited her, too.

Jo held up a pair of silver sandals with low heels. "What do you think? Are they perfect or are they perfect?" she asked, beaming proudly.

Holding her hands up in surrender, Allie laughed. "I guess they're perfect."

"Now, for your hair . . ."

Jo led her back to the chair and sat her down. She ran a comb through her thick waves and pulled it up into a loose ponytail. Without the henna she'd used at home to color it bright shades of red, Allie's hair was gradually fading to its natural dark brown.

Jo worked in silence for a while, but Allie could see she was thinking. After a moment she said, "So, why do you care about who Carter takes to the ball?"

Allie squirmed uncomfortably. "I don't really care. . . . I just wondered. How do you know for certain that Sylvain's going to ask me?"

Jo twisted a strand of hair into a glossy loop and pinned it into place. "A little bird told me. A very knowledgeable bird."

"I wish he'd get on with it," Allie muttered, watching her hair take stylish shape. "Everybody else already has a date."

"There." Jo stepped back and smiled at her in the mirror, obviously pleased. "Sylvain will be lucky to have you."

Allie's usually unruly hair looked sleek and shiny, loosely twisted with white silk ribbon into a chignon. A few loose strands framed her oval face, drawing attention to her gray eyes.

"That's amazing," Allie breathed, looking at herself in astonishment.

"That's how you'll wear your hair," Jo said, adding modestly, "if you like it."

Allie hugged her. "I love it. Where did you learn to do all this stuff?"

"Girl school," Jo said blithely as she gathered up shoes from the floor. "Which I think you're now enrolled in, too."

Allie was quiet for so long that Jo, who was busy putting shoes away, stopped and looked at her worriedly. "Are you okay? I didn't mean anything by that."

Allie smiled at her. "I'm fine, don't worry. It's just that I had the weirdest thought."

"What's that?" Jo had returned to organizing her shoes.

"Even with everything that's going—even with Carter being an ass, and Sylvain not asking me, and classes being super hard—with all that, I think I'm sort of . . . happy."

"That's because you're crazy." Jo laughed.

"No, I mean it. I'm really happy. For the first time in a long time. You know, I thought I'd hate this place. I was ready to hate it. And the old me would have hated thinking about dresses and dances and shoes and having my hair done and worrying about how I look. But I don't hate it. I . . . kind of like it."

Kneeling by the wardrobe arranging shoes, Jo looked up at her. "And that's a good thing, right?"

"Yeah," Allie said thoughtfully. "I guess it is."

An hour or so later, Allie carried the dresses back to her room, and tucked them away in the wardrobe. She fixed her hair back into a ponytail, carefully laying the ribbons in the top drawer of her desk. Glancing at the clock, she dashed out—only twenty minutes left before they closed the dining room after lunch.

"Hey, Allie." At the sound of the voice behind her, she turned to see Jules walking in the same direction.

Great. Just what I need right now. Will this be another prefect talk about how I'm doing, or has Katie sent her to warn me off Sylvain . . . ?

"Oh. Hi, Jules."

As ever, Jules's blunt-cut blond hair was perfectly smooth, and she wore her cute pink Birkenstocks. Allie thought again how unfair it was that she got to wear her own shoes.

"I was just wondering," Jules said, "are you going to the ball? You really should. I know you're new, but it's an experience you really won't want to miss. You don't have to have a date."

Allie bristled a bit at the last line. "Yes, I'm planning on going," she said.

"Oh, great! You know, you might never be here for summer school again, so it would be such a shame not to see the Summer Ball."

Allie frowned. "Why would I never be here for summer school again?"

Jules looked puzzled. "Oh, I didn't mean anything by it. It's just that, you know, it's usually only for the top students. I understand that you're here for . . . other reasons."

Allie felt as if she'd been punched. "What do you mean? What reasons?"

"Oh, didn't you know?" Jules looked increasingly uncomfortable. "Isabelle made special arrangements for this one term. After that, I assume you'll join the other . . . you know, regular students."

Allie straightened her shoulders and took a step forward.

"What are you trying to say, Jules? That I don't belong here?"

"Oh, of course not!" Jules took a hurried step back. "I hope I haven't off—"

"Offended me? Yes, Jules, you've offended me." She turned and ran down the hallway, her fists clenched so tightly, her nails dug crescent moons into her palms.

At the foot of the stairs she turned and skidded around the corner, nearly colliding with Sylvain, who caught her easily.

"Don't you ever just walk anywhere?" He laughed, holding her up.

"Only when appropriate," she said, her voice more brusque than she meant it to be. She took a deep breath and tried to calm down.

"Hey. What's the matter?" He studied her face with concerned eyes. "Is everything okay?"

She shrugged. "I just ran into Jules. Never mind, it's not worth going into. She's just a pain in the—"

He looked amused. "Oh, she can be rather difficult. But I wouldn't take her too seriously. She means well."

He had this way of smiling with his eyes that she simply couldn't resist, and after a second she smiled back. "You're right. I shouldn't let her get to me."

"I've been hoping to run into you, to be honest." He leaned against the wall and, taking her hand, pulled her closer to him so that their conversation felt more intimate.

He's so cool. How does he do that?

"I wanted to ask if you have a date for the ball yet."

Allie felt her cheeks go red as her heart began to pound. She forced her breathing to stay steady. *I must look as calm as possible.*

She shook her head. "No, not yet."

His eyes still held hers. "I was hoping you'd agree to go with me."

Oh my God. What took you so long? Yes!

"That would be great," she said calmly.

"Fantastic. I cannot wait." He gave her a sleepy, sexy smile and looked genuinely pleased.

They stood for a moment as if loath to leave each other; then he lifted her hand, kissed it lightly, and let it go. "You'd better go have lunch before they close up."

She nodded. "See you later."

"*À bientôt.*"

Allie floated into the dining room on a cloud of happiness and almost didn't see Jo waving at her from their usual table. She was eating a green salad as Allie walked up.

"Nothing but salad for me until the ball or I won't fit into my dress—what happened?" Jo moved so quickly from the statement to the question and Allie was so drunk on romance that for a second she just stared at her.

"You look like something happened. Tell me—what happened?" Jo demanded.

Allie smiled dreamily. "Sylvain asked me."

Leaping from her seat, Jo squealed and danced around the table, pulling Allie into a hug. "I knew it! Didn't I say? I'm, like, omniscient."

"You're a genius." Allie laughed. "And I guess I better have salad, too, if I'm going to wear that white dress."

Back in her own seat, Jo passed her the salad bowl. "This is going to be the best Summer Ball ever."

But as Allie served leaves onto her plate, she looked up to see Carter staring at her from a nearby table. When he realized she'd seen him, he stood up and stalked from the room.

TWELVE

The two weeks until the dance seemed to last months, and Allie felt as if the entire school was in a state of suspended animation. Classes dragged. Teachers refused to give in to student apathy and distraction, so coursework piled up, but, for the first time, the library was largely empty in the evening.

"If I get behind this week . . . so be it," Jo pronounced, the drama of her statement somewhat undermined by the fact that she was sitting on her bed and waving a tiara. "I'll catch up next week."

"Hear hear!" Allie was lying on her stomach on the floor, flipping through a beauty magazine and contemplating hairstyles. "Maybe I should get my hair cut short?" She held up a picture of a pixieish model.

Jo tilted the tiara in her direction. "A new haircut lifts your spirits, young Allie. Never forget that. But that's too short for your face shape, FYI."

Allie turned the page. "Wise words, Josephine. Wise words."

Back in her room, the white dress hung tantalizingly from Allie's wardrobe door, with Jo's shoes arranged neatly on the floor beneath it. Every morning when she woke up, that was the first thing she saw, and each night she ticked another day off a mental calendar.

While Allie was trying to keep up with her classwork, she was finding it nearly impossible to concentrate. So a few days before the ball, when she found herself reading the same paragraph in her history book for the fifth time, she gave up on the entire enterprise. Standing up from her desk, she stretched, then stood looking out the window at the sunshine.

I've got to move.

She pulled on her running clothes and gathered her hair into a short ponytail. As she slipped down the stairs she passed only one other student, and on the landing, when she leaned over to look down at the main floor, she could see nobody at all. Outside, the sun beat down on the soft green grass. From the front steps she could see a number of bodies basking on towels and blankets spread out on the lawn, but she never could understand the attraction of just lying in the sun. Instead, she struck out at a brisk pace. Movement had always helped to calm her down, and now she threw herself into it, running faster down the footpath. She counted each footstep quietly.

"Two hundred and ninety-six. Two hundred and ninety—"

"Why do you do that?"

The voice seemed to come from nowhere, and it startled Allie so much that she tripped and had to grab a tree branch for support.

Carter stood on the edge of the path, his hands on his hips. Panting, she bent over to rest her hands on her knees while she caught her breath.

When she stood up, she tossed her ponytail over her shoulder. "What? You're speaking to me now, Carter? I'm honored."

He acted as if she hadn't spoken. "That counting thing. I've heard you do it before. Why do you do that?"

"It's none of your business, you stalker. Now get lost."

Turning back down the path, she took off running again, but he easily matched her stride.

"It was a simple question."

Allie gave a frustrated squeak and sped up, anger propelling her. But he didn't fall behind, and finally she shouted at him in short bursts.

"You don't. Ignore somebody. For weeks. And then. Ask them. Personal questions. You. Asshole."

"Temper."

"Whatever."

Silence fell as she concentrated on not speaking to him.

"Allie, don't trust Sylvain."

"I'm ignoring you."

"I can't go into why. But he's not who you think he is."

Slowing down, she shot him a glare. "What's that supposed to mean?"

He started to speak, then stopped. Shaking her head in disgust, she ran away down the path—after a while she couldn't hear his footsteps behind her anymore.

Ahead of her, the summerhouse roof appeared above the trees, and even through her rage, Allie gasped. She hadn't been able to really see it properly that night in the rain. It was beautiful—a fanciful construction, with a narrow, pointed roof rising twenty-five feet high, covered in brightly colored Moorish tiles in an intricate design. Six delicately carved pillars supported the vivid roof.

Although she'd meant to go on a long run, Allie had to stop and check it out.

She climbed up the steps into the shady, open-air interior, where a stone banister and benches circled the edges. Sitting down on a cool seat, she rested her chin on her arm as she looked out into the woods. Carter was nowhere to be seen.

What was he going on about? Was it just jealousy? Or was he serious?

He sounded serious.

She tried to think of anything Sylvain had done to make her doubt him. He'd always been there for her when she was in trouble. He'd protected her from Zelazny. Yes, he was slick, and yes, apparently he was super rich, but he didn't act like a snob. He seemed kind. Carter, on the other hand, had been difficult, pushy, judgmental, and threatening.

It was obvious who she should trust.

Lost in thought, she nibbled the edge of her thumbnail. *I just don't understand why Carter cares so much.*

That night at dinner, when Allie arrived at the table, Jo, Lisa, and Ruth were talking animatedly in low voices.

"You have to do it, Lisa," Jo said. "It's tradition."

"I'm going to do it, and you know I hate this sort of thing," Ruth said.

Clearly reluctant, Lisa stirred food around her plate, her long, straight hair swinging forward around her face. "I don't know. It's just a bit weird."

"What's weird?" Allie asked pulling up a chair. "What's for dinner tonight? I hope it's lasagna."

"The Summer Splash!" Jo's eyes were bright with enthusiasm. "It's always the night before the Summer Ball, and Lisa doesn't want to do it. But she has to. And I thought you were only eating salad."

"Oh, balls," Allie said. "I'd forgotten about the salad thing. And what the hell's a Summer Splash?" She poured herself a glass of water from the pitcher on the table.

"Oh my God—I completely forgot to tell you about it." Jo let go of Lisa's arm and turned to Allie. "It's a tradition. Juniors and seniors sneak out at midnight the night before the ball and go swimming in the pond."

Puzzled, Allie looked at Lisa. "What's wrong with that? Can't you swim?"

Raising her chin, Lisa shot an accusing look at Jo. "Not just swimming. Tell her the whole truth."

Jo rolled her eyes. "Okay, fine. Skinny-dipping. Must you be such a prude, Lisa? It's going to be awesome!"

Allie choked on her water. "What? All of us? Guys and girls? Naked?"

Ruth pounded her on the back.

"It'll be dark, Allie." Jo was beginning to sound exasperated. "And it's no big deal. You just dive in and then jump out and put your clothes back on. It's not a porn movie. It's good, clean, wholesome fun and it's a tradition and you have to do it because I don't want to do it alone."

Allie leaned toward her. "Let me make sure I'm getting this—you, me, Ruth, Lisa, and our dates for Friday night and a bunch of strangers are going to get naked in a pond. Together. For fun."

She imagined being nude in a pond with Sylvain and felt both horrified and excited. She wondered if he was going, but something told her this wasn't his sort of thing. He was far too sophisticated.

"Exactly!" Jo said brightly. "And we're all going to be there, right?"

Lisa looked nauseous.

"Surely Allie's not invited." Katie stood by their table, as beautiful as ever. "She's too new. This is for real Cimmeria students."

"Oh, fuck off, Katie. Seriously." Jo glared at her.

Katie stood her ground. "I mean it, Jo. I really don't think it's fair. I'm going to speak with Jules about it."

"So what if you speak with Jules about it, you moron?" Jo said. "It's unofficial. What's she going to do? Tell us not to go? We're not supposed to do it in the first place."

"Jo," Allie said, her jaw set, "when did you say this splash thing happens?"

"Midnight Thursday," Jo said with a wicked glint.

"Great. I'll be there."

Katie shot her an icy look and walked away.

Jo snickered. "Forget her. I'm glad you're going to do it. I've been looking forward to this since I got to Cimmeria. If Lisa and Ruth come, too, we can just all do it together, and it will be even better."

Looking miserable, Lisa stared at her empty plate. Allie

smiled at Jo, but her heart sank. Already she regretted her rashness. Still. How bad could it be?

"But how do we get out of the school without getting caught?" she asked. "I mean, do the teachers just let you go dive naked into a lake in the dark?"

Jo's face told her the answer before she said a word. "They do whatever they can to stop us. I mean, imagine the wrath of furious parents if one of us got hurt." She smiled cheerfully. "Getting out is half the fun."

As the kitchen doors opened and the staff walked in carrying platters of lasagna, Allie groaned. "I'm not sure which is worse, being forced to skip lasagna or swimming naked with Katie Gilmore."

"Gabe and I have a plan for getting out," Jo said. "Let's talk about it after dinner. Come to my room at eight and we'll plot." She began filling her plate with salad. "I love plotting."

At ten past eight that night, Allie walked into Jo's room. Jo, Lisa, Ruth, Gabe, and Lucas were sitting in a circle. Allie took a spot on the floor between Ruth and Lucas and, pulling her feet up so that they were underneath her, wrapped her arms around her knees. Gabe was pointing at a point on a map of the school grounds.

"... so, given all of that, I think the only safe way out is through the classroom wing."

Lucas looked skeptical. "Wait. All we know is that the other doors will be watched. Why wouldn't they guard that one, too?"

"Two reasons," Gabe said. "First because The Rules say we can't go in that wing outside of class hours under any circumstances—so the amount of trouble we'd get in if we were caught is pretty serious. Second, because it's marked as an alarmed fire door."

"What will we do about the alarm?" Allie asked.

Gabe's reply was simple. "There is no alarm."

There was an uproar, and Gabe, who seemed to enjoy their astonishment, held out his hands for silence. "There are no alarms anywhere in this building at all. Any sign that says 'alarm' is a lie."

Stunned, Allie looked around the room. Everyone looked shocked. Even Ruth and Lucas seemed taken aback.

Lisa's quiet voice broke the silence. "Why?"

"I don't know," Gabe said. Watching him closely, Allie got the feeling he was lying. He knew precisely why. He just didn't want to say.

No fire alarms. No burglar alarms. Nothing to warn anybody about anything.

"So"—Jo brushed aside the alarm conversation—"how do we get into the classroom wing without attracting attention?"

"I know that one," Lucas said. "Here's what we do. . . ."

THIRTEEN

"Ouch!" Hopping up and down in the dark, Jo grabbed her toe.

"Shhh." Allie held a finger to her lips and they both froze.

It was eleven thirty Thursday night, and they were standing on the stair landing in the dark, the polished wood floor cold against their bare feet. They'd worked on the plan until late Wednesday night and talked about it half the day today.

Now they listened for any sounds, any sign that they'd been noticed, but the old building was silent. After a moment they began feeling their way down the stairs again, each holding her shoes in one hand and clinging to the banister with the other. Lucas had reminded them that the third from last step creaked, so they carefully stepped over it. When they reached the bottom, Allie looked toward Isabelle's office—no light shone under the door.

Her eyes were adjusting to the dark—she could see a little better now.

As they stealthily tiptoed down the wide hallway to the classroom wing door, Allie stopped.

"Did you hear that?" she breathed, her lips barely moving.

Jo shook her head, but at that moment they both heard the sound. Footsteps. Nearby.

Allie spun around, looking for a place to hide. Thinking fast, she ran behind a stone column, pulling Jo with her. A few seconds later, a lithe shadow flitted down the hallway. Allie pressed back against the wall, but Jo leaned forward, squinting into the darkness. Before Allie could stop her, she dashed after the shadow.

"Jo!" Allie whispered, but there was no reply. Cursing under her breath, she hurried after her.

At first she could see nothing, but then she bumped into Jo, who was standing just down the hall with Lisa.

"Found her!" Jo whispered, clearly delighted.

Lisa looked less thrilled, and Allie wondered why she'd come. She'd been so reluctant in every conversation about it. Now she seemed unable to stand still, hopping nervously from one foot to the other like an anxious dancer before a show, her eyes enormous in her delicate face. Allie gave her a sympathetic look and then pointed at the door to the classroom wing.

Jo nodded.

"What about Ruth?" Allie whispered.

"She's late—we can't wait."

Allie turned the handle. If the door creaked, they were dead.

It swung open silently on hinges Gabe had oiled that afternoon.

They slipped through and then ran as fast as they could down the long corridor. The door at the end was marked with ominous, official-looking signs that warned of alarms and security; there were numbers to call in case of emergencies. Allie wondered: if she dialed them, who would answer?

Standing still for one brief moment, they exchanged a look in the shadows. Then one at a time they each put a hand on the door and, at Jo's nod, they pushed it.

It opened without a sound.

Rushing through, they tumbled onto a path covered in gravel that dug into their bare feet. They hopped around comically pulling on their shoes and trying not to cry out from the pain. Thinking how ridiculous they must look to anyone watching, Allie stifled a giggle.

"Go, go, go!" Jo whispered, and they ran recklessly into the night, reaching out for each other until all three held hands.

By the time they reached the tree line, Jo and Lisa were winded, and they stopped for a moment to catch their breath. But Allie was nervous.

We're still too close to the school.

"Which way from here?" she hissed, trying to keep them all motivated enough to continue. Jo nodded toward the right, and Allie motioned for them to move. They moved on at a slower pace.

At first the woods were almost silent, but gradually Allie began to notice rustling noises and the sound of snapping twigs. The hairs on the back of her neck stood on end.

Reaching out for Jo, she squeezed her hand and nodded in the direction of the sounds. She could see Jo's white teeth in the darkness as she smiled.

"The others," she whispered.

As they put distance between themselves and the school, people were less careful, and soon they could hear other sounds: muffled giggles, occasional whispered oaths as somebody tripped, fake birdcalls followed by more smothered laughter. Allie felt the tension between her shoulder blades begin to ease.

Jo stopped so suddenly, Allie and Lisa nearly tripped over her.

"We're here," she whispered, and disappeared behind a shrub. Peering into the darkness, Allie couldn't see a pond—just trees and brush. But she and Lisa followed Jo into a hiding spot.

"Why are we hiding?" Lisa whispered.

"Nobody can know who's here until midnight," Jo said. "It's tradition."

"How do you know all this?" Allie asked.

"My brother told me about it," Jo explained.

Jo's watch had a glow-in-the-dark dial, and the three stood looking at it as the minute hand moved inexorably to midnight.

"Where's Ruth?" Allie asked.

Jo held out her empty hands. "She was supposed to meet us either in the school or along the way, so I presume she's here already somewhere." She checked the watch. "It's nearly time," she whispered, grinning widely. "Get ready."

Allie could feel Lisa trembling. She longed to comfort her, but she was too scared herself. She took a deep breath and looked out toward where she presumed the pond must be.

Am I really going to do this? I mean, who skinny-dips, anyway? Isn't that something that only happens in films?

At that moment a deep male voice rang out in the silence, making her jump. "It's time, kids. Drop trou."

As Allie and Lisa hesitated, Jo started undoing her shorts, but when she saw that they hadn't moved she paused and gave them a warning look.

"You may as well," she said. "At this point, it would be worse going back without doing it."

Lisa and Allie exchanged a look of dread. "I will if you

will," Lisa said finally.

Allie could now hear people splashing into water and screaming with laughter. She sighed heavily.

"Oh, what the hell." As she pulled down her exercise pants, Jo cheered and ripped off her shorts. In seconds they were all naked. Lisa and Allie crossed their arms protectively across their breasts, but Jo grabbed their hands.

"If you're going to do it, do it proudly," she said, pulling them out onto the path.

In the dark, Allie saw only flashes of skin as people jumped into and out of a pond she couldn't quite make out in the gloom.

"On three," Jo said, giggling. "One. Two . . ."

They leaped into the dark water, hitting with an icy splash. Allie, who could only barely see the pond in the black night, heard the loud shrieks of laughter around her muffled into silence as she sank below the surface. Jo's hand slipped away almost immediately.

She was surprised by how deep it was—she'd never been a strong swimmer. As she splashed toward the surface, a sudden flash memory came to her: A hot sunny day. She was seven, and Christopher was teasing her for sinking like a stone in the pool. "You run like a rabbit, but you also swim like a rabbit. . . ." He'd laughed while she paddled wildly.

When she came up for air now, sputtering and shivering, she couldn't see Jo or Lisa anywhere.

"Jo?"

How had she lost them in seconds? But the pond was crowded with laughing students—none of whom looked familiar. As she thrashed in the cold water looking for a familiar face, Allie grew increasingly panicked. Hot tears of fear and shame burned her eyes. Suddenly she realized she was struggling to breathe. She hadn't had a panic attack in weeks, but now she wheezed three labored breaths in a row as she fought to stay afloat.

I can't . . . breathe. . . .

She tried to make her way to the edge, where the water would be more shallow, but it was hard to swim when she couldn't breathe. She hadn't imagined the pond would be so deep—she couldn't touch the bottom.

She went under for just a second and kicked hard to find the surface again. Under the water, somebody's foot hit her shin and pain shot through her leg. She didn't cry out—she didn't have enough air left.

Thrashing in the water, she wheezed a paltry breath in before slipping under again. Her heart pounded as she fought to make her way out of the middle of the pond. Around her she heard screams of laughter and slippery bodies slithered by her, but nobody seemed to notice her in the dark. Nobody seemed to see her. Her limbs felt heavy—she was so tired.

Again the cold water closed over her head, but this time water entered her lungs and she splashed violently on the way up, trying to summon the air to cough.

Her lungs ached and she felt so weak. *This is how people die,* she thought with horrible sudden clarity. *This is what it feels like.*

But at that moment, two strong hands grabbed her shoulders and pulled her to the surface. Gratitude rushed through her, but then she saw who was helping her and she struggled to free herself while trying to cover her breasts with her hands.

"You're okay, Allie. Look at me." Carter's voice was calm and commanding, and his eyes were locked on hers. "Breathe slowly through your nose. Don't look away. Keep your eyes on me. Just breathe slowly."

She tried to explain to him that she was dying, but no words would come out.

"Breathe in," he said, demonstrating, his eyes willing her to try. "And now out." He blew air out forcefully.

When she tried to do what he asked, she wheezed ineffectually, and as the lack of oxygen became worse, she felt fear seeping away.

If I can just rest for a second . . .

Her eyes fluttered shut, and darkness seemed to blanket her.

Carter slapped her face, and it startled her so much that her eyes shot open and she took a sharp reflexive breath.

Oxygen burst painfully into her lungs.

"You can do this, Allie. Breathe with me."

His hands were so tight against her arms it hurt, and she could sense he was trying to keep his voice steady. She got the feeling he was frightened.

He took a deep breath, and she tried to do the same. A little air entered her lungs.

"Good!" he said. "Again."

A deeper breath, and she could feel the tightness in her chest begin to loosen. He urged her on, but she was trembling violently now, and on the fourth successful breath she burst into tears.

He wrapped his arms around her, his skin cold against hers.

"You're okay, Allie. Just keep breathing."

Shielding her body with his, he led her out of the water to shore. She could hear people laughing and splashing around them, but she didn't know or care if they were laughing at her.

His voice was gentle. "Where are your clothes, Allie?"

"I don't know," she whispered hoarsely.

He half smiled. "Why am I not surprised to hear that?" He helped her off the path into relative privacy behind a large tree. "Stay here. I'll find something for you to wear."

Only when he walked into the shadows did she realize that he was naked, too. As she watched the muscles move in his hips and back, she forced herself to keep breathing.

He's beautiful, she thought. Her heart fluttered in her chest.

When he reappeared a few minutes later, he'd put on a pair of shorts. In his hands he carried a guy's shirt and a pair of girl's shorts.

"This is the best I can do," he said apologetically.

Since he was shirtless, she had a feeling the guy's shirt he'd brought was his own.

She turned away as she pulled on the shorts, then turned back toward him and held out her hand for the shirt. He handed it to her wordlessly. She couldn't see his face in the darkness, but as she shrugged on the oversize shirt, she felt her heart pound in her chest so loudly that she thought he must surely be able to hear it.

"Ready?" he asked, expressionless.

"Yes."

Reaching for her hand, he helped her out of her hiding place and onto the path. The warmth of his hand was comforting—his fingers were strong, and she clung to them.

"I couldn't find any shoes for you," he said apologetically. "This might be hard on your feet—do you want to wear mine?"

Though the sharp pebbles cut into her feet, she shook her head. "I'm okay," she said.

As they walked away from the lake, the noise and laughter

faded behind them. After a few minutes the only sound they could hear was their own breathing.

When she was certain they were alone, Allie stopped and looked up at him. "Carter . . . thank you."

Dropping her hand, he looked down at the ground. "It was nothing."

"No, Carter." She grabbed his hand back. When he looked at her, his eyes were so vulnerable she couldn't tear hers away. "It was *something*."

They stared at each other for a long moment, but just as he started to speak . . .

"Allie! Carter!" Jo's voice broke the spell as she raced up the path toward them with Gabe and Lisa right behind her.

Grabbing Allie by the shoulders, Jo gave her a worried shake. "Where have you been? Are you okay? I looked for you *everywhere*."

Even as she nodded, Allie felt the unwanted tears begin again.

"I couldn't find you. Carter helped me"—she turned to look at him, but he was gone—"out," she whispered.

Breakfast the next morning was a muted affair—the students who'd spent much of the night in the woods were easily identifiable by their bed-hair and the circles under their eyes. Jo and Allie sat in near silence with Lisa yawning beside them. None of them was hungry. Allie clutched a steaming cup of tea as if it were the only thing keeping her alive, while Jo shredded a piece of toast into minute particles.

Allie had spent the night on the floor in Jo's room after they'd crept back into the school unnoticed through the same door through which they'd departed an hour earlier.

They'd talked until four in the morning, after which she told Jo she felt better, but she didn't really.

I mean, how do you get over having a naked panic attack in front of half the school?

At least she now knew what had happened after they'd jumped into the pond. During the night, Jo told her the whole story. How Gabe and Lucas had been in the water and had spotted the girls as they ran to the water. How Gabe had grabbed Jo as soon as she'd hit the surface and pulled her over to where they were swimming near a tree. How she'd managed to hold on to Lisa and pull her along even while Lisa tried to hide from Lucas. And how in all the commotion she'd lost Allie.

"The pond filled up with people so fast and it was so dark, when I went back to where we started, or where I thought we started, I couldn't find you anywhere," Jo said. It was Jules and Ruth who eventually told her that they'd seen Allie with Carter, and that Allie looked ill. "Ruth had gone with Jules in the end, because Jules didn't want to go on her own. And Jules thought we'd been drinking and that that's why you were ill, and she gave me a bollocking, which is why it took me ages to find you."

"I never saw Sylvain there, but then I didn't see anyone, really," Allie said.

"I don't think he was there," Jo said. "But just about everybody else was."

Allie, who had prepared a bed of coats and sweaters on the floor, buried her face in Jo's spare pillow. "I wonder how many people saw me freak out."

Up on the bed, Jo stretched out flat and yawned. "Not many, that's for sure. It seemed like nobody saw you all night except Jules."

"But she'll tell everyone."

"She won't. She's a prefect. She has, like, a duty to support you, or something," Jo said. "Anyway, what exactly happened?"

Allie explained about the panic attack and how Carter had rescued her. She didn't talk about the way she'd felt when he pulled her from the water and helped her breathe. Or about watching him walk away in the moonlight. Instead she focused on how calm he was, and how coolheaded he'd been amid crisis.

Jo thought for a moment, and when she spoke her answer was carefully phrased. "People here have a weird thing with Carter because he acts like he's better than everyone, and because he has really upset a lot of girls over the years—pretending he likes them and then suddenly not liking them anymore. And, you know, he does his own thing. I'm actually kind of surprised he was down at the pond at all tonight, or last night"—she looked at the clock—"this morning. Whenever. Because that's the kind of scene he usually avoids. So people think he's standoffish. But he can be a good guy—he really can."

She yawned widely. "Lots of people know he doesn't like them or that he thinks they're shallow. He makes it obvious."

"That's what I like about him," Allie had murmured, closing her eyes. "He's so honest."

"Honesty can be good." Jo said, turning out the lamp. Her last words floated out of the darkness, disembodied. "But it can be bad, too."

Now, as they sat stirring cereal around their bowls, nobody seemed to have anything to say. Lisa was the most cheerful of them all—she'd survived the Splash, and Lucas had walked her back to the school building afterward. She thought he was starting to like her. But even she was tired.

"God, I'm so going to need a nap before tonight," she said, resting her head on her hand.

"I feel like ass," Jo said succinctly, reaching for the sugar. "Who knew sleep mattered?"

"Ass about sums it up for me, too," Allie said, sipping the scalding tea and yawning.

By tradition, classes ended early on the day of the Summer Ball, so she only had to get through half a day. Carter studiously ignored her in biology, and in English she dozed off while waiting for the class to start and never saw him come in. When she looked up, he was there but not looking at her. It was just as well. In eight hours she was going to the dance with Sylvain. This really wasn't the time to be thinking about standing in the water with Carter's arms around her. Naked.

She pulled her textbook out of her bag and dropped it on the desk with a thump.

No—not the time at all.

Isabelle had taken her place at the edge of the circle of desks.

She glanced around the room knowingly. "My, some of you look very tired. Didn't you sleep well?"

They shifted uncomfortably in their seats. Somebody snickered.

Isabelle's expression was enigmatic as pulled on her glasses. "I'm sure that most of you are daydreaming of dancing in the arms of your dates, but we must get through today's class nonetheless," she said, opening her book. "So I thought we would talk about romance today. Let's start with a beautiful poem about secret love. 'Silentium Amoris' was written by Oscar Wilde. . . ."

She read the first two stanzas in her rich, powerful voice. Lost in the flowery prose, Allie almost instantly tuned out, drawing a sleepy butterfly on her notebook. She was giving its wings elaborate decoration when she heard her name.

Confused, she sat up straighter. Everyone was looking at her.

"Sorry?" she said, flushing.

"Good morning," Isabelle said as the class tittered. "I said, would you mind reading the third stanza for me."

Clearing her throat, Allie began reading—she started quickly, but slowed as the words began to take shape.

> *But surely unto Thee mine eyes did show*
> *Why I am silent, and my lute unstrung;*
> *Else it were better we should part, and go,*
> *Thou to some lips of sweeter melody,*
> *And I to nurse the barren memory*
> *Of unkissed kisses, and songs never sung.*

"What does that poem say to you, Allie?"

Horrified to find Isabelle was still focusing on her, Allie tried to think of what to say.

Her voice was nearly a whisper. "He's afraid to tell somebody how he feels about her, but it makes him sad that she doesn't know."

"And why would he be afraid to tell this other person of his feelings?" Isabelle said.

Somehow, when Carter answered that question, Allie wasn't surprised.

"Because she might not feel the same way he does." His voice was steady and calm, and something about it made her blush. "So he thinks it's better never to find out."

Keeping her eyes on her notebook, Allie drew a small cage around the butterfly.

"Why would he think that's better?" Isabelle mused. "Wouldn't it be better to tell the truth and take his chances?"

"Maybe . . . he's afraid of being hurt," Allie said very quietly, adding another bar to the cage she'd created.

The minute class ended, Allie was up from her desk and heading for the door with her head down, determined not to make eye contact with anyone.

Especially Carter.

She was the first one to the stairs, and her feet pounded on the stair boards as she hurried up, counting to herself.

. . . thirty-one, thirty-two, thirty-three . . .

Inside the sanctuary of her own room, she closed the door behind her and leaned her back against it, staring at the neat familiarity of the space.

What just happened? Was Carter trying to tell me he likes me? Or am I reading into it?

She was so tired, she didn't trust herself to think about serious things right now. She was still obviously freaked out after last night. Her brain was really not working.

And the bed she hadn't slept in seemed to call to her. Setting the alarm for six so she wouldn't miss getting ready for the ball with Jo, she pulled the shutter to, closing out the dazzling sunlight. Pausing only long enough to kick off her shoes, she climbed into bed fully clothed. It felt wonderful to be alone, and in the cool darkness she wondered once more about Carter, before forgetting about everything for a little while.

FOURTEEN

When Allie arrived at Jo's room at half past six, Jo and Lisa had already draped the room in dresses and cluttered it with shoes. Allie was feeling much better—more normal. Somehow, sleep had settled her. Whatever might happen tomorrow, tonight she was going to have a good time. So last night had sucked. So what? She'd been through worse. She hadn't cared what anybody thought before she came to Cimmeria, and she wasn't going to start caring now.

Lisa was flushed with excitement. "I just think it's the perfect dress."

"Frankly, it'll be great just to spend some time with Gabe." Jo sighed. "I've hardly seen him in days."

"Any clue as to what's going on with him?" Allie asked, hanging her silky white dress on the wardrobe door.

Jo shook her head. "Not a peep. Just 'working on the project. . . .'" She deepened her voice and made it mildly defensive, which sounded so much like Gabe that Lisa and Allie giggled.

"Yeah, Sylvain is more like, 'Eet ees amporTANT wot we are

doEENG,'" Allie said, and they all collapsed in giggles again.

A silver tray of sandwiches cut into triangular quarters dominated Jo's desk, along with jugs of juice. Jo insisted that they all must eat something before leaving the room. ("Last year I nearly fainted at the ball because I was too excited to eat all day.") Slim as a daisy stem, Lisa nibbled delicately at the edge of a cucumber sandwich before setting it down on a napkin. Jo shot her a warning look.

"Eat it, Lisa."

"But I'm not hungry . . . ," Lisa said.

But Jo wouldn't back down, and Lisa forced down another bite.

Allie, who had skipped lunch to sleep, grabbed a cheese sandwich and took a huge bite. "Oh my God, how can you not be hungry? I'm starving. To *death.*"

Lisa, still undecided about how to wear her hair and beginning to panic, wordlessly held up a magazine open to a picture of blond starlet with an elaborate updo.

"I wish you'd just let me work my magic and quit worrying about it," Jo said. "I can do better than that. In fact, Allie, I'm going to do your hair right now. I have a feeling Lisa's will take forever."

Allie stuffed the rest of the sandwich into her mouth. "Mmph," she said agreeably as she climbed into the chair.

"Exactly." Jo brushed her hair and then began twisting it gently with the ribbon.

"I love having my hair done," Allie said, closing her eyes. "It's like having a head massage."

"If this whole expensive education thing doesn't pan out for me, I'm opening a salon in Mayfair in London." Jo deftly twisted a lock up and pinned it into place. "I'll call it MayHair."

"You've really thought about this." Allie laughed. "Well, fine then. If your expensive education doesn't take, I'll be your first customer."

As Jo predicted, Lisa's hair took ages. In the end, and after much disagreement, she had it twisted into a simple chignon that made the most of her long, slender neck.

"It's perfect." Lisa smiled at herself in the mirror. "Jo, you're a genius."

"I know," Jo said, smoothing her own hair into a flattering gamine style. "But guess what time it is."

Allie looked at her watch and groaned. "Step it up, ladies; we've only got ten minutes."

They grabbed their dresses.

"I knew this would happen," Jo said, slipping her silver minidress over her head. Allie zipped up the back for her.

"Yes, you did. For all the good it did us."

While Allie pulled on the long white dress, Jo slipped on her strappy sandals and turned around to help.

Allie gazed at her admiringly. "You look like a film star."

Jo smiled at her. "Darling, I might, but you look like a princess in a fairy tale."

Lisa wore a silvery blue silk dress with delicate straps and a matching silk wrap. When she finally pulled her shoes on, Jo and Allie applauded their approval.

"You look gorgeous, but good Lord, it takes you forever to get ready," Jo said.

Lisa picked up her clutch bag and smiled without rancor. "Everybody says that."

"Wait! Nobody gets out of this room until I've taken a picture." Jo waved a small camera at them.

She pulled Allie and Jo over to the full-length mirror, and they squeezed close together, giggling. When they were all reflected, Jo held up her camera and snapped the picture.

"Perfect," she said checking the image. "We look amazing."

"We'll probably never look this good again," Lisa said somberly. Allie and Jo stared at her for a second and then burst out laughing.

"You're impossible, gloomy guts," Jo said, hugging her. "Don't make me mess your hair up."

They walked out the door together at eight o'clock on the dot. When they reached the top of the stairs, a noisy crowd of boys had gathered at the foot of the staircase, all clad in black tuxedoes with tails.

The girls stood still for just a second as the crowd looked up at them and fell silent. The moment felt unreal—dreamlike. Six weeks ago she'd been hanging out in bus stations and empty rail lines spray-painting walls.

It felt like she was living someone else's life.

Sylvain, Lucas, and Gabe stood in the crowd below. Instinctively her eyes swept the crowd for Carter—he wasn't there.

Straightening her shoulders, she took a deep breath. Jo caught her eye and gave her a wink, then held out her hand. Allie took it and then reached out to Lisa with her other hand. They walked down the stairs together in a butterfly's fluttering of silk.

Focused on not losing her balance in Jo's kitten heels, Allie kept her eyes on the steps ahead. When she glanced up, Sylvain was in front of her, smiling.

Jo dropped her hand to walk toward Gabe.

Sylvain took up Allie's hand, kissed it, then placed it on his arm.

"You look beautiful," he said.

She could see real warmth and desire in his eyes—it made her feel strangely powerful.

"So do you."

And he did. He belonged in that dark, perfectly tailored tuxedo. Its cut emphasized his lean and muscular shoulders.

He smiled his perfect smile and brushed his fingers lightly across her brow, smoothing an invisible hair. "I can't wait to dance with you. Let's go in."

As they joined the stream of beautifully dressed students flowing into the great hall, staff in tuxedoes stood by the doors holding trays of champagne flutes. They each took a glass.

Inside, Allie expected to find a disco. Instead, an elegant scene, like out of another time, unfurled in front of her. A small orchestra had set up in one corner, where it played a waltz. Everywhere candles sparkled on tables, in the chandeliers, in wall sconces, in the fireplace. Vases filled with white flowers topped every surface. The tables were covered in white linen, and the chairs were draped with white silk ribbons. The scent of jasmine floated on the breeze.

Isabelle appeared in a flowing white chiffon gown cinched at the waist with a gold rope belt. Allie glanced down at her own dress and thought that, compared to Isabelle, she looked like a little girl. She reached out and tugged Jo's hand to get her attention and nodded in Isabelle's direction.

Jo smiled knowingly. "What can we do? Our headmistress is hot."

Gabe led them to a table in a corner, and they stood around it for a moment a bit awkwardly.

"What are we waiting for?" Allie whispered to Jo.

"You'll see."

After a moment, Isabelle tapped a silver spoon against a champagne flute, and the room fell silent.

"Welcome to the two hundred twenty-third Cimmeria Summer Ball."

Everybody clapped enthusiastically, and she waited for the applause to quiet.

"Every year, this is a very special occasion when we gather to celebrate the school, its history, and all of you, for you are Cimmeria's future. Many of your parents attended this ball years ago, and many of your grandparents and great-grandparents before that. You stand now where they stood then. Young and hopeful as they were. You are now part of the circle. Unbroken."

She raised her glass. "To the Summer Ball. And Cimmeria Academy."

"To the Summer Ball," they chorused. "And Cimmeria Academy."

"Enjoy!" she called out, laughing at their raucous applause.

When Sylvain pulled a seat out for her, she was surprised by his formality, but then she noticed Gabe and Lucas had pulled out Jo's and Lisa's seats as well.

Tradition, I guess.

Allie, who had only ever had small sips of champagne at

Christmas, thought it tasted a bit like the cheap wine she used to drink with Mark and Harry. At the thought of their names, she stopped and stared at the glass, where bubbles rose in quick, endless lines.

How long has it been since I thought about Mark and Harry?

Guiltily, she wondered what they were doing right now. If they were still getting into trouble. Hanging out in that cold, dingy warehouse where Mark's band used to practice, terribly.

Whatever they're doing, she thought, looking around the ballroom, *it isn't anything like this.*

She raised her glass again. The second sip of champagne was better.

At that moment the orchestra began playing an extraordinary song. It sounded exotic, but Allie couldn't place it. Hungarian? Turkish? As soon as it started, she could feel the excitement in the air—it was electric. A few couples began dancing in a complex pattern that seemed to involve circles within circles. It was dizzying to watch, and after a moment she turned away, feeling light-headed.

"It's a traditional Cimmeria song." Sylvain had been watching her. "It was written for the school a long time ago by an Egyptian composer who studied here."

"I've never heard anything like it," Allie said.

She would have asked for more information, but at that moment waiters walked by with trays of hors d'oeuvres, and Gabe, Sylvain, and Lucas all took several. Jo and Allie each took one, but Lisa waved the tray away.

"Everything is so beautiful," Allie said, staring up at the

ceiling as she bit into a breaded prawn.

"They've been working on it since yesterday morning," Jo said. "I could hear them in here hammering away this morning, too."

"It's all perfect," Sylvain said, smiling at Allie. "I think we should definitely dance. But you must finish your champagne first."

At the thought of going out on that dance floor, Allie's heart jumped with fear. Glancing over, she watched the dancers move. A few of the couples were less than perfect and the others swirled past them, like water flowing around stones.

She took a quick gulp of champagne for courage, wrinkling her nose at the pleasant feeling of the bubbles. Then another.

"It really grows on you, champagne," she murmured half to herself. The others laughed at her.

"Yes," Gabe said cheerfully. "Champagne definitely grows on you."

"Don't drink it too fast," Jo cautioned, shooting Sylvain a warning look.

Allie dismissed her with a smile. "Remember, Mum, I used to drink quite a bit."

Jo didn't look placated. "Cimmeria champagne is pretty strong, Allie."

"She'll be fine," Sylvain said. Standing up, he held out his hand. "May I have this dance?"

"I have no idea how to dance to this music, Sylvain," she protested as she placed her hand in his. "I predict humiliation if we do this."

"Oh, I don't think it will come to that."

His face was so confident, she almost believed him. Or was that the champagne giving her courage?

They walked to the edge of the dance floor where the couples were still swirling in their intricate circles. They moved with impressive speed and practiced perfection, and Allie watched them in awe. She saw Isabelle moving gracefully in the arms of a handsome, dark-haired man she'd never seen before. She was incredibly elegant.

Allie sighed enviously. "How do they all know how to dance like this?"

"Most of us have had dance lessons since we were children," Sylvain said, holding out his hands to her.

"How weird that people still do that."

"Is it?" He pulled her into his arms and she looked into his bluer-than-blue eyes. His arms were firm around her, his right hand in the small of her back pulling her close to his chest, her right hand in his left. "It seems strange to me that anybody wouldn't do that. Tonight I will teach you one dance, a simple one. Just follow me. We'll start very slow. It's left right left left right. Like this."

He demonstrated, and she followed carefully. As they made their first circle, she stared worriedly at her feet and almost immediately tripped, falling against him and scuffing his glossy shoe as he held her up.

Blushing, she took a step back.

"I told you I can't do—"

He shook his head. "Don't say you can't, Allie. You can do anything."

With his fingertips, he gently lifted her chin so her eyes met his.

"Don't look down," he said. "Just watch my eyes. They will tell you where to go next. And it's left right left left right, over and over again. Ready?"

"No."

He laughed and twirled her out onto the dance floor.

"Left right left left right . . . Left right left left right . . ." Allie murmured the directions under her breath as she moved but kept her eyes locked on his. They twirled three slow circles without a mistake. Then four. Five!

She couldn't believe it.

"How are you doing this?" she laughed incredulously. "Seriously, Sylvain, I don't know how to dance."

He held her eyes with his, rising and falling with the steps. "We can do it because you're trusting me. I'm leading. You're following. It's very simple." He smiled. "Also, we're moving very, very slowly. . . ."

As they spun and she gained confidence, he gradually increased their speed until they were moving seamlessly around the floor.

When she was moving with confidence, he lightly kissed her neck just below her ear. All of her senses tingled and she nearly tripped, looking up at him, startled.

With a low laugh, he whispered, "You look so lovely tonight, Allie. Thank you for coming with me."

She felt the blood rush to her face, and her body responded to him as he pulled her closer. All the while they spun in a smooth and constant series of circles. Allie was growing dizzy—the rest of the room was a watercolor blur. It was exhilarating.

This is incredible.

After what felt like only a few minutes, the circles led them to the edge of the dance floor, and he guided her back to the table, his arm tight around her waist.

Allie's head spun, and she held on to him for support. "I feel dizzy."

"It's the dancing. You're not used to it." With one hand, Sylvain lifted two glasses off a passing tray. "What you need is more champagne."

Allie accepted the glass he passed her with a grateful smile. "Thank you. I'm so thirsty." The drink was ice-cold, and she gulped it down. "You know, I'm starting to really like champagne."

His chuckle was warm, and he was so close to her, she could feel it vibrate in her own body. "So you've said."

Allie looked for Jo in the crowd of dancers. Her very short dress made her easy to spot—it was definitely the tiniest dress in the room. She and Gabe were twirling around the dance floor with assurance. She saw Lisa's dress swirling a short distance away as she and Lucas spun easy circles.

She barely noticed when Sylvain took the empty glass from her hand and replaced it with a full one.

Glancing around the room, she noticed Ruth and Phil walking toward the dance floor holding hands—Ruth wore a pretty pale pink silk dress that made the most of her athletic figure. Nearby the teachers were at a table together. The science teacher, Jerry, almost unrecognizably suave in a tux, sat talking comfortably with Eloise from the library; she was in a sexy little black dress with a low back, and her long hair hung down her back in glossy curls.

"She's not very old at all," Allie said, surprised.

"Who?"

"Eloise. I always thought she was old. Or at least, you know, older."

Sylvain smiled. "Yes, I think she wants people to think she's older. If they knew she was so young, nobody would take her seriously. She was at school here six years ago." He gave the librarian an appraising glance. "Very sexy, Eloise."

Allie punched his arm lightly. "Hey! Watch it. Remember who your date is."

His smile was wicked. "I could never forget. But I think it's time for my date to dance with me again. Come on now, bottoms up." He finished his own drink, then waited until she'd emptied her glass before holding out his hand.

As they headed back to the dance floor, she felt a little unsteady on her feet, and reached for Sylvain's arm to steady herself. At that moment, Carter stepped in front of them. When their eyes met, Allie felt a spark of electricity. Then she noticed he had his arm around a petite girl in a blue taffeta dress. She was pretty, with long, curly blond hair. Before Allie could say anything to him, he turned away very deliberately and smiled down at his date, whispering something in her ear that made her giggle.

Allie flushed and must have tensed, because Sylvain looked over to see what had caught her attention. When he saw Carter, his eyes narrowed, and his arm tightened around her waist.

"Is everything okay?" he asked. His voice was cool.

Forcing a smile, she pulled him onto the dance floor.

"Everything is perfect." But she noticed she'd slurred the last word, and she frowned with concentration as she tried to figure out why.

Wait—am I drunk? Already?

"You look," he said as they took their first steps onto the dance floor, "like an angel."

Carter was right there at the edge of the dance floor, Allie was certain. He was probably watching them. With his date.

Fine, then. She'd give him something to watch.

She pulled Sylvain closer. "I don't feel like one."

He threw his head back and laughed as they picked up speed. This time the dance steps were easier, and at first Allie relaxed into the movement and the music and let Sylvain decide where they went on the floor. Her head felt light and pleasantly dizzy. She gave in to the feeling with a soft sigh, leaning back against his arm and letting him support her completely. She felt the air rush around them.

He pulled her closer until his lips were against her ear; as he nibbled sharply at her earlobe, she gasped and would have tripped were he not holding her so tightly.

"I'm sorry," he said, his voice taut. "You are irresistible."

His expression was so intense, it made her nervous.

He swirled them to the edge of the dance floor and led her hurriedly out of the room. Feeling a bit woozy, Allie clung to his hand as he rushed out into the dark night, past a small crowd gathered near the back door, then around the corner to a quiet empty spot, out of view.

She tried to talk without slurring her words. "Where are we . . . ?"

He shoved her roughly against the wall, and she cried out at the impact, although she felt it as if through a cushion of cotton wool.

"Stop! Sylvain, What are you . . ."

Her voice trailed off as she looked up at him. His eyes were luminous in the moonlight and she saw something like ferocity in them.

Then he kissed her so hard that her head hit the wall and she bit her tongue. Tears filled her eyes. Suddenly frightened, she struggled to get away, her fists pushing at his chest.

A vague memory of Carter's warning filtered through her confusion: *Don't trust Sylvain. He's a liar.*

Sylvain tilted up her chin and kissed her neck. For a second she liked it, but then he nipped at the skin so hard it hurt, and her body moved involuntarily against his as she tried to squirm away from him. But he was pressed hard against her and didn't seem to notice. His hands moved up from her waist to her breasts and she started to panic in earnest. A tear ran down her cheek as she shoved against his chest, but it seemed to have no effect on him.

"You want me," he whispered.

"Stop!" Her voice was just a whisper.

She clawed at his wrists, but he was too strong and her strength seemed to have fled.

"Say it," he said again, pressing harder against her. The rough stone behind her dug into her back through the thin fabric of her dress. "Tell me that you want me."

"Ask yourself a question, Sylvain. If you force somebody to want you, do they really want you?" Carter's voice came from right behind Sylvain's shoulder.

Sylvain's hold loosened just a little, but he didn't let go as he turned to face Carter.

"Oh, do go away, Carter."

Carter stood his ground. "What are you trying to force her to say, Sylvain? Spell it out for me. Like I'm stupid."

"This is none of your business, Carter. Your envy is pathetic."

"Tell it to Isabelle. And while you're at it, tell her what you were about to do to Allie. And then you can have a long talk about The Rules."

Dizzy and bewildered, Allie struggled to free herself as she looked from one boy to the other.

Carter kept his attention on Sylvain. "Which will it be, Sylvain?"

Their eyes met in an icy clash, and for a second Allie thought Sylvain would not back down and she wondered what Carter would do. But then without warning, Sylvain let go and stepped away from her.

"Fine, Carter. Be the hero. Save the girl. But we both know you're pathetic. And it's me she wants."

Tensing his shoulders and curling his hands into fists, Carter took a furious step forward, but before he could pounce, screams split the night air. Carter and Sylvain froze.

Carter turned to Allie, the rage gone from his expression. Now he looked alert—on guard.

"Allie, stay here. Don't move."

Sylvain didn't look back at her as the two of them ran away around the building.

Trembling, Allie stood right where they'd left her. When she reached to touch the back of her head, she could feel a lump under her fingertips.

What the hell just happened?

She wrapped her arms tightly across her chest. She was sore all over—she knew she'd have bruises on her arms in the morning, and her head pounded. Sylvain had been out of his mind, but she hadn't fought properly. She hadn't stood up for herself.

Too drunk, she thought disgustedly. *Too stupid.*

She wasn't an inexperienced drinker, but she'd never got drunk on one glass of cheap wine, either. And she'd only had a few glasses of champagne. As the idea took shape, a horrified look crossed her face. Or was she merely drunk? Could he have put something in her drink?

Would Sylvain do . . .

Before she could complete the thought, piercing screams came again. The sound was close—just around the corner. She jumped back into the shadows.

Crashing; sounds of fighting. Then, silence.

She held her breath.

After a moment, in the darkness, footsteps. Running toward her. Fast.

"Carter?" she said, her voice tentative.

The footsteps stopped.

With a gasp, Allie realized her mistake.

The rush of adrenalin surging through her veins cleared the haze of alcohol better than coffee or time could have, and she pressed back against the wall, making herself as small as possible. Although she could see nothing, someone was there—she could feel their presence. Someone was watching her. Frozen, not breathing, she counted her heartbeats.

. . . ten, eleven, twelve . . .

Footsteps moved toward her again. Slower this time.

Flinging herself from the wall, Allie raced around the corner toward the door. The footsteps followed—fast.

Speeding up to evade them, she tripped over something soft on the ground. With a sharp scream, she lost her balance and pinwheeled to the ground.

On the cool, damp grass, she curled up into a ball and covered her head, waiting for the attack. But none came. Instead she heard footsteps moving away from her, then gradually fading into the night.

Allie stayed still until she was certain she was alone. Then, moving cautiously, she pushed herself up and peered around her.

Her hands were covered in something wet and sticky. As her eyes adjusted, she saw that she'd tripped over a girl in a pale dress, lying prone on the ground. She touched the girl cautiously, but she didn't move. With her hands on the girl's shoulders, she rolled her over onto her back.

"Hey, are you okay?"

Then she saw. She sucked in her breath.

The world seemed to go silent.

Scrambling back away from the girl, she stared at the shape of her body in the dark.

Numb, she stumbled to her feet and walked with slow steps to the back door. Inside, the lights had gone out and the hallway was dark and chaotic. It smelled of smoke. People were shouting and running past her. Allie felt disembodied—distanced from everything around her. She looked straight ahead, her bloodied hands out to either side.

Over and over in her head she thought the same words: *None of this is real. It cannot be real. None of this is real. It cannot be real. . . .*

As she made her way back toward the ballroom, the smoke grew thicker, bringing tears to her eyes. The grand room—so beautiful earlier that night with its sparkling candles and white flowers—was on fire. The only light came from flashlights held by teachers, and from the flames themselves. In that half-light, boys in tuxedos and girls in gowns beat flames with wet table-cloths and carried water using anything they could find: ice buckets, punch bowls, flower vases. The floor was littered with abandoned high-heeled shoes and broken champagne flutes.

The fires were small and already beginning to go out—it was clear the students were winning the battle. But the intense smoke was the biggest problem—it was hard to breathe.

"Open a window!" somebody shouted.

"Don't!" came Zelazny's firm reply. "It'll make the fires worse. Get out if you need a break."

His stern voice was somehow comforting to Allie, who stood stunned in the middle of the room, unable to take it all in.

"Allie! Are you all right?" Jo appeared at her side, her face smeared with soot, an empty vase in her hand. "Jesus. Where did the blood come from? Are you hurt?"

Dropping the vase, she grabbed Allie's bloody hands and turned her around looking for obvious wounds. Allie shook her head, but for a second she couldn't find her voice. Her lips moved, but no sound emerged.

"Allie, you're scaring me." Tears sprang to Jo's eyes. "Please, please, please tell me you're okay."

Her words jarred Allie, and words burst out of her as she

gripped Jo's hands so tightly it must have hurt. "Oh my God, Jo. There was screaming, and . . . There's blood . . . everywhere."

Jo's cornflower blue eyes were wide with fear.

"Allie, please try to explain—where is the blood from?"

Allie stared at her hands. "Jo, this is Ruth's blood. She's out back. Her throat is . . . it's cut. I think she's dead."

Swallowing hard, Jo whipped around, calling urgently, "Jerry!"

Allie watched through the dark and smoke as Jo ran to the teacher, who had been beating smoldering embers with a soaked tablecloth. His face was black with soot. Eloise stood nearby, her long hair tangled down her back. She'd taken off her heels and stood barefoot, spraying foam from a fire extinguisher.

Jo spoke quickly, her face panicked. Allie couldn't make out her words.

Jerry and Eloise exchanged a look. Eloise handed the extinguisher to another teacher and the two ran out of the room.

When Jo returned to her side, Allie looked around. "Where's Lisa?"

Jo bit her lip. "I couldn't find either of you anywhere."

"So you haven't seen her at all?" Allie could hear the hysteria in her own voice but was helpless to stop it. "Jo, she could be hurt! She could be . . . like Ruth."

Tears filled Allie's eyes and she fought them back as Jo grabbed her bloodied hands.

"Stay calm, Allie. I haven't had a chance to really look for her." She glanced around the room. "It looks like most of the fire is out now. Let's look for her together."

Moving quickly, Jo headed across the room, pulling Allie with her. They walked through the lingering smoke, checking every room.

Nothing.

"Out front." Jo was moving swiftly now, and Allie was right beside her. They headed for the front door and then skidded to a stop. In the entrance hall a frail body in a silvery blue dress lay still on the stone floor, a long, filmy wrap stretched out on either side of her, as if blown on a breeze only she could feel. A tall wooden candleholder lay across her body.

"Oh no." Jo's words were a whisper as they rushed to Lisa's side.

Crouched beside Lisa, Allie picked up her cold hand. "She's alive," she said.

Jo pulled the candleholder off her and threw it to one side. Lisa's hair had fallen across her face and Allie gently smoothed it back, revealing a deep gash across her cheek. Jo gave a small cry and her hand covered her mouth, her eyes filled with tears.

"Lisa? Lisa, wake up. Can you hear me? We really need you to wake up." Allie said the last word with such force that it seemed to reverberate.

She saw droplets fall on Lisa's dress, and it took her a moment to realize that she was crying. Burying her face in her hands, she sobbed as Jo cried beside her.

"Wake up."

FIFTEEN

In the chaotic hours after the attack, teachers shepherded the students into the darkened dining room and attempted to calm the panic. Staff carrying boxes of flashlights handed them around, while nurses set up a triage in one corner. The injured queued to have their wounds bandaged, burns assessed, and ankles splinted.

The room was generally clear of the choking smoke that lingered in the hallways, but the air was filled instead with the stifled weeping of students and the brutally efficient conversation of medical staff.

"Hand me those bandages."

"This ankle needs an ice bath; you got one free?"

"Antibiotic by injection."

Lisa remained unconscious and was carried away to the nursing ward by two silent members of the staff. At first Jo and Allie insisted on going with her, fluttering around the stretcher like shrill birds. But Eloise convinced them to stay.

She was still in her little black dress, and her eyes were bright and tireless. "I promise you she's going to be all right. She needs to rest. And we really need your help down here. Please tell me I can count on you."

They nodded reluctantly, and she sent them upstairs to wash off the blood and change clothes.

As they climbed the stairs, the fearful rumble of the aftermath gradually faded into the pitch-black silence of the dormitory wing. Jo held Allie's hand. Allie's head pounded, and her stomach was churning. She thought she might throw up.

When they separated at the top, Jo said, "It's safe up here, right?"

"She wouldn't have sent us here otherwise," Allie replied, but her voice was uncertain.

"Okay. Be really, really fast. I'll meet you in the bathroom."

Allie opened her bedroom door slowly and flashed the light around to verify its emptiness. In the dark it felt foreign—as if it had no attachment to her at all and her belongings had been placed randomly. Hurrying across the room, she rifled through the dresser, grabbing whatever clothes came to hand.

Later, in a dark, cold shower lit only by a flashlight propped up against Jo's borrowed silver kitten heels, she scrubbed the blood off her body fiercely. The cold and the water cleared her head, as if she were washing the whole night away. Jo waited for her by a sink, swinging her light around the room. Occasionally they called out to each other for reassurance.

"You still alive?"

"Yep. You?"

"I think so."

When she was finished, Allie left the ruined white dress and the sparkly silver shoes in the shower changing room.

She and Jo hurried downstairs, where the air of panic had transmuted into grim efficiency. Flashlight beams bobbed down hallways as students carried scorched furniture out of the ballroom. Outside the back door a generator rumbled steadily, and thick black cables snaked down the corridor to the great hall, where the klieg lights they powered gave the still-smoldering space an unearthly glow.

Teachers armed with clipboards orchestrated the work. Some stood on chairs and called out instructions while others were sequestered in small, whispering groups around the walls.

Jo and Allie stood side by side, surveying the room.

"Well, I guess we should find Eloise," Allie said, her voice shaky.

But instead of the librarian they found Isabelle, perched perilously atop one of the dining room's wooden chairs issuing orders calmly to the teachers and students who milled around. Her white dress was smudged with soot but otherwise perfect, although her hair had escaped from its clips and flowed in waves over her shoulders. She looked relieved to see them—especially Allie.

Crouching down, she took Allie's hands and pulled her closer. Speaking so quietly no one else could hear, she said, "I'm so sorry that you had to be the one to find Ruth. Are you all right?"

As she looked into Isabelle's concerned eyes, a flood of conflicting emotions swept over Allie. She wanted to cry for Ruth and for herself. She wanted to hug the headmistress for caring. Instead, she willed her tears back and nodded to show she was fine. Giving Allie's hands a final squeeze, Isabelle stood up again.

"Okay, you two," she said, businesslike again. Handing them a clipboard with a pencil connected to it by a string, she continued, "I need to be sure that everyone is accounted for. There are fifty-two students here this term altogether. Identify everybody you can find. Search the central ground floor—not the wings. Do not go outside under any circumstances."

A group of teachers approached her, and she turned away to deal with them.

At first Allie and Jo were overwhelmed—it was so dark, and people rushed by them in the haze. But then they came up with a system, ticking off names of everybody they'd already seen, then searching only for the remaining names on their list.

The work steadied their nerves. They wandered from room to room as the number of missing students dwindled. After about an hour electricity was restored, making their chore easier. The bitter burning smell lingered, but the air gradually cleared.

Throughout it all, Allie had a strange sense of distance—of watching herself on television as she moved around the school doing what had to be done. She couldn't even feel her own exhaustion. Her body moved, but she felt disconnected from its actions.

By the time the sun came up, about twenty-one students were still not ticked off their lists. These included Gabe, Carter, Sylvain, Jules, and Lucas.

"Where do you think they are?" Allie asked.

"Night School." Jo's voice was weary as she rubbed her forehead. "They're all Night School. We've looked everywhere—this is all we're going to get. Let's go turn it in."

After searching the dining room and the library, they found Isabelle with Jerry and Eloise in the empty great hall. The stench of scorched wood and plaster was thick and nauseating. The electricity was still out in here, and the generator had been turned off, so it was dim and hard to see. Faint ambient light coming in from the hallway shimmered on the smoke particles still dancing in the air. They looked, Allie thought, like tiny black crystals. She could see that one wall was entirely blackened as far up as the ceiling. Small piles of rubble still smoldered here and there. But otherwise, the room was less damaged than she'd expected.

Isabelle scanned the list quickly and handed it to Jerry, who looked it over and nodded.

"Thanks, you two," Isabelle said. "You did a brilliant job."

"But so many are still missing!" Allie protested.

Isabelle had circles under her reddened eyes. She looked tired.

"We know where they are, and they're fine," she said, putting her arm around Allie. "Don't worry about them."

"It's all the Night School guys, right?" Jo's arms were crossed tightly across her chest.

"You know we can't talk about Night School with you, Jo. But I expect you also know the answer to your own question." Eloise's voice was sharp.

Jo held her ground. "I'm sorry, Eloise—I just think it would be good if we were all a bit more honest right now than we usually are."

Isabelle squeezed Allie's shoulder gently and let go before turning to Jo. "And a lot of teachers would agree with you," she said, to Allie's surprise. "But right now, we just have to get through the next twenty-four hours."

"How many people were . . . killed?" Allie's voice was small.

"One, Allie." Isabelle's voice was filled with sympathy.

As Jerry and Eloise turned to go, Jerry squeezed her arm in a comforting, dadlike way. Eloise wrapped her in a warm hug.

"Hang in there, lovely," she whispered.

When they'd gone, Jo turned back to Isabelle. "How's Lisa? Can we see her?"

"She's not awake yet. The nurse said she needs to rest." Isabelle gestured down the hallway. "There's some food in the dining room. I'd really like you to take a break and get something to eat. I'll come find you there if we need you."

Although it was hard to even imagine eating, at her insistence Jo and Allie decided to try. It was early morning now, and light streamed with inappropriate cheeriness through the dining room windows. Tired, dirty students sat or slept at most tables, plates of half-eaten food in front of them. At one end of the room a buffet table was piled high with sandwiches, and big copper urns held steaming coffee and tea.

They stood in front of it, staring at the food. It just seemed weird to care about eating right now, but after filling their plates they found an unoccupied table, pushing aside the used cups and saucers to make room. For a while they ate in exhausted silence. Jo sat lotus style, her white blond hair fluffed around her head in a disarrayed halo. Allie bent her leg to pull one foot up onto her seat and leaned her elbow on her knee. She finished a sandwich and pushed her plate away.

"What did you see?" She asked the question with no warning.

Jo looked puzzled for a second. "Last night?"

Allie nodded.

Jo's face clouded over. "Oh, Allie, it was crazy. Where were you, anyway?" She didn't wait for an answer. "At first, everything was beautiful, you know? Gabe and I were dancing, and then suddenly there was a noise—like a big bang—and the lights went out. Then it all got really confusing because it was so dark; everyone was running to where they thought the door was. But the door was locked. People were screaming that they couldn't get out. Then we smelled smoke. It was . . . awful. Just awful.

"Gabe and I got down on the ground so that we could breathe, and we made sort of air masks out of napkins. We got to where we were far from the fire, and then he said he had to go see what was going on—like, why people weren't getting out of the room. And then he was . . . gone."

Allie waited for more, but Jo stopped and tore the crust of her sandwich into little pieces.

"What happened then?" she prodded.

Wrapping her arms tightly around her torso, Jo continued, her voice grim. "It was dark. I could just . . . hear screaming, and the smoke was really bad. Suddenly there was a crashing sound—I guess somebody broke the door open. Then there was fresh air, but that made the fire worse. Then people started putting the fire out with water and fire extinguishers, and people could get out, and then you walked in." Her voice trailed off; she shoved her plate away. "You know the rest."

"Have you seen Gabe since?"

Jo shook her head, and a tear traced down her cheek. "I'm trying not to be stupid. Eloise says everyone's fine, so he's fine. It's just . . . he just left me there. In a fire."

She covered her face in her hands.

"Oh, babe." Allie reached out to squeeze her arm and tried

to think of something to say. "He made sure you were safe first, right? That was the very first thing he did. And you know what? He has faith that you're tough, and you can take care of yourself. And that's kind of cool."

Jo nodded, although she was clearly still unconvinced., Then she closed her eyes and leaned on her elbow. "God, I'm so tired."

Allie scooted her chair closer and pulled Jo's head onto her shoulder. "Me, too."

In a few moments they were both asleep, their arms wrapped around each other.

The sound of movement woke them a short while later. The Night School group had returned.

Gabe was the first one through the door. Despite everything she'd said earlier, the second she saw him, Jo flew across the room and flung herself into his arms. They disappeared out the door talking in whispers.

Sylvain wasn't far behind Gabe. Allie, who felt that she hadn't had time yet to process what had happened between them last night, wasn't ready to see him. Sliding down low in her seat, she stared into her empty teacup and hoped he wouldn't notice her.

As she thought about last night, she ran her fingers absently across the lump on the back of her head. It was smaller now, but it still hurt.

When Carter and Lucas walked through the door a few minutes later, she felt a surge of relief. They both looked tired and filthy—dirt smeared their faces and their hair was matted with sweat.

She was still keeping her head down, so Carter didn't notice her as he filled his plate and grabbed a coffee. But Lucas saw her immediately and hurried over to her table.

"Any word about Lisa?" he asked.

She shook her head. "Nothing yet."

His lips tightened. "I feel so awful about . . . I just wish I'd been with her."

It occurred to Allie that when the worst happened, they'd all been alone. She, Jo, and Lisa. Their dates had left them to . . . to do what? She wanted to shout at him that yes, he should have stayed with Lisa. And Gabe should have stayed with Jo.

But he looked so worn out and defeated, her anger left her. She pulled him into a hug. "Isabelle says she's going to be okay, and I believe her." He nodded against her shoulder. "I think you should get some rest, Lucas. You look awful."

He managed a smile before he walked away. "Thanks, Allie. You sound like Carter—he was just telling me the same thing."

At the mention of his name, Allie turned to look for Carter. He sat alone at one of the farthest tables with his legs sprawled out, eating with mechanical thoroughness; his eyes were fixed on his plate as if he didn't want to see anything else.

Weariness made his face so vulnerable that her breath caught—he looked like a little boy. But as she walked up to him, the guarded look returned.

Pulling out a chair, she didn't wait for him to invite her to join him.

"Hey," she said.

"Hey back." His voice was distant.

She studied his face. "Are you okay?"

"I'm good." His eyes searched her face. "You?"

She shrugged. "I'm alive."

"I heard about Ruth...."

Almost reflexively she lifted her hand to stop him. "I don't want to talk about that."

"Sorry," he said.

"No. It's just..." She willed bloody images of Ruth's body out of her mind. "I just... can't talk about it right now. I'm not ready."

For a fleeting moment she saw sympathy in his eyes.

"I understand. We don't have to talk about it."

Silence fell between them; he studied his coffee mug as if it held a secret. She waited three breaths.

"Carter?"

His eyes flickered up to her. "What?"

"Have you seen Phil? Is he okay?"

"Not okay." He shook his head. "He's devastated. He blames himself for not being with her when it happened, the poor bastard. I think he's going home."

Allie absorbed this information before speaking again.

"About last night..."

"Allie..." He shot her a warning look, but she ignored him.

"Was I drunk? Or, I don't know... drugged? I mean, I've been drunk before, and I know how you get drunk, obviously. But I just had *three* glasses. And I was... well, I don't really know what I was."

"I don't know what you were either, Allie."

His tone was accusing, and she leaned away from him, stung. "Hey. That's not fair."

"You want to know what I think?" His dark eyes flashed with repressed anger. "I think you drank too much and you trusted

Sylvain. I tried to warn you."

"I know! I know you did." She was angry, too, but her anger was directed at herself. "And I'm sorry I didn't listen. But . . . I didn't realize . . ."

His expression softened. "Look, Allie, it's not your fault Sylvain's a dickhead. But . . . I've told you before. You haven't been at Cimmeria long enough to understand how things are here. So be careful, okay? Things are not what they seem. People aren't always who they seem to be."

Even though his tone was more kind, his warning chilled her.

What kind of school is this, anyway? Who are these people? Worry burned her stomach. *Can I trust anybody? Even Carter? He's always been such a pain in the ass, but has he ever lied to me?*

She studied his serious face, then reached out and put her hand on his arm. "Thanks, Carter."

He raised one suspicious eyebrow. "For what?"

"You kind of rescued me last night. That's twice in twenty-four hours you've saved me. In some countries, I'd owe you my life or my firstborn child or something."

He half smiled, but she thought his eyes still looked guarded. "Just . . . believe me next time, okay?"

"Okay," she said, wondering if she would.

As he leaned back in his chair and took a sip of his cooling coffee, his eyes narrowed and he stared hard at something behind her. Allie turned. Across the dining room Sylvain sat alone, his eyes boring into them. She could feel anger radiating off him like heat.

Carter returned his glare, unflinching.

"Oh, balls," Allie muttered.

"You're going to have trouble with him," Carter told her, turning to face her. "He is powerful around here, and he's not going to be happy if he doesn't get what he wants. And what he wants is you."

Staring fearlessly back at Sylvain, Allie said, "Well that's too bad. Because he can't have me."

Pushing back her chair, she stood and stalked over to where Sylvain sat at the front of the room. His expression was intimidating, but she was sober now. All the rage of the past hours seemed to roil inside her. Her hands curled into fists at her side. It was comforting to hate him. Indulging her anger felt good. She leaned over until her hands rested on the arms of his chair and her face was just inches from his.

When she spoke, her voice was a threatening whisper.

"That was the worst date I ever had. And we. Are so. Over."

She waited just long enough to clock the surprised look on his face; then she walked to the door. Out of the corner of her eye, she saw Carter smile.

They were sent back to their rooms a short while later. As she climbed the stairs to the girls' dormitory, Allie counted every single step. When she reached her own room sixty-one steps later, she opened the door.

All was as she'd left it hours ago—dresser drawers were still open and clothes strewn on the floor from her hurried late-night search for something to wear.

Taking a deep breath, she took the sixty-second step into the room.

But even when she was inside and the door was closed behind

her, she couldn't relax. She felt fearful and threatened. So she began the process of making it feel safe again. First she picked up the clothes and put them away, then she straightened the already straight desktop and closed the wardrobe door. Finally, when everything was perfect, she closed the shutter over the window to block the daylight, kicked off her shoes, and lay down on top of the duvet.

For half an hour she tossed and turned as last night's events swirled through her head like the dancers at the ball. *Who killed Ruth? . . . Carter must think . . . I don't know. Was I drunk? Jo said the champagne was strong . . . But Ruth was . . . She was . . .*

Dark and cloudy images of Ruth's bloodied body made her retch, and she sat bolt upright. Her heart was pounding and her hands dripped with sweat.

She couldn't breathe. She could hear herself beginning to wheeze.

Air. I need air.

Springing from her bed, she scrambled up onto her desk and flung the shutter and window open. Daylight poured in and she took a strangled breath of warm, fresh air. . . .

"Ouch!"

The voice outside her window startled her so much, she nearly fell off the desk as she scrambled backward. Clutching the chair as if it would protect her, she wheezed breathlessly.

"Who . . . ?"

"Allie? What's the matter?"

"Carter?" she wheezed. "What the . . . hell are . . . you . . . ?"

Reaching through the open window, he pulled her closer—his hands were firm but gentle on her shoulders, and her body slipped easily along the polished wood of her desktop. His hands slid down her arms to take her hands, and his dark eyes were serious as he watched her struggle to breathe. "Remember what you did the other night? You need to do it again. Breathe in through your nose. Slowly. And out through your mouth."

Still wheezing, she tried to process what was happening. "Were you . . . spying . . . ?"

He glared at her. "Bloody hell, Allie. Will you just shut up and breathe?"

With her eyes on his, and his hands gripping hers, she breathed in sync with him, raggedly at first, but gradually more easily. When she seemed to be breathing normally, he let go and the questions burst out of her.

"Are you a total *pervert*? How on earth did you get up here? And how did you find my room? And . . ."

Sitting as casually on the window ledge as if he were in an easy chair in the common room, Carter laughed. "Come on, Allie. I've lived at this school my whole life. I know every inch of it. Including the roof. Which is, by the way, easy to get up on, and I'm kind of surprised you haven't tried it yet."

Allie looked for any sign that he was lying to her but saw nothing but amusement.

"Did you come here from your room?" She paused, looking around. "Where is your room, anyway?"

He pointed across the building. "Look, the guys' dorm is on the top floor of the main building. My window is the third one down—do you see it?"

She counted the dormer windows. "Yes."

He turned back toward her. "It's easy to get here from there."

Suddenly she had a flashback to a few weeks ago. She stared up at him.

"You've been here before." Her voice was accusing. "When I first came here, I thought I heard somebody outside my window late one night. It was you, wasn't it?"

He had the grace to look embarrassed. "I didn't think you heard. Sorry about that."

"You freaked me out, Carter," she said. "What were you doing?"

He squirmed uncomfortably. "I was . . . actually on my way to see somebody else, and you opened your window and nearly knocked me off the roof. I'm not a Peeping Tom or anything."

At the thought of him passing her window to go see another girl, something tightened in Allie's chest. She wondered whose room it was. Tilting her head to one side, she studied him speculatively.

Who the hell are you anyway, Carter West?

Having him on the defensive made her feel more in control, and she crossed her legs and rested her elbows on her knees. "So, why are you here now, Carter? On your way to see some other girl again?"

He leaned against the window frame, avoiding her eyes. As he did it, he dislodged a pebble from the ledge, and she could hear it clicking its way to the ground three stories below.

"No. Of course not." His dark eyes glanced off hers. "I was just . . . worried about you, I guess," he said finally. "It's been a pretty terrible night and you get these panic attacks, so I just . . . you know . . . worried."

They held each other's gaze for a moment. Panic attack or

not, Allie thought now would be a good time to look completely together and in control, but his eyes were so limitlessly dark they seemed to summon images of last night's awful events.

She covered her face with her hands to block them out.

"I keep seeing Ruth and remembering. . . . It was bad, Carter. Really bad. It was dark, but I could see that her throat was cut. There was so much blood. . . . And then the footsteps. I thought I was next."

"What footsteps?"

Something in his voice wasn't right—it was as if he spoke without air. She looked up to find him staring at her, and for the first time it occurred to her that in all of the chaos she'd never had a chance to tell anybody about everything that had happened outside.

When she filled him in, he kept returning to the footsteps she'd heard. "You're quite certain the footsteps came from the school and then headed away?"

Allie nodded—she could see that his mind was working.

"How many footsteps did you hear? I mean, how many people do you think there were?" he asked.

Frowning with concentration, she tried to remember, but it all blurred into a haze of fear and danger and blood.

"One, I think, but I'm not certain. I was too frightened. Carter, who could have done this? Do you think it could have been a student? Or . . . a teacher?"

Until she said it aloud, the idea that a teacher might be involved had not occurred to her, but suddenly it all seemed appallingly possible. She hoped he'd laugh at her, or tell her she was being stupid.

Instead, he rubbed his eyes wearily.

"I don't know. I don't think so—but I don't know anymore."

"Why didn't they kill me, too?" Her voice was plaintive as she finally said the words she'd been avoiding since last night. "Carter, why am I still alive?"

Looking out over the school grounds, he didn't speak for a long moment. When he did, his voice was rough.

"I don't know, Allie. But if it's possible the killer saw you, and maybe thinks that you saw him . . . Well, you need to be very careful from now on."

It was a warm morning but Allie shivered. She lowered her voice to a whisper. "Carter, what is going on here?"

His eyes locked on hers, and she could feel how much he wanted to tell her something. But the moment passed and he shook his head.

"I can't, Allie. I just can't."

She was so tired she couldn't bear to argue—she'd had almost no sleep in two days. Resting her head on her hand and closing her eyes, she yawned.

"I want to stay awake and fight off murderers, but I'm too tired," she murmured. "It really sucks being alone right now, Carter. I wish you could stay."

She hadn't meant to say that aloud. A long silence passed between them, but she'd dozed a little and didn't notice until Carter spoke again.

"Scoot over," he said.

She made room for him on the desktop and he climbed lithely through the window, then closed it behind him.

A sudden rush of adrenalin made her feel very awake. "We'll

be so busted if Jules finds out," she said, although she didn't really care.

"Oh, I can handle Jules," he said. Sitting on the floor beside the bed, he stretched out his legs with a groan of pleasure—his lanky frame had been compressed on the window ledge and he'd probably been running all night. "Besides, everything's crazy today. Nobody will notice. Get into bed and let's both try to sleep."

After a second's hesitation, Allie climbed off the desk and onto the bed. Feigning nonchalance, she pulled the blue blanket off the footboard and handed it to him. But when their fingers touched as he took it from her, they both froze for a second.

"Do you need a pillow?" she asked, forcing her voice to be steady.

"Thanks—no, this is good." He sounded calm, but she could see how tight his jaw was as he unfolded the blanket.

Allie stretched out and tried to relax, but her body was rigid—every muscle tensed as if for flight. With a groan of despair she covered her face with her hands.

"I can't do this. I'll never sleep."

Gently, Carter lifted one of her hands off her face and held it in his. His fingers were strong and warm. "Did I ever tell you that I used to have panic attacks?"

Surprised, Allie rolled onto her side so that she could see him, careful not to lose his hand in the process. "Did you? When?"

"A few years ago." He was lying on his back, staring at the ceiling. "I was going through a rough patch and I started having these . . . episodes. A good friend helped me through it. And one thing he taught me was to stop thinking about what was freaking me out, and to concentrate instead on things that made me feel safe, even . . . happy. To force better thoughts into my head. What makes you happy, Allie?"

She thought hard. *Christopher, alive and well and normal. Being part of a normal family. Being here. Until last night anyway. You holding my hand.*

"I don't know," she whispered.

Carter was quiet for a while, holding her hand against his chest. The steady beat of his heart seemed to thump inside her own body. When he spoke again, she could feel the rumble of his voice through her fingertips.

"Imagine . . . we're somewhere else. Somewhere really beautiful. Maybe on a beach with white sand and blue water."

She tried to see herself sitting with Carter in the shade of a palm tree, sand between their toes.

"You're safe here," he said, his voice low and steady. "Maybe later we'll snorkel and watch the fish swim. Bright, colorful fish. Can you see them?"

Focusing on his words, she thought she could see the fish flashing by in the blue water. She began to hear the rhythmic rumble of waves. His voice was so calming, her shoulders relaxed at last as bright shoals of tiny blue, red, and yellow tropical fish scattered across her imagination. Her breathing became more steady. She felt herself sinking into the warm water—slowly and deliciously.

"It's beautiful." Her voice was thick with sleep.

"Yes, it is," he said, still holding her hand.

In her mind she surfaced and saw a ship on the horizon, sails unfurling as she fell asleep.

SIXTEEN

When Allie woke some time later, she was alone, but she had the not unpleasant feeling that Carter had been with her most of the time. She'd half woken several times from bad dreams and in her exhausted daze thought she'd heard him whisper, "It's okay. Sleep."

Sitting up, she looked at the alarm clock. It was just before seven o'clock.

Morning? Or night?

A glance out the window revealed a summer evening. She'd slept all day.

As she stretched her tired muscles, her stomach rumbled so loudly, at first she didn't know what she was hearing.

"Starving," she announced to the empty room.

Jumping out of bed, she headed straight for the door, only skidding to a stop when she caught a glance of herself in the wall mirror. Her hair stood on end, her face was smudged with soot, and she still wore the same clothes she'd put on in the middle of last night, now almost unrecognizably wrinkled.

She made a face at her witchlike self.

Even I can't go out looking like this.

Grabbing a hairbrush off the desk, she forced it through the tangled waves, then quickly changed clothes, hopping up and down on one leg and swearing under her breath when her skirt caught on the shoes she'd put on first.

Still buttoning the waistband, she rushed out of her room and down the empty hallway to the landing, where she stopped.

It was quiet. Unnaturally quiet.

An awful thought crossed her mind: *What if everybody left while I was sleeping, and they just forgot me?*

Even though she knew it was absurd, a rush of fear she wouldn't completely acknowledge made her race down the empty staircase, accompanied only by the rubber patter of her shoes on the wooden steps. As she neared the ground floor, though, she could see crowds of students moving in a subdued hush to the dining room.

Feeling ridiculous, she slowed her pace.

Of course they hadn't left.

You're losing it, she scolded herself. Taking a calming breath, she joined the throngs.

The smell of food mingled unpleasantly with the acrid scent of scorched wood and plaster. As she looked around for a friendly face, she noticed that several of those around her had visible bandages. One hopped on crutches.

In the dining room, the night's chaos had all been cleared away, but the tables had not been reset for supper with the usual crystal and china. Stacks of plates stood on every table, and students were handing them around to one another. No candles glimmered (after the fire she was glad of that). Everyone sat quietly as if nobody knew quite what to say.

She noticed with relief that Jo, Gabe, and Lucas were at their normal table, and she headed straight for them, but then Carter walked up beside her.

"Hey."

As she turned to look into his dark eyes, her stomach flip-flopped. Suddenly shy, she shoved her hands in her skirt pockets.

"Hey back."

He'd showered and changed—his cheeks were still rosy from the water, and his hair was damp on the ends. The tiredness was gone from his face. "Did you sleep okay?"

She nodded, trying to stay cool, as if boys slept in her bedroom every day. But heat rose in her cheeks, betraying her. "Did you? When did you leave?"

"An hour or so ago."

He had a way of talking so quietly, she was forced to lean closer to him in order to hear.

"I needed to change," he continued. She was hyperaware that her arm was rubbing against his. "I didn't want to wake you—it took you so long to fall asleep."

The tension between them was unbearable. One of them was going to have to look away, but Allie didn't want to be the one.

What's happening to me? she wondered. *I can't like Carter. I just . . . can't.*

"Yeah," she said breathlessly. "I mean . . . I had to change, too."

Looking around, Carter noticed that most of the room was seated. "We better go or Zelazny will start shouting."

He steered her to the table and waited until she was seated, then, to her surprise, pulled out the chair next to her. He never sat with her group at meals, and she tried not to let her face show how pleased she was.

Gabe had no such qualms.

"Carter!" He leaned back in his chair with a teasing smile. "You do us an honor."

"Oh, you know how it is, Gabe." Carter shrugged. "Sometimes I just need to be close to you."

Jo, who still looked tired, leaned toward Allie. "Did you sleep?"

"Eventually," she said. "You?"

"Not really." Jo gave a weary smile. "But I think I might be starving. Does that make me a bad person?"

"I hope not," Allie said. "Turns out death and destruction can really negatively impact a low-calorie diet. Who knew?"

"Any news on Lisa?" At Carter's question, Allie felt instantly guilty for making even a mild joke.

Lucas was the one to answer. "I tracked down Eloise an hour ago, and she said Lisa's awake and doing okay. We should be able to visit her soon."

Allie felt herself smile for the first time since last night. The mood lightened, and for a while conversation buzzed in an almost normal way.

Then Lucas's voice rose above the hum. "Hey, did everyone hear about the announcement?"

Allie glanced around the table, but she could tell nobody knew what he was talking about.

"What announcement?" Carter asked.

"Isabelle's making some sort of big announcement tonight about what happened. There's a rumor that they're sending everybody home, shutting the place down for the rest of the summer."

"No!" Jo's voice was vehement, and the murmuring at the table stopped.

Puzzled, Allie watched as Gabe put a hand on her arm and she looked up at him with wild eyes. "They can't send us home. They *can't.*"

"I'm sure they won't." His voice was soothing.

Feeling as if she were trespassing somehow, Allie looked away as he tried to calm her.

The doors at the end of the dining room opened and the kitchen workers emerged in their usual orderly black-clad ranks, carrying steaming bowls and platters. Even though she was ravenous, Allie watched with strange uninterest as they set food on the table. Eating seemed so pointless, somehow, after all that had happened.

But the first bite tasted pretty good, and Allie found the second went down even easier. In the end she emptied her plate and sopped up the last of the gravy with a roll, then sat back in her chair with a satisfied sigh.

"You really were hungry," Carter observed, amused.

"My brother always says I eat like a boy . . . ," Allie said without thinking, and her smile faded as suddenly as it arrived. She never talked about Christopher.

The low hum of conversation in the room grew as rumors spread about the impending announcement, and Allie was relieved that things felt, if only momentarily, slightly more normal. But as she glanced around the table, she saw Jo looked wan and worried as she picked at her food. Before she could say anything to her, though, a voice spoke from the front of the room.

"Can I have your attention, please?"

Dressed neatly in pressed black trousers and a pale blue cardigan, Isabelle stood still until the room quieted. The man she'd been dancing with the night before stood a few feet behind her, his hands folded in a position of calm. His alert eyes seemed to miss nothing. Then Allie felt her heart pound—Sylvain walked through the door and stood nearby, as if he were part of a triumvirate.

Isabelle's face was somber, but Allie marveled at how normal she looked.

"I know many of you were up all night, and I appreciate how tired you are. We are all so grateful for your efforts putting out the fire."

Glancing over at Carter, Allie saw he was watching Isabelle with a slight frown.

"What happened last night was unprecedented in the history of Cimmeria," Isabelle continued. "It is disturbing and will require considerable work on our part to set right. The fire alone has damaged ancient walls. Bits of our history are gone forever. But we will restore this school, have no doubt, and it will continue as it has always done."

Faltering applause from the students seemed to take her by surprise, and she waited for it to fade to silence.

"I am very sorry the events of last night occurred. It was upsetting for all of us. Our hearts go out to those of you who were close to Ruth Janson—she was a lovely, if disturbed, girl, and we will miss all her terribly. Her suicide came as a horrible shock."

Allie gasped and covered her mouth with her hand.

Suicide? What is she talking about?

"We know that some of you might have problems dealing with her death. We are all—the teachers and I—ready to help at any time if you need counseling or just someone to listen." Isabelle's eyes were suffused with understanding, "You don't have to suffer alone."

A murmur swept across the room, and Allie noticed that some students were weeping. Turning to catch Jo's eye, she saw that she was biting her lip and trying not to cry—Gabe had his arm around her.

"A memorial service will be held at the chapel next week. I'm sure those of you who knew her well will want to attend."

After waiting a moment for all of that information to be absorbed, Isabelle continued in a more brisk manner. "Some students injured in the fire will be leaving us tomorrow to recuperate at home, and we wish them all the best. We hope to see you all back in the autumn term. For those of you remaining—the work to repair the damage done by the fire should take about a month, and I fear there will be some disruption in the meantime; it's annoying but necessary. The great hall is, of course, off-limits for now."

She took a step back. "In the meantime, curfew is early tonight—we'd like everyone to be in their rooms by nine o'clock—and you are all to all remain indoors at all times for at least the next forty-eight hours."

As soon as she finished speaking, the teachers clustered around her and the students began trooping toward the door in a low rumble of hushed conversation.

As the table emptied, Allie spun to face Carter, whispering, "What the hell . . . ?"

Tight-lipped, he held up his empty hands.

Allie leaned forward. "I don't get it. Won't the police be able to take one look at her and know it wasn't a suicide?"

He met her gaze. "What police?"

She gaped at him. "Are you serious? You think they haven't called the cops?"

"Haven't," he said. "Won't."

"But . . . how . . . ?"

He just shook his head, and she could tell from his expression he wouldn't say any more. Anger and frustration made her chest hurt; she was cold with anger.

Looking toward Isabelle, Allie stood up. "I need to find out when we can see Lisa. I'll catch up."

Carter grabbed her arm. His eyes contained a warning. "Allie . . ."

"I can handle it," she said, shaking off his hand. "I promise I won't lose it. I really want to know about Lisa."

She needed to look Isabelle in the eye. And to see if she could look back after lying to everybody in the room. After lying to *her*.

"I'll find you after." Carter gave her one more warning look before hurrying after Gabe and Lucas.

Standing at the edge of the group of teachers, Allie waited for a break in their conversation. They were clearly agitated, but they were whispering so quietly she could only make out a phrase here and there.

"Too dangerous . . ."

"Send them home!" (Said with great force by Jerry, who was shushed.)

". . . about Nathaniel."

Then Eloise noticed her. "Can we help you, Allie?"

Everyone fell silent as they all turned to look at her. Allie crossed one ankle behind the other in an unconscious gesture of nervousness.

"I was just wondering if we can see Lisa."

Isabelle stepped through the crowd and put her arm around her. "She's doing fine, Allie. She's awake, but she's groggy. You can see her tomorrow."

Allie held Isabelle's eyes challengingly. Up close she looked more anxious than she'd seemed from a distance—she had dark circles under her eyes. But she didn't back down under Allie's gaze.

"Is there something else you need, Allie?" she asked evenly.

For just a second Allie imagined saying, *"Yes. Why are you pretending Ruth slit her own throat from ear to ear?"*

But she knew this wasn't the time or place to challenge Isabelle. That time would come, though—she was sure of it.

"No . . . thanks," Allie said, hurrying to the door.

Just before she reached it, she heard the whispers begin again.

Outside the dining hall Jo stood alone, leaning against the wall. She looked less pale than she had during dinner, but Allie didn't like the way her hands clenched and unclenched.

She seemed to cheer up briefly when Allie gave her the good news about Lisa, but something still wasn't right.

As the two climbed the stairs toward the girls' dormitory wing, Allie glanced over to see Jo staring down, near tears.

"What is it?" she asked. "What's going on?"

"It's nothing." Jo didn't meet her eyes, and Allie knew she

wasn't telling the truth, but she didn't think pursuing the issue would help.

When they reached Jo's room, Allie walked in with her, suddenly afraid to leave her alone. Jo sat down on the bed, kicking off her shoes in her usual way, but she was wringing her hands.

Allie leaned back against the desk. She spoke in calm tones. "Is there anything I can do?"

"I need to talk to Gabe," Jo said, then she repeated the phrase in different ways. "I just . . . I have to talk to Gabe. I need to see Gabe."

"But we just left Gabe," Allie said, puzzled.

"I need to talk to him alone." Jo shook her head so hard, her short hair flew in all directions. "I'm not keeping it together. He'll know what to do."

Studying her pale face, Allie made a quick decision. "Okay, don't worry. I'll go find him. Do me a favor and just rest for a while, all right? You're wiped out. Have you slept at all today?"

"I'm not tired," Jo said, sitting down on the bed. "I'm way too wired to sleep."

"I was, too," Allie said. "But try, okay? Just lie down and I'll stay here until you're asleep. I'll find Gabe, I promise."

"I need to talk to him." Jo's voice was blurred with exhaustion, and her eyes fluttered shut even as a tear slipped down the side of her face. Finally, she leaned back against the pillows.

"Just rest for a second," Allie said softly. She stood by the open window—the breeze was still cool. "I'll find Carter and get him to send Gabe back."

"How will you find Carter?" Jo's voice was drowsy.

Looking out the window at the lengthening shadows on the grass below, Allie said, "I can always find Carter."

When Jo's breathing was regular and steady, Allie quietly closed the window and shutter, then tiptoed out, closing the door behind her with a nearly silent click.

Downstairs, she found the ground floor mostly empty. All the students who had been milling around had disappeared to their rooms. She wasn't sure where to start looking—she'd never been to the guys' dorm, and she wasn't even sure how to get there aside from going across the roof, which didn't seem like a great idea right now.

A familiar slapping sound caught her attention, and she looked up to see Jules, with a clipboard held against her chest, walking purposefully, her pink Birkenstocks hitting her heels with every step.

She remembered Jo's words when she'd asked her if any girls were in Night School. *"Maybe Jules . . ."*

Allie stepped into her path. "Hey, Jules. How's it going?" She used her friendliest tone, and Jules looked a bit startled.

"Hello, Allie." She slowed her pace but didn't stop, and Allie swung into step with her.

"Do you know where Gabe and Carter are?"

"Why?" Jules asked suspiciously.

Allie attempted a friendly but exasperated approach. "It's a long, crazy story, but Carter has something of mine and I really need it and Jo thought he might be with Gabe. Do you know? Like . . . where they are?"

Jules studied her face.

"No," she said crisply, hurrying her pace.

Cursing silently, Allie rushed after her.

"Look, Jules. It's super important. I wouldn't ask otherwise."

Jules stopped and turned to face her. "They're in a meeting in the classroom wing where you're not allowed to go. But if you hang out near the door, you'll probably catch them as they come out. On the other hand, I don't have any idea how long they'll be."

Allie wanted to shake her, but she wasn't giving up.

"So," she said, dragging one toe in a straight line on the floor, "where are you headed right now?"

Tucking the clipboard under her arm, Jules affected exaggerated patience. "What's your point, Allie?"

"Just that if you're going to that meeting, could you please send Carter back here. Now? Or just tell him I'm waiting here and I need to speak with him. It's really important."

Looking like she couldn't believe what she'd just heard, Jules began walking again.

"Of course, Allie. And would you like me to get you some tea and chocolate while I'm there? Because I've got nothing better to do today than to be your messenger girl."

Dropping behind her until she was out of her line of sight, Allie flipped her off.

"No thanks," she said, her voice cheerful and steady. "I can get my own tea."

Jules's sarcastic voice floated back to her as she turned the corner. "How lovely."

"Thanks," Allie muttered when the prefect was out of earshot, "and you have a great day, too, Jules."

Leaning against the wall with her arms crossed over her chest and the rubber sole of one shoe propped on the antique wood paneling behind her, Allie waited. After ten minutes, she slid down the wall and sat on the floor, crossing her legs. In this spot she was hidden by the baroque marble-topped occasional table next to her, so Isabelle didn't see her when she walked by with her dancing partner a few minutes later.

". . . Lucinda needs to know that Nathaniel is out of control." Her voice was icy with rage. "Last night was unacceptable. She's got to do something about it. At least pick a side. My God, Matthew, people got hurt. *Children* got hurt. This can't continue."

Matthew murmured something in reply that Allie couldn't make out.

"Well then, you will just have to go see her personally," Isabelle snapped as the two walked out of earshot.

Isabelle's words had an electrifying effect on Allie, who leaned forward to peer around the heavily carved mahogany legs of the table.

Nathaniel? She tried to think of a teacher or student with that name and came up blank. *Was Isabelle saying that Nathaniel was the murderer?*

Hadn't she heard that name earlier?

The teachers. One of the teachers mentioned Nathaniel.

She drew her knees up close to her body and wrapped her arms around them as a strange feeling of relief washed over her. At least the murderer wasn't somebody she thought of as a friend.

More footsteps.

Leaning forward again, Allie saw Carter looking up and down the wide corridor.

"Carter." She scrambled to her feet.

"Allie!" He hurried over to her. "What's wrong? Jules said you were looking for me."

I can't believe it. Allie almost smiled. *She did tell him.*

Then she remembered why she was there. Stepping closer to him, she lowered her voice.

"Is Gabe in that meeting you were just in?"

He nodded.

"He needs to go to Jo's room—she's being really weird," Allie said.

Carter didn't seem surprised. "I'll tell him. I could see something was wrong at dinner—he didn't want to leave her, but . . ."

"She's acting very strange, Carter," Allie said. "She doesn't sound like herself."

"I told him that would happen." There was a pause while he seemed to come to a decision. "Allie, we need to talk."

"Sure. What's up?"

He looked around. "No, I mean in private. Can you meet me at the chapel in twenty minutes?"

She looked at him dubiously. "We're not supposed to leave the building on pain of wrath-of-Isabelle, and it's after nine already."

"It's the perfect time," he said. "Everybody's in meetings or gone to their rooms for curfew. The teachers are all distracted."

Allie thought about saying no. The last thing she needed was detention. But Carter looked so determined. Maybe what he had to say would explain some of what was going on.

"Okay, but if I get expelled, I'm so narking on you."

Even though his lips curled up in a smile, his eyes were serious.

"Good. See you there. Give me a ten-minute head start so that I can let Gabe know about Jo. Then run fast."

As he walked away Allie muttered under her breath, "Run fast? I thought you said everyone would be too busy to notice."

Nobody passed her as she paced *(three hundred and ninety-one steps)* while waiting impatiently for ten minutes to pass. At the eight-minute mark, she began walking toward the front *(thirty-three steps)* with feigned nonchalance. The entrance hall was quiet, and Allie reached the door without encountering anyone, but as her hand touched the door handle, she heard voices coming down the hall.

Aside from large candleholders and tapestries, there was no furniture in this space save for one wrought-iron table draped in heavy fabric. Allie darted behind it just as Eloise and Zelazny rounded the corner.

"Will this take long?" Eloise was asking as their footsteps approached. She sounded irritated.

"I hope not." Zelazny opened the door. "But it depends on what we find."

"Where do you want to start?"

As they walked out the door, Allie could just make out Zelazny's reply. "Where we found Ruth's body."

The click of the latch echoed in the empty stone hallway.

In her hiding place, Allie frowned. *What are they looking for?*

At first she thought there was no way she could get out of the building with Zelazny and Eloise now outside, but then it occurred to her that Ruth's body had been found at the back of the building. The chapel was in the woods across the front lawn. Although she hadn't heard all that Zelazny was saying, if they were starting at the back, she should have plenty of time to get to the shelter of the tree line before she could be seen.

To give them time to get away from the front, she counted to one hundred before opening the door. It swung silently on its hinges and she peeked outside.

Not a soul in sight.

Stepping out into the late-evening light, she closed the door behind her with care.

It was well after Isabelle's nine o'clock curfew, and the sun was thinking about setting at the end of the long summer day. Standing on the top step, illuminated in the golden glow, Allie looked upward for a long minute as if she were trying to absorb the light into her soul. Then she darted across the lawn and hurled herself toward the forest.

Once she'd made it safely to the tree line (*ninety-seven steps*), she slowed a bit to catch her breath, then jogged down the path through the darkening shadows. All was silent and dim. When she reached the churchyard gate, the quiet was oppressive.

If Carter's in there, I certainly can't hear him.

Lifting the latch, she winced as it opened with a metal clang that seemed to ring out in the peaceful glade like a church bell.

Instinctively she headed to the yew tree where they'd sat talking on detention day. As she neared it, she saw a foot clad in a dark shoe dangling down. Reaching up, she grabbed it, and it was instantly retracted.

"Hey—you made it."

He was sitting on the same broad branch, his back against the tree trunk. As she climbed up onto the branch beside him, he reached down to help and she could see the muscles in his shoulder move through his T-shirt.

Shifting herself onto a smooth spot, she turned to face him, her knees bent and her feet flat on the branch between them.

"So . . . what's this all about, Carter?" she asked. "Why did you want to meet all the way out here in detention land?"

"Because I didn't want to be seen or overheard."

Something in his posture looked uncomfortable. He seemed to have trouble deciding what to say, and she couldn't catch his eye.

"Couldn't you just . . . come to my room?" She felt her cheeks flush even as she said the words.

"Someone could walk in," he said. "Jo . . . somebody. They'd ask questions."

"Fair enough." She leaned back a little, studying him. His muscles were taut, and worry lines creased his forehead. "What's up, Carter?"

"It's just . . . ," he said, then stopped. After a moment he tried again. "There are some things you need to know."

Well, thank God for that, Allie thought. *Some answers at last.*

She didn't wait for him to start. "Carter, what do you know about all of this? Why are they pretending Ruth killed herself? Her throat was . . . There is no way she did that to herself. And there was somebody out there. I heard them. And Isabelle knows who it was."

Carter had started to interrupt her before she mentioned Isabelle. Now he stopped and stared at her. "What makes you think Isabelle knows?"

Quickly she told him about overhearing the teachers and then Isabelle talking about someone named Nathaniel and the implication that he was involved in what had happened.

"Who's Nathaniel?" she asked as she finished. "Because whoever he is, Isabelle thinks he did this."

Carter raked his fingers through his hair. "I've never heard of anybody called Nathaniel. Whoever he is, he's not in Night School, and he's not a teacher." Allie could see the frustration in his face.

"Who else could he be?" The question was directed as much to herself as to him. "Somebody Ruth knows . . . knew?"

The verbal stumble made her wince. *Knew. In the past. When she was alive.*

"I just don't know."

He looked so lost and worried, she knew he was telling the truth. But she also knew there were things he did know.

She leaned forward until he looked at her. "In the dining hall, earlier, you said they wouldn't call the police about Ruth. How could they possibly get away with that?"

His reply was immediate. "The police have no idea what's going on here, and nobody's going to tell them. They will never know Ruth died here. The teachers tell us it's a suicide, but her body will turn up in an alley somewhere, and her parents, who spend most of their time in France, will tell the cops she was a runaway. And the cops will believe them because her dad's an investment banker and her mum wears designer clothes and those kinds of people don't lie, right?"

Allie couldn't believe what she was hearing. "Are you serious? Carter, are you saying this will all be covered up?"

"Of course it will, Allie. There's a reason you'd never heard of Cimmeria before you came here." His tone was bitter. "Don't you get it yet? Don't you know where you are?"

"You know what, Carter?" Her voice was tight and she swallowed hard. "You're right. I really don't know where I am."

"Then you need to find out," Carter said. "And you need to decide pretty fast who you're going to trust."

He was so intense and angry, it made her nervous. She swallowed. "Carter, what is going on here, really?"

"That's what I'm trying to figure out." He stared out over the churchyard. "Nothing is making sense right now. Look, Cimmeria is a very unusual, tightly knit place. Everybody knows everybody. Everybody is here for a reason. Remember when we had sort of an argument when we first met? You thought I was saying that you didn't have a right to be here?"

Flushing at the memory of her humiliation, Allie nodded.

"We don't get new students here in the middle of summer term who don't have a strong connection to the school. Strong like their parents are on the board. Or their whole family studied here. Something like that," Carter explained. "All I was trying to find out was which one of those you were. But you're none of them. You don't seem to have any connections to the school at all."

He met her gaze directly. "That just doesn't happen."

Clinging to the branch with her knees, Allie chewed on her thumbnail as she tried to process what he was telling her. Evening was encroaching on the summer sun, and it was getting harder to make out his features in the fading light.

"I don't know what to tell you," Allie said. "My parents said the police recommended Cimmeria. Or at least"—she stopped to think—"they sort of said that. But they were all top secret about it before we came here. They wouldn't even tell me where the school was. I still don't know the name of the nearest town. The whole thing was all rushed and weird and James Bondy."

Carter shook his head. "The police in London wouldn't recommend this school because they've never heard of this school. So your parents lied to you. Now, why would they do a thing like that?"

Feeling her heart pound, Allie tried to breathe normally and not panic. *(Five breaths in, four breaths out.)*

"If they lied to me about that—" she began, but Carter finished the thought for her.

"Maybe they lied to you about a lot of things."

SEVENTEEN

This was too much for Allie to handle. Shivering now, she wrapped her arms around her torso. "Carter, if you're trying to scare the crap out of me, you've totally succeeded. So, can you stop now?"

For a long minute he said nothing; then he sighed heavily. "I'm sorry to dump all this on you. And I really don't want to scare you. But I do want you to realize this is serious."

"I knew this was serious the second I fell down in a puddle of Ruth's blood," she snapped. "I get it, okay? I freakin' get it. We're in a lot of trouble. Something messed up is going on. People are dying. Everyone's lying. This school is really weird. And I don't belong here."

"I'm sorry. I shouldn't be doing this to you. I just don't want you to get hurt," he said.

Taking a tremulous breath, she steadied her nerves.

"I have to tell you something." Carter leaned back into the shadows. "I came out here tonight to convince you to go back home."

Her head snapped back and she looked up at him in shock. Seeing her expression, he continued, fumbling with his words.

"I figured they'd let you go because of, like, mental stress or whatever."

She opened her mouth to argue, but he continued before she could speak. "Only I decided that I really didn't want you to. Go, I mean. What I mean is . . . I really hope you'll stay. We'll figure out what to do."

Confused emotions swirled through her.

"I think we'll have to figure something out," she said finally. "Because I haven't got any place else to go."

In the darkness, Allie couldn't see his eyes when he replied. "Then you're just like me."

For just a second she let the warmth of those words wash over her. She wasn't alone.

A cool breeze caused the branches above them to sway, and Carter looked up at the sky where the last light was now fading away. "We better go in. It's getting late."

Jumping down from the branch with athletic grace, he turned to help her down. But she leaped from the branch, landing solidly on her feet right next to him. A half smile crossed his face as his eyes held hers for a second. Then he turned toward the gate.

"Step on it, Sheridan," he said, his voice rough.

"I'm right behind you."

As they hurried back down the wooded path, the sun disappeared entirely, and with the dark came disquiet. Allie looked around as they jogged in the gloaming, trying to sense movement or danger in the forest around them. The breeze blowing through the tops of the pine trees made a mournful hum. She could tell that Carter, too, was aware of every sound—his eyes were watch-ful—and she stuck close to his side, matching him stride for stride. Neither of them spoke until they reached the tree line and the school came into view. They stopped to catch their breath at the edge of the school lawn.

Even though Allie knew nothing was safe anymore, she was still glad to see the school, light shining through its leaded win-dowpanes as if it were any ordinary night. Her spirits rose just a little.

"Okay." Carter was panting after their rush through the woods. "Here's what we do: I think the front door is the least likely entrance to be watched right now. Sprint as fast as you can across to it. I'll be right behind you."

Allie gave him a challenging look. "Like you could pass me."

"Fine then." A wicked glint sparkled in his eyes. "I'll race you."

"What does the winner get?" Allie asked, arching one eyebrow.

Carter chuckled. "I'll think of something."

"Or maybe I will. OnetwothreeGO!" Catching him off guard, Allie took off, her arms pumping and her legs powering her across the lawn. She could hear as he scrambled to react behind her before she gained too much ground.

"That's . . . cheating," he panted.

"Deal with it," she replied, speeding up.

She had to admire his power—despite her head start, they reached the steps at almost the same time. Fighting to be the first to the door, they sparred for space and grabbed the door handle at the same time, Allie's hand on top of his. Playfully, they shoved at each other to be the one to open it.

"Shhh!" Carter hissed suddenly, and they both froze, listening.

Then she heard what he'd heard first: footsteps inside. She didn't dare move. They were all tangled up—his arms wrapped around her grabbing for the door, while she had one hand on the door and the other on his arm. The lean muscles in his arms and chest were hard against her body. Her heart pounded as she inhaled his distinctive scent of sandalwood and cinnamon. She thought for a moment she felt him shiver, and looked up to find he was watching her, his eyes as dark as the night above them.

"I think they're gone," he whispered, his eyes still locked on hers.

His face was so close, she could feel his breath on her hair.

"Ready?" he asked.

Not trusting her voice, she nodded.

Tearing her eyes from his, she turned to face the front, pressing back into the warmth of his body for just as long as it took to turn the handle. Then the door swung open silently—the entrance hall was empty.

"Act cool," Carter hissed, giving her a light shove into the room.

The push seemed to bring her back to reality.

"Always," she replied, raising her chin and sauntering across the stone floor.

He latched the door behind them, and they strolled down the hallway.

Allie was still recovering from whatever had just passed between them, but Carter talked in his usual laconic fashion as if nothing had happened.

"You're fast," he said.

"I've always liked running." She tried to strike the same casual tone. "I like knowing I can get away."

A smile played on his lips. "Somehow, that doesn't surprise me." They were near the staircase now. "Right. I'm off to the guys' dorm. You okay from here?"

"Totally," she replied.

"All right," he said, holding up his fist. "See you later, then."

She bumped her fist against his and then turned toward the stairs. But as he disappeared down the wide hallway, she whispered after him so quietly there was no way he could hear: "Good night, Carter."

Sun poured through the windows on the main staircase as Allie bounded down the next morning, her hair damp on her shoulders. She'd been so worn out the night before that she'd fallen asleep within minutes. She must have slept soundly, because she had no memories of nightmares, or any dreams at all for that matter.

Now, after a hot shower, she felt almost like herself again.

The dining room was busy, if less raucous than normal, but neither Jo nor Gabe was anywhere to be seen, so she sat down next to Lucas.

"Hi," she said, only glancing at him as she focused on the scrambled eggs and bacon piled high on her plate.

Lucas barely waited for her to sit down. "Gabe and Jo have been MIA since last night. Is something up?" Lucas asked.

Chewing enthusiastically, she shook her head. "Haven't seen

them today," she said, swallowing with effort. "Seriously, I'm so hungry."

"Have you been to see Lisa yet?" he asked.

"No, have you?"

He nodded. "This morning. She's pretty beaten up, but she's awake and talking."

For a moment Allie was so relieved, she forgot to eat. "Oh, Lucas, that's great! I'll find Jo after breakfast and we'll go see her."

After rushing through the rest of her breakfast, she hurried back upstairs to find Jo, moving so fast she was nearly running when a door opened right in her path. She had to skid around it as Katie stepped out, blowing on her nail varnish.

"Will you watch where you're going, Allie?" she snapped, holding a hand tipped in perfect pale pink up out of harm's way. "You're always thundering down this hall like a herd of wildebeests."

"Sorry, bi . . . I mean, Katie," Allie said, keeping her voice sweet as she walked by at a slower pace.

But Katie followed her. "Where are you going? Are you looking for Jo?"

Allie didn't turn around to look at her. "Why, Katie? Are you her press agent?"

"Don't be stupid. I was just . . . worried about her."

She didn't sound at all worried, and Allie felt her nerves tingle. Warning signs flashed in her mind. Stopping in her tracks, she turned.

"Why are you worried about her? What's happened?"

Katie blew on her nails with deliberate languor. "Nothing's

happened. I just saw her this morning looking upset. You know, I'm no expert, but I thought she looked like she was on something."

Allie's stomach tightened. "What do you mean 'on something'? Jo doesn't do drugs."

"And I thought you two were friends," Katie said. "Well, if she hasn't told you, then I guess she doesn't trust you. So I better not say anymore."

Curling her hands into tight fists at her side, Allie turned back toward Jo's room. "Whatever, Katie. Go peddle your evil gossip to Jules or your other stupid friends. Just leave me out of it."

"With pleasure," Katie replied, walking in the other direction. "But you are going in the wrong direction. The last time I saw Jo, she was going into your room."

Refusing to react, Allie continued on to Jo's room, but she moved in a quick staccato rhythm as Katie's words rang in her ears.

Why would Jo be in my room?

She rapped her knuckles twice on Jo's door before opening it without waiting for an answer.

The room was empty.

The shutter was open but all the lights were out, and the bed was rumpled but didn't look slept in. Clothes were piled on the floor in an uncharacteristically messy fashion. Her desk drawers were half open, as if Jo had been in a hurry and looking for something.

Determined not to listen to anything Katie said ever, Allie sat at the desk and waited for a moment in case Jo was nearby and might soon return, but after a while she was forced to concede she wasn't coming back.

Heading back down the hall to her own room, she moved more slowly. As she opened her bedroom door, she felt a vague sense of dread.

Nothing was as she'd left it. The light was on, and the room was a wreck. Her desk drawers had been thrown open and ransacked—pens, books, and papers littered the floor.

Allie looked around cautiously before taking a step inside, but the room was empty. As she walked across it, she picked up her scattered belongings numbly, stacking papers and gathering books in a neat pile. By the time she reached her desk, she realized that what she was holding was her copy of The Rules, which had been torn apart.

Someone had scratched a thick line across the front page and scrawled on it:

THIS IS BULLSHIT!!

Flipping it over, she saw a note on the back. The angry scrawl was hard to read, but she knew it was from Jo even before she read the message.

A

Everything's ruined. Everyone's lying. You need to know the truth but nobody will tell you. Come talk to me: I'm on the roof. DON'T TELL GABE where I am.

J

"Shit." Even as Allie breathed the word, she noticed the window above her desk was wide open.

She ran back across the room and closed the door. Her mind was whirling. *What should I do? What should I do?*

Climbing up onto her desk, she looked out the window. The dormitory rooms were just below the attic. She leaned over and looked down to the ground below.

It was a long way down.

But Carter had done it and he said it was easy. If he could, then she could. Taking a deep breath, she cautiously eased herself out until she was sitting on the ledge where he'd perched the other day, resting her feet on the old Victorian gutter beneath it.

"Jo?" she whispered tentatively.

There was no response.

From far below her came voices and the crunching sound of people walking on the gravel drive.

Holding tightly to the window frame, she tested the strength of the gutter she was standing on. It was solid. She turned around so that she was facing the wall and, clinging first to the window and then to slate roofing tiles, she slid along the edge of the gutter for about two yards until she reached another ledge and hoisted herself up onto it, finding fingerholds in the brickwork. Once there she stopped and breathed heavily, looking around.

"Jo?"

A rustling sound above her head made her look up, but she could see nothing. Then she heard a bitter giggle.

"Finders keepers."

Grunting with the effort, Allie pulled herself up onto the next ledge; from there she could see the roof. Jo was sitting on the very top, leaning against a chimney stack. Her hair was a tangled mess, and Allie could tell she'd been crying.

"Jesus, Jo. How'd you get up there? And how will we ever get down?"

Jo waved her hand dismissively. "Don't be such a coward, Allie, for God's sake. Take a chance now and then, why don't you?" Then she leaped to her feet and stood up fearlessly, balancing on the very tip of the peaked roof.

Holding her breath, Allie began looking for a way to get to her. She spotted a jagged section of roofing tiles where she figured she could get a grip and pull herself up, and cautiously made her way over to it. Once she'd begun the climb, she saw how the tiles formed a natural series of hand- and footholds.

On the last stretch, though, her foot slipped. As she felt herself slide, she tried to scream, but no sound came out.

Her fingers grabbed a chunk of masonry and held on. Once she had a solid grip, she felt along the wall with the toes of her shoes until they located a jagged tile.

As soon as both feet connected to the roof, she pushed herself up with a mighty shove, sprawling onto the roof in an ungainly heap.

Leaning back against the broad chimney stack, Jo—who had made no move to help her—clapped sardonically.

"Hooray for Allie. She climbed to the very top of the Cimmeria ladder of success in no time at all. I think she deserves a drink. Don't you, audience?"

Reaching down, she pulled a bottle of vodka from behind her feet and held it out to Allie. It was half empty.

"Have a drink. The audience and I think you should."

Angry now and still shaking from her near fall, Allie ignored the bottle. "What audience, Jo? What the hell are you talking about? And what are you doing up here?"

Shrugging, Jo pulled the top off the bottle and took a swig, making a face.

"You know, this just does not get better with time," she said, putting the top back on the bottle. "I really question Isabelle's choice of vodka. You'd think she'd have Grey Goose or Absolut, but no, just this nasty Russian stuff."

How can she be drunk at eight o'clock in the morning? Allie wondered.

"Jo, have you been drinking all night?"

"No! Don't be ridiculous. Just for the last few hou . . . What time is it?" She turned her arm over to look at her watch, spilling vodka on the tiles. "Oops!"

Allie tried to look calm. "Please sit down, Jo, and talk to me."

"Of course, Allie!" Jo smiled at her as cheerfully if they were in the dining hall chatting after lunch. "I want to talk to you. But I've been sitting for ages. It feels great to stand up and stretch."

Spinning around on one foot, she wobbled wildly. Gasping, Allie covered her mouth with her hands, but then Jo caught herself and laughed. "That was a close one!"

Allie's heart was pounding so rapidly, she feared she might have a heart attack. "Please, Jo. Please sit down and talk to me. I'll drink your vodka. Just . . . sit down."

As if it had only just occurred to her, Jo slowly lowered herself until she was sitting on the roof. The smile had disappeared from her face. Now she looked mournful, and tears slipped silently from her eyes.

"Nobody understands me, Allie. Not even you. You're my best friend and I can't tell you the truth. That makes me so sad."

Sniffling, she picked up the bottle and took another drink. Then she swiped her arm across her eyes and handed the bottle to Allie. Allie tilted the bottle back and pretended to take a drink. Then she held on to the bottle carelessly, as if she'd forgotten she still had it.

She leaned toward Jo. "Oh, honey, I'm so sorry you're sad. Has something happened?"

Jo looked at her as if she were crazy. "Of course something's happened, Allie! Ruth's dead! She's dead. And nobody will tell the truth about what happened. Everybody's a liar."

Swinging her arm up, she pointed at Allie. "And you don't know anything. Everybody's keeping you in the dark because they don't know why you're here. Or who you are. Who are you, Allie Sheridan?"

Allie held up her hands. "I'm just . . . me, Jo. I'm nobody."

Shaking her head vehemently, Jo looked increasingly angry. "No, no, no! That's not true, either. You don't know anything. You really don't know. And that's . . . . stupid. And nobody will tell you. Nobody will tell you." Suddenly she looked up and met Allie's eyes in what felt like a parody of complete clarity. "I know things and I won't tell you."

Allie swallowed hard. "What do you know, Jo? Do you know who killed Ruth?"

Jo narrowed her eyes slyly. "Yes, I do, Allie." She added in a singsong voice, "But I won't tell you. . . ."

"Jo, you have to tell me." Allie's heart was pounding, but she struggled to keep her expression blank. "It's really important.

The police have to know."

Shaking her head back and forth, Jo looked tearful again. "My parents don't want me around, did you know that, Allie? They don't care about me at all."

Baffled by the switch in direction, Allie tried to keep up. "I'm sure they do, Jo. They must. They're your parents. But tell me about Ru—"

"No they don't!" Jo shouted. "My parents love money, and they love New York and Hong Kong and Cape Town. But not me. Not me."

She was sobbing now. While she was distracted, Allie scooted across the roof closer to her—close enough so that she could, if necessary, grab her.

"Oh, Jo. I didn't know." Jo had completely lost it, but Allie had to get her to talk about Ruth. "Tell me who hurt Ruth, Jo. And then we can talk about your family some more."

Jo's glare was accusing. "Don't try and trick me, Allie."

As she spoke, Allie heard movement just below them. Before she could react, Carter appeared nearby, climbing nimbly up onto the roof beside her.

"Hey, ladies." His voice was studiedly casual. "How's it going?"

Through her tears, Jo beamed at him. "Carter West! I love you, Carter West. You're so handsome and you have those deep dark eyes. I would have chosen you if I hadn't chosen Gabe." Then she looked confused for a second. "No, I would have chosen Lucas if I hadn't chosen Gabe. But if that didn't work out, I'd choose you. Definitely. Or maybe Sylvain."

Allie didn't know whether to laugh or cry, but Carter didn't hesitate. "And I'd have chosen you, too, Jo. Because you're the prettiest girl at the school."

Smiling shyly, her face red and puffy, her hair standing on end, Jo said, "Really? That's the nicest thing anybody ever said to me. Give me a hug."

Jumping to her feet without warning, she wobbled wildly, her arms pinwheeling. Allie gasped and reached out for her, but Carter was at Jo's side in an instant, wrapping her in a bear hug and laughing with her.

"Careful, Jo, we're up a bit high here."

She ignored his words. "I love you, Carter West. You're much nicer than Gabe."

He gently lowered her down to a sitting position again, his eyes on her all the time. "You know Gabe loves you, right? Would you talk to him if he came up here?"

"Gabe doesn't love me. He doesn't tell the truth about anything. He's a liar like everybody else." She gave Carter an appraising look. "But I'm not sure if you're a liar, too."

She rose unsteadily to her feet again, brushing Carter's hands away when he tried to stop her. "Carter, you know what Gabe is. Allie doesn't know anything. But you do." She turned to Allie. "Gabe is important—much more important than me or you or Carter. He's in Night School—do you know what Night School is, Allie?"

Carter was frozen, staring at Jo as if he didn't know what to do. Allie shook her head. "No. What is it, Jo?"

"It's a bunch of boys and girls pretending they're knights or soldiers or gods, or something. They think they'll be kings of the world." Jo pointed at Allie. "They don't trust you. Did you know that? They think you're lying about who you are. Where's my bottle?"

Spotting the bottle at Allie's feet, Jo took a quick step toward her. Climbing to her feet, Allie picked up the vodka and looked wordlessly at Carter, but before they could decide what to do, Jo lunged for it.

Carter reached out for her, but it all happened too fast; a loose tile caught her foot, and Jo lost her balance. Falling out of control, she rolled down the steep slope of roof and, with a piercing cry, disappeared.

The vodka bottle fell from Allie's nerveless hands, rolled off the roof, and hit the ground below with a crystalline crash. In the awful moment that followed, Allie could hear a voice screaming far away and realized it was her own.

Carter stared at the space where Jo had been, his face empty. And one second seemed to stretch beyond the limits that physics allow.

Then they both heard a scrabbling sound from the edge of the roof. Before Allie could move, Carter had thrown himself to his stomach and begun inching down the steep roof to the edge. Allie followed suit, and they both saw bloodied hands trying to hold on. They lunged for Jo at the same moment. Carter grabbed Jo's left wrist, and a few seconds later Allie had her right hand. Looking over Jo's shoulder, she could see the steep fall down to the ground.

Now she could hear a high-pitched whining sound from below the rooftop, as if Jo were too frightened to cry. The blood on her hands made them slippery, and as Allie struggled to hold her,

Carter shouted tersely, "Get her wrist."

But even after Allie had Jo's arm in a firm grip, she couldn't pull her up. Because she was facing down the steep slope of the roof, she had to use all her strength just to hold on to Jo without falling off herself. Carter's face was purple with effort, but at this angle even he was having difficulty.

"Okay, let's try something different. Let go of her arm," he said, panting. "I'm going to try and swing around so that I'm sitting up. Then I can get some traction to pull her up. Grab me around the waist and hold on." Catching her eye, he added, "Don't let us fall, Allie."

So frightened she couldn't breathe, Allie nodded her understanding. Holding Jo's arm in an iron grip, Carter swung himself into sitting position with a groan of effort. As soon as he was ready, Allie let go of Jo's arm and, moving as quickly as she could, scrambled into position behind Carter, bracing her feet hard into the roof tiles. As Allie wrapped her arms around his waist, he shouted, "On three, pull me back as hard as you can. One, two . . ."

At three, Allie dug in her heels and heaved.

Jo's torso appeared over the edge of the roof.

Carter and Allie scooted back and then, "Again!" Carter shouted. "Pull!"

This time Jo was fully on the roof, and they both reached for her arms to pull her to safety.

Relieved tears burned Allie's eyes. Panting from the exertion, and she crawled over to Jo. "Are you okay?" She grabbed Jo's hands to see her injuries and winced. "Oh, Jo," she said. Several of Jo's nails had torn clean away, and she had a deep cut to the palm of her left hand that was bleeding freely.

"Allie? Jo? Are you up there?" Gabe's voice came from below them.

Carter and Allie exchanged a look. But it was Jo who answered. "Gabe," she cried out, sobbing, "Gabe, help me!"

"Jo?" he shouted, fear in his voice.

Allie could hear him climbing fast up toward them, apparently taking the same path Carter had earlier.

Leaping onto the roof, he stood staring at them for a second, astonished, before rushing over to Jo.

"What the hell happened? What's wrong with your hands?" When she didn't answer, he turned toward Carter. "Carter?"

Carter's voice was dull with exhausted tension. "She fell off the roof. I think she hurt herself trying to hold on. We need to take her to the nurse."

"Jesus Christ." Gabe wrapped his arms around Jo and lifted her up so that she was on her feet with him supporting her. Looking at Carter over her shoulder, he mouthed, "Vodka?"

Carter nodded. Although Gabe looked saddened, his voice was calm. "I've got you, babe. I'm going to get you down. Carter, can you help me?"

Turning to Allie, Carter said, "Stay here. *Do not move.* I'll come back and show you the safe way down."

Beyond speech now, Allie nodded, and Carter hurried after Gabe. As she waited, she noticed her hands were still sticky with Jo's blood, and she rubbed her fingers fiercely against the fabric of her skirt. As if from far away she could hear the boys lowering Jo down to the ledge and then maneuvering her through the window. There was a low murmur of conversation that she couldn't make out.

Wrapping her arms tightly around her body, she rocked back and forth, counting every movement. (*One hundred seventeen, one hundred eighteen, one hundred . . .*)

The sound of counting drowned out Carter's footsteps, and she only realized he'd returned when he stood next to her.

"Are you okay?" Carter crouched down beside her so that his face was even with hers. She could see the worry in his eyes as he wiped a tear from her face with his fingertips.

Straightening, she nodded.

"Then let's get off this crazy roof," he said.

He helped her to her feet and then led her past the spot where she'd climbed up earlier to a section where the roof sloped more gradually down toward the ledge. It was easy from there to make her way down to a sturdy ledge, and then walk the short distance to her bedroom window.

He helped her up onto the windowsill, and she climbed through onto her desk, banging her head hard on the top of the window in the process. Inside, she reeled around the room, clutching her head as he slipped gracefully through the window and looked at her in amazement.

Despite what they'd just been through, she saw him try not to smile. "Allie, what have you done to yourself now?"

Her eyes watering from the sting, she pointed at her head.

"Come here." He grabbed her arm and pulled her over to him and examined her head briefly. "Seriously, if you survive Cimmeria, you're going to end up with no brain cells at all."

He kissed the wounded spot, his lips as light as a wish. "There. I think that's all the medical treatment you need.

It was probably a coincidence, but her head *did* feel better.

"How did you find us?" she asked.

"Jules said there might be a problem. I came looking for you. You weren't here, but I saw that." He pointed at the note on her desk. "Then the open window, and I put two and two together."

"Thank you, Carter." Her voice was fervent. "I think you saved Jo's life."

"I'd rather you two just didn't get into trouble in the first place," he said, but he smiled. "Now, should we go find Gabe and Jo and make sure she's okay?"

Allie nodded, astonished to find herself smiling back. "Thanks."

"You're welcome," he said. "Now try not to hurt yourself walking down the hall." She punched him in the arm as she opened the door, and then jumped back.

Isabelle stood in the hallway outside, her hands on her hips.

EIGHTEEN

Allie and Carter walked down the hallway, with Isabelle stone-faced beside them. Allie had the feeling they were being marched. There had been no discussion. Isabelle had said, "Carter, Allie. Come along please." And off they'd gone.

They walked quickly to Isabelle's office. She held the door open for them and then walked in last before sitting in the chair behind her desk.

"I've called you here because I want to know if I've made a mistake." Isabelle fixed her eyes on Allie.

"What . . . what do you mean?" Allie replied warily.

"I broke a lot of rules to let you into this school." Isabelle's voice was clipped with anger. "Was I wrong?"

As Allie felt fear uncurl in her stomach, there was a quick tap at the door.

"Come." Isabelle's voice was a command.

Sylvain stepped into the room. He glanced around, avoiding Allie's eyes, then shut the door behind him and leaned his back against it.

Her heart sinking, Allie turned back to the front. "I don't understand," she said. "What have I done?"

"I gave explicit instructions that students were not to go outside, and I find that not only have you been sitting up on the roof drinking with Jo Arringford, you've been out to the chapel as well. I ask you, Allie, what am I to think except that you are insubordinate?"

Allie stared at her, mouth agape. *How did she know about the chapel?*

Carter leaned forward. "Wait a minute, Isabelle. She went to the chapel because I asked her to. I was with her all the way. She was safe."

"And Jo was very upset," Allie said. "She left me a note to find her on the roof. I was afraid she'd get hurt. I was just trying to help her."

Isabelle's glare was icy. "A bottle falling off the roof missed a student by inches. If he'd been hit, we would have been liable. Glass, and might I add, vodka, are scattered around the front door."

Allie was so stunned and angry, she had to drop her eyes so Isabelle couldn't see the rage in her expression. *Ruth dies, the school burns, and she's worried about being sued over broken glass?*

Isabelle shifted her attention to Carter. "And why, may I ask, were you with her all the way? You know the rules."

"After what happened with Ruth and Lisa, Allie was upset. She was thinking of leaving the school," Carter explained. "I wanted her to be able to talk freely without fear of being overheard."

Impressed at how smoothly he used truth to, well . . . lie, Allie shot a glance at Isabelle to see how she was taking it. She didn't look impressed.

"I appreciate that Allie was upset, but there are places where that conversation could have happened in this building, Carter," she said dryly. "And I do not like it when my rules are blatantly ignored, particularly when they have been set out so clearly, and so recently."

Carter held out his hands, palms up. "Well then, I should apologize, not Allie. I was the one who suggested the chapel. At first she even refused to go because she didn't want to break your rules, but I convinced her. If anyone was insubordinate, it was me. But I did it for reasons I thought were right."

Carter's voice was surprisingly confident, Allie thought. His tone was more like that of a son placating an angry mother than a student addressing a headmistress.

"May I, Isabelle?" Sylvain looked at the headmistress inquiringly, and she gave him a brief nod.

"Carter, you not only disobeyed Isabelle's instructions but mine as well," he said, his elegant French vowels curling around each word. "And in doing that, you put Allie in danger, and that is unacceptable."

For the first time in this conversation, Carter looked tense. Allie saw him clench his hands into fists and then very deliberately relax them in his lap. He said nothing.

Isabelle sighed. "Enough. Carter and Allie, this was a serious infraction of the rules I set out last night. I understand that you're both still upset because of what happened on Friday night, otherwise you would both face detention and written warnings. Instead, I am telling you now that another such infraction will not be permitted."

"What's going to happen to Jo?" The question burst from

Allie's lips before she could stop herself.

Isabelle shot her a sharp look. "Let's start with what exactly happened on the roof this morning, Allie, shall we?"

Allie told her about finding the note in room, noticing the open window, and then climbing up to find Jo on the roof, and all that transpired.

"I really didn't know what else to do except to help her," she explained. "Is she okay?"

"Four of Jo's fingernails were torn off," Isabelle said, "and she's badly bruised. All of these wounds were presumably incurred when she fell. She is also drunk. As her wounds are largely superficial and drunkenness is temporary, she's been treated by nurses and sedated. She will remain in the infirmary until we decide her punishment. Her parents will be notified."

"Will she be . . . expelled?" Allie gripped the arms of her chair so tightly, her knuckles paled.

Isabelle looked disapproving. "I will not discuss disciplinary actions regarding other students with you, Allie."

Sylvain walked over and whispered something in her ear. Isabelle turned to Allie. "You may leave now, Allie. I would like to speak with Carter in private for a moment."

Allie glanced at Carter, but he was looking straight ahead as she walked from the room. She noticed that Sylvain stayed behind.

Not all that private, then.

Closing the door behind her, she leaned against it trying to listen but could hear nothing through the solid wood.

Turning, she ran up the stairs to the girls' dorm, stopping at room 335.

She knocked, then jumped back when the door opened almost instantly.

Jules was, as ever, immaculate—her uniform crisp and her hair perfect. "Allie. What can I do for you?"

If she was surprised to see her, she didn't show it.

"I want to visit Lisa," Allie said, "but I don't know where the infirmary is and I figured you would."

"I heard she woke up at last," Jules said. "Go to the ground floor and all the way through the classroom wing. Then up the staircase at the end. It's on the first level you'll come to. You'll know it when you see it."

Allie hesitated, wishing she trusted Jules enough to really talk to her. When she didn't move, the blond prefect raised her perfectly arched eyebrows and asked, "Is there something else?"

"It's just . . ." Allie twisted the hem of her shirt around one finger, "Carter told me you gave him my message last night. And I wanted to thank you for doing it. You didn't have to."

Jules crossed her arms loosely. "You're welcome. Although I'd feel better if you'd told me the truth about why you wanted him. And now, with all that's happened with Jo Arringford, I'm wondering if I should regret my decision."

"But all I did was try to help Jo!" Allie burst out in protest. "I didn't give her vodka or take her up on the roof. I just tried to save her life. I don't see why that's so awful."

"Well, why didn't you come get me first?" Jules asked.

"Why would I do that?" Allie replied. "You'd only try to get her in trouble."

Jules looked exasperated but also, Allie thought, a little hurt. "You and Jo are my responsibility while you're on this floor, Allie. You should never put yourself in danger like you did today. I'm not here to get you detention or yell at you. I'm here to help you. But no matter what I do, you treat me like I'm your enemy."

This came as such a surprise that for a moment Allie was struck speechless.

"I just . . . I thought you hated me," she said at last.

"I never hated you," Jules said. "I just didn't know how to make you see that I'm not the enemy."

"But you're friends with Katie Gilmore, and she really does hate me."

To her surprise, Jules gave a brief laugh. She held up her hand apologetically.

"I am friends with Katie and, yes, she does hate you, but she's just jealous. She likes Sylvain and Sylvain likes you, and she's used to getting what she wants. I tell her all the time she needs to grow up and leave you alone, but"—she shrugged—"she's her own person."

Her expression grew more serious. "Don't judge me by her behavior. Judge me on my own."

Sheepish now, Allie rubbed the toe of one foot against the other. "I'm really sorry, Jules. I've been a complete ass."

"It's okay," Jules said. "I should have sat you down and talked with you before. I'm the prefect, and I should know how to handle this sort of thing. But I'd really like it if we could put that stuff behind us."

With a challenging look she held out her hand. "Friends?"

After a split second of hesitation, Allie took it. "Friends."

"All right, now go to Lisa—she's probably lonely over there by herself," Jules said, stepping back into her room, adding in her more normal, officious voice, "But Jo is not ready for visitors yet, I'm told. And no more rooftop excursions, please."

As Allie hurried along the route Jules had described to the nursing ward, she replayed her conversation with Jules in her head.

How could I have been so wrong about her? Was I that wrong, really?

She remembered Carter and Sylvain both laughing at her for not liking Jules—they seemed to think she was great, although Sylvain agreed she could be difficult.

But difficult isn't bad.

It used to bug her that they defended her, but maybe if she'd completely misjudged Jules, it all made sense.

She tried to remember the things the prefect had said that upset her, and suddenly all she could remember was her baffled expression when Allie got angry or upset.

But still, it seemed odd that Jules suddenly wanted to be her friend. Jo's drunken words from the rooftop rang in her ears: *"They don't trust you. . . ."*

The lights were turned off in the classroom wing, and she felt along the wall for a light switch. When she failed to find it, she walked quickly. Her footsteps echoed as she half ran down the corridor past the doors opening onto vacant classrooms, where empty chairs and desks sat in ghostly rows and circles.

At the end of the hall, an unmarked door had a frosted-glass window through which daylight poured.

That looks promising.

She pushed it open.

Behind it a narrow, utilitarian staircase climbed upward, brightly illuminated by windows on every floor. The first level she came to was a mezzanine between the ground and second floors. Stepping off the staircase, she immediately entered a corridor where the low ceilings and linoleum floors contrasted with the soaring spaces and polished wood elsewhere in the building. On one side of the corridor a row of closed white doors each had a frosted-glass window subdivided by a neatly painted blue cross. The other wall was lined with windows through which light and fresh air streamed.

"Hello?" Allie called tentatively.

Her voice echoed in the empty hallway.

It was so quiet, she felt unnerved as she knocked tentatively on each door she passed and tried handles. Nobody answered, and the first three she tried were locked.

But the fourth opened.

The room was tiny and dark, with just one bed. Instead of Lisa's long dark hair, Allie saw Jo's bright blond head on the pillow.

"Jo?" she whispered, taking a tentative step into the room. "Are you okay?"

There was no response, but something told her Jo was awake. Leaving the door open, she tiptoed across the room to crouch beside the bed. Jo's eyes were closed, but her breathing was uneven.

"Hey," Allie whispered, "are you all right?"

A tear escaped from Jo's eye and trickled down the side of her face. She wiped it away with hands mummy-wrapped in bandages.

"I don't want to talk right now, Allie." Her voice was hoarse and dull. "Please go away."

Wounded, Allie thought about arguing. Instead, she decided to do what Jo wanted. As she opened the door, she looked back—Jo was staring up at the ceiling as if she were already alone.

Back in the hallway, Allie tried the other doors. Two doors down from Jo's room, she peeked in to see a sunny, white-painted space in which two rows of four hospital beds were separated by white curtains fluttering in a light breeze that whispered in through a half-open window. Only one bed was occupied.

Lying under a white duvet on a white bed, Lisa was pale and her eyes were closed—her thick lashes made shadows like bruises on her skin. Her long straight hair was strewn across the pillows, and a large bandage covered one side of her face. One arm was bandaged.

Allie was struck by how thin she was. Did she ever eat? She looked so . . . breakable.

As she sat down in a wooden chair at the edge of the bed, it made a faint creaking sound and Lisa opened her eyes.

She smiled drowsily. "Allie."

Allie smiled back, but worry lines clustered between her eyes. "Hey. How are you? Are you okay? I heard you were awake."

Lisa pushed herself back against the pillows. She had a bandage on her wrist where an IV had been connected at some point, and dark purple bruises stained her upper arms.

"I'm okay. I'm pretty drugged up, I think. I just don't know how long I've been here."

"Not long." Allie had to stop and think about it. "I mean, it's . . . what day is it? Sunday, I think." She flushed at her own confusion, but Lisa seemed satisfied.

"Good. I thought it was longer." She looked out the window and a shadow crossed her face. "But what happens when it gets dark?" She looked so fearful that Allie took her hand and squeezed it.

"Don't worry. You're totally safe in here."

Lisa didn't look convinced, but the drugs seemed to affect her ability to hold on to a thought, and a moment later she seemed relaxed again.

"Lisa, what happened to you?" Allie asked. "Jo said she lost you when the lights went out, and she never saw you again until we found you . . . well, you know, in the entrance hall."

Her eyes darkening, Lisa frowned with concentration. "It's all really hazy. I remember dancing with Lucas. Then we decided to go walk and get some air. We were going to go out the front door because the back was crowded. But then the lights went out. At first it was no big deal—in fact, it seemed kind of fun. The candles were lit in the entrance hall, so we could still see and everything. But then people started screaming.

"Lucas told me to stay there, that he would come back for me. And he ran back to the great hall to see what was happening."

She stopped and looked up at Allie with empty eyes. "And that's it. I don't remember anything else. It's just a big, giant blank."

Allie patted her hand. "Isabelle says you're fine—have you got a concussion or something? My brother had one once, and he couldn't remember falling down until two weeks later."

"Yes, the nurse said I hit my head on something when I fell, and cut myself somehow—I have twelve stitches." She touched her bandage unconsciously.

"What about your arms?" Leaning closer, Allie carefully pushed up Lisa's short hospital gown sleeves so she could see her skin better. "Those bruises—they look like . . . like handprints."

Looking looked down at her arms, Lisa said, "Do they? I have no idea how they got there. And I sprained my wrist when I fell, I guess."

"Did they . . ." Allie faltered and started again. "I suppose they told you about Ruth?"

Nodding, Lisa looked as if she might cry. "I don't believe it, though," she whispered. "How could she . . . kill herself? She never seemed sad or depressed. And she had all these plans for when she was older. She wanted to travel around the world, you know? I don't understand why she would do something like that."

Allie thought about telling her about her suspicions about the official story surrounding Ruth's death, but she didn't feel like Lisa was the right person to confide in. It wasn't that she didn't trust her, but more that she didn't want to worry her.

For a while after that they sat quietly, and Lisa dozed, but when Allie shifted in her chair, the creaking sound woke her up again.

"You're still here." Lisa's drowsy voice sounded pleased.

"'Course I am," Allie said. "You shouldn't be alone all the time. It's too boring. Where are the nurses, anyway?"

Lisa glanced around as if she expected to see them jump out from behind a cabinet.

"I don't know. It's weird—they were here a lot yesterday, but I've hardly seen them today." She yawned. "Tell me what's going on out in the real world? What's been happening?"

Allie wondered how much to tell her. Then she decided that Lisa knew Jo even better than she did.

"Not much. Everything just feels kind of weird. And . . . Lisa, Jo kind of freaked out this morning, and now she's seriously busted."

Lisa looked more alert. "What do you mean? Why is she in trouble?"

Allie told her what had happened that morning on the roof. When she finished, she expected Lisa to look shocked, but instead she just shook her head.

"Oh, poor Jo. She must be so upset. I wish I could go talk to her."

"Lisa, Carter told me she's done this kind of thing before . . . ?"

Lisa nodded. "You know Jo," she said. "She's absolutely lovely. But her parents ignore her. They always have. I think she used to do this sort of thing to get them to notice her. Then it just sort of became a habit, I guess. They got tired of it and sent her here. But she's happy here, so it hasn't happened in a long time. The only thing I can think is that what happened at the ball was too much."

She looked sorrowful. "Gabe was close to Ruth, you know? Jo wasn't so much, but I think she liked her."

Allie nodded. "I guess it makes sense. I've just never seen her like that before. I didn't know what to do."

Lisa reached out for her hand and squeezed it. "Poor you. You must think Cimmeria is a madhouse. It's really not, you know. Not usually, anyway."

Allie put her hand over Lisa's. "When are they letting you out?"

Lisa shrugged. "Nobody's said."

Glancing at her watch, Allie stood up. "I should probably go see what's happening out there. Things have been so weird. I feel like if I'm not there, the whole school could just . . . blow up. It's freaky."

She leaned over to hug Lisa, who felt so fragile in her arms, she barely dared apply any pressure at all.

Lisa smiled up at her. "Thanks for coming to check on me."

"I'll come back," Allie promised. "If you feel well enough to see her, Jo is two doors down. But give her some time to sober up first."

As Allie shut the door, she heard Lisa say: "Don't forget about me. . . ."

NINETEEN

"Hey, Allie!"

The voice came from the common room as Allie walked back across the school building from the nursing ward, and she turned to see Lucas waving her over.

"Hey, I was just with Lisa," Allie said. "She looked good."

"Great!" he said. "I know she wanted to see you. Did Jo go, too?"

Allie shook her head. *Does he still not know what's been happening?*

"Have you talked to Gabe lately?" Her tone was cautious.

"No, I haven't seen him, or Carter or Jo for that matter. Do you know what's going on?"

She lowered her voice. "There was a thing this morning." She told him briefly about what happened up on the roof.

Lucas rolled his eyes. "Oh God. Not this again. She just snaps sometimes. Drinks too much, does drugs, then nicks someone's Porsche, gate-crashes a stranger's wedding. . . . You know. The usual Mummy-doesn't-love-me thing." He didn't look sympathetic. "All that drama queen crap gets old."

The picture he drew was disturbing. It wasn't the Jo she'd known since she got to Cimmeria. Her Jo was fun, bouncy, laid-back, silly. This Jo was mean, selfish, irrational.

"Do you think they'll kick her out?" she asked finally.

Lucas laughed as if she'd made a joke. "No way. Her parents are so connected and so loaded. She could kill somebody and they'd still let her stay until graduation and throw her a little party on her way out."

Before Allie could respond, he continued, "Anyway, at least that explains where Jo and Gabe are—she's in trouble again and he's trying to help, poor guy. But where's Carter?"

Allie gave him the short version of how she and Carter had broken curfew the night before. "I hope he's not in too much trouble," she said as she finished the tale.

"Oh, Isabelle will get over it, don't worry. She pretends he's just another student, but everyone knows she loves him like her own child." He glanced at her appraisingly. "So, what's up with you two, anyway? Are you an item now?"

Blushing, Allie shook her head. "No, of course not. We're just friends."

"Mm-hmm." Lucas didn't seem convinced. "Friends who sneak out after curfew to be alone in the woods. The best kind."

Allie felt her color rise further.

"Don't be silly," she said. "Anyway, I don't know where he is now."

"I hope Sylvain isn't giving him a hard time. He'll be so jealous about you spending time with Carter now that you've dumped him."

Allie had been staring at the floor to hide her red face, but now her head shot up. "How did you know that?"

Lucas smiled again. "There are no secrets at Cimmeria—especially when it comes to relationships. Katie Gilmore's been annoyingly happy ever since Friday night, and she's telling everyone that Sylvain dumped you," Lucas said. "Given that he's being miserable, we all assumed that, actually, you dumped him. I'm guessing we're right?"

Allie nodded.

"Good. He can be a complete dick. That's what happens when your parents are billionaires and you're their only son." Lucas smiled wickedly. "He's not good enough for you. Carter's much cooler."

As Allie tried to interrupt, he laughed. "Whatever. I'm so bored. I might be forced to study if something doesn't happen soon. Total nightmare."

As he was saying good-bye, though, a tall, graceful girl walked over. "Did I hear you threaten to study, Lucas? Please don't. The Earth might stop turning and we're having pasta for dinner tonight. I don't want to miss it."

"Fine then," Lucas replied. "I'll find something else to do—wouldn't want you to miss your spaghetti."

Allie thought she recognized the girl, but she couldn't place her. The two looked at each other expectantly for a moment before Lucas noticed. "Oh, sorry. I didn't realize you two didn't know each other. Allie Sheridan, this is Rachel Patel. Rachel, meet Allie. You should talk. You might like each other. You're both freaks."

"Asshole," Rachel said affectionately.

Feeling left out of their friendly teasing, Allie studied her shoes, but after Lucas walked away, Rachel turned to her with a wide smile that showed off her even, white teeth. "Lucas is cool. He's that guy I'm such good friends with that we can never date. Have you got one of those?"

She had golden brown skin and almond-shaped eyes, and her long, curly dark hair was held back with a thin, braided silver band. Her smile was irresistible, and Allie found herself smiling back easily.

"I guess everyone does," she said, thinking about Mark back in London.

"Totally. It's like a rule of nature." Rachel studied Allie for a moment. "We've met before, you know. Well, sort of, anyway."

"I know," Allie said, "but I can't. . . ."

"At dinner, one night, a few weeks ago?"

Allie had the faintest memory of Rachel sitting at the table with Lucas and not talking much.

"Of course," she said, with false brightness that Rachel clearly saw right through.

"Never mind." Rachel grinned. "I wasn't super memorable that night. I don't usually hang out with Lucas's pack."

Allie liked her voice—it was almost honeyed, with the faintest hint of a northern accent.

"I guess I just feel like I know you already," Rachel continued. "I've heard so much about you."

"Oh, really?" Allie's voice was cautious. "What have you heard?"

Her brow wrinkling with thought, Rachel went down the list, rapid-fire. "Oh, you know, first that you were going out with

Sylvain, then that you weren't; that you're friends with Jo, and then that Jo went crazy; that you're the one who found Ruth's body the night of the ball. . . ." She paused. "Which sucks, by the way, if it's true."

Allie dropped her eyes and Rachel's breath hissed between her teeth. "Yikes." She glanced at her watch. "Where were you headed anyway? Are you busy?"

Allie shook her head.

"Let's go get lunch," Rachel said as they walked down the hallway. "I want to know everything. Along with the whole Ruth thing, I want to know what's up with Jo Arringford. What happened? Did she really throw herself off the roof? The gossip on this is unbelievable. . . ."

To her complete astonishment, sitting in a quiet corner of the dining hall with cups of tea and sandwiches, Allie found herself telling Rachel everything. All about finding Ruth and then Lisa, as well as the entire story about what had happened on the roof. Rachel hung on every word as her sandwich sat uneaten in front of her.

Why she could tell her things she hadn't told anyone else, Allie didn't know. *Maybe I just need someone to talk to who isn't a guy and isn't going to throw herself off a roof,* she thought. Whatever the reason, she couldn't seem to stop herself from talking and talking.

There was something inherently honest about Rachel. She seemed both knowledgeable about Cimmeria and critical of it. She knew everything about everybody at the school, and yet she clearly kept her distance from most of them. Lucas seemed to be her only good friend, but when Allie asked why she didn't sit at the table with him, Gabe, and Jo for meals, she made a face.

"That's just not my scene," she said.

Rachel didn't just listen, though. She proved to be a veritable gossip columnist of Cimmeria intrigue.

"How do you know all of this?" Allie asked at one point.

"I just listen," Rachel said. "You'd be amazed how much you can learn if you sit quietly not minding your own business. Maybe it's in my blood. My dad's a sort of investigator."

"Like a cop?" Allie asked.

"Kind of like a cop."

As the room had emptied and the two of them were alone, Rachel issued a challenge. "Name anybody at this school and I will tell you everything about them—known or suspected."

"Seriously?" Allie laughed.

"Seriously."

"Okay . . . Katie Gilmore," Allie said.

Rachel smiled. "Good choice. Unbelievably rich. Her father's on the board with mine. He's an investment banker, lives in Kensington, shags the housekeeper. Buys the kids off with holidays in the Seychelles and buys off their mum with a black AmEx." She poured herself a glass of juice. "Her brother finished here last year, now goes to Oxford, where he is learning to mint money like his daddy."

"Impressive," Allie said, with a look of respect. "What about Jules?" she asked.

Rachel nodded. "Jules Matheson—very clever, perfect school record, perfect looks—perfect everything. It's a bit scary. Her dad's a bigwig attorney. Her brother went here a few years ago, just graduated with honors from Cambridge in ancient history. Nothing tawdry there. Want to know about Jo?"

Swallowing hard, Allie hesitated before she answered. This felt just a little bit like betrayal. But Jo had never told her much about herself, really. And after what had happened . . .

"Yes," she said.

"Jo Arringford," Rachel reeled off. "Daughter of banker and former government minister Thomas Arringford, who is now an executive with the International Monetary Fund living in Switzerland, with homes in Knightsbridge, Cape Town, Manhattan . . . you name it. Her parents are divorced. Daddy has a new wife, who is six whole years older than Jo. Mum lives in the Cape Town house most of the time. An older brother is at Cambridge. Jo's very bright—with perfect scores. She's had three breakdowns and one suicide attempt—"

"Stop!" Allie said, too late.

"—a year and half ago," Rachel finished.

"Jo tried to kill herself?" Allie whispered.

Rachel nodded somberly. "Christmas break. Her parents . . . neither of them asked her to come home. She stayed here . . . took some pills."

Allie felt sick. "How did they . . . ?"

"Lucas found her. He'd stayed here to spend Christmas with her. When she didn't come down to dinner on Christmas Day, he went up to her room to check on her, and . . . Happy Christmas, everyone." She sighed. "They pumped her stomach, made her see a shrink. Lucas stuck by her. When she was better, he broke up with her."

"No wonder . . ." Allie's voice trailed off.

"What?" Rachel asked.

"After Jo . . . you know. Lucas didn't seem surprised."

"Yeah, well. He wouldn't have been," Rachel said dryly.

"But why is everybody—why is *Lucas*—still her friend?"

"You've met her," Rachel said. "Ninety-nine percent of the time she's the sweetest, kindest girl you've ever met. People forgive her the one percent. Besides, she's one of them."

"One of them?" Allie asked.

"You know, her family's wealthy, her parents went to school here, some of them knew her when she was little. She's Cimmeria all the way," Rachel said.

As Allie sat still for a moment, thinking, a somewhat horrible thought occurred to her.

"What do you know about me?"

Rachel looked doubtful. "Are you sure you want to know?"

Allie nodded. "I can take it."

Obviously uncomfortable, Rachel thought carefully before answering.

"Okay, I know very little about you and I consider what I do know to be unsubstantiated." She paused, looking apologetic. "But here goes. The name Sheridan is unfamiliar to everybody, so you're not legacy unless it's on your mother's side. You're an only child as far as everyone knows. Your parents have government jobs of some sort. You grew up in south London. You have a criminal record. Your parents sent you here as punishment. You're on scholarship. You found Ruth's body."

Allie swallowed hard. When it was all reeled off like that . . .

"God, I sound like such a loser."

"Hey, I didn't mean it that way." Rachel looked worried. "I

don't really know much about you. I don't think you're a loser."

Allie considered this, then shot Rachel a challenging look.

"What about you?"

"What about me . . . what?" Rachel said, puzzled.

"Tell me the gossip about you."

She smiled. "Fair enough. Okay. Let's see. Rachel Patel, daughter of Rajesh and Linda Patel. Born in Leeds. Father Indianish, mother not. Father was a scholarship student at Cimmeria, now an international security expert; works for a couple of governments. Top-secret stuff. On the Cimmeria board—*very* influential. Rachel has one sister, Minal, who is twelve. Rachel's mother has two PhDs—overkill, if you ask me—and runs a private medical research firm not far from here, where the family has a palatial home on several acres, with a pool and a horse paddock. Rachel has perfect scores in most things, especially science, and wants to be a doctor when she grows up. Okay?"

Allie smiled, but her eyes were serious. "Okay."

They were even.

Throughout the next week, the school returned to a kind of battered normality. The distracting percussion of hammers and drills soon became a tedious part of daily life.

Lisa was sent home to recover from her injuries, and without her or Jo around, Allie found that she spent most of her time with Rachel. This meant she spent most of her time in the library, as that was where Rachel appeared to live. So Allie was not at all surprised when Rachel suggested they go to the library to study after class on Friday afternoon. Lucas came along reluctantly, on the grounds that he had a paper due on Monday and he hadn't yet even looked at the coursework.

Rachel had proved to be an ideal study companion, since she knew everything.

"You really are a science geek," Allie marveled, making a face as Rachel explained the biological structure of tapeworms, her eyes fairly glowing with interest.

Looking up from his books, Lucas said: "Why do you think I hang out with her? It's not like she's fun or anything."

Rachel elbowed him in the ribs and turned to Allie. "Science is my thing, but you can help me with French. French is definitely *not* my thing."

"Don't mention French to Allie," Lucas warned her. As they both looked at him blankly, he mouthed "Sylvain."

"Oh, don't." Allie buried her face in her hands.

"Too soon?" Lucas asked.

Allie nodded, but Rachel was struggling not to giggle.

"What?" Allie asked.

"It's just"—Rachel snickered—"you broke up with *Sylvain*. That's like breaking up with, I don't know, God or something."

She and Lucas were both now giggling uncontrollably. "Just about every girl in this school wants to go out with him, and you just dumped him."

Allie felt her face redden, and she looked around to make sure nobody had heard them.

"Will you shut up?" she hissed. "Seriously!"

As they tried to control themselves, with Rachel wiping the tears of laughter from her eyes, Allie turned the pages of her book, frowning.

"Well, he was a dick," she muttered defensively.

That set them off again, only this time Allie found herself joining in. It was, she had to admit, kind of funny. In an awful way.

That night after dinner, bored of the library, Allie retreated to the common room to read her English assignment. But by nine o'clock, she was half asleep, curled up in a deep leather chair near the unplayed piano in one corner of the room with her head resting on one hand and the words on the page in front of her starting to swim. When a piece of paper folded into a tiny square was shoved in front of her, it took her a moment to absorb what was happening.

"Your friend Carter asked me to give it to you," Lucas whispered, grinning and putting a sarcastic emphasis on the word "friend."

"What? Where is he?" Allie asked, sitting up and looking around her.

Lucas shrugged. "I passed him in the hall a few minutes ago. I gotta run. We're playing cricket out front."

Glancing around to make sure nobody observed her, Allie unfolded the piece of notebook paper. Carter's neat handwriting filled only a few lines at the center of the page.

Allie,

> *We need to talk.*

> *Come find me at 9:30, in the library. I'll be in the ancient Latin section in the back left corner. Don't let Sylvain see you looking for me.*

C

Allie's heart beat faster. As soon as she finished reading the words, she folded the note in half to hide its message and slipped it between the pages of her book.

The next twenty minutes went by slowly as she tried to read but found it impossible to concentrate. Finally, at 9:25, she gathered her things, and stretching theatrically to indicate how tired she was in case anyone was watching, she rose from her chair.

"Well, I guess I'm off to bed," she said to nobody before heading for the door.

Once out in the hallway, she stopped and flipped through her papers, waiting to see if anybody followed her out. When nobody came out after her, she headed for the library, stopping to look over her shoulder before opening the door.

Inside, the room was full but hushed, and as she walked across the soft rugs, she flipped through the pages of her notebook as if looking for something. Occasionally she peered at book numbers on shelves, then, as if she hadn't found what she sought, moved on.

I should be an actress, she thought. *So convincing.*

Gradually she made her way past the wall of elaborate paneling where the senior student study cubicles held their strangely violent murals, and then on to the section on ancient languages. The farther back she went, the fewer people she saw. By the time she reached the bookshelves lining the back wall, there was nobody around at all.

Unsure where the Latin books were kept, she moved aisle by aisle, pulling heavy books off the shelves to determine the language. But although she found rows of dusty leather-bound books in Greek and entire stacks in Arabic, she found no Latin.

"Why have they hidden the Latin books?" she muttered. "Is this some sort of clever joke? Like, if you want to read Latin you have to go the—"

"Allie."

The whisper that cut off her random thoughts came from somewhere ahead of her, in the very back corner of the room.

"Carter?" The lighting was dim. As Allie squinted to see who'd spoken, a hand reached out of the shadows and pulled her into the space between two towering bookcases.

"Jesus," Allie said. "A simple 'hello' would do."

Carter didn't smile. "I'm sorry, I just wanted you to get back here before everybody in the library wondered what you were doing hanging out the in the ancient languages section talking to yourself."

"A paper on ancient Rome for history class."

Allie was delighted with her cover story, but Carter didn't look impressed. "We're studying Cromwell."

"I'm working ahead," she said defensively. "Or behind. Anyway. We must study Rome at some point."

"Very convincing."

As she took in his humorless face, her heart sank. "What's wrong, Carter? What's with all the intrigue? Why didn't you just come get me in the common room?"

"Look, we have a problem." Crossing his arms, he leaned back against a bookcase as if he was trying to put distance between them.

"Right," she said. "What's our problem?"

"From now on, if anybody asks you what you saw Friday night, you tell them that Ruth killed herself, okay?"

Allie opened her mouth to protest, but he held up his hand and kept talking. "Because as far as everyone's concerned she did. She killed herself."

Silence fell as she thought about what he was saying. "But I know that's not true," she said.

"Do you?" he said. "How do you know? Because of your background in forensic science? It was dark, Allie. There was a lot of blood. You got scared. But there is no way you know whether or not Ruth killed herself. So quit playing detective."

"Did Isabelle send you to tell me this?" she asked angrily.

"Nobody sent me." She locked her eyes on his looking for any sign of evasion, but he did not look away.

He reached out for her hand. "I'm on your side, Allie. I really am."

"Then I don't get it!" she said, yanking her hand free. "Why are you doing this? I saw what I saw."

He stepped closer to her. "Look, Allie, word is getting around that you were with her when she died."

"That I . . . What?" Allie stared at him.

"And that you were the last person to see her alive and the only person to see her dead body."

She shook her head. "I don't . . ."

He chose his next words carefully.

"Allie, there's a rumor going around that you had something do with Ruth's death."

"How can anybody think that?" she asked, aghast. "That's insane. I hardly knew her. Why would I want to hurt her?"

"It's a setup, Allie." His face was grim. "They're also saying that you got Jo drunk up on the roof, and that you've got . . .

mental problems." She opened her mouth to protest, and he held up his hand. "Whoever is spreading this stuff knows it's not true. They're messing with you."

"But why? Why would anybody want to do that?"

"Some people feel threatened by you."

"How am I threatening?" she asked plaintively. "I'm nobody."

"I've told you before, I don't think that's true," he said. "And neither does anybody else."

"I don't get it." She ran her hands through her hair, pressing her fingers hard against her temples. "My parents are normal people. They're not rich. Most of the people here are millionaires' kids. How can they be threatened by me?"

"That's what we have to find out," Carter said.

TWENTY

The next morning, Allie walked down the stairs well before seven. Her hair was pulled back snugly in a ponytail that bounced with every step. She looked drawn, but resolute.

When she'd left Carter the night before, she'd gone to the bathroom and splashed cold water on her face. She'd stayed there for some time, staring at herself in the mirror, replaying their conversation in her head.

Afterward she couldn't sleep. More than once the thought passed through her mind: *Could it be Rachel? I trusted her. She's the only one who knows everything. I didn't tell anyone else. She loves gossip. But she wouldn't . . . would she?*

She thought that perhaps she'd dozed off at around five, but not for long. When the alarm went off at a quarter past six, she was wide-awake, staring at the ceiling.

And now she had to get through breakfast.

By going down to the dining hall as early as possible on a Saturday, Allie hoped to avoid most people. She and Carter had decided she should go about her day as usual. But she didn't really want to deal with Katie Gilmore and her gang right now.

When she walked in, nobody seemed to pay any undue attention to her, and as she filled her bowl with cereal, she allowed herself to feel relieved. *Maybe this whole rumor thing isn't going to be a big deal.*

She looked around the room for her usual dining companions, but she was so early, nobody was there.

"Hey, Allie. Come sit with me." Rachel sat alone at a table to her right.

For a moment Allie hesitated, her thoughts from last night swirling queasily. But it would look weird if she didn't sit with Rachel.

She's the most gossip-aware person in the school. If she doesn't mention the rumors about me, I'll know it's her.

She made her way over and set her food down. "Thought for a second I was going to have to sit by myself."

"I'm always here this early," Rachel said. "My dad kind of beat the whole early riser thing into me when I was little, and now I guess I'm stuck with it. Abusing children is just wrong."

Rachel had created a toast, egg, and cheese sandwich, and as she poured milk into her cereal, Allie had to admire how she was systematically demolishing it. "Your breakfast looks better than mine," she observed.

"Most important meal of the day, girlfriend," Rachel said, chewing. "Hey, did you know people are spreading a really sick rumor about you?"

Allie froze, her spoon halfway to her mouth. "I've heard something about that," she said cautiously. "I heard it's something crazy."

Rachel nodded. "The whole 'Allie's a psycho killer'? That's the one I heard anyway. I got it from Sharon McInnon—do you know her?"

Allie shook her head.

"Well," Rachel said taking a bite of her sandwich, "I told her to go screw herself."

A wave of relief washed over Allie. *It wasn't Rachel after all. I knew it wasn't.*

"How'd she take that?" she asked.

"She was okay with it," Rachel said. "I think she's used to me telling her that because she's such a bitch."

Allie smiled halfheartedly, but her heart felt heavy.

"Who's saying these things, Rachel?" she asked. "They're such horrible lies—who would do that?"

"I've been trying to figure that out all night," Rachel said, frowning. "Don't worry. I'll get to the bottom of it."

She raised her cup of tea. "With you on my side, Rachel, they don't stand a chance."

But for some reason, she still felt uneasy.

As she walked down the hallway after breakfast, she was lost in her worried thoughts.

I can trust Rachel now. Right?

She'd nearly made it to the stairs when Katie's straight-razor voice sliced the normal Saturday-morning quiet.

"Hello, killer! How are you feeling this morning?"

Allie spun around to face her. "Fuck off, Katie."

"Language." The redhead's perfect lips curved into a vicious smile. "We should have known if they let you into the school, standards would slip."

Her circle of glossy acolytes giggled around her, whispering to one another while waiting for Allie's response.

"What the hell are you talking about, Katie?" Allie fought to keep her voice steady, despite the anger coursing through her. While she was trying to think of the best way to handle the situation, the overwhelming desire to punch Katie in the face was winning out. Her hands curled into fists.

As her internal battle raged, Katie took a step toward her. "I hear you have anger issues." Her voice was low and malicious. "Is that what happened to Ruth, Allie? Did she upset you? Make you angry?"

Allie felt her fist go up before she knew what she was doing, but before it made contact with Katie's pert nose, someone grabbed her from behind and pulled her back so quickly, her feet briefly left the ground.

"Katie, shouldn't you be binging and purging?" Sylvain's silken voice asked as Allie struggled in his arms.

Katie stared at him in disbelief. "You can't be serious, Sylvain. What are you doing? Why are you defending the little nobody? What on earth do you see in her?"

Allie had quit fighting now, but he still held her firmly. The warmth of his body against hers brought back unwelcome memories.

"I see somebody with more class than you will ever have in your miserable life." His clear blue eyes swept her group of friends. "And that goes for all of you. Now you can all go on with your business, please."

After a brief fluttering of indecision, the group began migrating to the dining hall. Katie led the way, her head high.

When they were completely out of sight, Allie wrenched herself free.

"I wish you'd let me hit her," Allie said ungratefully.

"The thought did cross my mind," he said.

"She's so horrible. I just . . . Anyway." Allie scuffed at the floor with the toe of her shoe. "You can go now. Emergency over."

"I am afraid that you will have many problems now. These rumors, they are"—Sylvain swirled his finger around in the air—"everywhere. And she will use them against you."

Allie did not want advice from Sylvain right now.

"I know," she said, keeping her distance from him. "I just wish I knew who was saying these things."

He looked at her seriously. "When everybody is saying it, I think it no longer matters who said it first. But I believe the first rumors were spread by somebody who is known to be jealous of you."

Allie glared at the dining room door. "Like Katie."

"Like Katie," he said.

For the first time she met his eyes. "Is she behind it all?"

"I do not know for certain. But it is something I have . . . heard. I will ask around. And if I find out, I will speak with Isabelle."

Allie didn't want to be beholden to him, not after what had happened.

But what if he could stop this from getting worse . . . ?

"Fine," she managed, staring past him.

"Don't worry about it. As you British say, I owe you one."

She flushed but he continued, his accent thickening as he talked.

"I have to say this, Allie. The night of the ball—I am sorry about how rough . . . I hurt you, I know. It was wrong of me. You are different from the girls I have been with before. I know that I cannot treat you like them."

Allie's cheeks burned, but she faced him squarely. "You shouldn't treat *any* girl like that, Sylvain. Ever."

To her astonishment, he looked humble.

"You are right. *Absolument*. Please accept my apology."

She'd expected arrogance. Even resentment. But regret wasn't on her list.

"I—I'm just—don't," she stuttered.

She didn't want to forgive him. She wanted to stay angry at him. But then a thought occurred to her.

"I have to know one thing." She watched his face closely. "Did you put something in my drink that night?"

He looked horrified, and at that moment she knew the truth.

"My God. Of course not. What do you think I am?" he said.

"Fine . . . I'm just . . ." *Not sorry. Don't say you're sorry.* She kicked the wall behind her. "I just had to know. Because things all got so blurry. . . ."

"Cimmeria wine is strong," he said. "If you're not used to it and you drink it too fast, it will go to your head. And I let you drink too fast, that much is true. And I did try to use that to my advantage. I know that was wrong of me."

His humility and apparent honesty left her with no choice. But she still didn't trust him. She just didn't want to talk to him anymore. Ever.

"Fine, Sylvain," she said, her voice cool. "I'm over it. But just . . . Never again."

Before he could speak, she added, "Look, I'm going to run

away before anybody else calls me a murderer or apologizes for practically date raping me, okay? I can't take any more excitement before nine o'clock."

Just before she turned to run for the stairs, he said. "Be careful, Allie." His eyes were intense. "There is real danger around you at the moment."

"Oh, awesome," she said wearily. "I was hoping you'd say something like that."

Allie would never have used the word, but she hid in her room for much of the day. By Sunday morning, though, she'd finished all her homework and was looking around for something to do. She packed her backpack with a blanket.

Unable to face another meal in the crowded dining hall, she sneaked down just before most students arrived for lunch and grabbed several sandwiches, packing them away in her book bag with bottles of water and an apple.

But as she walked down the hallway to the front door, a group of younger students passed her, and she heard one of them whisper, "That's her. The one they say did it."

Some giggled and others gawked at her fearfully.

What could she do? She couldn't fight them all. So she pretended not to hear and kept going.

When she walked down the front steps a few seconds later, though, one of Katie's friends passed her, and made a wide circle around her as if she were toxic.

"Gross," the girl said, looking her up and down before hurrying away.

Her chin up, Allie kept going. But the lawn was crowded with students stretched out in the sunshine, and she imagined that she could hear whispers and laughter all around her. Before long she was running across the grass and into the forest.

Away from them all.

At the summerhouse she stopped to catch her breath. It was completely empty—she could see nobody. Sitting on the steps, she dropped her head to her knees and breathed slowly until she calmed down.

Why did this always happen to her? For a brief moment she'd thought she'd found a place where she could just . . . be. Where she was safe. Where she was almost accepted.

But it was always the same.

Everybody turns on me. Everybody leaves me.

She wanted to cry, but she couldn't. Staring into the trees, she allowed herself to think about Christopher. He hadn't just gone. First he'd shut her out. Treated her like there was something wrong with her. Like he didn't love her anymore.

Now it was happening again. Only this time it was everyone.

Well. Almost everyone.

In her head she added up a rough tally. She had Carter. And maybe she should trust Rachel. There seemed to be something inherently good about her. And maybe she had Lucas.

So . . . she wasn't alone this time.

After a while, she realized she was starving. Relishing the peace in the glade by the summerhouse, she spread her blanket on the grass and ate a sandwich in the warm sunshine. No whispers, no laughter, no craziness. Later, she stretched out with her head on her bag. She was asleep within minutes.

When she woke up, the summer sun had moved lower in the

sky, and she was now in the fast-cooling shade.

Gathering her things, she headed back up to the school building with some reluctance. Her afternoon of peace had been so pleasant; she wasn't ready to deal with the situation she was in.

Nearing the building, she realized it was later than she thought—the lawn was empty of sunbathing students, and in the hallway she could hear the buzz from the dining hall. It must be after seven; everyone was at dinner.

Climbing the stairs to her room, she felt a pang of hunger, then remembered that she'd thought to set aside a sandwich and some cookies for dinner.

I won't have to face anybody until tomorrow morning.

She knew she was being cowardly, but right now, she didn't care.

As the evening wore on, though, the flaws in her plan became clear. She hadn't spoken to one person all day. She had no television, computer, or video games, and she wasn't at all tired. By eleven thirty she was sitting on her desk staring out the open window, wide-awake and very bored.

Lights had been coming on in dorm rooms around her for the last hour as students returned from the games she'd heard them play on the lawns. Half an hour ago, she'd heard Zelazny's gruff bellow of "Curfew!" followed by the low rumble of voices and footsteps in the corridor outside her room.

Now, sliding across the desktop to the windowsill, Allie climbed out onto the ledge, less timidly than the last time. Her skirt fluttered against her thighs in the cool evening breeze. Following the path Carter had showed her the previous weekend, she had to pass a few windows belonging to the girls' wing before making her way along the ledge to the spot where the roof sloped at a gentle angle and she could pull herself up. From there, she would make her way safely across the rooftop to the main building. There a similar sloping spot made a natural exit onto a ledge that would lead her past the guys' windows.

But some students were still up—light poured from the two windows she had to pass before she could make it to the relative safety of the roof.

When she reached the first window, she peered cautiously through a corner of the glass. The lights were on, but the room appeared empty and she scuttled past it, exhaling only when she was well beyond it.

The next window was wide open. As she neared it, she could hear voices and laughter. Peeking inside, she saw three girls talking. One—a pretty girl with olive skin and straight, dark hair that swung just above her shoulders—sat on the bed facing the window. Allie recognized her as one of Katie's acolytes.

The other two sat on the floor, their backs to her. Even from behind, the familiar short blond hair made Jo impossible to miss. The girl next to her had a distinctive, vivid auburn ponytail.

Katie.

What is Jo doing hanging out with her? I thought she was still in the infirmary.

Astonished, Allie hung on to the bricks and tried to decide what to do. The girls looked relaxed, and they could be planning to talk for hours. There was no way she could pass the window without the girl on the bed seeing her. But she couldn't pull herself up onto the roof from here. She was trapped.

Her fingers were sore from holding on to the bricks, and

she was trying to find a way to shift her position on the narrow ledge to get more comfortable, so she wasn't really paying attention when Katie's words floated out the open window. It took a moment for her to realize who she was talking about.

". . . and I think something needs to be done," Katie was saying. "Isabelle has no right to let somebody like her loose among us. We don't know anything about her. First Ruth and then . . . well. She could have killed you up on that roof, Jo. It's a miracle you survived."

Wait. What is she saying?

She waited for Jo to tell Katie she was crazy.

"I used to think she was my friend," Jo said. "But now I don't trust her at all. That scene up on the roof was so scary. I could have died."

I saved your life! Allie glared at the wall in front of her as if she could cut through it with her eyes.

"Of course you could have," Katie said. "Just look at what happened to Ruth. It's no coincidence that Allie didn't go get help first. She went up there so she could be alone with you when you were vulnerable. God knows how you survived."

"Carter was up there, too," the acolyte said, sounding surprisingly reasonable.

"Yes, Carter did help me . . . ," Jo said uncertainly.

"But why didn't he stop her from pushing you off?" the acolyte asked.

Pushing who off? Nobody was pushed!

"Because he's in love with her." Katie's voice rang with contempt, but Allie felt her heart skip a beat.

He's in love with me? She smiled stupidly at the old brickwork in front of her. *Really?*

"He's done here, too," Katie finished.

Allie stopped smiling.

"We should never have accepted him in the first place," Katie continued. "I've never understood Isabelle's obsession with him. He doesn't belong here. He's not legacy any more than Allie is. Standards are really slipping here. I'm going to tell my father—he needs to intercede."

Her caustic tone seemed to amuse the acolyte. "That should scare Isabelle," she giggled.

"It better. He's on the board," Katie said. "And Jo, you need to write to your father, too. He's incredibly influential. Tell him what happened on the roof, how some crazy new girl tried to kill you and Isabelle won't lift a hand to protect you."

Allie held her breath, waiting for Jo to tell her this was ludicrous. That she wouldn't have anything to do with it. That she knew Allie and she deserved to be here.

"Okay," Jo said.

Okay? Allie thought, betrayed. *Okay? You spoiled little . . .*

Someone knocked on the door.

Allie leaned around to peek through the edge of the window. Jules stood in the doorway.

"Katie, Ismay, can you come with me for a moment? I need to talk with you." Jules sounded stern, Allie thought, but Katie just rolled her eyes.

"Seriously, Jules?" She stood up and walked past the prefect, her every stride conveying irritation. "This is so boring."

I wonder what that's about, Allie thought, watching them go.

The acolyte, who Allie now knew must be Ismay, was right on

her heels. Jo trailed behind them.

Though she was overwhelmed with the desire to throw herself into the room and demand an explanation from her ex–best friend, Allie waited right where she was. As soon as they were out of sight, she shot past the window like a Fury. A few seconds later she was climbing across the roof to the main building and then skidding down the slope to Carter's open window.

Sitting at his desk working, he didn't notice her right away. She studied his face, taking in his fair skin and slightly mussed straight dark hair. The way his long lashes cast feathery shadows against his cheeks. She liked his hands—his fingers were long but strong, his nails square and neat.

She felt an unexpected warmth spread through her as she watched him.

He really is lovely. . . .

As if he'd heard her thoughts, Carter looked up and their eyes met.

With a startled shout he leaped from his chair so quickly it fell over. Allie tried not to giggle out loud as he slowly returned to his desk and peered out the window.

"Allie?" He looked embarrassed and grumpy, although she thought the latter was probably just to hide the former. "What the hell . . . ?"

"Hi," she whispered. "I can't sleep. Want to come out and play?"

He opened the window. "You're crazy. Get inside before you kill yourself."

"Katie is such a *bitch*," she complained as she clambered across his desk.

Carter raised his eyebrows. "No argument."

"You don't understand." Allie paced the floor. "I heard her talking through a window. She's trying to 'finish us' and she hates us both and she's planting awful thoughts in Jo's head about me—that I tried to kill her on the roof. I think she's behind these horrible rumors about Ruth."

As she ranted, he closed the window behind her, then picked the wooden chair up off the floor and propped it under the handle of his bedroom door, testing it for stability.

Finally he turned back to her. "What exactly did you hear?"

She told him what had happened that morning—with Katie and her friends, and how Rachel had known all about the gossip by seven a.m. His eyes narrowed when she mentioned Sylvain's intervention, but he said nothing. As she told him about what had transpired in Katie's room, his face darkened. She could see he was trying to stay calm.

"Okay, so there are two possibilities," he said. "Either she didn't spread the first rumor and she's just taking advantage of it to spread more rumors about you and Jo, or she did spread the first rumor and this new rumor is just part of her evil plan." He punched his right fist into his left palm. "That socialite bitch."

"What should we do?" Allie asked. Then for the first time she paid attention to where she was. "And why is your room bigger than mine?"

He had two bookshelves to her one, and space for an extra chair in the corner. While the walls were whitewashed like hers, all the fabrics in the room were dark blue, giving it a more masculine feel. Allie noticed that all his shelves were filled with well-thumbed books. And that a battered football rested on the seat of the spare chair. She pointed at the neatly made bed and he nodded. Sitting down on the edge, she stretched out her legs.

"I've been here longer," he said absently.

Turning the desk chair to face her, he sat across from her. "These rumors are intended to cause the most damage possible, even to get you to leave the school. This feels like a campaign to me. To get rid of you."

Allie slid forward on the bed until her knees nearly touched his.

"Okay, Carter. Enough with secrecy and all that crap. It's time. Tell me about this place."

"Allie . . ."

He leaned away from her, but she ignored the warning look he gave her.

"Uh-uh. Not this time. Someone *died*. And somebody else is trying to ruin my life here. For all I know, whoever killed Ruth could go after me next. You know things. You are allegedly my friend. So tell me everything. Now."

Jumping up, he stood against the wall by the door, his previously relaxed posture now all tight insecurity, his arms crossed.

"You don't understand, Allie. I can't. If I did—and if anybody ever found out . . ." He shook his head. "It's just bad. Trust me."

"How can I trust you if you won't tell me the truth?" she asked. Under her breath she muttered, "Maybe I should just go ask Sylvain. . . ."

Carter's cheeks reddened. He stalked back over to where she sat and leaned over her. "Do you want to know what you mean to Sylvain? Well, I'll tell you. Every year he picks a pretty new first year girl, shags her, and dumps her. It's his thing. And each one thinks she's *so* special. The last one left school afterward because everyone made fun of her. But when her parents withdrew their offer of a generous donation to Cimmeria, Isabelle warned him never again." He spat the words out at her as if it sickened him to say them. "So that's who you are to him, Allie. His newest naive conquest. Who thinks the gorgeous rich boy chose her. Just her."

"Stop it!" Feeling sick to her stomach, Allie shoved him away and jumped to her feet. "If that's true, why didn't you tell me before, Carter? Why didn't Jo tell me?"

They stood inches from each other, both furious. She could feel his breath against her face.

"I tried," he said. "I just . . . didn't think you'd believe me." But she wasn't letting him off that easily.

"From what I hear, you're a bit of a lady-killer yourself. How is what Sylvain does any different from you?"

He winced but didn't look away. "The difference is Sylvain does it to be cruel. I don't want to hurt anybody. I'm just looking for the right person."

"People say you're into one-night stands," she said accusingly.

"Are these the same people who say you killed Ruth?"

She hadn't thought of that.

"Point taken," she conceded. "So, you tell me. Is what they say about you a lie?"

His eyes locked on hers. "Yes, Allie. It's a lie. Or at least an exaggeration. I got this . . . I guess, reputation . . . because if I go out with someone and I can tell they're not the right one for me, I break up with them right away. And they're never the right person." His eyes seemed to hide nothing from her—she saw only vulnerability. "I don't want to hurt anybody, Allie. I really don't.

I just want the right girl."

Standing so close to him, she thought she could feel the warmth of his body crossing the space between them, and without really knowing why she was doing it, she held her hand up, her palm facing him, her fingers spread.

"Okay. I believe you."

He pressed his palm against hers. "Thank you," he said softly.

"For what?"

"For believing."

He glanced at their hands quizzically. "Is this some sort of London thing?"

As Allie laughed, he entwined his fingers with hers. Her laughter fading, she looked into his eyes questioningly.

"You big city kids have all these crazy traditions," he said.

"Yeah," she said, her voice low. Her throat tightened. She thought of Katie saying *"He's in love with her."* "You country kids don't know what you're missing."

"I've heard that. And, you know, someday"—he pulled on her hand until she took a step toward him—"I'd really like to find out."

Their faces were so close now it was inevitable—when he brushed his lips very lightly against hers, she gave a little gasp, then reached her hands behind his neck and pulled his head down.

The warmth of his mouth exhilarated her as, with a groan of surrender, he wrapped his arms around her, his lips moving in delicate butterfly kisses along her chin.

"I've wanted to do this," he whispered when he'd reached her ear, "for so long."

Her entire body tingled, and she pulled him harder against her. Heat spread through her as though he radiated it. His kisses were more insistent now, as if he would devour her.

Suddenly he wrenched himself away with obvious effort, walking as far away from her as he could get within the room's limited boundaries. He stood against the far wall, his eyes dark and his hair rumpled where her fingers had tangled it.

He was breathing heavily, and she knew what he'd say before he spoke. "God, I hate to do the grown-up thing, but we should—"

"No, you're right." They stared at each other for a moment. "Okay," she said. "So. There's that."

"Yes. There's absolutely that." Carter laughed—a warm, intimate chuckle. "You just . . . stay over there for a minute, if that's okay. Now, what were we talking about before we were so . . . interrupted?"

His smile had almost as strong an impact on her body as his kiss—she felt like she was the only girl in the universe. It was hard to focus on his words.

"I was . . . I think I was asking you to tell me everything," she said.

His smile faded. She was sorry to see it go, but the conversation needed to happen.

"There are reasons why I haven't told you everything, Allie. It's not just that I'm a jerk who wants to keep things from you."

"I get that." They were calmer now, and she felt like he was really listening. "But I think I need to know where I am. What this school is about. People are getting hurt. I don't want to get hurt, Carter."

He looked troubled. "I keep my word. It's the one thing you

can say about me. If I tell you, I'm breaking a vow. "

"But aren't you starting to wonder just who you made a vow to?" Allie asked. "Tell me, Carter. Tell me about Night School. And I swear I will never tell another living soul."

Carter's eyes searched her face as if he were looking for a sign telling him the right thing to do. Finally, he sat down in the chair, gesturing at the bed.

"You may as well sit down." He sighed. "This could take some time."

TWENTY-ONE

"The first thing you need to know is that I don't know everything," Carter said. "I'm a new initiate as of last term. There's a full year of training before they accept you."

"Okay." Allie sat on the bed with her arms wrapped around her knees, her eyes watching his intently. "But you grew up here. You must know something."

"I know what they've told me," he said. "And it's pretty serious stuff."

He leaned his elbow on the back of the chair. "All of this—the school, Night School—is the first step to a larger organization. Kids are recruited to Cimmeria specifically to join Night School, because people in this bigger organization want them for life—does that make sense?"

"Kind of. . . ."

But she must have looked confused, because he tried again.

"Okay, what I'm saying is, you start Night School at Cimmeria, then you continue it at college—and if you're in Night School, you *will* get into Oxford or Cambridge, without doubt. And you're a member of a club there. Then, when you graduate, you go work for a company run by a member of the organization. And eventually you run a company that hires people who started in Night School. And you do what you're told. What I'm saying is this is *for life.*"

Frowning, Allie tried to process what he was telling her. "What is this bigger group called?"

He shook his head. "I have no idea. I'm not sure it has a name. It just . . . is."

"So . . ." Allie was still trying to understand. "You're in Night School now, and when you finish at Cimmeria, you'll go, let's say, to Oxford, where you'll be in the university-level version of it; then you'll go to work and get really rich. . . . I don't get it. Wouldn't that happen anyway, because you've got all these connections and education? What's the point?"

Carter lowered his voice to a whisper.

"I can only tell you what they tell us, Allie. And what they tell us is that this organization and a few just like it elsewhere . . . they run the world."

"Run the . . ." Allie stared at him. "What do you mean?"

"I mean presidents, prime ministers, MPs, ministers, CEOs, journalists—the people you see on TV, the ones you read about in newspapers, people who run the world—Night School is everywhere."

As Carter ticked the professions off, she frowned doubtfully. "What? All of them?"

"No. But a lot of them. And at all levels. Night School runs media corporations. Government departments. Militaries. Everything. It's everywhere."

"And it all starts here?" she asked doubtfully. "Carter, that's impossible."

"It's not just here, though. We have exchange students all the time from schools in other countries—like Sylvain."

She tried to process what he was telling her. "So, it's like a giant kind of . . . conspiracy?"

"Yes."

Stunned, she searched his face for any sign that it was all some elaborate joke. But there was nothing.

"How does it work?"

He shook his head. "That goes beyond what they tell the neos."

"Neos?"

"Neophytes," he explained. "It's what they call us the first year."

"How embarrassing," she said dryly. "So what *do* they tell you?"

"We get the big marketing pitch—the whole 'society of power' speech—and a fancy dinner with a bunch of rich guys in tuxedoes who used to be us," he said.

"Okay, but what do you do?" she asked, wrinkling her brow. "I mean, here, at Cimmeria. All this training you all do, what is it?"

He took a deep breath. "God, it's hard to explain. They've got all these theories of war and strategy being the basis of everything—so, I know it sounds weird, but the first thing they do is teach us how to play chess. We play chess for *days*. While they feed us all this stuff about how knights are warriors and pawns are foot soldiers. . . ."

"Wait, I've heard that before." She stared at him. "Jo said those exact words to me a few weeks ago. Is Jo . . . ?"

"In Night School?" He looked uncomfortable. "Not exactly. Her dad is, and he's insisting that she should be, too, but Isabelle think she's not ready. She has these . . . problems, you know. So they've given her, like, introductory to introductory training, and Gabe keeps an eye on her."

"What? Her own boyfriend?" Allie was horrified. "Is, like . . . spying on her for these guys?"

"No!" Then he paused. "Well, sort of, I guess. But it's not like he's pretending to like her."

"No," she said sarcastically. "He would never do something like that."

He held his hands up in surrender.

"So," she continued, "after chess, it's like . . . what? War games? Is that what you're doing out in the woods at night?"

He nodded. "More or less. Combat training, techniques in subterfuge. That kind of thing."

"Crazy. Why are they teaching you that? You're just kids."

"War is a strategy for life and for business. And some of us will end up running militaries. And governments." He shrugged as casually as if he were talking about a math test. "Look, this is what Cimmeria is about, to an extent. And everybody at this school is connected to it in some way."

He gave her a direct look. "Except, apparently, you."

"Except me," she said, frowning.

"So," he said, "what are you doing here?"

Allie sat staring at him for a long moment. Then she slid to the edge of the bed, poised to bounce off it.

"I don't know. But I'm ready to find out. Are you with me?"

"In theory . . . ," he said cautiously, "yes. What do you have in mind?"

Her face was animated with a mixture of excitement and determination. "You know how yesterday in the library we decided I should pretend nothing was going on and nobody was talking about me, while you tried to find out what was happening?"

He nodded.

"Well, balls to that. Whatever is going on here, the place to find out is Isabelle's office. Let's go there. Now."

"No way!" He looked shocked. "That's insane, Allie. If we got caught in Isabelle's office, they'd kick us both out. No question. It would ruin everything."

"Why do you care?" Allie asked. "I thought you didn't buy into that stuff?"

A look flashed across his face that she couldn't quite read. "I don't buy into all of it," he said, avoiding her gaze. "But that doesn't mean I want to get kicked out. This is my home, Allie. I have no place else to go. And if I don't go on to Oxford from here, where will I end up? You've got your family. I've got no one."

"But here's the thing. I know how we can avoid all of that," Allie said, jumping to her feet.

"How?"

"By not getting caught."

She headed for the door.

"Allie . . ." She ignored his warning tone and opened the door, but he reached past her to close it again. "Wait a minute."

He lowered his voice to a whisper. "What exactly are you looking for? What do you think you'll find?"

"Two things," she said. "Why Ruth died. And why I'm here."

When he didn't appear convinced, she raised her chin defiantly. "I'm going, Carter. I'm doing this now. I'm not waiting for later, or for someone to maybe someday decide to tell me this information out of simple human kindness. That's not going to happen. So are you coming with me? Or is being the future president of Cimmeria Incorporated really that important to you?"

He stared into her eyes for a long minute, then seemed to make up his mind.

He opened the door.

TWENTY-TWO

"Is that your foot? Or somebody else's?" Allie's whisper was so quiet, it seemed to fade into the inky darkness around her.

"Of course it's mine," Carter whispered. "Who else's foot could it be?"

They were tiptoeing down the grand hallway from the staircase toward Isabelle's office. Around them the old building was unnaturally quiet—it didn't creak or settle. It was as if it held its breath.

Carter had explained that, as part of their training, Night School students patrolled the hallways of the school at night, but not constantly. So on the way down, they'd hidden in an alcove on the second floor and waited until a pair of shadows walked by, silent as death.

After that, Carter figured they had more than an hour before the patrol would be back again. So they'd slipped down the stairs, skipping the creaky step near the bottom.

Now they stood outside Isabelle's nearly invisible office door, waiting until they could be certain that the headmistress wasn't inside.

"Why would she be in there?" Allie whispered. "It's one o'clock in the morning."

Carter shrugged, but the look on his face told Allie it was possible.

After hearing nothing through the door, he finally decided it was okay to go in. With his hand on the door handle, he held her eyes.

"Three," he whispered, "two . . . one . . ." He turned the handle.

The door was locked.

Carter swore under his breath and Allie stifled a giggle. "Plan B?"

Reaching into his pocket, he pulled out a twisted wire. "Two minutes," he said. "Time me."

Leaning down, he pushed the wire into a lock Allie couldn't see and moved it gently with his fingertips until, without warning, the door gave way.

"Whoa. Less than two," she said admiringly. "Where did you learn to do that?"

He gave her a look. "Where do you think?"

"Church?"

He smiled and pushed the door. It swung open with a sound like a sigh.

"So," Allie whispered, walking into the office, "how does burglary make you a better future prime minister?"

Closing the door behind them, Carter took a cream-colored cashmere throw off one of the leather chairs and pressed it into the base of the door.

"I have no idea," he said.

Then, with a click that seemed to echo in the quiet school, he turned on a small desk lamp. Standing beside the desk, the two of them looked around the headmistress's office. An empty teacup with the Cimmeria seal sat on the desk amid stacks of papers. The air smelled faintly of Isabelle's distinctive citrus perfume.

"I feel like a criminal . . . again," Allie whispered, suddenly unsure.

"Oh no, you don't." Carter said. "We're here now. Let's get this over with."

She knew he was right. It was too late to turn back now. But now that she was here among Isabelle's things, she felt slightly sick thinking about how hurt the headmistress would be if she found out. In the past when she'd broken the law, she'd *wanted* to hurt someone.

What's changed?

"I'll take the bookshelves. You start with the cabinets." Carter's voice shook her from her reverie, and she moved toward the low cabinets. Kneeling in front of the first one, she hated herself as she opened it.

For half an hour they worked in hurried silence. Carter started on the left side of the room and moved from shelf to shelf, looking for anything unusual. Allie sat on the floor, looking through the low cabinets.

The first one held mostly maintenance records, phone bills, receipts—nothing of interest. The second one held academic files, graded papers, and other bits of schoolwork from years past.

As soon as Allie opened the third cabinet, she knew she was on the right track.

"Bingo," she whispered.

Carter looked up. "What is it?"

"Student records."

He stopped what he was doing and walked over. Looking for Ruth's records, Allie started to flip through the Js. Then stopped.

"It's not here."

He looked puzzled. "It has to be. Look again."

"Janson," Allie muttered under her breath. "J-a-n-s-o-n. No. It's not here."

"It could be in the wrong place or something," he said. "Start at the beginning."

Impatiently, Allie flipped through the neatly labeled manila folders, passing familiar names as well as many she'd never heard of, until she reached one that stopped her.

"Found it?" Carter asked.

"No . . . it's mine."

Her fingertips rested on a thick file with her name written on the top in black ink.

"Pull it."

She could hear the tension in his voice.

"Do you think?" she asked.

"Two things, remember?" he said. "We're looking for two things."

With reluctance, she set her file aside and went through the rest of the records, lingering on the one labeled "Carter West."

"You want yours?"

Shaking his head, he said curtly, "I know what it says."

"Okay." Allie flipped through the last few files. "Ruth's file isn't here."

"They must have pulled it." Carter walked over to Isabelle's desk. "It could be in the desk—I'll start looking. You look through your own file."

Allie sat on the floor, staring at the blank expanse of the folder cover, her fingers poised to open it. Now that the moment had come, she was scared.

Do I really want to know the truth?

From above her came the sound of Carter shuffling through pages and opening drawers. He was moving quickly—she knew she didn't have much time.

She opened the folder.

The first few pages were all the normal things: admission forms with no surprises, transcripts from her last two schools. Looking at her old grades, she winced and quickly flipped the page.

Then things got weirder. A copy of her birth certificate. Photos of her as a young child with her parents. A photo of her as a baby with a woman she didn't recognize, laughing at the camera.

A letter addressed to Isabelle in her mother's handwriting hurt her heart, and she held it up into the light to see it better. Then her breath caught. Words and phrases seemed to jump out at her.

"We need your help, Izzy" ". . . we don't know what to do" "Christopher could have been taken . . ." "We don't want to involve Lucinda, but we think the time has come . . ." ". . . danger . . ."

"We need your help, Izzy?" She calls her "Izzy"?

She turned the page. This one—on thick, expensive paper—contained a short note in an elegant handwriting she did not recognize. It was dated July this year.

Isabelle,

Admit my granddaughter immediately under Protect Proto-col. I believe Nathaniel is a threat to her as he was to Christopher. She will be safer with you than in London. As per the protocol, the school should also increase security patrols.

Be careful, Isabelle. Nathaniel will be watching you, too.

I will be in touch soon.

Lucinda

For just a moment Allie stopped breathing.

Why is that note in my file? Who is Lucinda?

Increasingly anxious, she turned the page. The next few pages were photocopies of old Cimmeria school records, but they were not her own.

They were her mother's.

Her hands shaking, Allie flipped through them quickly, scanning each page and then turning it. Scanning and turning. Scanning and turning.

The last page was a note on a yellowed card. She recognized the handwriting from the earlier note from Lucinda.

G,

So pleased to hear my daughter is doing well in Night School. Blood will out, as they say. I'd appreciate weekly updates on her progress from now on.

L

Allie dropped the file as if it could bite. But Carter's voice interrupted her whirling thoughts.

"Hey. You better come look at this."

His tone was ominous, and she hurried over to where he stood at the desk, holding a paper under the light. Allie peered over his shoulder to see it.

When she'd read the whole thing, she looked up at him, stunned.

"Oh my God, Carter. What are we going to do?"

They couldn't linger in Isabelle's office. Allie returned her file to its place in the cabinet while Carter straightened the desk. He folded the throw back over the arm of the leather chair and then switched off the light.

They both leaned against the door, listening for what seemed to Allie like a very long time. Carter opened the door and slipped outside while she waited. When he was sure the hallway was empty, he came back for her. They closed the door behind them, standing frozen as the click of the latch sliding into place echoed in the preternatural hush like a shout.

It was nearly two in the morning. If they were caught in the hallway now, they'd have no excuses at all.

They'd only walked about twelve feet when, without warning, Carter stopped. Holding out his arm just as they rounded a corner toward the staircase, he held Allie back. After looking around, he slipped into the thick darkness under the stairs; he didn't need to say a word—she was right on his heels.

They pressed together in the corner, and he whispered almost soundlessly into her ear.

"Someone's coming."

With her head against his shoulder, inhaling his clean scent of sandalwood, she nodded, then turned so she could see what was happening around them. His arms were wrapped around her protectively.

Now she could hear the footsteps, too. Very quietly, someone was padding down the hallway toward them.

Holding her breath, Allie tried to make her heart beat more softly.

They watched as a shadowy figure walked past them to Isabelle's office door and tried the handle. Finding it locked, the figure paused for a moment as if considering the options before walking away.

When Allie looked up at Carter questioningly, he pressed his finger against her lips. For five minutes they didn't move. Then, after they'd stepped out to ensure the hallway was completely empty, Carter took her hand and they hurried up the stairs.

They made it unseen down the empty hallway of the girls' dorm into Allie's room, where she pushed the door closed behind them and clicked on the desk lamp.

"Who was that?" she whispered.

"I couldn't see him," Carter said. "He wore a school uniform, though. So it's one of us."

"Do you think he saw us?" she asked.

He shook his head. "He never looked our way."

At that she relaxed a little. "I guess we're not the only ones trying to figure out what's really going on around here."

The adrenaline that had propelled her through the night's activities seemed to flood out of her body all at once, and she yawned hugely.

"We both need some sleep," Carter said. "Tomorrow's a school day, after all."

"But we need to talk about all of this." Allie tried to force herself to feel more awake. "My file and that letter . . ."

"After classes tomorrow—meet me at the chapel," he said. "And I'm going to breakfast at seven—go at the same time and I'll protect you from the gossipers. In the meantime . . . get some sleep."

He opened the window, then turned back to her. "One more thing. Earlier tonight? In my room?"

Her eyes shot up to his, almost challengingly. If that was his cue to tell her it was all a mistake, she was ready.

"Was fantastic." He smiled that sexy smile of his with his hair falling into his eyes and climbed through the window.

A flood of warmth spread through her whole body. All the stress of what they'd learned tonight faded away, and she smiled at the darkness.

"Right back at ya," she said as she closed the window behind him.

On Monday morning Allie walked to breakfast at seven o'clock precisely. Carter stood waiting for her at the dining room hall.

"Is my lady ready for her escort?" he asked as she walked up.

"Your lady could murder a bacon sandwich," she said.

"How ladylike of my lady."

They walked into the dining room laughing but felt the chill in the room instantly.

"Whoa," Carter murmured.

Everyone was staring at them. Allie stiffened but kept her face blank as they filled their plates. Walking over to where Rachel sat with Lucas, she could hear the whispers and harsh laughter all around them.

"This sucks," Lucas said as they sat down. "What are we going to do?"

"I think Isabelle has got to step up," Carter said. "There's not much we can do, unless Allie wants us to follow her everywhere."

"Isabelle wouldn't usually let this sort of thing get so out of control," Rachel agreed.

"Maybe she's trying not to show favoritism," Lucas suggested. "Everybody knows she has taken a special interest in Allie."

"Whatever." Anger made Allie's hands shake as she stacked bacon onto a slice of fresh bread. "All I know is I'm going to kick Katie's ass if she comes anywhere near me today."

Taking a gigantic bite, she looked up to see Carter smiling and shaking his head.

"What?" she said, her mouth full.

"Nothing," he said still grinning.

"I think what he's thinking," Rachel said, "is 'That's our girl.'"

"Could I have everybody's attention, please." Isabelle's voice rang out over the dining hall rumble.

Silence fell.

Standing at the front of the room in a lavender cardigan open over a crisp white skirt and blouse, a silk scarf over her shoulder, she looked more stern than Allie could ever remember seeing her. "I would like to remind all students that bullying is grounds for expulsion on a single offense. I trust I won't have to mention this again."

As she walked out, her footsteps echoed in the crowded room.

When Allie pointed at herself and mouthed, "Is that about

me?" Rachel, Carter, and Lucas nodded.

Later, as they walked to class, they were divided over whether or not Isabelle had done enough to put an end to the gossip. Rachel didn't think so, but Carter and Lucas thought she'd done all she could for now.

Walking into biology, she saw that Jo, freed from her house arrest, was already at their table—her blond hair neatly combed and her expression subdued. She still had bandages on her fingers.

Allie didn't know how she was going to handle this. She couldn't really let on what she'd overheard last night, because how could she explain hearing it? And she couldn't ask to move to a different seat—Jerry would never allow it.

"Uh . . . hi." Keeping her voice cool, Allie sat in her usual seat.

Jo's blue eyes glanced off her gaze. Allie could see the tension in the way she held her shoulders stiff. Taut lines had formed at the corners of her mouth.

"Hi." Looking down at her notebook, Jo pretended to see something fascinating there, but Allie knew how little she cared for this class.

"How are your hands?" Allie hoped her eyes conveyed the anger and hurt she felt about the things Jo allowed to be said about her.

But aside from a brief glance, Jo scarcely looked at her.

"Fine," she said, flipping a page.

As Jerry called for quiet and class began, Allie felt futile rage simmer inside her. Yanking her chair, she allowed it to drag and make an irritated squawk until she sat facing away from Jo. For the rest of the class they sat, side by side, without saying a word.

At lunch Jo and Gabe avoided their usual table, sitting off in a corner of the dining room. Allie joined Rachel and Lucas, who, she observed, were sitting together more and more these days.

"Hey," she said, dropping a bag in a chair. "What's up?"

Rachel and Lucas exchanged a look she couldn't quite translate.

"The gossip," Rachel said after a second, "is that Jo was so drunk, she now can't remember what happened on the roof. And so she has decided that she believes the gossip about what happened."

"At least that's some explanation. However lame." Allie plopped down into a seat. "This would be funny if it weren't happening to me." She sighed.

"It's not happening to me and I don't think it's funny," Rachel offered.

"Look," Lucas said, "I'll speak to her later, see if I can talk some sense to her."

"Or at least get her to remember what really happened." Carter pulled out the chair next to Allie and sat down. "Like how she got so wasted she nearly killed us all. If you ask me, it's pretty convenient that now that everybody knows something crazy happened that day, she suddenly can't recall behaving like a lunatic."

Looking around the table, Allie thought, *These are my only friends in the world right now. Everybody else hates me.*

As if he knew what she was thinking, Carter brushed the side of her head with his lips.

"Don't let her get you down," he whispered, and she found herself smiling at him in spite of everything.

She was aware that Lucas and Rachel were both watching them with dawning recognition. The whole school would soon know that they were together.

"I'm good," she said. And she meant it.

For the rest of the day, Allie could not say she was bullied. Instead she was treated like a ghost—as if she wasn't there at all.

Nobody outside of her immediate group of friends spoke to her. Even Katie, when she passed her in the hallway, merely turned her head away and flounced by.

As Allie walked to her room after classes ended, Jules stopped her in the hallway. "I just wanted to tell you that I'm sorry how everyone's behaving," the prefect said. "I spoke with Isabelle about it yesterday, and she has given Katie and two of her friends written warnings about this."

"You're sure Katie's behind the rumors, then?" Allie said.

"I've known Katie all my life, Allie." Jules looked frustrated. "But I've told her we can't be friends unless she fixes this. It is incredibly unfair to you. And it's just not going to happen on my watch. She knows how I feel, and I expect her to sort this out."

"Thanks, Jules." The gratitude in Allie's tone was genuine. "It feels weird to have people say things about you that aren't true."

"If anybody harasses you or bullies you, come to Isabelle or me," Jules said. "We'll deal with them. But look, I know what happened between you and Katie this weekend, and I'd rather this didn't end up in a fistfight."

Allie flushed guiltily. "Okay, okay... I'll try to control myself."

When Jules had gone, Allie put on her running clothes and headed outside. It was another unusually warm afternoon—the sun felt hot on her shoulders as she jogged out to the chapel. The sensation was soothing—as if it could heal her soul. She decided to go the long way, taking in the summerhouse as well. She was almost sorry when she arrived at the chapel twenty minutes later, but at the same time . . . there was Carter.

As she opened the gate, she saw him immediately, leaning against the ancient wooden door of the chapel, watching her with eyes like pools of melted chocolate.

"Hey," she said, running down the stone path.

"Hey back," he said. His tone was brisk, but she got the feeling he was trying not to smile. "Look, before we go inside, there's something that we need to get out of the way."

Reaching for her hand, he pulled her gently toward him, and in the shadows of the doorway he lowered his mouth to hers. She smiled against his lips and pulled him closer until she could feel the warmth of his body. Spurred on by her response, he kissed her more urgently, holding her so tightly her lungs felt compressed. When they stopped a minute later, she was flushed and breathless.

"I'm glad we got that over with," she said.

"Me, too." He held the door for her. "So now we can hopefully focus on all the bad, scary stuff without being distracted by the fun, romantic stuff."

His voice echoed off the cool stone walls as he stood aside to let her walk inside. As she passed him, Allie paused to run her fingers tantalizingly down his arm from his shoulder to the tips of his fingers. Goose bumps formed in their path.

"Uh-huh," she said, laughing.

He tried to grab her but she danced just out of reach, laughing.

"Not in church, Carter. We'll go to hell."

"Then lead me not into temptation," he said, following a few steps behind her.

"Fair enough," she said, still just too far away from him. "As long as you deliver me from evil."

"Deal."

She let him catch her near the pulpit. He pulled her down giggling onto a dark wooden pew beside him, his arm light across her shoulders.

"This place is amazing," she said, looking around, as his thumb pulled up the short sleeve of her T-shirt and stroked the warm skin underneath. "I've never seen anything like these paintings in my life."

"I think lots of churches used to look something like this." His lips were against her ear now, and she closed her eyes, feeling her body quiver. "But they changed."

"Sad for them," she whispered.

"Isn't it?"

Their kiss was more passionate this time, and after a moment he lifted Allie up onto his lap. Pulling the band from her ponytail, he ran his fingers through her hair until it fell around his face in soft waves as she leaned forward to kiss him. Turning his head, he ran his lips lightly between her ear and the corner of her mouth. Her breath came in soft gasps.

After a few minutes, though, she pushed herself away. With a regretful sigh he let her go, and she slid off his lap onto the pew beside him.

"So much for getting that out of the way," she said with a wry smile.

"I warned you about the leading and the tempting," he said.

She laughed. "How could I tempt you? I'm sweaty runner girl."

He tugged a strand of her loose hair. "Tempting."

But after a moment he sighed. "Right, so now we must destroy the lovely mood we've created and talk about what's going on."

All the warmth seemed to leave Allie's body, and she shivered. But it had to happen.

"Yes, let's do it."

"Let's start with your file. Tell me more about what you found in there."

"It was strange," she said. "It had all the normal Allie-isn't-very-good-at-science stuff and then a lot of weird papers that weren't mine."

He looked puzzled. "Like what?"

"Like . . . my mum's school records." She gave him a significant look. "From here."

"From here . . . as in, from Cimmeria?" His voice rose incredulously.

"Exactly. So it turns out my mum wasn't very good at science either when she was my age. Oh, and she attended Cimmeria, a school she pretended she'd never heard of until the week I came here. In fact, she knows the place so well she called Isabelle 'Izzy' in a letter."

"'Izzy' . . . ?" Carter stared at her. "Allie, what the hell is going on?"

She held up her hands in a helpless gesture. "I have no idea. But there's more. There was also a note in my file from somebody named Lucinda to Isabelle dated a month ago. It *ordered* her to

336

admit 'my granddaughter' immediately, and 'protect her from Nathaniel.'"

Carter let his breath out in a low whistle. "Him again." He arched an eyebrow. "I don't suppose you have a grandmother named Lucinda?"

"One of my grandmothers died before I was born. The other one died two years ago," Allie said. "Her name was Jane."

"So . . . ," Carter said.

"Who's Lucinda?" Allie finished the thought for him. "Good question. It also mentioned my brother, Christopher, saying Nathaniel was a threat to him, too. There was also a note in Lucinda's handwriting to somebody with the initial *G*, talking about how well her daughter was doing in Night School. It was very old."

Carter pushed his hair back out of his eyes as he absorbed all of this information. "Allie, did your parents tell you anything that was true, ever?"

She was surprised to feel tears burning her eyes.

"I don't know," she said, forcing them back.

He squeezed her hand.

"Okay, so let's sum this up." He ticked the facts off with a tap on the back of her hand. "You're rubbish at science. Your mum probably went to school here. Lucinda either is your grandmother or thinks she is and your parents forgot to mention her to you—for your whole life. And whoever this Lucinda is, she's important enough that she can order Isabelle to do things." He seemed to be finished but then he added, "Oh, and Isabelle has a daft nickname."

Allie forced a smile. "That's about it, I think."

"So . . . not much then."

"No," she said feebly. "Not much."

"Okay, so let's just leave that there for a minute, because it seems to me we'll need time to think about how to handle all of that." He looked up at the old painting of the yew tree on the wall. "Let's talk about the letter."

The letter he'd found on the desk was from Nathaniel to Isabelle and dated several days earlier. It had been short and angry. "What happened on the night of the Summer Ball was just a taste of what I have to offer," it said. "Give me what I deserve or I will destroy Cimmeria with my own hands."

It listed a date and time for a "parley at the usual place." The night was tomorrow, the time was midnight. But the place was never described.

"What's a parley?" Allie had asked at the time.

"It's a military term," Carter had replied. "It's a meeting of enemies to talk terms."

"Oh," Allie had said. "Awesome."

Now, curled up on the church pew next to him, she asked the question that had been eating away at her all day. "Do we both think Nathaniel killed Ruth?"

He looked serious. "I don't know. He all but said as much in that letter. But the main problem I have with that is why? Why would he do that? Who the hell is he? What does he want that Isabelle won't give him? And why does he want it so desperately that he'd do something like that?"

Allie twisted a strand of hair around her finger as she stared at the yew tree on the wall. "I read somewhere that most people who are murdered are killed by people who know them—like their family or boyfriends." She dropped the strand of hair. "God, I wish we could have found Ruth's file. I mean, what if Nathaniel's, like, her evil stepdad or something?"

Carter shook his head. "If it was something like that, why would he be making demands to Isabelle, acting like they have this long history and she's done something bad to him at some point? It doesn't make sense to me."

"None of this makes sense to me," Allie said. "The thing is, there's so much going on that we don't know about—there's no way for us to figure out what's happening unless somebody tells us."

Carter stared at her as if she'd something brilliant. "That's it, Allie! We'll get them to tell us."

She leaned away from him, her expression dubious.

"Um . . . like . . . how?"

His cheeks were flushed with excitement. "Simple. Isabelle's meeting Nathaniel tomorrow night. I'll follow Isabelle to the meeting. Then I can listen to what they say, and we can decide what to do next."

"That's a great idea," she said. "I'll come with you."

He glared at her. "No, you most certainly will not."

"Yes, I most certainly will."

"Allie . . ." His eyes warned her to drop it but she ignored them.

"Why should you go and not me? So much of this involves me and my family, and although I know more now, I still don't understand what's really going on." He tried to speak but she held up her hand. "This is my *life*, Carter. And I want to find out who's messing it all up."

"It could be dangerous." She could hear frustration in his voice. "And you could get expelled. Allie, this is not a good idea."

"It *is* dangerous," she said. "But I'm doing it. Look, there's one thing in my file I didn't mention. In the letter from my mother, she mentioned my brother. And she says 'Christopher could have been taken.'" She leaned forward intently. "Don't you see, Carter? I could find out what happened to Christopher. I have to go."

For a long moment his eyes searched her face. She could see the moment when he gave in.

"Okay," he said, resigned. "I don't like it. But I know if I don't let you go with me, you'll just go on your own and get in even more trouble."

"Thank you!" She threw her arms around his neck.

"But I have one condition," he said, holding on to her. "We have to do it my way. Agreed?"

"Agreed!" Allie said, hugging him tighter.

"Now, how many hell points will we get if we desecrate this chapel?" he asked, breathing in the scent of her hair.

TWENTY-THREE

Clinging to the ledge outside the girls' dorm rooms, Allie inched along toward the low, sloping section of roof where she could make her way up and across to Carter's room.

It was after curfew. The night was dark and clear—perfect sneaking-out weather.

And she'd already made her way past the first window—now there was only Katie's window to get by. Standing on her toes, she leaned across the window frame tentatively to peek inside.

The lights were on, but it appeared empty.

Stretching out her arm to reach the other side of the window, she scuttled across.

Home free, she thought.

But as she took the next step, she kicked something off the edge of the gutter—perhaps, she would think later, a roofing tile, or a stone—and it clattered to the ground with the percussive impact of a tiny drumroll. Frozen in place, Allie couldn't decide whether it would be better to rush the rest of the way onto the roof—risking making more noise—or to stay right where she was now.

"Who's there?" The demanding voice came from about three feet from her right elbow.

Standing still as a corpse, Allie held her breath. She wore her running clothes—dark blue stretchy trousers and a dark blue T. Together with dark rubber-soled shoes, she figured she must be practically invisible.

Think Catwoman, she told herself.

"Jo? Is that you?" Katie's voice pierced the night. "Or is it Allie, the crazed killer? If it's you, Allie, just so you know, I'm going straight to Jules to turn you in."

Allie tried to breathe in time with the breeze so that the sound would disappear. After a few minutes—silence. She counted to one hundred, then raced to the sloping roof and climbed up, then hurled herself across to the boys' side. Practice was making her faster. She skidded down the slope on that side until she reached a drainpipe, then slid across to Carter's room.

His window was open, the light was on, and he was standing across the room, waiting for her. She thought that his dark eyes grew lighter when he saw her.

As she climbed through the window, he walked over to lift her off the desk.

"Hey," he whispered with that sexy half smile that drove her crazy.

"Hey back."

She'd already decided not to tell him what Katie had said about turning her in to Jules—she knew it wouldn't take much incentive for Carter to insist that she stay at the school while he went out alone.

Instead, she reached up and pulled his head down toward hers.

A few minutes later he lifted his head to look into her eyes.

He stroked her cheek. "We need to go follow Isabelle now and find out who the killer is."

"*Quel* drag," Allie said, lifting her lips for another kiss.

"My German is terrible—what does that mean again?" he murmured.

She laughed against his cheek. "It means why are you talking?"

After a minute he stepped away with a regretful sigh. "Let's go do our spy thing before we forget what we're supposed to be doing."

Allie straightened her clothing. "Okay. Let's go kick some ass."

"Ooh, very convincing."

"Thanks," she said. "I've been working on it all day."

Opening the door to make sure the hall was clear, Carter then stood aside for her to pass and they slipped down the stairs, stopping on each level to listen for footsteps or voices.

At the back door he crept out first as she waited in the shadows. Then, perfectly in step, they ran around the east wing to the front of the building, following a course they'd chosen earlier that day. At the tree line they ducked down among the tall bushes, settling in with a clear sight line to the school building. As long as the meeting didn't happen somewhere behind the school, they were well positioned.

"Now," Carter whispered, his eyes on the door, "we wait."

Above them a full moon cast the grounds in a ghostly blue glow. In its light they could see quite clearly. So when a group of shadowy figures slipped out the front door twenty minutes later, they saw their every move.

After the figures made their way to the footpath that led to the chapel, Carter signaled her to follow, and they jogged slowly, avoiding twigs that could snap underfoot and give them away.

They were nearly to the chapel when they heard voices. Carter grabbed her arm and they dropped back into the shadow of the churchyard wall.

Just ahead of them the gate stood open and, after creeping up to look around, he motioned for her to follow him inside.

"These theatrics, Nathaniel, are tedious."

Isabelle's voice. Allie could hear her clearly but could see nobody. *Where* was *she?*

As he crossed to the yew tree, Carter, who knew the graveyard well, easily avoided gravestones, rocks, and other dangers. A good distance behind him, Allie picked her way gingerly around the hazards.

"Hurry," he whispered.

She frowned into the darkness. "I *am* hurrying."

By the time she reached the yew, he'd already pulled himself up onto the big low branch. Reaching down, he helped her up, and then they climbed the ancient tree together until they were sitting well above the fence top. The branches were thinner up here, so Carter sat on one branch with Allie just below him on another. She couldn't actually see him without craning her neck, but she could still sense tension in his body. He was alert, poised.

Looking between the narrow and twisted branches around them, they could see the stream that ran behind the chapel through a clearing. The moon helped fully illuminate the scene.

A man stood on the far bank, meadow grasses up to his knees. A large German shepherd sat beside him, still as a statue. Isabelle stood directly across from him on the near bank, her arms crossed. Allie could see irritation in her posture.

Leaning forward in her high perch, Allie studied Nathaniel with fascination. Wearing dark trousers with a black, short-sleeved shirt, he was neither particularly tall nor short. He had thick, dark hair and stylish glasses. In fact, he was ordinary looking in every way. But he exuded power, more panther than lion.

Tearing her eyes away from him, she looked across at the headmistress. Her clothes were unusual for her—a simple black tunic and leggings with knee-high boots. Allie got the feeling she was trying to look tough.

"All I want to know, Isabelle, is this." Nathaniel's voice was a not-unpleasant baritone, but something about it made Allie's skin crawl. "Are you willing to do the right thing at last?"

Isabelle ignored the question. "What set this off, Nathaniel? I thought you were satisfied with our arrangement."

The wind picked up, and for a moment Allie lost their voices in the rustling of trees. When she could hear them again, Nathaniel was speaking.

". . . so I agreed to try to do things your way. I've been patient. Now it's my turn."

For the first time, Isabelle moved, stepping toward the

stream, closing the gap between them. "What you did the night of the ball was barbaric, Nathaniel. Why would anybody give you control of this school after that?"

"I did what I had to do to send a message. You didn't seem to hear me before then." His voice was steady. "If you had just honored our arrangement, none of that would have been necessary."

"What you had to do?" Her voice rose in anger. "Setting fire to my school and killing one of my students in cold blood was something you had to do?"

Nathaniel arched one eyebrow. "One of your students was killed? I had no idea. Perhaps you should talk to your staff. Nobody was killed by me or my people."

Allie saw Isabelle's shoulders stiffen.

"A student's throat was cut from ear to ear," she said. "Are you telling me you had nothing to do with that?"

He had a predator's grin. "Sounds to me like your school is a very dangerous place, headmistress. I wouldn't want my children to go there."

She looked at him skeptically, and he held up his right hand. "I swear we had nothing to do with that. On my honor."

"Your honor . . ." Isabelle's tone was disdainful, but something in her voice told Allie she believed him.

"Let me tell you what I think is behind all of this," Isabelle said. "I think you can see that the school is successful. That the tide is turning against you and your views. And that many of those on the board who once disagreed with me are now reconsidering their stance. But you're so arrogant that you still want to prove that your way is better."

"Enough of this." Nathaniel stepped closer to the water. The dog stayed where it was, its eyes fixed on Isabelle. "Here are my terms, Isabelle. You will tell the board that you have changed your bizarre beliefs. That you realize how wrong you have been. And that you wish to turn the running of Cimmeria over to me."

Every word dripped malice.

If Isabelle was surprised by any of this, she didn't betray it. Instead, she sounded amused. "Oh, Nathaniel, don't be ridiculous. You know these terms are absurd. I reject them all."

He took a step back. "Then you will suffer the consequences."

As he turned to leave, the dog right by his side, Isabelle shouted after him, "Lucinda will know it was you, Nathaniel. She will deal with you."

He disappeared into the trees without looking back. After a moment Zelazny and Eloise walked out of the trees to Isabelle. They conferred briefly and then walked back into the forest. When they reached the trees, two other shadowy figures joined them.

Her back pressed against the tree trunk behind her, Allie sat frozen, her thoughts in turmoil. When Carter looked down at her, she could see from his expression that he was as confused about all this as she was.

"Let's get out of here," he said.

After climbing down from the tree, they made their way through the gate; Carter latched it behind them, then held out his hand.

"Ready?"

She nodded.

They began to run.

TWENTY-FOUR

Carter took a different route back to the school on a narrow path she'd never noticed before that ran through the depths of the forest. At one point they passed a small stone cottage sitting quietly in a garden filled with flowers. The scent of jasmine and roses wafted to them on the breeze.

"Whose house is that?" Allie whispered.

"Bob Ellison's," he said.

It was far behind them when he added, "I grew up there."

Allie stopped. "That was *your house?*"

"Don't stop," Carter said without looking back.

The trees around them made ghostly shapes in the moonlight, but as they ran side by side, Allie still felt safe. Things that had frightened her in the past—a rustling in the undergrowth, the sound of a twig snapping in the distance—didn't bother her at all.

But when she heard a voice ahead, they both skidded to a stop. With his finger over his lips, Carter motioned for her to stay where she was and then ran ahead.

He was well ahead of her and around a bend in the footpath

when heard him speak to someone, but she knew immediately something wasn't right. The tension in his voice set off warning signals so strong, the hair on the back of her neck stood on end.

Acting on instinct, she ducked off the footpath and crouched behind a tree surrounded by thick undergrowth. Sinking down on one knee, she held her breath.

". . . nothing at all," Carter was saying.

Then the other voice—Gabe's voice: "So you're just out patrolling on your own, even though it's not your shift?"

She could tell that he didn't believe Carter.

"Why, what's wrong with that?" Carter asked. "I do this all the time."

"Not tonight," Gabe said. "Didn't you hear Zelazny? We're only to go out on our own shifts after curfew. You better go talk to him. He's not going to be happy."

"Fine," Carter said. "See you later."

As the cool breeze chilled the sweat on her skin, Allie heard the faint sound of his footsteps disappearing in the distance. A minute later footsteps and voices headed her way—several people, she thought.

Carefully, she leaned over to peer around the tree. In the moonlight she saw Gabe talking to somebody, but his body hid whoever it was from her view.

". . . such a screwup sometimes, you know?" Gabe was complaining. "He really needs to get it together. I don't know why Zelazny puts up with it."

"Did you believe him?" the other person asked—Allie couldn't see who it was, and she didn't recognize the voice.

"I don't really care," Gabe said. "If he keeps screwing up, it won't matter whether or not he's telling the truth." He walked down the path. "I never understood why Isabelle pushed us to let him in Night School in the first place."

At that moment a crashing sound in the woods behind Allie made her jump, and she ducked down so low, her cheek pressed against a stone. Soft fronds of bracken curled above and around her, tickling her neck.

Still as a stone. Still as a stone. Still as a stone . . .

"Who's there?"

Gabe's voice sounded closer—he must have stepped to the edge of the path. Visualizing him standing a few feet away, staring directly at her hiding place, Allie stayed frozen, her heart pounding in her ears.

She could hear him breathing.

She knew Gabe. They'd always been friends. But something was really wrong here. He sounded different. Angry. Even threatening.

All of her instincts told her to stay hidden.

Lucas's voice came from the woods nearby. "It's me, dude."

"Jesus." Gabe sounded disgusted. "Subtle, man."

"Sorry! I tripped over a freakin' log. It's dark in the trees."

"Whatever." Gabe had returned to the path. "We're moving on."

After waiting until quiet returned and she was certain they were far down the path, Allie picked her way silently back to the path and then ran at full speed toward the school.

She'd made it to the tree line when a figure stepped out of the bushes and into her path. Jumping back, she opened her mouth to scream as a hand clamped over her lips and an arm wrapped around her.

"Allie," Carter whispered, "it's me."

She relaxed in his arms. "You scared the crap out of me, Carter."

"Did Gabe see you?" he hissed.

She shook her head.

Obviously relieved, he pointed to their right. "This way."

Sticking to the shadows at the edge of the lawn, they looped around to the back door.

They crept through the door, but the stealth wasn't necessary—the hallways were empty. Raised voices floated out from Isabelle's office, but they didn't linger to listen as they ran up the stairs.

"What the hell is going on?"

Raking his hands through his thick, dark hair, Carter paced back and forth across Allie's bedroom floor.

As she watched him from her perch on the edge of her desk, she didn't have any answers.

"Who is Nathaniel?" Carter muttered to himself. "Why is he doing this?"

"He has a dog!" Allie said inanely.

Carter shot her a look, and she explained: "It was a dog Jo and I heard that night growling in the walled garden. Nathaniel must have been there."

He pivoted and paced the other way. "I still don't understand what's going on. Who is he?"

"Okay, let's think about what he said. He talked about the board," Allie said. "He told Isabelle to go to the board."

Carter glanced at her inquiringly.

"Well, why doesn't he go himself?" she asked. "I mean, if he's so powerful. And if he can't go to the board, there has to be a reason."

"Yes." Recognition dawned on Carter's face. "Because he's either been in trouble with them or they don't like him."

"Or they don't know him." She twisted up her face in thought. "He could be a complete outsider. But I got the feeling he and Isabelle knew each other well. Like old friends gone wrong, or bad family or something."

"Yeah. Or ex-boyfriends," Carter said.

Their eyes met.

"Totally," she said.

They thought that through for a minute—Allie swinging her foot, Carter pacing.

"And Lucinda." Allie broke the silence. "She said 'Lucinda will know.'"

"I heard." He pivoted and paced.

"Lucinda again . . . ," she murmured, watching him pace. "Did you believe him? Nathaniel, I mean. Do you think he didn't kill Ruth?"

"I don't know." His tone betrayed his frustration.

"I think Isabelle believed him."

"Brilliant," he muttered. "This is just brilliant."

"So that would mean . . ." Her voice trailed off. She didn't want to think about what that meant. Pulling her feet up onto the desk, she wrapped her arms around her knees. "God, this is a nightmare. . . . What do we do now?"

He stopped pacing. "I have no idea."

For the rest of that week, Allie felt isolated. All the students were in their normal seats, and the teachers continued the lessons in the usual way, but to her nothing was the same. Something awful was going to happen—Nathaniel was going to do *something*—and out of all the students, only she and Carter knew about it.

Worse than that, she was still treated as if she were invisible by many students. They ignored her when she walked with them down hallways, passed them on the stairs, brushed her teeth next to them in the bathroom. And although she refused to admit it to anyone, it was getting to her. It was an oddly disembodying experience to be treated as if she weren't actually there.

On Thursday morning a girl she couldn't remember seeing before dropped a pen near her in French class, and when Allie picked it up and held it out for her, the girl acted as if she couldn't see it, even when Allie waved it back and forth in front of her. Eventually she let it fall back to the ground.

"Whatever," Allie muttered, turning back to her notebook.

On Friday Jules took her aside and told her she was doing all she could to get Katie to stop the campaign against her.

"I'm trying, Allie, I really am," she said. "But she's stubborn. I've tried talking to Isabelle about it, but I've never known her to be so busy."

Allie knew perfectly well why Isabelle was busy, but she couldn't tell Jules that.

"Jerry's spoken to the boys and told them they could all face punishment if they don't stop—so I think you'll see the guys getting back to normal soon. Of course, some may be more scared of Katie than they are of Jerry." Jules looked uncomfortable. "But with time this will all work out. The term ends next week and fall term will be better. . . ."

Or, next term, Katie poisons even more kids against me. And then this whole thing becomes impossible, Allie thought.

By Friday she'd had enough. After her last class ended, she stormed down the hall to Jo's room, knocking perfunctorily before shoving the door open.

Jo sat on the bed reading a fashion magazine. "You could knock," she snapped.

"I did. And you could not be a bitch," Allie replied.

Sighing heavily, Jo returned her attention to the magazine, flipping the page with a sharp, irritated crack.

"Look, Jo," Allie said, leaning against the desk, "we need to talk . . . now."

"Fine. Talk." Jo kept flipping pages.

Crack. Crack. Crack.

"What can you remember about what happened up on the roof that day?" Allie asked.

Jo's normally sunny clear blue eyes were like chips of ice. "I can't remember much, but I know that somehow I ended up nearly dying."

Involuntarily, Allie glanced at Jo's hands, where bandages still covered the tips of two fingers.

"It's the not remembering that's the problem here," Allie said. "Because I do remember. I remember everything. And what I can't figure out is why you never once came to me or Carter to ask what happened."

Jo closed the magazine with exaggerated patience and looked at her.

"I didn't come to you because I don't trust you, Allie," she said. "See, the thing is, lying in my bed in pain with my hands wrapped up in bandages for nearly a week, I had plenty of time to think about everything. And I realized that I have no idea who you really are or where you come from. All I know is what you've told me. And I also know that ever since we met, everything's just fallen apart."

Color flooded Allie's cheeks and she stared at Jo in disbelief. "Are you telling me you think what's been happening here is my fault?"

"Think about it, Allie," Jo said. "Isn't it your fault, at least a bit? It seems to me bad news just surrounds you. Maybe Katie's right. Maybe you really are crazy."

Her tone was venomous and her words stung. For a moment Allie was speechless.

Jo was supposed to be her friend.

She fixed Jo with a hard stare.

"You want to know what happened on the roof, Jo? Fine. I'll tell you. You drank half a bottle of vodka and you danced on the roof. You *danced*. You threw yourself around like a drunken fairy. You didn't know where you were and you didn't care who you took down with you. Both Carter and I risked our *asses* to save you that day. And right now, I've got to say, I'm kind of regretting that."

Jo tried to speak but Allie talked over her. "If you don't believe me, for God's sake believe Carter. You've known him for years. Or believe Jules; she's been trying to talk to you. Just don't believe people who are only using you to get at me. Because that's kind of pathetic."

Her face red with anger, Jo threw the magazine at her. As it fluttered across the room, Allie caught it easily.

"What I'm regretting right now is that I ever thought I could be your friend." Jo spat the words out at her. "Now get out."

Fighting back tears, Allie stumbled down the hallway toward the sanctuary of her own room.

I will not let them see me cry.

But at that moment, Rachel stepped in front of her with an armful of books. She took one look at Allie's face and grabbed her hand.

"With me," she said firmly, pulling Allie back into her room.

Dropping the books on the desk, Rachel sat down on the bed beside her. "What happened?"

And that was all it took.

Her body shaking with sobs, Allie told her about confronting Jo and how she'd reacted. She added in the things she'd overheard Katie saying (although she left out the bit about being on the window ledge clinging to a wall at the time).

Rachel held her hand and listened, occasionally tutting sympathetically but mostly just letting her pour out her heart.

"I just don't understand how she could say these things to me . . . or about me," Allie said finally as her sobs lessened.

"Jo has . . . problems," Rachel said diplomatically. "She's fragile. But she's good at heart. We all know that. She's being manipulated by Katie and her gaggle of hags to believe this rubbish about you. I know it hurts—I just wish there was something more I could do."

She handed Allie a box of tissues. "I think she'll come around. And when she does, she'll be sorry she said those things."

"Is this the reason you never really hung around with Jo and

Lisa before?" Allie asked, drying her eyes. "Because Jo's a little, what did you call it? Fragile?"

Rachel hesitated before replying. "I had my own . . . encounter with Jo's group a long time ago. Do you remember how I told you once Lucas was the guy friend I could never date?"

Allie nodded.

"Well, that wasn't completely true." Rachel looked down at her hands. "I had a huge crush on Lucas when I first started here two years ago. He kind of took me under his wing. There aren't many Asians here, and I was a bit self-conscious. But he made me feel completely welcome. I was just a kid and, well, you know how it goes. A fun, good-looking guy almost adopts you . . . I fell completely in love with him."

Allie looked up at her in surprise, and Rachel shrugged. "A few weeks later a pretty blond girl arrives late in the term, Lucas takes one look at her, and . . ." She slapped her hands together and let them fall apart. "Lucas became my best guy friend forever."

Allie looked at her, puzzled. "But . . . they broke up, right?"

"Oh yeah." Rachel rolled her eyes. "They broke up. After she had a complete meltdown." She sighed. "But I guess some part of me could never forgive him for choosing her over me. And some other part of me could never forgive her for letting him make that choice. Or maybe that was all the same part of me."

"That sucks," Allie said.

Rachel smiled sadly. "Yes, it does."

For weeks now Rachel had been Allie's rock of support. She seemed so wise and mature beyond her years—Allie had longed to tell her what she and Carter had learned. If anybody would know what to do, she reasoned, Rachel would. She had held off because she had promised Carter she'd tell nobody. But keeping all that information to herself was just about impossible. And there was nobody else to tell. And maybe she and Carter could use Rachel's help.

She looked at Rachel for a long moment as she fought an inner battle.

"What?" Rachel asked, puzzled.

Allie wiped the last tears from her eyes. "There's something I have to tell you."

"You did *what*?"

Carter's incredulous voice echoed in the summerhouse. It was after supper and the sun dipped low in the sky, gilding the tops of the trees around them. They were sitting on a stone bench in a pool of warm light.

Allie raised her chin stubbornly. "I trust her, Carter. And it can't be just us dealing with this."

"No, but we should both be involved in deciding who to tell, Allie. It's not going to be a secret for long if we both go around telling people we think we can trust without talking about it first," he said. "I mean, I didn't just go off and tell Lucas."

Allie thought about Lucas crashing through the woods.

"Don't do that," she said quickly.

Carter shot her an exasperated look. "Seriously, Allie, how much do you really know about her? Have you, for example, ever wondered if she had anything to do with spreading the gossip about you finding Ruth's body?"

Allie thought her heart might have stopped.

"What? Are you saying she did?" she asked, fighting to stay calm.

"I'm saying I don't know and neither do you," he said. "I'm saying she loves to gossip. I'm saying it's a bloody big coincidence that you told her about it and suddenly everybody knows."

"She wouldn't . . ." Allie faltered. Who could she trust anymore, anyway? Why should Rachel be any different from Jo or Sylvain? Both of whom she'd trusted. Both of whom betrayed her trust.

"You don't know that, Allie." Carter's voice was more gentle now. "I don't know enough about her to know whether or not we can trust her. She's always kept to herself."

"Like you," Allie pointed out.

"Like me," he admitted. "But her father is very big in Night School. He runs security for huge corporations, advises governments. . . . He's an insider, Allie."

"I know that. Rachel told me her dad was some bigwig on the board," she said. "But Rachel isn't in Night School, is she?"

"No," he conceded with obvious reluctance, "and that is unusual."

"So it's possible she's not an insider like her dad," she said.

"Yes. But you just took a pretty big chance on 'possible,'" he said.

She knew he had a point. "You're right. I'm sorry. I'll be more careful."

Mollified, he sat thinking for a moment.

"What did she say when you told her?" he asked.

"She didn't know what to think. But she was quite certain

she'd heard her dad talking about some guy named Nathaniel and complaining that he was causing trouble." She looked over at him cautiously. "She wondered if she should ask him about it."

"*What?*" Carter nearly shouted the word, and Allie ducked.

"She's not going to do it," she hastily reassured him. "She just wanted us to talk about the possibility. She thinks we can trust him."

"Oh, bloody hell." Carter buried his head in hands.

"What?" Allie asked innocently.

"This is how you keep a secret Allie? Seriously?"

"No . . . I mean, yes." She shot him a look. "I've only told *one* person, Carter. I think you're overreacting."

"Al, we could get in a lot of trouble."

"I know that," she said defensively.

"Well then?" he said. "Should we maybe try *not* telling people our secrets?"

She narrowed her eyes. "So I guess you want me to tell Rachel you'd rather she didn't tell her father?"

"Yes, Allie. That's what I want."

"Fine," she said icily.

"Great."

They sat in silence for a long minute.

"Did we just have our first fight?" Carter asked, looking up at her with that half smile that always made her melt.

"No," Allie said. "I'm pretty sure we fought a lot before we got together."

"True," he said.

"Anyway," she said, "whether you like it or not, we now have somebody else to help us if and when we need help. And she happens to be very clever."

"That could come in handy," he conceded grudgingly.

"Yeah," she said. "That's what I thought."

He lightly punched her shoulder. She tickled him back, and before long they were both laughing. Draping his arm across her shoulder, he brushed his lips against her temple.

"I'm sorry," he said. "I shouldn't be so cross. It'll be fine."

"It *will* be fine," she agreed, "if we make it fine. Somehow."

"Which reminds me, I wanted to tell you what I learned today," he said.

Even though he sounded serious, she found it hard to focus on his words when she looked into those big dark eyes.

"Okay," she said, thinking dreamily: *He's really mine. Voluntarily!*

"Allie, this is important."

"Sorry." She untangled herself from him and sat up straight. "Hit me."

"Night School is starting late night drills again."

She frowned. "What does that mean?"

"It means we've been given really weird instructions. We'll be patrolling the grounds in shifts all night, every night. Taking turns, so everybody gets some sleep." He looked off at the trees. "We've patrolled the grounds before for training purposes, but this is different. It's very intense. They're telling us it's a new training project to teach us what they call 'protect and defend.' They're going to stage fake attacks that we have to fend off. They've even told us we can take time off from morning classes the day after our night shifts. And that's never happened before. It starts tonight, and they've got us doing training all weekend."

Watching his face, Allie could see the worry in his eyes.

"They're getting ready for Nathaniel to do something," she said.

He nodded.

"I guess there's no way they'd call the police and ask for help?"

"Hah."

"So . . . no more sneaking out at night?" she guessed.

"Absolutely not," he said. "The security is about to get intense around here."

"Okay," she said quietly. "So he's coming."

"Oh yes." Carter's eyes scanned the horizon. "He's coming."

TWENTY-FIVE

For Allie, that weekend seemed to drag on forever, slowed by a toxic mix of dread and loneliness. Carter and Lucas were both tied up in Night School, and Katie's anti-Allie campaign was still under way.

For the first time, she realized how much she'd come to rely on Carter. She rarely saw him, and even when she did, there was only time for a quick hug. When she asked him how it was going out there, he said only, "It's intense." But his eyes told her everything she needed to know—he was tired. And worried.

She dealt with it all by not dealing with it. She spent most of her time in the library. Next week was the end of the summer term, and she had essay papers to finish and exams to prepare for. In all the excitement of the last couple of weeks, she'd let herself get behind. After all she'd been through this summer, she did not intend to get bad grades.

Rachel was there all day every day, so Allie always had someone to work with.

"Study buddies," Rachel liked to say with inappropriate cheer.

But the seeds of doubt Carter had planted still lived in Allie's mind.

Did Rachel spread rumors about me? Can I trust her?

Rachel was so supportive and so open and honest about things, it seemed impossible. But Allie had come to realize nothing was impossible.

The librarian's desk was staffed by student volunteers, a fact Rachel observed with raised eyebrows.

"I guess Eloise is off playing war games," she muttered after the volunteers brought her the wrong book for the third time. "I wish she could save it until the term is over."

"Did you know Eloise was in . . ." Allie gestured vaguely.

Rachel nodded. "She's an old friend of my dad's. I think he was one of her trainers or something when she was a student. Anyway, Eloise has no secrets from me." Closing her book, she added, "I think, anyway. Who knows anymore?"

"That's how I feel about everything." Allie didn't meet her eyes.

Rachel glanced at her watch. "It's noon—want to take a break and get something to eat?"

Leaving their notebooks open on the table to reserve their places, they headed to the dining room. They chose a table in a quiet corner where they could talk without being overheard.

"Any news from Carter?" Rachel asked.

Allie shrugged. "A little. He says it's all really intense, and they never get a break. What does Lucas say?"

"The same."

Rachel bit into her sandwich, frowning. Allie could tell there was something on her mind but waited until she was ready to talk.

"Allie Sheridan?" A younger student Allie didn't remember ever seeing before stood at their table looking at Rachel.

"Her." Rachel pointed at Allie.

"Me," Allie said, looking at him curiously.

"Isabelle asked could you come to her office, please?"

She couldn't hide her surprise. "What? Why?"

He stared at her blankly.

"Allie . . ." Rachel was trying not to laugh. "What have you done now?"

Allie shrugged. "She probably just wants to tell me how amazing I am. Again."

"Uh-huh," Rachel said. "Well, I'll be in the library all afternoon—come find me when you're free. If she doesn't throw you in the dungeon or something."

"Thanks for that," Allie said, gathering her things. "I've got to say, at this point, if I found out there were a dungeon here, it really wouldn't surprise me."

Isabelle's office was empty when Allie arrived, but the door stood open, so she sat in one of the chairs. As she waited, she glanced around nervously, as if even now she'd find that she and Carter had left something out of place that could give them away.

Isabelle strode in a few minutes later looking distracted, her glasses pushed up on top of her head.

"Would you like a cup of tea?" she asked, turning on a kettle on top of a small refrigerator in a corner. "I could really use one myself."

"Sure," Allie said politely, although she didn't feel like tea.

The electric kettle rumbled to life as Isabelle rummaged

about for an extra cup and tea bags. When it was ready, the head-mistress handed her a cup, then sank down in a chair next to her and pulled her feet up, curling like a teenager.

"That's better." She sipped her tea reflectively before focusing her gaze on Allie. "There is nothing wrong in the world that isn't made better by a good cup of tea. Thank you for coming, Allie. I don't want to take you away from your studies for too long. But with the term ending on Friday, I wanted to spend some time with you to find out how you are. I know this has been an unusual term, and I wondered if you wanted to talk about anything."

For a moment, Allie was speechless.

Is she joking?

Isabelle was looking at her expectantly, and she knew she had to say something.

What should I say? "Well, the murder was a little upsetting, and the fire did worry me a bit. I was nearly date raped, and my ex–best friend is crazy. But, hey, at least I'm making an A in history"?

"Okay . . . ," she said, cautiously.

Her head was full of things she couldn't talk about—things she wasn't supposed to know. And she knew Isabelle didn't want to know how she was doing in biology, or why she was late with her essay last week.

As her silence stretched on, Isabelle raised an eyebrow and offered her a lifeline. "How are things between you and Jo?"

Allie winced. This was not a conversation she wanted to have.

"I've noticed that you're less close than you were. Why is that?"

Allie told her in basic terms what had happened. Dismayed, Isabelle closed her golden brown eyes as she listened.

"I'll speak with Jo," she said when Allie finished. "She is going through a difficult time, too. So you may have to be patient with her. But I know your friendship is important to her."

"*Was* important," Allie muttered.

"And will be again," Isabelle said with confidence. "If you're patient."

She set down her teacup. "Katie's little campaign is another issue I'm dealing with. I know Jules has talked to you—and I'm sorry I haven't had a chance to before now. But Jules has been updating me about this every single day, and she has been fighting your corner with Katie.

"You have been remarkably patient in dealing with her, but I think we're at the point where I will have to consider suspending her if she doesn't stop," Isabelle said. "She knows The Rules perfectly well, as do her parents. I've written to them about this and they have not responded. So I'm giving her a final warning today. I very much appreciate your restraint."

"Be careful!" Allie spoke before she could stop herself.

The headmistress looked at her curiously; Allie's voice faltered. "I mean . . . aren't her parents on the board? I think they're super powerful; she's always bragging about it. They'd be . . . you know. Bad enemies . . . I think. If they're like her."

Isabelle leaned forward. "You're very sweet to worry about me, Allie. But don't worry—I'll be careful."

They talked for a few minutes about her classwork. Isabelle pointed out that all of her grades had steadily improved. Even Zelazny had praised her paper on the Civil War.

"So, actually, my only concern is what happens now," she said finally.

"What do you mean?" Allie asked, puzzled.

"I can't help but notice that you haven't called your parents while you've been here," Isabelle said. "During that time I've spoken to your mother many times. She's worried about you. They both miss you."

Immediately tears burned Allie's eyes, and she fought them back. She was surprised how much this hurt. She'd avoided contacting her parents because she was so angry at them. But she didn't know why they hadn't got in touch with her.

At the same time, she felt betrayed by what she'd found in her student file. Isabelle knew her mother well and had never told her. Hadn't they all lied to her?

Maybe now was time for truth telling.

"Do you know my parents well?" Allie asked.

Isabelle's expression tensed. "Why do you ask that question?"

"Something my mother said when she brought me here has been bugging me," Allie lied. "She called you 'Izzy,' as if she knew you. And then Katie and Jo both said something about everybody here being legacy. That made me wonder what I was doing here if I wasn't legacy."

She stared hard at the headmistress. "Am I legacy, Isabelle?"

Emotion flashed across Isabelle's face as she hesitated a second too long, but in the end her answer was simple.

"Yes, Allie. You are very much legacy."

TWENTY-SIX

After leaving Isabelle's office, Allie stopped to splash cold water on her face before returning to the library.

"What? Was the dungeon occupied or something?" Rachel asked with a teasing smile. But when she noticed Allie's reddened face, her expression changed to concern. "Hey, what's the matter?"

Allie smiled wanly. "It's nothing, really. It just turned into an unexpected therapy session."

"I hate it when therapy jumps out and surprises you like that," Rachel said, but her eyes were still concerned. "Want to take a break and talk about it?"

Her sympathy made Allie feel tearful again, and she nodded. She didn't want to cry in front of everyone.

Rachel led her to a nook down the hall from the library before heading off in search of tissues and returning with two cups of tea.

"Tell me everything," she said, settling down. "Or at least everything you want to tell me."

Allie started to speak, but then stopped. *If today is a truth-telling day, then why stop with Isabelle?*

She couldn't think of a good reason.

"Before I tell you, I need to ask you a question," she said. "It might hurt your feelings. But I hope you'll understand why I need to ask this."

Rachel's almond-shaped eyes were wide with surprise, but she never lost her cool.

"Okay," she said. "Ask me anything."

"Have you ever gossiped about me?"

Rachel didn't even hesitate.

"Before I met you I did," she said. "Because I gossip about everybody. But as soon as I met you, I stopped talking about you and I have never done it again. Ever."

Watching her closely, Allie saw not a flicker of hesitation. Not the slightest sign that she was even uncomfortable with the question. She just seemed . . . herself. All of her instincts told her she could trust her.

"The thing is," Allie said, "everybody seems to lie to me. My parents. Isabelle. Jo. I'm losing faith in—"

"Everyone?" Rachel finished for her. Allie nodded.

Rachel put her hand on her heart. "I swear, Allie, I'm not one of them. You can trust me."

Somehow, Allie knew it was true.

Leaning forward, she pulled Rachel into a hug. "I believe you. I'm sorry I had to ask."

"I understand," Rachel said, hugging her back. "Maybe more than you know. Remember, I've been here awhile. There's a reason I don't choose to have many friends. Now, tell me what happened that upset you."

Allie told her briefly about her meeting with Isabelle, and about asking her if she was legacy. When she told her Isabelle's answer, Rachel breath hissed through her teeth.

"She admitted it? Blimey. What did you say?"

"I tried to make her be specific," Allie said, remembering the look on Isabelle's face—she'd seemed torn. "I had to ask her about my family."

"My mum went to school here, didn't she?" she'd asked the headmistress. "You knew each other then."

Isabelle nodded. "She did. We were in the same class. She was one of my closest friends."

Allie's brow creased. "Then why have I never met you before? Or heard of this school?"

"It's a very long story, Allie, although I want you to know that your mother never fell out with me. She fell out with Cimmeria. And the people behind it." She looked somber. "I think you should really talk about this with her. She wouldn't want me to be the one to tell you her story. It's not my place. But I can tell you that when she completed her education here, she left all of this behind. I don't think she ever looked back. She hated it here. And I believe that's why she never told you about it."

Setting her teacup down on a table, Allie had pulled her legs up, wrapping her arms around her knees. "But she sent me here."

Isabelle nodded.

"Why would she send me to a school she hated?" Allie's voice rose querulously.

"She couldn't handle you," Isabelle said. "And that's not your fault; it's hers. And she knows that. After Christopher . . . left, she wasn't herself. She worried herself into a place where she couldn't be a good mother to you anymore."

An unexpected wave of grief washed over Allie, and she bent forward until her head rested on her knees, trying not to cry.

"Sending you here was one of the bravest things she's ever done in her life, Allie," Isabelle said gently. "She knew you were in trouble where you were. But to send you here, she had to ask for help from people she'd left behind her long ago. And that was hard."

Allie watched a tear fall onto her knee.

"Why didn't you ever tell me before?" she asked, her voice muffled. "You and Mum are friends and neither of you ever told me. Isn't that like lying?"

Isabelle rested her hand on Allie's shoulder. Her voice was low and calm.

"She begged me not to tell you, and I had to honor her wishes because you are her daughter, not mine. I think she was wrong not to tell you the truth, and she knows I think that. But I couldn't betray her trust." She sounded like she, too, was fighting tears now. "But I didn't want to betray your trust, either. And I'm so sorry I didn't tell you."

Allie took a shaky breath. "Are you keeping other things from me, too?"

There was a long silence.

"Adults," Isabelle said carefully, "can't tell young people everything they know. That isn't how things work. They tell them as much as they can to keep them safe. So, yes, I'm keeping some things from you until I think you're ready to know them. But please believe that I will tell you when you're ready."

Allie's grief was usurped by anger. *Why do adults always think*

they're better at handling important things just because they're older?
Why do they think that gives them the right to lie?

But Isabelle wasn't done yet. "And some of this—a lot of this—needs to come from your own parents. Not from me. You need to ask them these questions first, and give them a chance to be honest with you. If they won't tell you, or you think they're not being honest, then come to me. And I will tell you what I can."

"How can I ask my parents anything?" Allie's voice rose. "I haven't called them because I was waiting to see if they would call me. It seemed to me if they missed me, they'd call. Or at least write. But they haven't. They're *useless*."

"Your mother hasn't talked with you because she wanted you to have time to think." Isabelle's voice was sorrowful. "Time to decide whether or not you wanted to stay here. And whether or not you could forgive her. I know without a single doubt that she is sorry about how hard this has been on you. Because she is who she is, she can't tell you that."

She added in a whisper, "But I can."

Allie buried her face in her hands so Isabelle wouldn't see her cry, but she felt the headmistress wrap her arms around her.

Later, when she'd quieted, Isabelle gave her a tissue and put her teacup back into her hands.

"You need to understand, Allie," she said, "that you still have much to learn about yourself. Your family has a long and unique history. Your mother rejected that history, so she chose not to tell you about it. I think that's a shame. You have a most astonishing bloodline. Ask her about it.

"And I hope you will forgive your parents. They did what they thought was right."

When Allie finished telling the story, Rachel leaned back in her seat. "Wow," she said. "That is so intense. And I don't care what she says. Your parents are profoundly lame. But I'm super curious about what she means about your bloodline."

"It's got to be Lucinda," Allie said. "Whoever she is."

"Your mysterious would-be grandmother . . . ," Rachel mused. "No doubt—she's the key. You didn't ask Isabelle about her?"

"No. I got sidetracked with all that my-parents-are-crap crap."

"It's driving me crazy," Rachel said. "Who is she?"

"I wish I knew."

Rachel gave her a challenging look. "You know what I'm going to say."

Allie sighed. "Your dad . . ."

". . . knows everything," Rachel finished for her. "Let me tell him what's going on."

"Carter doesn't want to tell anybody else—particularly a board member like your dad," Allie said. "He's still cross with me for telling you."

"Fine," Rachel said. "But it's not his family we're talking about here. It's yours and mine. This is our decision to make."

She had a point.

"Let me think about it," Allie said. "I might need to work on Carter a bit."

"Okay," Rachel said, "but don't take too long to think. The term ends on Friday."

By Monday, Allie still hadn't made up her mind what to tell Rachel about her dad, but when she walked to the dining hall at lunchtime, all thoughts of the end of term, Lucinda, and danger flew out of her mind when she saw Lisa standing in the doorway. She was pale and even thinner than before, and the only visible reminder of the attack she bore was the red scar on her cheek.

"Lisa! Oh my God." Allie ran over to hug her. "When did you get back? How are you?"

"Hi, Allie. I got here a couple of hours ago." She smiled wanly. "My parents didn't want me to miss my exams. . . ."

"That sucks," Allie said. "But welcome back! It's been all wrong without you. I'm glad you're here for, like, five whole days."

"Thanks." Lisa looked around the room, clearly puzzled. "What's going on? Nobody's at our table. And Jo's off over there with . . ." She gestured at the corner of the room where Jo sat with Ismay and Katie.

Allie nodded. "It's bad. Jo hates me now."

"Get out." Lisa looked at her doubtfully.

"No, I'm serious. A lot of stuff happened while you were gone. The group is pretty much over for now. Everybody's divided. I sit with Rachel Patel and Lucas most days if they're around, and Carter."

"Why? What on earth happened?"

"Oh God, it's the longest story in the history of stupid." Allie sighed. "Just trust me: Jo hates me. But somehow I'm surviving."

Lisa seemed lost. "I have no idea where to sit now," she said plaintively.

Allie's lips curved into a wicked smile. "Well, you could sit with Jo and Katie Gilmore. Or you could sit with me and Lucas."

"Lead the way," Lisa said with a guilty giggle. They walked

over to where Rachel and Lucas were already piling sandwiches onto their plates.

Over lunch they took turns filling her in on all that had happened while she'd been home recovering.

When Carter appeared, he lightly brushed his lips to Allie's hair before he slid into the seat next to her. Lisa's eyes widened, but Allie turned to smile at Carter as Lucas elbowed Lisa lightly in the ribs.

Aside from that, though, there were no sparks between Lisa and Lucas. In fact, at one point Allie noticed Lisa watching Lucas and Rachel with concern, and for the first time she realized how closely they sat together and how companionable they seemed.

Maybe Rachel was thinking about forgiving him after all.

She didn't like the idea of finding herself in the middle of a Rachel-Lucas-Lisa triangle, but at the same time, she wanted Rachel to have the guy who made her happy.

A worried frown briefly lined her brow.

Why does love always have to be such a mess?

At eleven that night Allie raised her head from her books.

"Sustenance," she muttered. "I must have sustenance."

She was studying in the library with Carter, Lisa, and Rachel, and had been since dinner ended. Library curfew had been extended to midnight for the week, and even at this hour the place was packed.

"I'm going to get something to drink," Allie said. "Any takers?"

"I'm fine," Lisa said, barely looking up from her book.

Rachel said. "I don't want to be pedantic about this, but we *did*

376

just take a break an hour ago."

"Allie likes breaks more than she likes studying," Carter observed.

"How is that not normal?" Allie said, getting to her feet. "Fine. You stay here. I shall return when I've found food. And when you all faint from hunger later, don't think you can just feed on me."

Emerging from the room bleary-eyed, she headed straight for a table stocked with power bars, bowls of fruit, and thermoses of tea and coffee outside the library doors. The hallway was lined with students taking study breaks, stretching, sleeping, and chatting before diving back into their books.

"Coffee," she mumbled, stumbling over to the table.

As she poured her coffee into a white china cup with the Cimmeria insignia in blue, she surveyed the food with dismay. "Why are there no cookies here?" she asked nobody in particular. "And where is the chocolate? How am I supposed to work under these conditions?"

"I will bring you chocolate."

The voice came from nowhere and Allie jumped, barely saving her coffee.

"Sylvain! Don't *do that*."

"*Désolé*," he said, clearly startled by her reaction. "I didn't mean to frighten you."

"Whatever."

As he poured himself a cup of coffee, Allie turned to leave.

"Well, it's been really great chatting with you, Sylvain. . . ."

"Allie, wait." He took a quick step toward her. "Please. I'd like to talk to you. . . ."

"Oh God, do we have to?" Talking to him was the last thing she wanted right now.

"No, of course not," he said. "But I'd appreciate it if you would give me just a few minutes of your time."

Glancing back longingly at the library door, she sighed.

"Five minutes." She held up her hand with her fingers splayed. "Then I have to get back to work."

"Agreed."

Carrying her coffee cup, she followed him down the hallway to the empty entrance hall. Their footsteps echoed in the spacious corridor.

As soon as they were alone, his demeanor changed. He seemed uncomfortable, and he looked around to make sure that nobody had followed them. His tension made her uneasy.

"So . . . what did you want to talk about?" she asked, keeping her distance from him.

Without warning, he stepped close to her. Before she could step away, he whispered just loud enough for her to hear the words: "You're in danger."

She was so alarmed by the concern on his face, she didn't step away from him.

"What the hell are you talking about?" she whispered back.

"I cannot tell you much," he said, "but I believe that you are in danger. That somebody will try to hurt you."

She looked for any sign that he was kidding, but he wasn't smiling. For the first time, she felt a stab of fear.

"Who, Sylvain? Who wants to hurt me?"

He shook his head. "I can tell you nothing. I shouldn't even tell you this. But, I am worried for you. Please believe me, this is real."

"Is it Nathaniel?"

As soon as she said the words, Allie's hand shot up and covered her mouth.

A spark of interest glittered in his eyes. "How do you know about Nathaniel?"

Carter will murder me.

"I . . . I just . . . must have heard a rumor or something. . . ."

He searched her face as if looking for clues.

"Who threatens you," he said smoothly, "matters less than what could happen if we do not keep you safe. I think you should stay with friends as much as possible—do not spend time alone. Especially not outside."

It still seemed strange to Allie that Sylvain was the one telling her about this. She tilted her head to one side dubiously.

"Does Isabelle know?"

"Yes, but she does not want to scare you and thinks she can protect you. Everyone thinks they can keep you safe. I am not so sure. Please believe me. This is real."

Standing so close to him was disturbing. His familiar scent reminded her of how she'd once felt about him—of kissing him. And what had happened at the ball.

Suddenly she needed to be far away from him.

Exhaling, she took a quick step back. "Okay. Fine. I'll stay with friends, and I won't go outside much. Deal?"

She expected him to walk away at that point, but he stayed where he was, his eyes holding hers.

"What? Is there more?" she asked. "Please say there's not more."

"No. I am still trying to figure out how you know about Nathaniel."

"And I'm still trying to figure out who's trying to hurt me," she said tartly. "So I guess we're even."

Turning away from him, she picked up her coffee and began walking back down the hallway. He stayed right by her side but she didn't look at him.

When they reached the library door, just before he branched away from her, he said quietly, "Remember. Be careful."

"On it," she replied, her voice grim.

With Sylvain's warning hanging over her, Allie slept poorly that night. By Tuesday night, after another day of intense classes and an evening spent finishing her essay in the library, she was exhausted when she climbed the stairs to her room at midnight.

Her teeth had only the most fleeting visit from a toothbrush, and she was half asleep by the time she pulled on her pajamas.

Leaving the window open to the warm night breeze, she muttered, "Night-night, room," and fell into a sleep so sound, she couldn't recall a single dream.

When she awoke about two hours later, at first she didn't know what had disturbed her. Her eyes fluttered open. Still deep in the hazy space between asleep and awake, she saw a figure bent over her bed, watching her. At first she thought she was dreaming.

Then she heard him breathe.

"Carter?" she murmured, stirring.

She sensed rather than saw the sudden movement as the

figure jumped lithely onto the desk and then slipped out the window with the ease of an acrobat.

That isn't Carter.

That realization yanked her from her torpor and she sat bolt upright in bed, staring at the open window for a split second before leaping up to turn on the overhead light.

The room was empty. But somebody had been there, she was certain of it. The books and papers on her desk had been disturbed. A pen that had rested on a notebook when she went to sleep now lay on the floor.

She hadn't been dreaming.

Forcing herself to keep breathing steadily, she climbed up onto the desk and looked out the window, but all she saw was countryside, bathed in the faint glow of a sliver of moon.

Shivering despite the warm night, Allie closed the window and latched it tightly—testing the strength of the lock before climbing back into bed and wrapping her arms around her knees. She sat awake for a very long time.

TWENTY-SEVEN

"Maybe you were dreaming," Carter suggested, but she could see that his muscles had tensed.

"I wasn't," Allie insisted. "Things were moved. Besides, I saw him."

They were sitting with Rachel at the summerhouse. Classes had ended for the day a few minutes before. The sky was gray and ominous, but it hadn't yet begun to rain.

"I sat up in bed as he went out the window. It wasn't a dream. He was in my room." She shuddered. "He was *in my room*."

"Hey, it's okay." Rachel put her arm around her. "We believe you. Tell us exactly what you saw. What did he look like?"

Screwing up her face, Allie tried to remember everything. "He was shorter than Carter, and more slight. He wore all black. I'm pretty sure his hair was almost blond."

For a while they went halfheartedly through a list of all the students who could conceivably match that description but dismissed them all.

"Nobody in Night School right now looks like that," Carter

said finally. "Gabe is blond but he's not slim and he's taller than me. And only Night School can get up on the roof right now without getting caught because of the extra patrols."

"Night School and whoever was in my room last night." Allie looked up at him, worry twisting her stomach. "Carter, there's something else I have to tell you. . . ."

She told them about her conversation with Sylvain. As Carter listened, his jaw tightened. When she'd finished, he jumped to his feet without a word and strode out of the summerhouse to the edge of the woods, where he stood with his back to them.

"Uh-oh." Allie half stood to follow him, but Rachel gave her a warning look and she sat back down again.

"Give him a minute. He'll be fine." Rachel said. "And then I'll really piss him off with my news."

"News?" Allie raised an eyebrow curiously.

"Let's wait," Rachel replied, watching Carter. "I kind of only want to tell this once."

Allie saw that he was walking back toward them now. The rush of color that had flooded his face as he listened to her story had receded, and he seemed calmer.

"I believe him," he said. "He's an asshole, but if anybody would know, he would. He should have told me. Not you." He looked angry. "But he has this thing for you, so he decided to do it this way. Fine. Now we know."

Allie looked over at Rachel, who winced before leaning toward Carter. "You're not going to like what I have to say."

"What?" he growled. "Are you telling me this day gets better?"

"I told my father what's going on."

"Oh, good. It *does* get better!" Carter ran his hands through his hair. "I had no idea that was possible. You know, between the two of you *everybody's* going to know *everything* about us before the term ends on Friday. Should we just take out a billboard and put all our secrets on it? Maybe we could set up a website—AllOurSecrets dot com."

"There are no computers here," Allie reminded him.

"I am fully aware of the lack of internet technology at Cimmeria," he snapped. "But thanks for reminding me."

She ducked behind Rachel.

"I am truly sorry," Rachel said. "I know you don't know that you can trust my father, but I know you can. And I'm scared for Allie. So I borrowed Isabelle's phone and I told him everything. He knows who Nathaniel is."

The last sentence seemed to hang on the air.

Allie was the first to gather her wits. "Who is he?" she asked eagerly.

"Here's the thing," Rachel said, shooting Carter a worried look. "He won't tell me."

"Of course not," he said sarcastically. "But he's *completely* trustworthy."

"He really is." Rachel was fighting to stay calm. "He said he couldn't tell me that. But he did tell me some things about him. He said Nathaniel is for real. That he and Isabelle used to be very close—those are the precise words he used—but they had some sort of falling out and now he is determined to take over Cimmeria and Night School—to sort of be the new her. If that happened, my dad said, it would be a disaster. He loathes Nathaniel. Says he's ruthless. Possibly insane. And that he'll stop at nothing to have what he wants."

"Oh, good," Allie said.

"There's more," Rachel said. "Some members of the board are on his side. There's something Isabelle's doing that they don't like. It has something to do with the larger organization. Anyway, some people would like to see Isabelle gone, and they think they could use Nathaniel to do it. Just let him get rid of her, and then they think they'll get rid of him. But Dad says it won't work and that it could ruin everything.

"He's going to talk to Isabelle about it on Friday when he comes to get me. But he said something else."

She looked at Allie, her brow furrowed. "He said for you to watch your back."

Images of last night flashed in Allie's mind and she shuddered. Then she stood up, her eyes resolute. "Let's go talk to Isabelle."

"What . . ." Rachel looked a bit scared. "Now?"

"Now."

"She's right." Carter stood and walked to Allie's side. "I'm out of ideas. And somebody was in Allie's room last night. It's time."

"Well"—Rachel sighed as she joined them—"maybe she won't expel all of us."

"And you're certain you weren't dreaming?" Isabelle's eyes were piercing, but Allie didn't falter under her gaze.

"Positive."

After they'd approached her with their story, Isabelle had invited Sylvain to join them.

Now they were all crowded into her office. Allie and Carter perched on the top of the cabinets they'd rifled through two weeks before. Rachel sat cross-legged on the floor beneath them.

Sylvain and Isabelle sat in the headmistress's leather chairs.

"It will be one of Nathaniel's people," Sylvain said.

Isabelle looked incredulous, but he didn't back down.

"Don't worry. They all know about Nathaniel already. Isn't that right, Allie?" He looked at her steadily.

Flushing, she nodded.

"How do you know about Nathaniel?" Isabelle's voice was taut with anger.

Allie glanced quickly at Carter, then back at Isabelle. As she thought about what to say, she twisted the hem of her shirt around her finger.

"Does it really matter?" she asked finally.

Isabelle held her gaze for a long moment and Allie couldn't read her expression.

"No. I suppose it doesn't." The headmistress turned to Carter and Rachel. "Do you all know?"

They nodded mutely.

"Fine, then. There are two days left in the term," Isabelle said. "Already Night School is stretched to capacity trying to ensure the grounds are safe. But there are not enough of us—somebody made it through and we noticed nothing. I don't know what you think you know about Nathaniel, but I can tell you he is very dangerous and vindictive. He was behind the attack the night of the Summer Ball. So we need to change our strategy. I will speak to the others but, in the meantime, Sylvain and Carter, your role from now on will be to stay close to Allie at all times. Night and day. At least one of you will accompany her constantly. Never leave her side. Work in shifts. Agreed?"

Carter glowered at Sylvain, but he nodded.

Sylvain kept his eyes on Isabelle. "Agreed."

"Allie." Isabelle turned toward her. "I want you to continue your life as normal. Go to class. Sleep in your own room. But do not go anywhere without Carter or Sylvain."

Although she was unable to imagine how this was going to work (*What about the bathroom?*), Allie nodded mutely.

"Rachel, I know you're doing this already, but stay with Allie as much as possible, too. She will need your support."

"Of course," Rachel said.

Isabelle continued, "I will speak with your father to make sure he's fine with this, but I'm sure he will be.

"Now." Isabelle's eyes swept the students. "You have work to do."

In the hallway outside her office, tension was thick in the air. Carter gripped Allie's hand possessively.

"Would you like me to take the first shift?" Sylvain's voice was pure silk.

A tendon worked in Carter's jaw.

"I want you to go f—" he started, but Allie grabbed his arm.

"Carter, no. Calm down. You can both stay with me until one of you has to go somewhere, Okay? Then the other will take over." She looked from one to the other of them. "No fighting. With each other, anyway."

Neither of them responded.

"I'll be in the library with Rachel for the rest of the day. We can all study together," Allie continued. "It will be fine. It's just two days."

"That is fine with me," Sylvain purred.

Carter still hadn't spoken, and now Allie looked up into his face, squeezing his tense hand in hers.

"Come on," she whispered.

"Fine," he said through clenched teeth. "We'll both take care of you."

Allie breathed out. "Good."

"Anyway . . . there's a chemistry book calling my name," Rachel said, clearly uncomfortable.

Allie shot her a grateful look. "And I've still got to finish that endless history paper. I just need to run up to my room to get my notes."

"I'll go with you," Carter and Sylvain chorused.

They glared at each other.

"Oh God," Allie muttered. "This is just *perfect*."

For the rest of the evening, aside from a brief break for dinner, the four of them worked in the library where the no-talking rule meant no fights, something for which Allie was grateful. But whenever she took a coffee break, Sylvain and Carter both stood up to accompany her. Carter would glower at Sylvain, who always innocently shrugged. "But I am thirsty."

"Dickhead," Carter would mutter, reaching for Allie's hand.

Allie turned to Rachel as he pulled her away, mouthing: "Help me."

Rachel grimaced sympathetically.

Later, when Rachel suggested a bathroom break, Allie followed her eagerly. Sylvain and Carter waited outside the door.

"So, basically, this is my worst nightmare. My current and former would-be boyfriends at my side constantly . . . together." Allie splashed cold water on her face.

"Carter's handling this really badly," Rachel said. "I wish for his own sake he'd have a big steaming cup of calm the hell down."

"No way can I take this for two whole days." After drying her face, Allie applied a sweep of pale pink lip gloss. "I'll lose it."

For a second she stared at herself in the mirror. Her hair had grown while she'd been here, and the henna had faded away. Now it hung in glossy dark waves to her shoulder blades. Her wide-set gray eyes were framed by long lashes, feathery black against her pale skin. She wore only minimal makeup; she didn't need more. The crisp white blouse and pleated short skirt of her uniform emphasized her curves and made the most of her athletic legs. It struck her that she didn't look anything like the tomboy she'd always been. For the first time, she thought she could see something of what Carter and Sylvain saw when they looked at her.

I've changed, she thought, and saw a surprised expression in the mirror. *I'm kind of, almost . . . pretty.*

"Ready?" Rachel asked, tossing her paper towel in the trash.

Allie tucked her lip gloss into her pocket.

"Ready."

"It's got to stop, Carter," Allie said. "It's just two days. I really want you to do this."

"But I can never forget the way he treated you . . . ," he said, his shoulders tense.

"I know. More than anyone. But he's apologized and I've . . . well, *mostly* forgiven him, so now you have to," she said. "He's helping me. He's earning back trust. And Isabelle wants us to work together, so please stop being so macho. It's not like you."

It was after midnight and they were sitting on the bed in

Allie's room. The window was closed and locked, and a bar had been affixed across the shutter to secure it more snugly. Isabelle had decided one of them should spend the night outside Allie's room, but they were both insisting on staying. Sylvain was waiting outside the door now.

"I'm sorry," Carter said. "I know I'm being jealous."

"Ya think?" Allie laughed.

He smiled back, shamefaced. "A little, maybe."

"You're the one I want, Carter West." She climbed up onto his lap so that her legs straddled him and her face was inches from his. "You have nothing to be jealous about."

His hands slid down her back as she wrapped her arms around his neck. "Only you," she whispered, leaning forward to kiss him.

They kissed until all thoughts of Sylvain left their minds and they were entirely focused on each other. Carter's hands slid down to her hips and pulled her tightly against him, and she did not resist. When his hands pulled her blouse out of the waistband of her skirt and ran up and down her bare back, her skin tingled. When she nipped at his ear with her teeth, she could feel his heart race.

When she pulled back from him, they were both breathless; Carter's face was flushed.

"I'll be the grown-up this time," Allie said.

"Do you have to?" he whispered. Her skirt had hiked up, and he stroked her bare thighs.

"Unfortunately." She climbed to her feet and, leaning forward, lightly brushed her lips against his, pulling back before he could grab her. "Somebody's got to, and I get the feeling it's not going to be you."

"Not this time," he said.

Running her hands through her hair to smooth it, she said. "So, I'm glad we had this little talk. . . ."

He laughed.

"Will you try and not be so jealous?"

"I'll try," he said. Standing up, he reached for her, but she was at the door in two seconds and flung it open.

"Good night then." She looked around outside until she saw Sylvain sitting with his back to the wall watching her door, expressionless. "Good night, Sylvain."

"Good night, Allie." She thought she heard regret in his voice.

Carter walked past her out the door, leaning over to kiss her lightly. "If you hear or see anything at all, just shout, okay?"

"I promise."

As soon as he was gone, she changed into clean pajamas and climbed into bed. After she turned out the light, she reran the evening in her mind, remembering the way his lips had felt. How much he'd wanted her.

Not once did she think about Nathaniel, or danger, or needing bodyguards. Instead, suffused in the warm glow of happiness, she floated into sleep.

Later, she would wonder what woke her. Maybe it was footsteps in the corridor. Or voices outside the door. Either way, when her door burst open and the light switched on, she was already sitting up in bed. It was three o'clock.

"Get up, Allie." Carter's face was grim. "Nathaniel's coming."

TWENTY-EIGHT

Allie worked to stay calm. Still groggy from sleep, she tried several times to put on her slippers but couldn't seem to make her feet slide into them.

"Leave them. There's no time." Carter reached for her hand and pulled her into the corridor, where Sylvain stood alert, waiting for them.

"This way," Sylvain said, leading them away from the staircase.

"Where are we going?" Allie whispered.

"Out of here," Carter said.

They ran to the end of the hallway, where Jules waited for them by an unnumbered door Allie had always assumed was a broom closet. Without a word she pushed it open to reveal a narrow, winding stone staircase, dimly lit by exposed bare bulbs.

They ran down at breakneck speed, Sylvain in the lead, Allie and Carter in the middle, and Jules bringing up the rear. Nobody spoke. When they reached the bottom, Sylvain opened a door leading into a room Allie had never seen before—a cryptlike space that seemed to be hewn from rock, with thick limestone pillars covered in elaborate carvings, lighted by flickering gaslight. The stone floor felt dusty and cold beneath Allie's feet.

I don't believe it. There is *a dungeon.*

"Where are we?" she whispered.

"Cellar," Jules said.

She, Sylvain, and Carter had formed a ring of sorts with Allie at the center. They each had their backs to her, peering into the shadows.

"Should we get her out of the building?" Jules asked.

"Isabelle said get her out if it's safe," Carter said. "But how do we know if it's safe?"

"Stay here." Sylvain's voice came from behind Allie.

Soundlessly he disappeared into the shadows.

The other three stayed where they were in silence. After about five minutes Sylvain reappeared and gestured for them to follow.

In the same formation they'd adopted on the stairs, they ran to a door hidden in the shadows. He motioned for them to wait as he slipped through the door; then he returned again and nodded at Carter.

They followed him up a flight of stairs and through a door so small, they had to duck to get through it. Once outside, they stood in a line with their backs against the school wall. Carter's arm stretched out across Allie protectively.

The night was cool and damp—clouds covered the moon. Allie could see nothing at first, but gradually her eyes adjusted.

It reminded her of the night that she and Carter had followed Isabelle to her meeting with Nathaniel. Uneasy, she looked off to the tree line, black on the horizon.

Is somebody there now, watching us the way we watched them?

Carter tugged her hand: they were on the move. They ran around the west wing to the back of the school building, past the terrace lawn and toward the walled garden. Stones cut into Allie's feet, but she ignored the pain. Just before they would have reached the garden gate, Sylvain turned off the path and disappeared. One at a time they followed him.

The gazebo he led them to was so well hidden behind trees and thick foliage that Allie had never noticed it before.

She couldn't fully make out its features in the heavy darkness, but she could feel that it was made of stone, and she could just make out a statue of a graceful nude woman dancing in the middle.

Communicating only through hand gestures, Carter, Sylvain, and Jules again formed a protective shield in front of Allie, looking back toward the school. Allie tried to be as still as the statue behind her.

For a long time nothing happened. Allie had counted one hundred thirty-seven breaths when she saw Jules gesture at a tiny point of light in the distance. Allie narrowed her eyes to try and focus on it.

Within seconds there was another. And another.

Then there were half a dozen of them, moving so smoothly that they seemed to float. And they were getting closer.

Allie stood between Jules and Carter trying to get a better look.

"What are they?" she breathed.

It was Sylvain who replied. "Nathaniel."

Allie's breath caught in her throat. "What are we going to do?"

"Wait," Jules said.

It took five minutes for the points of light to become flaming torches. And they were close enough that Allie could see the shadowy shapes holding them when she heard Isabelle's voice ring out.

"Nathaniel! Stop this. It's not too late."

"I know it's not too late." That familiar disdainful voice chilled Allie's blood. "That is why we're here."

"Leave this school alone," Isabelle said. "No matter what you do, you will never have Cimmeria."

"You sound so certain," he said. "But then you were always arrogant."

"Lucinda doesn't want this, Nathaniel." Her voice held a warning. "You go against her wishes at your peril."

"If that's true, then where is she?" he scoffed. "I don't see her rushing here to protect you."

As they argued, something in the air caught Allie's attention. A change in temperature? Or was it . . . smell?

What is that?

Her hand shot out and she grabbed Carter's arm urgently. "Smoke. I smell smoke."

Sniffing the air, Sylvain turned to Carter, and for the first time she saw alarm on his face.

"There!" Jules pointed to the boys' dormitory wing. Smoke poured from a second-floor window and flames danced behind the glass.

"Oh my God," Allie whispered.

"Jules, stay with Allie," Sylvain said. "Carter, come with me."

Before following him, Carter grabbed Allie by the shoulders.

"Stay here." It was dark, but she could see fear in his eyes.

Wordlessly she nodded, reaching up to grip his hand in hers so tightly it hurt.

And then he was gone.

Now alone, Allie and Jules stood side by side watching the school.

Isabelle's voice had lost none of its confidence. "Is that your plan, Nathaniel? To destroy what you cannot take by lying? By cheating? By demanding? I always knew you were petulant, but this act will destroy you. Not Cimmeria."

He laughed. "Please don't insult me, Isabelle. I'm smarter than that."

A light on the top floor of the west wing caught Allie's eye. Touching Jules's shoulder she pointed. It flickered in a window.

"The girls' dorm," Jules whispered, staring at it.

"What should we do?" Allie asked.

"Sylvain and Carter will take care of it," Jules whispered.

But time stretched on and nothing happened. The flames in the girls' wing seemed to take confidence and grew quickly. The smell of smoke was strong now.

"Jules, we have to do something," Allie said urgently.

"I promised Sylvain . . . ," Jules said, but Allie could hear the worry in her voice.

Allie made up her mind. "We'll stick together. Let's go."

She didn't wait for Jules to talk her out of it—she shot out of the gazebo toward the tree line, but Jules caught up with her quickly and grabbed the sleeve of her pajamas, directing her around the side of the school to an entrance away from Isabelle and Nathaniel.

They ran through the door together into a light haze of smoke. They were in a dark room with shelf after shelf of books.

We're in the back of the library.

They were near where she'd met Carter several weeks ago— Ancient Latin. She'd never known there was a door there.

"This way," Jules whispered.

And then she disappeared.

Bewildered, Allie spun in a circle looking for her, but she was alone.

"Jules?" she hissed into the darkness. "Where are you?"

There was no answer.

"Jules?" Allie could hear the panic in her voice. Taking a shaky breath, she tried to decide what to do.

Something was wrong. She was sure Jules wouldn't have left her . . . or would she?

Her heart beat frantically. *Did she lead me into a trap?*

She coughed. The smoke was getting thicker.

Suddenly she knew what to do.

Dashing out into the main library, past the study carrels and the tables where she'd sat with Rachel and Jo so many times, she burst through the library door. There was a fire alarm switch right next to it, and she yanked it down.

Nothing happened.

She stared at it, baffled. Then a memory came back to her— something Gabe had said before the Summer Splash: *"None of the alarms in this building are real. There are no alarms."*

Without stopping to think, she ran up the main stairs toward the girls' dorm. As she reached the landing and turned toward the next staircase, she saw a figure at the end of the hall. He held a flaming torch in his hand.

She froze. He hadn't seen her yet. If she stayed very still, he would never notice her, and then she could get upstairs to the girls' dorm.

But then he would set more fires. The school would burn down. Nathaniel would win. She felt torn. What was more important? Warning the girls or stopping him?

It was an impossible situation. There was nobody there to tell her what to do.

An unexpected surge of rage shook her and she took several steps toward him.

"Hey! You!" she shouted at the top of her lungs, and she saw him stop and turn.

For a moment that was as short as forever, neither of them moved and they stared at each other. The flame was close enough to his face that she could make out his features.

"Christopher?" she whispered.

She saw recognition in his eyes, and something else. And then he ran.

"Christopher!" She was screaming now. "Christopher! Don't leave me!"

Through the tears that ran down her face, she saw that he was gone.

The world spun, and she leaned against the wall for support while she took a steadying breath. But the smoke was too thick now, and she coughed so fiercely that she thought she might faint.

Okay, she thought, gasping for air. *Calm down, Allie.*

She could hear Carter's words in her head, telling her to focus on her breathing. She took slow, steady breaths, filtering the air through the fabric of her sleeve. When the world stopped spinning, she looked around. The smoke was getting thicker.

She didn't have much time.

Pulling her pajama top up over her mouth, she bent down low and raced up the remaining stairs (*seventeen steps*) to the girls' dorm. She threw open the first door she saw. Smoke hadn't made it in here yet and she could breathe. The girl in bed sat up.

It was Katie.

"Fire!" Allie shouted, taking a welcome breath of clean air. "Katie, get up and help me. We have to get everyone out."

"What?" Katie's voice was groggy and confused, but she soon focused on Allie. "What the . . . ?"

"The school's on fire, Katie. Please!"

Smelling the smoke, Katie jumped out of bed.

As Allie ran out the door, she shouted over her shoulder, "Every door! Knock on every door! Tell them to follow me."

Katie took one side of the hallway and Allie the other and they raced down the hall, throwing open doors and, if necessary, shaking girls in their beds to wake them.

Allie dashed to Rachel's room, but she was already up, disturbed by the voices.

"Help me," Allie said, breathlessly.

"Right behind you," Rachel said.

By the time Allie reached Jo's door, most of the girls were up. Closest to the fire, Jo's room was full of smoke, and Allie could see her blond head still on the pillow. She dropped to the floor and crawled across the room.

"Jo," she gasped, her voice a hoarse croak. "Wake up."

But she didn't move. Even when Allie shook her violently, she didn't react.

Reaching back, Allie slapped her face hard.

Her eyes fluttered.

"Ow," she whispered faintly, and Allie felt a hysterical urge to laugh.

"Get up, Jo. You have to get up."

With her arm under Jo's shoulder, Allie shoved her upright, but she was too heavy for her to lift alone. When Rachel walked in a few seconds later, she quickly assessed the situation and put her arm around Jo's other shoulder. Together they got her on her feet.

"Lisa," Jo whispered.

Allie shot a panicked look at Rachel.

"I've seen her," Rachel said. "She's in the hall."

As they half carried Jo from the room, Allie looked around worriedly.

"Is this everyone?"

"I did a count." The voice was Katie's. "The only person missing is Jules."

Allie felt like she'd been punched.

"She was with me downstairs," she said breathlessly. "I lost her."

"Let's get out of here first," Rachel said gently. "Then we can look for her."

Allie could see the sense in her words. "This way."

Jo's feet were moving now, and Rachel could support her alone, so Allie led them out along the route Sylvain had taken earlier that night. That stairwell was still free of smoke.

As they emerged into the cellar, Allie turned to Katie. "Do another head count."

Without hesitating Katie quickly tallied their numbers. "We're all here."

Allie gestured for everyone to follow her and led them up the short staircase to the door, praying it would open.

It did.

They poured out into the darkness, coughing and inhaling the fresh air deep into their lungs. Allie walked far enough away from them all so that nobody could see. Then she vomited onto the grass.

When she returned to the group, Jo was standing on her own, although she still looked woozy.

Allie straightened and tried to look like she had it all together.

"Jo, can you get everybody into the walled garden?" she asked huskily. "I think you'll be safe there."

Jo nodded and walked weakly down the path. All the others followed her except Rachel and Katie.

"Where are you going?" Rachel sounded suspicious.

"I have to find Jules," Allie said. "She could be hurt."

"Then I'm coming with you," Rachel said.

"Rach, no." Allie could hear the worry in her own voice. "You could get hurt."

"So could you," Katie pointed out. "And I'm coming with you, too. Jules is my best friend. We're not going to let you do this alone."

"Oh God," Allie groaned. "You guys, this is bad."

"Lead the way, Allie." Rachel's voice was firm. "Where did you see her last?"

Allie stared at them doubtfully, but time was passing. She knew she'd never talk them out of it anyway.

"In the library. There's a secret door."

"I know where it is," Rachel said.

"You do?"

"Of course I do," she said. "I know everything about that library."

Sticking to the shadows, they ran to the door and shoved it open. Smoke poured out in a thick gray wave.

Allie felt her heart sink. This was impossible.

"Stay low," Rachel hissed, and they dropped to their hands and knees, covering their faces with clothing.

"Where were you when you saw her last?" Katie asked Allie, her voice muffled.

Allie didn't want to tell her that in the thick smoke it all looked unfamiliar. That she wasn't sure at all. Holding her breath, she climbed to her feet and looked around, then dropped down again.

Ancient Latin dead ahead.

"Fifteen feet ahead. I think."

They crawled forward. But when they reached the spot, Jules was nowhere to be seen.

Rachel coughed. "I don't see her."

"Let's split up." Katie's voice was muffled by her shirt. "Go no more than ten feet in three different directions then meet back here."

"Carefully . . . ," Allie added.

Staying as low as she could, Allie crawled away from the others, counting her progress in her head. But she went more than ten feet in the end—when she didn't find Jules she went twenty. Then twenty-five.

But Jules wasn't there.

The smoke was thicker here, and it was difficult to see much of anything. Her eyes burned and the tears blurred her vision even further.

Too far. I've gone too far.

She turned to return to the others but was instantly disoriented—which way had she come? In the dark and smoke it all looked the same. Had she passed that tall bookshelf before? The one with book titles in Cyrillic? Had she ever seen it before at all?

She coughed viciously. When she tried to catch her breath, even through her shirt the smoke was so thick it was like being underwater. There was no air. There was no oxygen. Her breath came in short, futile gasps.

When she tried to move faster, the edges of her vision began turning black.

She wasn't going to make it.

Far away she heard a voice cry, "I've got her! She's here."

Another voice called her name. She tried to crawl toward the sound, but she couldn't move.

"Here," she croaked, but she knew the sound was too weak to travel.

She'd never felt more tired. *If I could just rest for a second, I'd gather my strength. A short nap and I'll be able to help more. I'm just so tired.*

Her head felt so heavy. She let it drop to the floor.

As unconsciousness wrapped around her like a warm blanket, she sighed with relief.

Suddenly she was flying, supported by something strong and loving. She leaned into it. Safe. Protected. Floating.

Warm air filled her lungs, and went away. Filled her lungs, and went away. Over and over.

And then a beautiful voice. "Please don't leave us. Don't go."

Warm lips on hers. Warm air in her body.

Pain racked her and she coughed so violently that her body shook convulsively. When the convulsion stopped, though, fresh air caressed her and she breathed in gratefully.

Her eyes fluttered open. She was lying in Sylvain's lap, his arms tight around her. She reached up and touched his face wonderingly.

"Why are you crying?" she whispered.

He didn't answer. Instead, he rocked her like a baby, his face in her hair. Listening to her breathe.

TWENTY-NINE

"This time Isabelle did call the fire department, then?" Allie asked in a hoarse whisper.

"For, like, the first time ever." Rachel smiled at her. "After you and Jules scared the crap out of everyone."

It was morning and they were sitting in a bedroom in the teachers' wing. Allie was propped up on pillows, clutching the cup of tea with lemon and honey that Rachel had brought to soothe her sore throat. Rachel was perched on the foot of the bed, filling her in on "everything that happened after you died."

"They put an oxygen mask on you, although they had to pry you away from Sylvain to do it." Rachel arched one eyebrow. "He wouldn't let you go."

"Was it Sylvain who found me then?"

Allie's memories of the library were fragmented and hazy.

"Yes."

"How . . . ?"

"He and Carter had cleared the guys' dorm. Then they saw the other fire. Carter went to get the teachers out. Sylvain was going to clear the girls' dorm, but when he realized it was empty he found us outside," Rachel explained. "Katie and I had just brought Jules out and saw that you weren't there. . . ."

She stopped in midsentence and Allie realized that she was crying. Reaching across the bed, she squeezed Rachel's hand.

"I'm okay," she whispered. Rachel nodded and wiped tears from her eyes.

After a second she continued, but now her voice shook. "When we told him you were missing, nobody could stop him. He ran into the library like he couldn't burn."

She took a deep breath.

"I didn't see you when he brought you out—I was giving Jules CPR. But Jo told me he gave you CPR for a long time before you came to. After that he wouldn't let you go. Guess he was afraid you'd stop breathing."

"Guess he was," Allie echoed.

"Anyway, as soon as Isabelle called the fire department, Nathaniel and his cronies melted away—and I wish I meant that literally." Rachel leaned back against the wall. "You and Jules and three members of the staff all needed oxygen. Jules and this one guy—Peter? Do you know him?"

Allie shook her head.

"He's one of the younger students. Well, they're both in the hospital for smoke inhalation. They wanted to take you, too, but nobody would let them. Isabelle, Carter, and Sylvain just weren't having it. So they put you in here and Carter sat with you all night to make sure you kept breathing. Which you did," she finished brightly.

"Yay me," Allie croaked weakly.

"Indeed. Yay you."

"How bad is the damage?" Allie asked.

"I'm not sure. I know three or four rooms are totaled. They won't let anyone into the dorms, and the whole building reeks of smoke." She wrinkled her nose. "The fire in the library was started at the librarian's desk and spread to the stacks nearby. They don't know how many books are gone."

She looked genuinely sad, and Allie had to hide a smile.

"They think the dorm rooms where the fires were set were all unoccupied, and a fire was set in an attic and on the landing near the stairs"—Allie had a flash memory of Christopher with a flaming torch—"but they're still assessing. Isabelle's running around like a madwoman.

"Contractors are coming in this afternoon to assess the damage, and everybody's being sent home. We're all writing essays to replace our last few exams. I think we should insist on doing ours on fire safety."

Allie's chuckle sounded like sandpaper on rough wood. "I could change my history essay to the Great Fire of London."

"Yeah, right? You've already done the research."

Someone knocked on the door. Allie tried to say, "Come in," but it came out as a whisper.

"Enter," Rachel called.

Jo opened the door and ducked in nervously, closing it behind her. She wore boys' pajamas that were about four sizes too big.

"Hey . . . are you okay?"

Allie smiled weakly. "I'm going to live—again—I think," she said. "Rachel was just telling me everything that happened last night."

"It was crazy," Jo said. "Really scary."

"But here we all are," Rachel said. "And I got to do CPR on a real person for the first time ever. So it wasn't all bad."

"Totally worth it," Allie agreed.

"That's what I thought."

Looking uncomfortable, Jo turned to Rachel. "I hate to ask, but would you mind awfully if I had a few minutes alone with . . .'"

Rachel jumped off the bed. "Of course. Allie, I'll go get you some food. What do you want?"

Allie's throat hurt. "Something cold," she said. "Nothing sharp."

An affectionate smile lit up Rachel's face. "Right. No sharp food. Leave it to me, babe."

When the door closed behind her, Jo sat gingerly on the edge of the bed.

"I just wanted to tell you I'm sorry."

Allie started to tell her it wasn't necessary, but Jo shook her head. Her face was red and Allie could see that she'd been crying.

"You saved my life last night—and you risked your own to do it. I believe you did the same thing on the roof a few weeks ago. Katie admitted she lied to me because she was mad at you."

Allie's eyebrows shot up. "She did?"

Jo nodded. "You saved her life, too, you know. She might be a bitch, but she's not an ungrateful bitch."

A hoarse laugh burst out of Allie before she could stop it, and soon they were both giggling, although that set off a fit of coughing from Allie.

"I'll tell her you said so," she managed to sputter.

When they calmed, Jo looked at her seriously. "I know I have a problem, Allie. I just have these . . . what the shrink called 'episodes' when I'm not rational. And I really shouldn't ever drink. I'm sorry you got caught up in it. I wish so much that it had never happened. If I could take it back, I'd do it in a second. But I want you to know I'm working on it."

"It's okay," Allie said, although it wasn't.

As if she'd heard her thoughts, Jo said, "It's not okay, actually. I know that."

"Good." Allie's voice was gentle.

But Jo wasn't finished. "The thing is," she said, "each time it happens, something sets it off. It used to be my parents. They'd do something stupid or forget about me and off I'd go. But this time it was . . . what happened to Ruth." She looked up at Allie. "It's just . . . knowing something awful and not telling anyone . . . I think it makes you crazy."

Allie felt a tingle of fear, like icy fingers against her skin. She couldn't tear her eyes away from Jo's. "What did you know that nobody else knew?"

Jo's round, cornflower blue eyes held hers. "I knew who killed Ruth. And I couldn't handle it. Just knowing. I couldn't . . . be the only one."

Two breaths in, one breath out . . .

Allie stared at her steadily as her heart pounded in her ears.

"Who killed Ruth, Jo?" she whispered.

"Gabe did it." Jo's voice was dull with grief. "Gabe killed Ruth."

When Rachel returned a few minutes later with yogurt, ice cream, and strawberries ("See? Nothing sharp . . ."), Allie was holding Jo in her arms as she sobbed.

Over Jo's head, Allie whispered to Rachel, "Get Isabelle." Without a word, Rachel dropped the food on the desk and ran.

"It's going to be okay," Allie whispered over and over, although she wasn't sure it would be. She felt sick, and took deep, settling breaths to try and steady her own nerves as questions rushed through her mind too fast for answers to catch up.

Gabe did it? Gabe killed Ruth? Why?

She remembered hiding from Gabe on the path that night she was out with Carter. Something in his voice—some element of menace—had kicked a self-protective instinct into action and led her to hide. She'd been as scared of him at that moment as she'd ever been of Nathaniel.

But murder?

That seemed inconceivable. Why would he do something like that? Ruth was his friend. What could she have done to make him want to hurt her? Much less to kill her.

"Jo, Isabelle's coming here in a few minutes and you have to tell her the truth," Allie rasped. "Will you do that?"

Her face puffy and red, Jo nodded. "That's why I told you. I think everybody needs to know. He's dangerous."

When Rachel and Isabelle ran in a few minutes later, Jo was still crying. The headmistress wore the same dark leggings and tunic she'd worn the night of the parley, and she smelled faintly of smoke.

"Allie?" she asked, taking in Jo's tears and Allie's pale face. "Is everything okay?"

"Jo has something she needs to tell you," Allie whispered.

Jo repeated to Isabelle what she'd told Allie. As she talked, Isabelle sank slowly to her knees beside the bed, never taking her eyes off Jo's face.

"But why, Jo?" she asked finally. "Did he tell you why?"

"He said Ruth talked. And that she knew too much about what was really going on. She wanted to tell people. I think she wanted to tell you," Jo said. "But then he wouldn't tell me what that meant—like what was really going on."

Allie could see the shock on Isabelle's face, but the headmistress kept her voice calm.

"Rachel," she said, "would you go get Eloise and Mr. Zelazny, please?" She reached out for Jo's hand, wet with tears and clutching a damp, crumpled tissue. "Did he tell you how he did it?"

"A little. Enough to scare me," Jo said. "It was during the ball. Everyone was happy and dancing. He only left me alone for a few minutes, but when he came back, I saw blood on his hand. I thought he'd hurt himself. He said he'd had an accident—a cut—nothing serious. But he didn't tell me then . . . about Ruth. He told me later. He thought Allie and I were getting too close. He didn't want me hanging out with her anymore. He told me what happened to Ruth could happen to Allie, too. Or any of her friends."

Remembering Ruth's body—her face all but unrecognizable and drained of blood, her pretty pink dress dark with gore—Allie swallowed hard. Gabe had been threatening her. That could have been her face. Her pretty dress.

She counted her heartbeats . . . *twelve, thirteen, fourteen* . . .

"What else did he tell you?" Isabelle asked.

"He didn't want me to tell Allie anything about Night School, or anything about what he was doing." Jo's voice was dull. "He said Allie was to blame for all the bad things that were happening, and that you and Mr. Zelazny . . ." She glanced up at Isabelle and away. "He said you were weak. He said Nathaniel was right and you should just let him have Cimmeria. . . ."

Isabelle and Allie exchanged a startled look.

"How did Gabe know Nathaniel?" Isabelle asked gently.

"I don't know," Jo said. "But they just . . . know each other. Like Gabe meets him sometimes. To talk."

Allie gasped.

"They're . . . friends?" Isabelle's voice shook, just a little. Jo wouldn't have heard it, but Allie did.

"Kind of." Jo thought about it. "I think Gabe admires him. After the ball, he kept saying Nathaniel should take over Cimmeria. And that his ideas for the organization were right, and you were just old-fashioned. Out of touch."

"But why did he kill Ruth?" Isabelle asked. "What did she have to do with it?"

There was a long pause as Jo took a sobbing breath.

"She talked," she whispered, "too much. He said he didn't trust her anymore."

At that moment Zelazny and Eloise walked in. After resting her hand on Jo's shoulder for a second, Isabelle rose to her feet and stepped outside to talk with them. She returned to the room alone and sat on the bed next to Jo and Allie.

"Why didn't you tell us sooner, darling?" she asked quietly.

Tears streamed down Jo's face. "I didn't know what to do," she sobbed. "I love . . . loved Gabe. I couldn't . . . I didn't know what to do. I'm sorry. I'm so sorry."

"It's okay," Isabelle whispered. But Allie could tell she was lying.

After Isabelle led Jo away, Rachel returned long enough to make Allie eat some melted ice cream and warm yogurt. She stayed until Allie fell asleep.

When she woke up, Carter was sitting on the foot of the bed watching her, his dark eyes unreadable.

"Hey," she rasped.

"How're you doing?" His voice was gentle.

"Never better." But waking up set off a round of coughing. Her throat burned as if the fire were happening inside it.

He handed her a glass of water with a straw; the cool liquid was soothing. After a second she scooted up in the bed until she was sitting.

"Did you hear about Gabe?" she whispered.

He nodded, his muscles tense. "I should have seen it, Allie. Why didn't I see that it was him?"

"Nobody could see it," she said. "Don't blame yourself or we'll all have to blame ourselves. Have they found him?"

"No—they're all looking."

She took a minute to digest this information.

Then she said, "Rachel told me that you saved lots of people last night. That's amazing."

"And you saved people, too." But he didn't say it was amazing and she could see the tension in his face.

"What's the matter?" she said.

He shook his head and didn't speak for a moment; when he did, his voice quivered.

"Why didn't you stay in the hiding place, Allie? You would have been okay if you'd listened to me."

"I'm sorry, Carter. But I was scared for the girls," she said. "I had to help. I couldn't just let them die."

"We would have gotten them out," he said.

"We didn't know that," she said. "The fire spread fast."

"Whose idea was it to go in? Yours or Jules's?"

Allie thought longingly about lying. "Mine," she said. "Jules wanted to wait awhile longer."

"And you both nearly died," he said angrily.

"But we saved people, Carter." Her hoarse voice was indignant. "We did help."

"I would sacrifice every single one of them for you."

She stared at him, aghast. "Don't say that," she whispered. "That's horrible."

"I know it's horrible." His fingers flicked a tear off his cheek and he avoided her eyes. "It's also true."

She had no idea what to say, and she studied him worriedly.

"I'm okay, you know."

"I know."

"So let's not lose sight of that? Let's just be glad that we're both alive." She reached for his hand and held it against her cheek. "I'm so glad that you're alive."

Saying nothing, he wrapped her in his arms.

"Carter and Allie save the world," she whispered.

That afternoon, Rachel brought Allie a skirt and blouse that smelled like a bonfire.

"They let me in the dorm for all of three seconds, and I raided your wardrobe for these," she said. "Sorry about the stench."

"No worries," Allie said. "I'm just psyched to finally get out of these char-grilled pajamas."

"They said we could go up to get the rest of our stuff tomorrow," Rachel said. "With supervision, of course."

"Of course." Allie gave a wry smile. "Wouldn't want anyone to get hurt. . . ."

After a shower in the teachers' bathroom to scrub the soot out of her hair, Allie began to feel human again. Rachel had forgotten shoes, though, so when she padded down the stairs later, she was still barefoot. But she walked with purpose straight to Isabelle's office and knocked. Isabelle and Eloise had already questioned her thoroughly about everything that had happened the night of the fire. But now she had questions of her own to ask.

The door opened before her knuckles left the wood, and without a word Isabelle wrapped her in a bear hug. Then she held her at arm's length and studied her face.

"How are you?"

"I'm good," Allie whispered, ". . . ish."

The headmistress held the door open for her. "Come in."

The normally neat office was in chaos. Papers and files lay on the floor and were stacked haphazardly on chairs.

Without waiting to be asked, Allie pushed some papers out of one of the chairs in front of the desk and sat down. Across the room Isabelle switched on the electric kettle and gathered cups.

Allie wasn't sure she could face more tea.

She opened her mouth to ask a question, then closed it again, afraid of the answer. But the question had to be asked.

"Gabe?" she whispered finally.

Without looking at her, Isabelle shook her head. "He's gone. When Mr. Zelazny and Eloise went to find him, he'd disappeared. We think he might have gone last night during the fire."

Somehow Allie wasn't surprised. She took a steadying breath.

After a second the headmistress handed her a cup of

strange-smelling herbal tea with a slice of lemon.

"For your throat. Drink it." She sat down beside her. "You sound terrible. Did the nurse see you?"

She nodded. "He said I'll live. But I'll never sing with the opera."

"Puccini will get along without you," Isabelle said with a strained smile. "It could have been much worse."

"That's what I thought." Allie asked the next question with trepidation. "Isabelle, I heard what Nathaniel said last night, and I don't understand it. Why does he want the school so badly? What is this all about?"

"Oh, Allie." The headmistress curled up in the deep leather chair next to her—the dark circles under her eyes betraying her exhaustion. "It's a very long story. Too long to get into now. But it has everything to do with the larger organization, of which Cimmeria is only a small part. Nathaniel was once a significant part of that organization, but he argued with those in power and was dismissed from it entirely. Since then he's been trying to get back in again. He has ideas that I—and quite a few others—don't agree with. But he's never taken no for an answer. And he uses people to get what he wants. So he's been using me—and my work at Cimmeria." She looked over at Allie. "And now, because of who you are, he wants to use you, too."

An unexpected surge of anger rushed through Allie, so intense it almost left her breathless.

"Well then, who am I, Isabelle? Can you tell me that much?" she snapped. "Because the person I thought I was really wouldn't interest Nathaniel at all."

For a long moment Isabelle didn't reply. Then: "I think you've already guessed some of it," she said in a low voice. "Haven't you?

But you need to start at the beginning. And the beginning, for you, is your mother. I want you to talk with her about this."

"But she's not here." Anger made Allie's voice shake. She gripped the teacup so tightly, the hot liquid scalded her through the thin porcelain. "I need answers *now*. I have waited long enough. And I have been through enough. I deserve to know why I nearly died. Why my brother . . ."

Isabelle rested a hand on her arm.

"You're right," she said. "And I think you deserve answers. I can tell you that your family is very important. Your grandmother, in particular, is very important in the organization. In fact, Allie, she runs the organization. And she has for many years."

Stunned, Allie couldn't think of anything to say. Her grandmother ran it all? Who was she?

Isabelle continued, "She's the key to everything that's been happening. You see, Nathaniel used to work for her. But she fired him. He's decided that he wants to run the organization now, and the only way he can do that is—"

"If my grandmother doesn't run it anymore." Suddenly it all made some sort of sense, and Allie's thoughts whirled as she tried to process it all. She was just a pawn in Nathaniel's game.

"Exactly." Isabelle's golden-brown eyes seemed to glow in the light of the table lamp. "But he can't get to her. Not physically, anyway. She is impossible to reach. She's protected at all times. So he found one way he could hurt her—through her grandchildren. First Christopher. And now . . ."

"Me." The word came out in a matter-of-fact tone, but Allie could hardly breathe. It all seemed so unfair. She didn't even know who her grandmother was. Some woman named Lucinda who she'd never met. And yet Nathaniel would throw away her life, as casually as somebody might discard a tissue, to get to her.

"But who is she?" Allie's eyes searched Isabelle's face for clues. "Who is my grandmother?"

"Allie . . ." Isabelle shook her head, very slightly, and Allie could tell she would say no more. "The rest, I think, really must come from your mother. I would feel like I was betraying all her trust in me if I told you more without letting you talk to her first. I must at least give her a chance to explain why she's kept this from you. This is her mother, after all. Her family as much as yours."

Allie wanted to ask a thousand more questions. She wanted to know everything right now, but she knew that look on Isabelle's face. She was done for now.

"So . . ." Allie asked, "what happens next?"

"We will look for Gabe," Isabelle said. "We'll let his parents know. We will try to make sure he's safe. We will take care of Jo. And then we will find a way to deal with Nathaniel."

"I want to help."

"You will," Isabelle said. "I promise you that."

"No, Isabelle." Allie's voice was firm. "I mean I want to *help*. I want to be involved in everything from now on."

The headmistress looked at her blankly, and Allie tried not to let the frustration and tension she felt into her voice. If she ever needed to act grown-up, now was the time.

"As you've said yourself, I'm right in the middle of all of this. Nathaniel has Christopher and now he wants me, too. All this term I've been rescued and saved and helped, and everybody's all about protecting me, which is wonderful, and I am grateful. But I want to protect myself. Right now I don't know how." She steadied her nerves. "But there's one place where I could get the skill to do that."

Isabelle spoke slowly. "You want to join Night School."

"Doesn't it make sense?" Allie wrapped her arms around herself. "I need to be stronger and faster. I need to know how to fight. And I need to know what's happening so that I can do the right things. I'm never just going to do what you say if you say, 'Allie, don't go outside.' But if you include me in things . . . that's different."

"I don't know if you know exactly what you're asking," Isabelle protested. "You haven't been here long enough to know what this entails." But then she stopped, and Allie could see she was thinking. When she spoke again, her voice was calm. "Still, I can't fault your logic. I think you would be safer with training. So . . ." She rubbed her forehead with tired fingers. "Okay, then. I'll talk to the others."

A thrill of excitement rushed through Allie.

As if she'd seen that, Isabelle hurried to quash it. "It's not my decision alone, Allie. The board will have to agree. But I will back you up."

Even though she heard Isabelle's caution, Allie didn't believe it. She knew Isabelle could do anything she wanted.

She was in.

Before she could thank her, though, the headmistress spoke again.

"There's one more thing. I'm sending you home, Allie, tomorrow."

She had thought she might stay through until next term. Allie's heart sank.

Back to that house, she thought. But then she raised her chin. *But back with questions. And knowledge.*

"You need to talk with your mother, and your parents want you home." Her eyes darkened. "But in London you'll be in more danger. I'll do what I can to protect you, but don't take any chances."

Allie thought about Ruth. "I'll be careful," she promised. "I'll lie low."

"The autumn term starts in three weeks," Isabelle said. "And I can't let you stay home that long. I'll give you a few days, but after that I really think you should go to Rachel's. Her father is completely capable of protecting you. I'll send a car for you. I will explain all this to your mother."

There was something awful about being told that home—once the safest place she had ever known—wasn't safe anymore. But Allie didn't argue. She'd seen what Nathaniel was willing to do.

"Okay," she said again.

Isabelle took a piece of paper off her desk and wrote something on it. "If you get concerned or frightened at any point—if anything feels threatening or just wrong"—she handed her the piece of paper—"call me, and I'll send somebody for you. Don't take any chances. Will you do that for me?"

The paper had Isabelle's name embossed on the top, and Allie saw that she'd written a phone number on it.

Allie nodded. "I promise."

Allie walked to the door. As she turned the handle, though, Isabelle stopped her.

"One more thing," she said. "When you ask your mother about Lucinda . . ."

Allie's eyes widened but she said nothing.

Isabelle finished: ". . . tell her I said it's time. Tell her if she doesn't tell you, I will."

THIRTY

"Come on, zip!"

Allie had stuffed the last few things into her bag, and now it bulged at the sides and refused to close. Even when she used all of her strength, she couldn't get it to zip up.

The girls had all been given fifteen minutes in their rooms to pack. It turned out most bedrooms were fine. But the teachers were worried the fire and water might have made the ceilings and floors weak.

"Oh, screw it."

Panting from the exertion, she flipped it open and looked for something to jettison. Her Doc Martens lay right on top. After pulling them out, she tried again.

It closed easily.

She clutched the boots to her chest lovingly. *No way am I leaving these behind.*

Holding them in front of her, she studied the scuffs on the toes, the way the dark red leather had molded to fit her narrow ankles. She'd been in love with these boots since the day she saw them in the window of the thrift store down the road from her school. When she found out they were the right size, she knew they were destined to be hers. For two months she'd gone to that shop every day to make sure they were still there. Eventually she convinced the workers to put them aside for her until her birthday. The thick soles, the sturdy leather, the sheer aggressive power of them made her feel strong again. They were like her armor.

I know I've changed while I've been here, she thought. *But I haven't changed so much that I don't think these are bitchin' boots.*

Kicking off her school-issued sensible shoes, she pulled on the Docs, lacing them up with happy familiarity. Paired with her school uniform, they looked . . . *perfect.*

Then she looked around one last time, running her hand along the top of her desk. She'd hated this place so much when she'd first arrived. Now she couldn't wait to come back.

She hoisted the bag to her shoulder and hurried out the door, crashing full force into Carter, who stood on the other side.

"Hey, Speed." He laughed, steadying her with a hand on each shoulder. "Where's the fire?"

"Ha-ha, you're hilarious," she said, rolling her eyes.

He smoothed her hair. "Are your parents here already?"

"They'll be here any minute." She made a face. "I'm only hurrying because my dad hates waiting."

His eyes clouded briefly, and she remembered that his parents would never come to pick him up again.

"Where will you live during term break?" she asked with a worried frown. "They won't let you stay in the guys' dorm."

"I'm moving into the teachers' wing while they're fixing the smoke damage," he said. "It'll be fine."

"I hope you won't be too lonely."

"I'll be okay," he assured her. "This is home for me, remember? And I won't be alone. Jo and Sylvain are staying, and Jules is only going home for a few days. Most of Night School will be back after a week or so."

Hearing Sylvain's name, Allie felt an unwanted pang. A cloud of confusion seemed to swirl around his name for her.

"Good," she said. "But I'll worry about you anyway."

"And I'll worry about you. Write to me," he said. "And I'll nick Isabelle's phone and call you."

"You still have my number?"

He held up his hand—she'd written her number just below his knuckles an hour ago.

"I'll have it tattooed while you're gone," he joked.

A somber silence fell, and Allie rested her bag on her foot and gently bounced it with her toe.

"You're going to be careful, right?" he said, tugging lightly at the hem of her shirt, pulling her a step closer to him. "You'll stay safe?"

Even though he kept his voice light, she could hear the seriousness behind his words.

"Don't worry. I'll be good as gold. I'm only home a week, then I'm off to Rachel's country estate, which is apparently as secure as Buckingham Palace."

"Good," he said, pulling her into a tight hug. "As long as you're careful. We need you around here, you know."

"Yes, you do. This whole place would fall apart without me," she said with an ironic smile.

Burying his face in her hair, he breathed in deeply.

"Time! Everybody out!"

Zelazny's voice rang out in the hallway outside the door. Allie lifted her face for a quick kiss, pulling away almost immediately. It was too late for long good-byes.

She picked up her bag and threw it over her shoulder.

"I'm going to go down by myself, okay?" Her eyes searched his face, but she knew he would understand. If he really kissed her properly or asked her to stay—if she just kept looking into those eyes—she'd never make it out the door.

Moving briskly, she walked to the door and opened it.

He called after her, "Nice boots, Sheridan."

She didn't look back.

"Stay cool, Carter West."

She was halfway down the hall when she heard his reply.

"Always."

ACKNOWLEDGMENTS

This book started on a dare. I'd always wanted to write a novel but was too cowardly to try. The industry is too competitive, I used to say. What's the point? But my husband dared me to do it. *Dared me.* I never back down from a dare, and he knew that.

Thank you, my darling Jack, for daring me.

Huge, gigantic thanks to everyone at Katherine Tegen Books, especially my brilliant editor Sarah Shumway and the very talented Laurel Symonds. They have surgical editing skills that should be *studied*. Thank you both so much for your time and your patience and your eyes that miss nothing.

I firmly believe there is no way you'd be reading this book now were it not for the enthusiasm, energy, and sheer genius of my agent, Madeleine Milburn, who is both my hero and my friend. There is no better agent on this planet.

Night School was shaped and honed with the help of friends who read it as it was written, and who told me the truth about it. Their honesty and brilliance made it so much better. Hélène Rudyck, Kate Bell, and Sally Davies—you are all *goddesses*.

I live in England, but while I was working on this book I spent a lot of time back in Texas, where I grew up. To the staff at the Starbucks on Memorial Drive at Dairy Ashford in Houston, Texas, thank you for letting me sit and write in your icy air-conditioning for hours on end—sometimes until you were stacking the chairs around me and sweeping the floor under my feet—without ever asking me to buy more coffee or get out of your way. Basically, thank you for ignoring me. *Night School* was fueled by your iced mochas.

Finally, I must mention the one person who I most wanted to read this book but never will. My mother passed away while I was writing *Night School*. She never got to see that everything worked out okay—that this wasn't just another one of my crazy dreams. They say sometimes people watch over you after they die so, just in case . . . Look Mom! I did it. I miss you.